MIDNIGHT

SIN

D0927587

MICHAEL TABMAN

TotalRecall Publications, Inc.
United States of America
Australia, Canada and United Kingdom

Exclusive worldwide content publication / distribution by
TotalRecall Publications, Inc.
1103 Middlecreek Friendswood, Texas 77546
6 Precedent Drive Rooksley, Milton Keynes MK13 8PR, UK
1385 Woodroffe Av Ottawa, ON K2G 1V8
281-992-3131   281-482-5390 Fax

ISBN   **978-1-59095-686-1**
UPC   **6-43977-46869-7**

1   2   3   4   5   6   7   8   9   10

FIRST EDITION

To my mom, who said I would do this....

About the Author

Michael Tabman served as a police officer for three years before joining the FBI. Michael investigated crimes ranging from white collar to bank robberies, organized crime, drug trafficking and money laundering. His professional travels took him to Israel, Russia, Vietnam, Singapore, Malaysia and Thailand. After retiring, Michael founded and still works at SPIRIT Asset Protection, LLC as a security and risk management consultant and public speaker.

Michael is the author of *Walking the Corporate Beat: Police School for Business People*, which draws amusing parallels between police work and decisions made in business and everyday life, based upon his 27 years of law enforcement experience.

Acknowledgements

With thanks to a great editor, Sigrid MacDonald.

Thanks to my son Garrett for the author photo.

Chapter 1

Crisp winter air was no match for the coldness of his conscience. Fiery thoughts fueled his rapidly pumping heart. Boiling blood excited him so much that he subconsciously grabbed himself just to feel the throbbing. Licking his lips, he anticipated the pain and humiliation he was about to thrust upon her. Oh, that tasted so good.

Hoping she would pick up her pace and turn along the path's bend to the south, he waited in the brush counting her steps and rubbing his hands together. When she made the turn, he would be behind her. She would never see him coming. It was dark. His clothes were as dark as his heart.

His plans were clear and deliberate: mentally mapping out every move. He was confident. Why shouldn't he be? He had done this before. And he would do it again. Who would stop him? The black wool scarf wrapped around his face muffled the condensation of his breath and covered his evil visage peeking out from behind the brush: a face that she would never see, yet never forget. Any other time, she wouldn't give him a second look. No girl did.

Raising her right wrist to look at her watch, Robin smirked as she realized that the sun had set and it was too dark to see. Running this late in the evening was not her usual routine. Guessing that her pace was a little behind her regular time, she decided to take longer strides. Her thin but firm legs tightly wrapped by the navy blue, sleek running suit, with pink stripes down the side, kept their cadence as she sidestepped patches of ice.

Brian did not want her to run that late in the evening, afraid she would get home late, then shower and be too tired for a little "don't forget me" sex. Catching an early flight in the morning for a business trip, Robin thought she may not have a chance to run again in the next few days. Not being a runner, Brian did not understand how important it was for her to stay on schedule.

Only about another half mile to go, she thought to herself. *Then I can shower and hit the sack. And then, maybe I'll give him that trip down south he's been bugging me about; after all, he won't have anything for a few days, I hope. Yes, give him something to remember me by while I'm away. Men are so easy.*

Just ahead, in about 20 yards, the jogging path turned to the east and in half a mile, it would end at the Meadow Woods Park parking lot. There, the darkness of the tree lined path would light up from the glow of the nearby Westland Park High School football field. Cheers and jeers were heard from the field where the home team was playing for the championship against their old rival, Bayview High, a school that lay just on the other side of Kansas City.

The break in the tree line let her know that she was in the final stretch of her run. Her warmly clothed body was starting to perspire despite the cold. She wiped her gloved hand across her running nose. And then, she felt a thud.

What happened? Did I slip? I'm off my feet, flying into the brush. I can't speak. I can't see! Bright, flashing lights. Was that a smash across the back of my head? I think I'm still alive. Or am I dreaming? A figure, a blur. Is it a person? I'm cold, so very cold. I feel the wind and chill. No, no, this can't be. I'm trying to scream, but when I open my mouth, no sounds emerge. Weight upon my body. I'm trapped. I hear his breath. Oh my god, it's happening.

What time is it? Am I still alive? Robin woke from her stupor, unaware of her surroundings. Feeling pain on her raw skin, there was also a sense of numbness over her entire body and mind. Tripping over her pants wrapped around her ankles, she started to walk, and walked right out of them.

Standing by the entrance of the field to keep out rowdy high school students, the off-duty, uniformed cops hired for security had their eyes trained on the football game. As the second quarter started, the excited, almost maniacal pointing of some saxophone brandishing band member alerted the cops to turn around. And when they did, they froze. Was this a joke? Was this a high school prank? The two veteran cops watched a young woman stumble towards them, naked from the waist down, wearing one running shoe. A thin line of blood on her neck, a bruised eye, she stared at them blankly. No words were spoken; she fell to the ground.

Flashlights, nightsticks and handcuffs jiggling off their belts, the two speechless cops ran to her. "What happened? Who are you?" Though they had a good idea of what had happened, they asked questions she could not answer, as some degenerate snuck through the brush of Meadow Woods Park on his way home, fully satisfied, at least for tonight. Indiscernible noise bounced around inside her head as cops barked questions at her. Unable to comprehend, unable to talk and completely enervated, she lay motionless, unaware of the circus environment surrounding her.

Students and over exuberant parents wearing high school sweatshirts stumbled over each other as a crowd began to form around this bizarre scene. Frenzied teenage boys, with nose rings, tattoos and other affectations of those who could not be on the football team, whipped out their cell phones and started snapping pictures, ready to be uploaded to the Internet for the enjoyment of twisted minds. No understanding of what they were witnessing, no clue to another's suffering, just pubescent laughing and horseplay.

*****

The cops radioed in for an ambulance and I heard the radio traffic, but was not sure what was going on. In a nearby sector, I was half asleep, still not used to working all night, as we patrolled the sector with no particular sense of purpose.

"Ya hear that, Hollings?" Mark Thompson, my training officer, asked me.

Not fully engaged mentally, I did not realize he was talking to me.

"Gary, wake up. I'm talking to you, rookie."

"I'm up. I hear you."

"No, you're asleep with your eyes open. Did you hear that last call? It sounds like some babe got raped in Meadow Woods Park."

"Are we responding?"

"Nah, plenty of units already there. They don't need us. What the fuck was this girl doing out at night by herself in the park? Probably out looking to get a little strange dick anyway."

"Yeah, Mark, I'm sure that's exactly what she was doing."

With that kind of conversation, I would rather have been sleeping.

*****

Twenty-four year old Jason Brooks, stopping at the game on his way back from his shift at a mall, made his way through the crowd, ripped off his official security guard jacket and covered her. "How about some decency?" he yelled at the crowd. The young men groaned in disapproval. Flashing red lights signaled the arrival of the ambulance. She was gone and the football game went on.

Two miles away, as Robin sobbed in pain and discomfort, awaking from her sedative induced sleep, the crowd collectively moaned in disappointment as the Westland Park quarterback got sacked and his fumble was run in for a touchdown with 20 seconds on the clock. Covered in two layers of white blankets, she heard the beeps and hums and sensed the sterile environment of a hospital room. It was not just any hospital room — it was one reserved for victims of rape. To the right she saw the detectives: the man in a plaid sports jacket, the woman in a smart black pants suit, badges dangling from their breast pockets, and writing pads in hand. The woman had her back to Robin, while talking on her cell phone.

Glancing to the left, Robin saw Brian. She stared, looking for a sign. The sign was there. No supportive smile. No caring touch of her hand. Just a coldness in his eye. She knew what that all meant. The flashbacks of what had happened came back at her like left jabs.

"Brian, I'm sorry. I know you told me not to go out." Robin did not know whether to feel guilty for not following sound advice or allow herself to feel her own pain.

"Yeah, I know, Robin, but as usual you didn't listen to me."

"I'm sorry," she struggled to cry out those words.

"It doesn't matter now. How are you feeling?" Brian asked with transparent disdain.

"Feeling? I feel like a dirty, disgusting crack whore. How do you think I feel?" Robin strained to speak without breaking down, as she subconsciously rubbed her fingers along the lumpy, dark bruise above her eye.

"Hey look, Robin, if you had just..."

The two detectives, who were on the other side of the room, quickly walked over and positioned themselves in between Brian and Robin as he started to walk towards her.

They had seen this before and knew where it was heading. With a gentle yet persuasive hand on the shoulder, the male detective escorted Brian out of the room.

"Sir, I mean no disrespect, and I know what you are going through, but you think you can cut her a little slack — show a little support?" Detective Frank Patelli said gently to Brian.

"Oh yeah, coming from a guy like you, that's easy to say," was Brian's response.

"What does that mean?"

"Look," as Brian held up his cell phone. "Look, there's already pictures being texted of her lying there with her pussy hanging out for everyone to see."

"Sir, I understand how disturbing that is, but..."

"But nothing. I can just see you and your cop buddies sitting around the squad room laughing about this, talking about what a great snatch she has."

"Sir, please. Give us a little more credit than that. Believe me, I do understand what you are going through. I have been at this a long time. But she needs you, man. If you don't support her now that may damage her forever."

Brian, hesitating and speaking under his breath, could only respond, "She's already damaged."

Then he walked back into Robin's hospital room.

Detective Patelli brushed back his thick black hair in frustration. While he had become a jaded police veteran, he still cared about each victim. He had seen hundreds of victims of rape and sexual abuse during his six years on the Sex Crime Squad. It never got easy, but it was becoming routine; that was how he knew it was time for a change. He had his 20 years in and could retire anytime. But, there wasn't much demand in the private sector for a sex crimes detective. His retirement was good, but he would still have to work.

Patelli knew the one sad reality of what had happened tonight. Robin was only one of many victims out there. For everyone else — the doctors, the detectives, and horny young boys sharing the cell phone photos of her half naked body — Robin's problems were meaningless. Patelli had seen many assholes like Brian before. He would be supportive for a week or two, maybe a month or two. Then he would find problems and pick fights with her. Then he'd be gone. He would never forgive her for letting someone else get between her legs. Looking at Brian, Patelli thought about how great it would be to punch his face in and then just walk away. But that was far from reality.

"Whatta ya think'n?" Detective Leslie Lake asked her partner Patelli as they got back in a police car that was so unmarked, it was obviously a cop car. Lake, of average height with short blonde hair, had a nice shape, but had adopted that butchy cop walk. Otherwise, she may have come off a little bit as a babe.

"Same shit, Les. She's a nice kid, and he's a dick. What you get from her?"

"Just what we thought. She was running down the paths and was attacked from behind. She didn't know what hit her. Next thing she knew she was walking around. I don't think she even knows that she wound up at the football game with no pants on."

"Well, I'm sure fuckface Brian will tell her. That was the first thing he talked to me about."

"You know men, Patelli. You're all assholes when it comes to things like that."

"I know. Anyway, was that her normal running routine?"

"No, it wasn't. She said she rarely ran at night. Was doing it 'cause she was leaving on a short business trip and didn't think she would have a chance to run in the next few days."

"So…" Patelli slowed his speech and began to think. "So, nobody knew she was gonna be there? Our rapist just got lucky?"

"Or," Lake continued, "maybe someone did know."

"Like who — Brian?"

"Who knows? Stranger things have happened."

"This shit is getting old, Leslie. I'm one bad day away from pulling the plug and retiring."

"Yeah, but every day around here sucks. What would be a bad day?"

"Fuck if I know, but I'll know it when I see it."

Chapter 2

Fourteen fuck'n years of this crap. No stripes on my arm, still in uniform, sitting on the midnight shift and writing up another report that's gonna be bounced back to correct a misspelling or something like that. Six more, long motherfuck'n years to go, then sweet retirement. Just hope I don't eat my gun before that, Jim Burkett was muttering to himself as he sat in his patrol car sipping his fourth cup of coffee for the night.

He wiped the white, flakey sugar crumbs of his last snack off his belly, which flaccidly hung over his shiny black police utility belt just far enough to capture each little morsel of food falling from his mouth as he took the next bite, before swallowing the bite before. His dark blue shirt collar was open and the gray fake tie, that all cops wore so it would break away if they got grabbed in a fight, was clipped to the button opening on the left side of his collar. He would have to button up if he got a radio call. Known for their professionalism, the Westland Park Police Department had a strict dress code. Three more hours and his shift would end. He was finishing up his report from the arrest he made at a fight that broke out at the end of the Westland Park High School football game. Nobody knew what really happened. Maybe it was a flirting look at another guy's girlfriend, but fights broke out easily at high school football games. Burkett remembered his time on the offensive line of his high school football team as he subconsciously ran his fingers on the right side of his plump neck over the three long, but superficial, scratches he got from the cheerleader who jumped on him during the scuffle. He started to laugh when he reflected on how Officer Carol MacKenzie pulled her off by tugging on the short, tight midriff shirt the cheerleaders wore. MacKenzie had been on Burkett's squad for about three years. She and Burkett did not speak to each other much, but Burkett knew he could always count on her when she backed him up.

If only MacKenzie had ripped that thing right off. Those young perky tits woulda bounced right out to everyone's pleasure. Then Burkett thought about MacKenzie, or Mac, as she was known. *How would she look in that police belt — just that police belt?*

Unaware of his surroundings, Burkett delved into his fantasy as a light drizzle began to drop, hitting his windshield in a soft, mellowing patter. That was not a good idea — a distracted cop was a dead cop. Ten of the parking lot's dozen overhead lights cast a dim florescent glow. Burkett parked under one of the two burnt-out lights in a dark corner. The whole point of escaping for a few moments was not to be noticed by some passing motorist who may think the officer wanted to hear about his problems. Like the rest of the cops, Burkett had a favorite parking area, and we all knew where to find each other. There was nothing much out of the ordinary happening on the streets tonight. It was four in the morning. In a couple of hours, the rush hour would start.

Considering the high possibility of an early morning commuter causing a wreck, Burkett convinced himself that some jerk was going to have an accident in his patrol district right before his shift was over. Getting out of this warm police cruiser, taking photos with either bulky gloves or freezing fingers, listening to both drivers bitch about the other guy, writing a ticket and all the bullshit paperwork that went with one stupid car accident seemed very unappealing.

I hate those fuck'n things, he thought to himself. *If it happens, maybe I'll get lucky and it will be a fatality. Then the Accident Investigation Unit will handle it and I can get my fat ass home,* he continued to converse with himself.

Why he was so eager to get home was a question Burkett could probably not answer if he thought about it. He knew there was nothing for him to really rush home to. Most of the day would be slept away. The sunshine would not bother him. When he awoke he would watch some television, maybe even doze off again on the couch, eat a little and perhaps do one or two errands. Then he would get ready to head off to work again. Only 35 years old, Burkett had few interests and little energy for anything more than watching sports on television.

Straining to reach the passenger side floor, Burkett grabbed the police radio scanner he bought, and keyed to the Kansas City Police Department frequency. Kansas City had a little more action going on tonight than Westland Park; they usually did. A couple of armed robberies, one high speed pursuit and a dead body found in a trash bin. That sounded like a little more fun to Burkett than what he was doing at the moment.

That's where I should be: a bigger police department than this crap hole. I would've made my mark there. I'd probably be detective by now. I'd be locking those maggots up left and right. I know how to work those city streets. Yeah, that's what I shoulda done. He kept on talking softly to himself and then stopped and mindlessly daydreamed for a while.

Ah, that's all right. I'll do my next six years sitting here in the car. If they don't appreciate everything I've done, fuck 'em. Then I'll retire and that's that.

Sitting there silently, slinking into his deep fantasies of what would have, could have and should have been, Burkett could not hear the wheeziness in his own breath. The passenger side window was opened a crack to let the chill in. Cops did that during the winter; otherwise sitting in the warm car during a quiet midnight shift may end up with them falling asleep. That would not be cool; a sleeping cop, like a distracted cop, was a dead cop.

Jumping up in his seat a bit, Burkett was startled when we hit him with the spotlight as we drove to pull up next to him. I noticed that he quickly picked up his cell phone and rolled down his window all the way just as I got window to window with him.

"All right, talk to you later, babe... miss you too," he said loud enough for me and probably my training partner, who was riding shotgun, to hear.

"Whatta ya doing, JB? Whacking off in there while talking to your mother?" Thompson yelled over to Burkett, whom the squad called JB.

Thompson really seemed to like busting on Burkett. I was not quite sure why. I did not know Burkett very well. I had only been out of the academy for three weeks. Burkett struck me as a little odd, but he seemed harmless. He was not a bad cop and he was there when you needed him. Thompson was young, good looking and fairly arrogant. From what I could tell, Thompson was a solid cop; a little aggressive in his approach to things, but that seemed to work for him. I had to learn as much as I could from him. He was going to be my training officer for at least the next three weeks, when hopefully, I'd be cut loose and get to patrol on my own.

"Fuck you, Thompson," Burkett barked back across my face.

"All right, c'mon, JB. I'm just busting your balls. Don't stress out on me. What's going on?"

"Nothing much tonight. But shit's happening over in Kansas City. If I was over in the city, I'd probably be breaking heads right now on some asswipes trying to gang bang some good looking bitch, instead of breaking up these stupid high school bullshit fights that I'm getting sick of."

"Well, you know, JB, it's not like we don't have our own problems right here."

"Not like KC we don't."

"Maybe not. But almost every roll call we hear about a burglary or rape that happened right under our noses while we were cruising around or drinking coffee. Maybe if you didn't just sit there bitching about things and started beating the bushes, you might actually catch someone in the act. Ever think of that?"

"Okay, hotshot. So why the fuck are you sitting here talking to me? Why don't you go out there and find some burglary in progress or something, and call me when you do? I'll back your sorry ass up."

"Well, I was gonna just shoot the shit with you while my rookie, Hollings, writes up the report from our last call. Some dude put a beating on his girlfriend and she won't press charges — typical bullshit, nothing new. But since you're in such a great mood, and it's so much fun to talk to you, I think we'll just leave you the fuck alone."

Thompson signaled for me to drive off and I got the feeling Burkett was happy to be left alone.

"What's up with him?" I asked, really trying to find out why Thompson was riding Burkett so hard.

"He gets like that a lot. I think he's just a bitter guy. He sees himself one way and everyone else sees him another. He thinks he's some great cop, and he's okay — he gets the job done — but great he ain't."

"Maybe it's just 'cause I'm a rookie, but I don't get it. If he's so unhappy, why doesn't he quit and do something else?"

"Two reasons, my young friend. First, there's something called that pension. You're too young to think about that now. But after you get more than 10 years in and you're more than halfway there, there's no looking back."

"Okay, I guess I can see that. That's reason number one. What's number two?"

"Well, for a dipshit like Burkett, if he wasn't a cop, he would be a plain fuck'n nobody. And, he'd have no way in the world to ever meet a woman. He'd probably never get laid."

"Does being a cop get him laid a lot?"

"Well, we all find our uniform chasers, you know — cop groupies. They're out there, and we all get a little bit of the action. Whatever Burkett tells you is probably more fantasy than reality, but who the fuck knows? And really, who cares, as long as I'm getting my share?"

"Your share? Uh, aren't you married, Mark?"

"Oh no, don't you become the department fuck'n chaplain on me. Tell you what, Gary. Learn to keep your mouth shut and I'll tell you some great stories and teach you a few things about the fringe benefits of this job. How does that sound?"

"Cool." Staying off that topic seemed like the right way to go at the moment. Besides, learning how to cash in on those fringe benefits did sound enticing. Wondering how much of a mistake I had made by stepping into such personal territory, I turned my stare out the window. It was like walking right into a cordoned off crime scene, stepping over the police tape and stepping on evidence. Then suddenly I felt that uneasy silence setting in and I wanted to break it. Being just a rookie and staying on the good side of my training partner was definitely the smart thing to do. Thompson was a well-liked and well-respected cop. My reputation hinged on what he said about me.

"So anyway, getting back to Burkett, he doesn't seem like such a bad guy to me. The only time I really ever talk to him is at roll call, though. What's the big chip he seems to always have on his shoulder?" I was trying to spark a little conversation, and Burkett appeared to be a good topic.

"I don't know. I think he's pissed because he failed the sergeant's test like three times."

"Three times? That sucks."

"Yes, it does. And to make matters worse, he never made detective, which was his big dream. I think that's bothering him even more than the sergeant thing."

"Why didn't he make detective? Do you need a certain amount of arrests or something? Or is it some kind of test?"

"Nah, it's none of those things. Supposedly, it's an interview, a review of your work record and a recommendation from your sergeant. But, you'll learn, rookie. It's all who you know and who you blow. Burkett is just weird. I can't see him as a detective. Let me put it this way; there's 800 cops in this department. For detective, I'd rank him 799."

"Oh yeah? So, who ranks 800?"

Thompson slowly and slyly looked at me. "Who else, rookie? You."

"Okay then, I guess I'll just pull over somewhere now and start writing that report before we get another call."

"Good call, rookie."

Behind a gas station, about a quarter mile away, there was a quiet, deserted, dark parking lot where Thompson usually liked to go to write reports, so that's where I drove to. Struggling to remember some of the facts of what happened, and who said what during the domestic dispute we just handled, I was fumbling with my report, but didn't want Thompson to notice. A good memory, and the ability to recall what you saw and heard were important to being a good cop, and I was going to be a great cop.

"Go ahead. Look at your notes, rookie. It's okay. That's why we write things down."

I felt a little relieved and embarrassed as well, but Thompson was a sharp cop. He picked up on what was going through my head right away. One day, I hoped, I would have his cop instinct. Besides that, I had an ever bigger plan that I could not share with anyone. I was going to make detective in less than three years, then start working my way up the ranks. I'd be aggressive, stay alert on patrol, make arrests, save some people, and be sure to get recognition. Just like Thompson said, it was just a game of playing the right people. I was not going to go the way of Burkett, becoming bitter as opportunities passed me by. I had it all figured out, all with only three weeks of street experience.

So we sat there quietly for a little while. I couldn't come up with any more conversation just for the sake of talking. About a minute later, the radio began to crackle.

"All units, 10-3," came over the radio. Then silence.

"What's that?" I asked. I had not remembered all the call signals.

"Shut the fuck up," Thompson hollered back, holding up his hand as if he were about to bitch slap me.

"318 Baker, 318 Baker," the dispatcher called.

"318 Baker, go," Burkett replied over the radio.

"318 Baker, we have a possible robbery in progress. A to Z gas station convenience store at 7814 6th Street. Customer drove by and did not see the clerk inside. Door was locked."

"318 Baker, roger. En route, ETA 2."

Thompson grabbed the radio off the car's console. "320 Baker, we'll respond as back-up. ETA 3."

Burkett had estimated his time of arrival in two minutes; Thompson said ours was three. I wanted to get there first. I had to focus.

Thompson turned to me. "It's probably nothing, but drop your work, put on your friggin' lights and siren, and get us the fuck over there. You know where you're going?"

"Yeah, I know where that is. Sorry, I forgot 10-3 meant to shut up and stand by for an emergency call."

Running Code 3 — speeding with lights and sirens — could get a rookie all worked up. And that's when you made mistakes. It was called the Code 3 syndrome. A few rookies washed up during probation, wrecking their cars while running Code 3. That was not going to happen to me.

The call was in Burkett's patrol district. Arriving on the scene first, Burkett called in on the radio. He had cruised along Shawnee Drive, which intersected with 6th Street where the gas station was located. Turning off the headlights about 50 yards before reaching the area was standard practice, so as not to alert any possible robber to our approach. Burkett waited for us, off to the side, not moving within view of the front door and window. Burkett knew this convenience store; it had been robbed a couple of times in the past. Most of the time these kinds of calls were nothing. Usually, the clerk was just in the back working and some good citizen jumped to conclusions. Ordinarily, the front door was not locked, making this a little more suspicious than normal, but only a little.

Thompson and I pulled up to Burkett less than two minutes after he got there. Everything seemed quiet from the outside. Four self-serve gas pumps positioned in a straight line, under the dimly-lit awning with one bulb quickly flashing on and off, were all unattended. That was not odd for this time of night.

"Okay, I'll approach the front door from the side and try to peek in. If I don't see anything I'll just knock. The clerk may just be in the back room. Thompson, why don't you cover the rear and have your rookie come with me, up front?"

"All right, JB. Just let me know as soon as everything is okay. Don't feel like freezing my nuts off out there for nothing."

Thompson ran around to the back of the store where there was a delivery entrance. These doors were always locked from the outside, but were normally the first place a robber would run out of, if he saw the cops coming in from the front. Burkett and I slowly approached the front door from the side, peeking around the corner. We saw nothing but a convenience store, brightly lit aisles filled with junk food, sodas and a magazine rack and the refrigerated shelves in the background. In the middle was the unattended check-out counter with the cigarettes stacked on the back shelf.

"All right, rookie. It's probably nothing, but you just don't know. I'm gonna knock on the door. You keep your eyes open and your weapon ready. Got it?"

"Got it," I answered nervously, trying to hide the quiver in my voice.

Knocking hard, two or three times, Burkett called out his presence. Within a minute or two, the clerk came out of a back room door, with cardboard boxes lined up on each side of the doorway. He was a short, Asian man with thick eye glasses. A white apron hung over his plaid shirt and blue jeans, and he was rubbing his palms together in a circular motion when he came to the door, passing the checkout counter. With a nervous, forced smile on his face, he struggled to unlock the door.

"Maybe he was just getting a little for himself back there," Burkett said half jokingly, turning slightly to me with a childish grin on his rotund face with red, dry, slightly peeling cheeks.

After fumbling with the keys, the clerk finally opened the door without saying a word. Burkett and I walked in slowly, our hands over our weapons still in their holsters. Burkett asked the clerk if everything was all right. The clerk told him that everything was okay. He said he had just locked up while he was taking inventory in the back. On the surface, that sounded rather plausible. Burkett hesitated for a moment, not saying anything; then he turned to me.

"Get your partner on the radio and tell him it's okay to come on in."

Tugging at my radio, which was fitting in tightly on my new police belt, I felt as if I was the nervous one, not the store clerk. I called Thompson to come in. Within a few seconds Thompson came running in the front door. Burkett was still talking to the clerk. It sounded as if he was asking the same questions over again. Thompson pulled me off to the side of the store.

"Okay, that was fun. Burkett can wrap this up without us," Thompson whispered to me as he rubbed his hands together and then blew on them for some warmth.

I could see that Thompson already figured that this was one of those false alarms: nothing really happening. At that moment, I was thinking that his ability to size up a situation quickly was what made him a good cop.

"'All right, JB, if everything's okay, we'll take off now," Thompson said to Burkett while Burkett was still talking to the clerk. Burkett held up his hand motioning for us to wait. Pointing his finger, he told the clerk to stay right where he was and then Burkett walked over to us. He spoke softly.

"You know what? This guy seems a little too nervous for me, though he's insisting everything's okay. Something may be going on. I don't know. I'll keep him talking. Why don't you two just check around? He came out of that back door there. I'll see if I can't get something out of him."

As Burkett walked back to the clerk, Thompson looked at me with a strange grin. I couldn't figure out what that look meant.

"Look, you know I don't think much of Burkett's gut feelings, but let's just play the game. We'll sweep the place and make sure there's not something going on and then get outta here. Okay?"

"Okay."

Watching every little thing Thompson did and every move he made, I tried to watch his eyes and see what he was seeing. He put his hand over his gun, but didn't pull it out of his holster. I immediately did the same. I knew he did not trust Burkett's instinct, but he was at least going to play it safe. Following Thompson's lead, we started walking towards the back door. Out of the corner of my eye, I noticed that the clerk was watching us closely. That bothered me. I was going to say something to Thompson, but as soon as we got close to the door, the clerk shouted.

"No, don't go in there! There's nothing there."

That was it. Thompson backed up immediately, pushing me and himself against the wall, knocking down the display stand filled with cupcakes. My heart was beating in my throat; I could not swallow though I felt that urge. A blank mind, with no idea of what to do, left me paralyzed. Before I could even think about the next move, a man came running out of that back door, shooting.

At first, all I saw was a figure in dark clothing running in our direction. I really did not know if it was a man or a woman, black or white, tall or short or anything. Then, I heard the gun shot. My knees buckled and my calves cramped; I found myself falling to the ground. In less than a second, I knew why. A sting and a burning on my skin forced me to look down at my failing legs. There they were: two clear bullet holes in my left thigh oozing blood. Agape, staring at my wounds, I remembered what they told me in the police academy. Getting shot does not mean you will die. The shock may kill you before the wound did.

Unable to believe that I had really been shot twice, maintaining consciousness was a struggle. Passing out was not an option. No shock for me. I was not going to die tonight. Wanting to get up, or at least shoot back from my position on the floor, I was unable to focus my thoughts. My movements were in slow motion. My gun was stuck in the new, hard and unyielding holster and sat there stubbornly. Maybe just as well. Not knowing what I was doing, sitting on the floor stunned, unsure if I was in pain, and unable to make sense of what was happening, rendered me the useless rookie I was. Nothing I was seeing or hearing seemed real.

Ears ringing and the room spinning... *Did I just hear another shot? Was I hit again?* I didn't feel anything. Managing to free myself of the fixation on my gunshot wound, I saw Thompson spin around in a 360 and fall to the ground as well; he had taken a round in the left shoulder. Burkett jumped on the clerk to bring him to the floor for safety. The robber headed for the door. Getting up on one knee, Burkett fired a round that missed and hit the exit sign above the door; sparks shot out. The robber turned back around and shot wildly, hitting nobody. Thompson fired off a round. It missed and went into a stack of newspapers, sending little pieces of papers airborne like feathers from a pillow fight. The robber spun around to run away just as Thompson fired a second and third round in rapid succession. We heard the shatter as the second bullet pierced the door's glass pane. The next shot hit the robber right in the ass as he was trying to run out. He didn't go right down, but fell face first through the front door's already cracked glass pane.

Thompson let his shooting arm drop, still holding on to his weapon and then stayed on the ground. Gripping his gun, he held his hand over the wound on his shoulder as it continued to bleed. Burkett ran out, through the now glassless doorframe with his gun in hand. The robber scrambled, trying to get up and run.

"I'll blow your motherfuck'n brains out. Drop it and get down," Burkett yelled, his voice three octaves higher than usual and cracking and quivering from his own fear.

The curly haired robber wearing baggy jeans and a black jacket stopped and hesitated, making no move, giving no clue as to his intentions. Probably just as well that the robber could not see Burkett's hand shaking; he might have been tempted to shoot it out. Finally, after a few moments of indecision, the robber leaned to his right and put the gun off to the side. He knew the drill and got down on his knees. Looking back over his shoulder, his partially crossed eyes flashed a sense of indignity at having been caught in the act again.

"Lie down, face on the ground, motherfucker," Burkett yelled out orders with a little more authority now.

The robber complied.

"Now put your hands behind your head, slowly." Burkett moved in closer. As he did, he quickly grabbed the gun off the ground and tucked it in his belt.

One thing the Westland Park Police Department was known for was giving their cops good training. Even for a mediocre cop like Burkett, the training kicked in when it was needed. He grabbed one of the robber's arms and then came down with both knees on his head and back. Burkett holstered his weapon, handcuffed the robber and set down that 250 pound frame on top of the hapless criminal. Catching his breath and trying to compose himself, Burkett let out a little cathartic laugh at the sight of the blood oozing from the robber's ass and flowing out onto the gas station lot. He was glad it was over. He was glad he was alive.

I went for my radio to call it in, but I was so flustered I didn't know what to say. Then I heard Burkett calling.

"318 Baker to dispatch. We have two officers down, one perp shot and in custody. Need medical aid and back-up ASAP."

Then there was a flurry of radio traffic. Everybody on the street was calling in to advise they were en route to give assistance. Sergeant Hughes was trying to get on the radio and give orders, but the radio traffic was chaotic.

Heavily, I breathed a tremendous sigh of relief. Laying there motionless, I too was glad it was over and help was on the way. Then I heard Thompson speak.

"Gary, you okay?"

"Yeah, yeah." It was good to hear Thompson's voice.

"How 'bout you?"

"Oh fuck, I'll make it. It takes more than one little pussy bullet to bring down Mark Thompson."

"Good." I wasn't about to get into one-upmanship of machismo with him. Actually, I didn't want to speak anymore, at all. I couldn't help wonder, was Thompson's reaction to being shot phony bravado or was he handling it better than I was? I did not care. I just wanted to get to the hospital and for this night to end.

Ineptly trying to tend to our wounds, the clerk and his wife were taking napkins from the dispenser and handing them to us. I could tell they were afraid to come near our blood. I could not blame them. They meant well, but with no idea of what to do, their frenzied actions were making me even more jittery than I already was. Waving them off with erratic hand gestures only added to the sense of confusion. The wounds were not life threatening, but we were both bleeding badly. I crawled to the wall just to hoist myself up into a sitting position. As I sat there I tried not to think about my wound. It wasn't hard to figure out what had just happened. The store was being robbed and the clerk's wife was being held with a gun to her head until the clerk could get rid of the cops. We walked right into it. Somehow, Burkett suspected something was wrong.

Four patrol cars were there within minutes. The red flashing lights gave me an inexplicable feeling of comfort, and I began to wipe off the sweat that was dripping down into my now stinging eyes. The ambulances were also there within a few minutes. All of a sudden, there I was, on the stretcher being interviewed by Sergeant Hughes, although I did not remember the paramedics picking me up and moving me; perhaps I had blacked out.

Sergeant David Hughes was a 20-year veteran who never rose above the sergeant level. Once a cop got on the career path, he usually kept moving. It was not fun to be outranked by someone you once supervised. Hughes seemed like a quiet and reserved man; I hadn't really had a chance to get to know him or much about him in my short time out of the academy. Our conversation was different than what I expected after being shot. Hughes was not trying to soothe me or engage me in any small talk.

"Gary, I just need to know a few things. I want you to answer only the questions I ask and nothing else. Anything specific about the shooting, you wait till you've had a chance to clear your head. Later on, you'll be interviewed by Internal Affairs. Until then, do not discuss the shooting with anybody except the department shrink. Understand?"

"Yes, sir," was the only appropriate response to that ominous warning.

"Okay, how many perps were there?"

"Just one. He came out shooting. I reached for my gun, but..." and Hughes held up his hand to stop me.

"What did I just tell you? The answer was one. I didn't ask for any more information, did I?"

I just nodded my head; he understood that I understood.

"Were any civilians hurt?"

"No."

"You saw the man Thompson shot who we now have under arrest, right?"

"Yes, I could see from inside the store."

"Was that the man who shot you?"

"Yes, it was."

"Okay then. Here's what happens now. As per department policy, you are on administrative leave with pay. You're gonna get treated at the hospital. Sometime after you're released, you'll be seen by the department shrink. Everything you tell her is protected by confidentiality. The courts, IA, even your mother can't get that information. So, if you are having any trouble coping, you let her know. Got it?"

"Yes, sir."

"Good. Only after you see the shrink and you are cleared to return to duty will IA interview you. Understand?"

"Yes, sir."

"All right. They're gonna take you to the hospital in a minute. Anything you want to ask me?"

"No, sir."

Sergeant Hughes knew the chief was on his way, and so was the press. In one night, two cops were shot in Westland Park and an armed robber was shot in the process. That was big news; it sounded more like Kansas City. The police department knew that, at that point, most of the questions the press would have could not be answered. The media was a tough game to play. Only the chief or the department's media representative was authorized to speak to the press. We were warned about that in the academy. If the cameras showed up and a microphone was thrust in front of your face, your only comment was, "No comment," and you were to refer them back to headquarters. I liked those instructions. I wouldn't want to tangle with those media people; they're a little too slick for me.

I was glad that I was not expected to talk too much to Sergeant Hughes. I did not want to say anything at this point. There was a lot on my mind I had to figure out. Thompson fired off rounds. So did Burkett. Stunned and unsure as to what was real, I didn't fire off any rounds, and I'd been hit. With shaky hands, I didn't even get my gun out of my stiff, new holster. What were they going to think about that? Could this be the end of my career, before it ever really started? Was I going to become the laughingstock — the cop who couldn't get his gun out of his holster? I needed time to think. I needed to know how to explain my actions, or actually my inaction. What was Thompson going to say? What was Burkett going to say? I just needed to escape for a few moments. With Sergeant Hughes not talking to me anymore, I closed my eyes; I did not want anybody else coming over to me. Within a few seconds the medics started to roll me into the ambulance. Before they pushed me all the way in, I glanced over to the convenience store.

The crime scene investigators were starting to crowd around outside of the store as they planned their next moves. They were looking and pointing, shining lights and calibrating. They had all sorts of fancy equipment. They would gather all the evidence and recreate the crime scene and chain of events — photographs, bullet trajectories, blood stains and fingerprints. They did it all. This was a major crime scene. There was no room for mistakes. Could they really recreate exactly what happened? I was not sure I wanted them to. Mackenzie and Paul Edmonds, another cop on my squad, helped two paramedics pick the perp up by his arms and gently place him face down on to the stretcher. Quietly, I fantasized that one of them would smack their nightstick right across his ass where Thompson's bullet remained. But they knew, as did I, that how they handled a handcuffed prisoner who had shot a cop would be closely watched. They had seen too many videotapes of their brethren on the west coast putting a beating on a prisoner. Once he was down and handcuffed, the fight was over. That may not be fair, at least from a cop's perspective, but that was the law. After the hospital visit, the perp would be driven down to the jail where he would be booked on robbery and attempted murder charges. Burkett would get credit for the arrest, but he had just been involved in a shooting. Like Thompson and me, he would also be put out on administrative leave for a few days — time to chill, collect his thoughts and pull himself back together before hitting the street again.

No matter how tough a cop was, or tried to appear to be, a shooting could shake him to the core. Before the ambulance took off, I cautiously opened my eyes, maybe halfway, and glanced over to Sergeant Hughes' car where Burkett sat quietly, by himself in the back, behind the Plexiglas that separated the driver from the prisoner. The darkness of the silhouette cast by his somewhat large head reflected the darkness that I knew was in his soul at the moment. Would anybody pay attention to what Burkett was feeling? Did anybody care? Probably not.

The flashing red lights that gave me some feeling of comfort were making Burkett uneasy and he tried unsuccessfully to shield his eyes from their glare. The shock was now going all throughout Burkett's body as he had time to replay the events in that big head of his. Like all cops, he would put on a brave façade; maybe not as much as Thompson, but he would not show weakness. I could just imagine the troubling thought that stuck in his mind: "Fourteen years on the job and I never fired my weapon at anybody. Now I do and I miss. Fuck."

Most cops never do fire their weapons. And when they do, they often miss their target. But two cops were shot tonight. A lot of questions were going to be asked. The answers would determine our futures. Burkett had his concerns, as did I. But the robbery was his call — his responsibility. Me, I was just a rookie following the lead of my more senior officers.

"This was not how I pictured my first shoot-out," Burkett was still muttering to himself as he kept playing the scene over and over again in his mind. *"Okay, I told Thompson to check things out. I protected the clerk when the shit hit the fan, and I returned fire. But I missed and Thompson shot the fucker right in the ass. I know how this bullshit cop game works, and I ain't looking like no hero."* His hands moving in random patterns, he kept explaining to himself why things happened the way they did. No matter how he looked at it, no matter what spin he put on it, he did not have a good feeling about how this would play out.

Chapter 3

"Okay, Mom, I'm leaving now. You need anything before I go?" Burkett yelled to his mother who was upstairs in their small, three bedroom, two bath house on a quiet residential block where most houses looked alike.

"Well, no. But you're not working tonight, are you?"

"Yeah, I am. Why?"

His mother started walking down the stairs in her flowered robe, holding on cautiously to the rail. "I thought you were off a few more days."

"No, Mom, I'm due back tonight. The admin leave is over. The shrink said I'm doing just fine."

"Are you sure you're ready? I mean getting shot and everything... maybe you need more time."

"I wasn't shot, Mom." In his mind, he was almost wishing he had been, not seriously, but just like Thompson and me. In the cop world, there was a badge of honor to be worn for getting shot on the job.

"The other guys were shot, Mom. I'm okay and it's time to get back to work. Sitting around here isn't doing me any good."

"But isn't it still kind of early? You're not due in for another couple of hours."

"I know. The whole squad is stopping by the hospital to visit Hollings and Thompson, before our shifts start. This should be their last night there. They're doing okay and should be back next shift."

Burkett was really hoping that Thompson would not be back so soon and would need some more time off. The thought of not listening to Thompson's crap for a while was appealing to Burkett.

"Well, that's very nice of you. Have a good time."

"All right, Mom. Good night."

"I love you, Jimmy."

"Yeah, Mom. I love you too."

Burkett walked out of the house he shared with his mother since his father died five years ago. Actually, he had never moved out of the house at all. He told everyone that he was staying home to care for his mother and to assure that he inherited the house all to himself and not have to share it with his two sisters. Nobody really believed that explanation; everybody saw Burkett as a man who just liked living at home with his mother. Westland Park cops did not make a lot of money, as most cops didn't, but certainly enough to live on their own.

Burkett stepped outside his door, cautiously walking down the three cracked concrete steps leading to the walkway. Holding on tightly to the black iron rail, he maneuvered his stout body cautiously around the icy spots. His patrol car was parked in the open carport next to the single garage door, which still sported the same green, peeling paint from when the house was first built. A long row of waist-high bushes separated his property from his next-door neighbor. Burkett reached in the car and turned on the ignition, then popped back out and started scraping the thin layer of ice off the front and back windshields. The condensation coming from the exhaust pipe was heavy. Burkett then sat in the car while it warmed up and listened to the police radio to get a feel for what was happening that night before he joined the rest of the squad at the hospital.

*****

Sharing the hospital room with Thompson made for one very long week of being too close to him physically: too much time talking to him and too much time getting to know the man, not just his cop persona. That was much more than I should've had to endure, with all the other pangs of a hospital stay. The wretched, urine soaked stench of the hospital was inescapable and permeated our room all day. But that was not the worst of it.

At home, I lived alone. Not used to sharing my bathroom with anybody, especially someone like Thompson who thought of nobody but himself; the stains and pubic hairs that he left on the toilet, and the odor, were noxious and nauseating. I dreaded going to the bathroom. The noise outside the room was a constant annoying hum. Old men and old women walking around in those stupid gowns with their flabby asses hanging out, while their blood-clotted arms held on to their portable intravenous stands.

There was only one thing to look forward to each day, and that was our visit from the nurse. Something about nurses plays right into the male fantasy; if only they still wore those virginal white uniforms. Cops and nurses had a certain, inexplicable compatibility. Whether it was the shift work, the dedication to public service or just the constant dealing with people at their worst, nurses and cops seemed to get along. Many cops were married to nurses. If it wasn't a nurse, it was a schoolteacher. My favorite nurse was Janie. Slender and petite with short, black hair that dangled freely in loose curls, she was not a beauty queen, but she had that look that just made me feel good. I usually liked long hair, and Janie was a little shy in the tits department, but she had a beautiful face, a sexy smile and most importantly, she seemed to have a heart of gold. I was not completely shallow.

From the moment she walked in to our hospital room, I knew I liked Janie and wanted to ask her out. But Thompson was too fast for me, putting the moves on her immediately. At our first encounter, she seemed taken by Thompson's shiny, thick blonde hair, blue eyes and Hollywood smile. Thompson was much more outgoing than I and exuded a whole lot more self-confidence — why not? He was replete with self- confidence, if not self-adulation. I thought for sure I would lose out to him, and pictured him tapping her right there in the room, with me lying in my bed choking the chicken. That disturbing worry only lasted until the next morning, when Thompson's wife and little daughter showed up to visit while Nurse Janie checked in on us before ending her shift. After that, I seemed to be able to get her attention and engage in some friendly conversation. Asking girls for dates was not my forte; I truly feared rejection. Nobody knew that, and I certainly could not let Thompson know that. Somehow, I would have to make my move, with Thompson in the room. That would not be easy.

We were not told that anybody was coming to see us tonight, but Thompson had dropped enough hints with the guys on the squad that we figured they would do something collectively. They had been coming by now and then on their own. Sergeant Hughes visited a few times with books he had bought for us. Neither one of us was big on reading; we tended to stare mindlessly at the television, talking intermittently about unrelated and unimportant matters. The boredom broke for me twice a day to get physical therapy for my bandaged leg. With two shallow bullet wounds that did not hit anything vital, I was not in terrible pain nor did I experience much loss of strength. Somehow, a little therapy with a cute therapist's hands all over my thigh was a lot more exciting than listening to Thompson.

One time, Hughes brought his wife, Melinda, with him. They met when she was a dispatcher and he was a hotshot SWAT cop. She was thin and attractive with a great set of knockers that seemed a little disproportionate for that thin frame: probably store bought. She liked flaunting those things, and Hughes liked showing her off. Nobody really minded looking, especially not Thompson. His eyes never left her and his words were probably more flirtatious than they should've been for his sergeant's wife. If Hughes had left them alone for even a moment, I was sure that Thompson would've made his move.

Tonight, Thompson was lying back, arms crossed behind his head, in his hospital bed situated closest to the door. I was on the other side by the window with the bathroom door between us. Thompson had a few flowers and balloons sitting on his night stand that his friends and family had sent. There were none from my family or any of my old friends. I couldn't let Mom find out about this. She was still mourning my dad's death from that nasty car accident two years ago. Her life was not an easy one; she had experienced too much loss for a woman not even 60. Nobody back in my hometown St. Louis knew I had been shot.

Thompson had the television on and he was looking in that direction, but once again, not really watching or listening. He had other things on his mind.

"Yeah, I got that fucker right in the ass. What a great shot. And I pulled that off while I was wounded too. Man, this is one great story I can tell. All a babe has to do is touch my shoulder. I'll act like I'm in pain and somehow, she'll manage to get the story out of me, hesitantly, of course. This is gonna bring me in some serious pussy, ya know what I mean?" Thompson asked, not really expecting an answer.

"You know, Hollings," he continued, "we did pretty good out there. Didn't we?"

"Yes, Mark, we did. But I think there's a lesson to be learned and we should just move on."

Thompson brought up how well we did at least two or three times a day. He never mentioned Burkett once. I was getting very tired of revisiting the shooting so many times.

"I think once we get past the Internal Affairs shooting review and everything, I should probably go on television and let everyone know what really happened. The public has a right to know."

"The public has a right to know? Whatta ya mean?" Thompson was getting way too caught up in himself, even for him.

"You know, how the shooting went down, how we saved two people from an armed robber who was probably gonna kill them."

"C'mon, you think…" and Thompson kept talking, not even hearing me.

"Not only that. I should probably speak at all the recruit classes in the academy, kinda let them know what to expect, just in case. There's nothing like hearing it from someone who has actually been through it."

"You know what else?" he continued. "I'm only the fifth cop on this department to ever shoot anybody. Only the fifth. Can you believe that? That's what Hughes told me."

"Yeah, Mark, that's something."

He had mentioned that every day since the moment Sergeant Hughes pointed that out to him. Hughes knew that number because Hughes was the fourth cop to ever shoot anybody. About three years ago, when Hughes was the SWAT commander, some punk took hostages in a botched bank robbery. When he came out, supposedly to surrender, he pointed his gun right at Hughes. Having worked his way up on the SWAT team to commander, Hughes was adept with his weapon. He quickly fired off two rounds, piercing the poor bastard's heart. The tragedy was that the perp's gun was not even real. It was a suicide by cop. Caught on film by the news, Hughes could not escape seeing it replayed several times a day that week. There was no question it was a righteous shoot. After that shooting, Hughes' name was kicked around as a shoo-in for the next lieutenant spot that opened up. That did not happen. Although the shooting was a good shoot in the police world, it was not a good shoot in Hughes' mind. A good cop, but also kind-hearted, Hughes always felt that there was just something un-heroic about killing an unarmed, distressed, poor slob — especially for the whole world to watch.

After the buzz of the shooting quieted down, Hughes requested a transfer back to patrol. He was never heard talking about wanting a promotion and he rarely talked about the shooting. I did not know him from back then, but word had it he used to be an outgoing, lively, guy's guy ready to take on the world. The shooting changed him. Now, he was quiet and reserved, even somewhat withdrawn. He seemed to shun confrontation, which was not a desirable quality in a cop.

"Internal Affairs Shooting Review is going to start their inquiry soon after we're released from here, you know." Thompson sounded like he was putting me on notice.

"Yeah, I know. I'm not really worried about it. What happened, happened."

"Very true, but there's a way to answer IA questions. Know what I mean?"

I hesitated for several seconds. I was afraid that I did know what he meant.

"No, not really, Mark. What do you mean?"

"Well, for example, you got to point out how we decided to search the store even though Burkett thought the clerk was getting a little."

"Yeah, well, uh, Burkett, didn't ..."

Thompson quickly interrupted. "Hey, that's what you said he told you. Let Burkett talk for himself. He's a big boy. He's gonna try to make himself out the hero. In the meantime, he shot out the fuck'n exit light while you and I took a bullet. He should've known there was a robbery going on. Maybe if he warned us, we would have been a little more ready. Maybe you would've gotten your gun out of your holster and returned fire like you should've. The way I see it right now, you didn't shoot because you didn't have a good shot. You know what I'm saying?"

"I think I do." And I did. Thompson knew how he wanted this to play out, down to the gritty details. He had more respect and credibility than Burkett. If he made me out to be the bumbling fool who could not get his weapon out of his holster, my career was over. And, bottom line, he was the one who shot the bastard robbing the place. I could either go Thompson's way or hitch my wagon to Burkett. I could come out looking good or looking foolish. I was getting the picture.

"You're right, Mark. We did a helluva job and I shouldn't hold back. I wish I had a clear shot at the guy myself; maybe I coulda plugged him too. But you had the shot, you took it and you did it. You the man."

"Exactly. You didn't have a clear shot. I'll be sure to let IA know how well you did for a rookie. Hell, just taking a slug as a rookie, your name is gonna get around. You'll see, play it right, and all those dreams you have may come true."

Whoa, I started thinking. *What did Thompson know about my dreams? Did he have me figured out that well after only a couple of weeks together? Or was I that obvious?*

"Hey, hey, there they are" called out Paul Stryker as he led the squad in to the hospital room. Chubby cheeks and straight black hair flopping on his forehead gave him a baby face awash in innocence, in stark contrast to his tall, strong cop build. Generally, the hospital did not let seven visitors in at one time. But for cops, on their last night, they didn't mind making an exception. On patrol, the car accidents, barroom brawls and domestic fights keep a cop in the Emergency

Room a lot; we get to know the hospital personnel very well.

The squad piled in with Liz Fiero holding a chocolate cake with vanilla frosting. I'm sure it was just a coincidence that vanilla frosting was my favorite. Liz was a somewhat attractive girl, but nothing extraordinary. In the nightclub arena, she probably would be rated a B. But in the cop world, where the standards were much lower, as there was limited competition, she was an A. And she knew it. She took advantage of that situation and played it well. There were rumors that she and a few of the guys got into some squad car sex antics, but they were just rumors. Nobody really knew the truth. We all thought Liz enjoyed having those rumors floating around; they kept her in the spotlight. As for being a cop, she was fairly well-respected. She would never lead the squad in arrests or even traffic tickets, but she did her job when she had to.

The message in icing on the cake read, "One for the good guys," an obvious reference to Thompson's shot to the perp's ass.

"How you guys feeling?" Liz asked as she put the cake down.

"We're doing..." I started till Thompson interrupted in a louder voice.

"We're both doing great. Nothing takes out the team of Thompson and Hollings. Let the next armed robber think twice about coming into Westland Park."

"Here, here," the squad chimed in, led by Stryker.

Sergeant Hughes then spoke up. "And let's not forget Burkett here. It was his call. He did the right thing. The perp was caught and no innocent people got hurt."

"Except the exit sign," Thompson tried to joke with an obvious attempt to not only keep Burkett from getting any recognition, but to embarrass him. With his comment getting only a few uncomfortable laughs by the squad, and Burkett sitting there with a forced smile, but no retort, even Thompson sensed the discomfort he had caused. He quickly, and adeptly, changed direction.

"Hey, and let's hear it for my rookie partner. Barely out of the academy, he takes two rounds, and he's ready to get back on the street. Now that's the kinda cop we want on the Westland Park Police

Department."

The squad followed as Thompson led a round of applause. Burkett hesitantly joined in. Sergeant Hughes looked over to Burkett and gave him a small, uneasy smile. Burkett returned it with a similar unenthusiastic smile. I could tell that Burkett was thinking what I was thinking — why did Hughes let Thompson talk over him like that and take away any credit from Burkett? Hughes was the sergeant; why wasn't he more forceful? This verbal exchange looked like Thompson was in command.

The squad did not stay very long; Hughes left about 10 minutes before everyone else. We ate the cake, told a few war stories, and passed rumors about some of the other cops on the department, whom I, of course, did not know. The timing worked out just right. They had to get to roll call and start their shift just as the conversation was running dry and the jokes started getting stupid. As they were leaving, Liz Fiero seemed to position herself to be sure to be the last one out the door with a calculated slow walk, allowing everyone to get in front of her. As the last one left the room, Liz turned back and said to both us, "Hey, let me congratulate our new heroes."

She went over to Thompson, leaned over and kissed the side of his mouth with the side of her mouth: kind of a kiss on the lips, but not really. He gently and lightly cupped his hand over her ass and at first, she did not react. Then, squirming slightly to get out of that position, she did not seem to be trying very hard and did not seem too uncomfortable. She stood up, moving away from Thompson and then gave him a playful wagging of the forefinger. Yeah, he had been a bad boy, and she liked it. Surprisingly, she then came over to me. I just sat there, because I didn't know what to expect from her. I hardly knew her. She leaned over me and placed her lips directly on mine. Not to the side the way she kissed Thompson, but landed those warm, soft lips right smack on mine. Then she gave my mouth a quick sweep with her tongue, like she was frisking a prisoner for weapons. It was pretty quick and so unexpected, I did not respond at all. I didn't know if that was a good way to react or not. I could not imagine she wanted to get into a long lip lock with me, right there in the hospital room, in front of Thompson. Was she hot for me, or was she playing games with Thompson? Or perhaps neither. She pulled her head back and said, "Get better," then gave me another quick kiss on the lips. Then she walked straight out the door knowing how we were watching that thin ass of hers sway side to side.

Once we knew she was out of earshot I heard Thompson. "Oh, you the man," he said and then gave a howl.

"Whatta ya talking about?" I asked, though I knew exactly where he was heading.

"Oh you are in, my man. I saw that kiss. If you ain't porking that thing within the first 48 hours of getting out of here, then you've got to be one gay motherfucker."

"Ah, c'mon. You were the one playing grab ass with her."

"Yeah, but I saw her shove that tongue of hers down your mouth. You don't think I see those things? Now cut the bullshit. If you don't do her, then I'll be afraid to drive with you anymore. I'm gonna think you're checking me out instead of trying to nail Fiero."

"All right, Mark, that's enough. I think we're getting stupid now. Let it go please."

"Okay, but if that was me, I'd be banging that thing any chance I could."

Of course Thompson would have to get the last word. I was trying to shake Liz Fiero off my mind, because if Nurse Janie walked in, I knew I would screw things up. I also knew I wasn't going to ask her out, at least not there in the hospital room and would have to come back some other time and do it privately. Getting that same feeling I had right after the shooting; I wanted to escape reality for a little while.

Ten and a half more hours and I would be out and home in my sparsely furnished, one bedroom apartment on the fifth floor of a 12 story high rise. Nobody would be there to greet me, but I didn't mind being alone. That was my choice when I left St. Louis in the middle of the night looking for a fresh start. I expected loneliness. This was home now. While a few of the guys on the department called to check on me, it was not like hearing from my old crew back home.

Eventually I'd call them and let them know what happened. Later, maybe. I closed my eyes and quickly fell off to sleep.

My dreams were vivid that night although they did not make any sense. They were a combination of child-like wishes and teenage sex fantasies. They must've awoken me three or four times during the night. The shooting, Nurse Janie, Liz's kiss; I had a lot on my mind. There was plenty to dream about, with many variations. The morning seemed to come quickly. I woke to the sound of a five-year old girl calling, "Daddy, daddy."

Thompson gave his daughter a big hug, picked her up and kissed her face three or four times. As Thompson hugged her, I was drawn in by her round cherubic face, with her mother's brunette hair; she was dressed in a black and white flannel skirt with white stockings and white snow boots. Even I, with no exposure to kids, could see how cute she looked. While holding her in his arms Thompson reached over and kissed his wife twice. Two long kisses and they stared right into each other's eyes. She really loved him. And, it looked like he truly loved her too. I did not expect someone like Thompson to display such true affection towards his wife and kid. But why not? Did being a player mean he did not love his wife? I didn't know. Even more importantly, it was not my business.

His wife was sweet and polite. She came over to me and asked how I felt. She then said that she would have me over for dinner soon and would probably want to set me up with one of her friends sometime. I doubted that either of those invitations would actually come to pass, but it was nice of her to at least make some small talk with me. I'm sure she was anxious to get her husband home. She was a pretty woman, with straight long brown hair complemented by her brown eyes. She seemed shapely, but was wearing loose winter clothes that did not reveal anything. I did not want to be looking at Thompson's wife from that point of view — the way he checked out Sergeant Hughes' wife — but I guess that's just the mold we were cut from. Checking out was okay; it was just how we went about it that mattered. It was all about discretion.

They left with Thompson's daughter waving good-bye to me with her tiny hand as he carried her out the door and down the hallway. I sat there on my bed, looking down at the floor, silently staring at nothing and nobody. I was kind of hoping that Nurse Janie would walk in so I could talk to her alone. Burkett would be there in a few minutes to drive me home. He volunteered, almost insisted that he do it. I wasn't quite sure why. I knew he disliked my partner, and I was just a rookie — nobody he needed as an ally. Maybe he was just trying to do the right thing.

"Good morning, I guess you're on your way out," Nurse Janie said as she walked in the door, half surprising and half scaring me.

"Hey, I was hoping to see you before I left," I blurted out, giving away more than I wanted to.

"How you doing today?" she continued with a caring tone.

"I'm doing good."

"When do you think you'll be back on patrol?"

"Oh, I'm hoping in about a couple of days."

"Hey buddy, ready to get the hell out of this joint?" a booming voice said as Burkett came into the room. His wide frame just about filled the doorway. He had a big smile on his face and seemed to be in an unusually good mood, wearing a dark knit cap around that big head of his and his cheeks were red from the cold. His huge gray jacket had no form; it looked like a big tarp just thrown over him. He had on blue flannel pants with just enough stains to make him look like he had been working at a gas station.

All conversation stopped as Nurse Janie and I first looked at Burkett and then at each other with embarrassed smiles. An uncomfortable silence set upon us, but Burkett did not pick up on it. He stood there with that awkward grin and his hands clasped together in bulky black gloves, just waiting for me to start moving.

"Umm, yeah, I guess I'm ready."

"Okay, let's do it," Burkett answered as he picked up my small black overnight bag that had my personal belongings. It was the gym bag I was given in the academy to carry my work-out gear. The words "Westland Park Police" were imprinted on it in white lettering. Most of the guys would use that bag when going to work out at the gym. How else would the girls know they were cops? Whatever it took to start a conversation.

"Well, I guess I'll see you around sometime," Nurse Janie said with a big smile that I could not be sure was flirtatious or just friendly. The way she tilted her head down and then glanced up at me made me feel confident. But now with Burkett in the room, there was nothing I could do. It was all about timing, and mine sucked. Janie walked out slowly and I watched her till she turned down the hallway and was out of my sight. Nurse Janie and Liz Fiero were two issues I knew I had to follow-up on.

We got into Burkett's personal car — a black Camaro with two racing stripes painted across the hood. He'd probably had that car for more than 10 years. Something about Burkett just did not seem to fit with that car. But he thought he looked good behind the wheel and that was about the sportiest of sports cars a cop could afford. Before I got in the car, I took several breaths of the cold, crisp air. It stung my lungs a little bit and made me cough, but what a relief from the hospital stench and sharing the bathroom with Thompson. It had been snowing on and off for the past week, but the snow had been reduced to muddy slush, with today's sunshine helping to melt it. Early Saturday morning, there was little traffic on the streets. That was good. I was anxious to get home.

"So what's been happening since I've been gone?" I asked Burkett, more out of desire to make conversation than true curiosity.

He turned down his radio, which was tuned to a country music station.

"Well, it's been a little busy. The Second Precinct had two rapes in one week. We had one sexual assault. She was able to fight off the attacker. We had a few burglaries, but nothing else out of the ordinary."

"No armed robberies. That's good."

"Yeah, ours is still the talk of the department. It was a pretty big fuck'n deal. I heard they're even talking about it in Kansas City. We made it into the big leagues."

"I guess. I got a long career ahead of me. I don't want getting shot in the leg to be the only thing I'm ever known for."

"I'm glad I asked you guys to stay and check things out, you know. I had a hunch. You know what I mean. Just sorry you guys had to get hit, but I had a feeling."

"You did a good job, JB. I gotta tell you, I really don't remember a whole lot of specifics right before the shooting started. I remember Thompson coming back in and then getting shot."

"But you remember me telling you that I didn't have a good feeling about this and to check the store. You remember that, right? Right?"

"Hey, JB, listen, I'm just getting out of the hospital. It's really been kind of a fucked-up week. If you don't mind, I'd rather not go over the shooting again. Internal Affairs is gonna make me repeat the whole thing."

"That's why you gotta remember things exactly, word for word. You know what I mean, right?"

"I got it, JB. I'm sure it will all come back to me. Besides, Hughes warned me about talking too much before I see IA. So thanks for picking me up. I appreciate it. I know we really haven't had a chance to become friends, especially with me riding with Thompson. What's up with you two — bad blood from something in the past?"

"No. He's just like that. He's always making some comment about my weight or my balding or whatever he can think of. I don't know why he's always busting my balls. I try busting his balls back, but I'm not good at that stuff and I don't even like doing it. Now with him shooting this guy, we'll probably never hear the end of his bragging and bullshit. What do you think of him? You're the one riding with him."

"Eh, he's not so bad. I think he likes to bash everybody, not just you." There was no way I was going to share my true feelings that Thompson was a brash, arrogant asshole who picked on Burkett just to pump up his own ego.

"He is a pretty good cop," I added. That was true, but did we really handle the robbery well? I knew I didn't have enough street time to make such a critical call, but the fact of the matter was, we both got shot. Fortunately, we both survived. But can two cops getting shot really equate to good police work? Thompson was well-liked and slick; I knew he'd already figured out a way to ride this shooting to something bigger for himself. I needed him to let me ride it too.

"So where do you live, JB?" I asked to change the subject.

"Oh, I got a house in Cherry Woods. Small house, but it works for me."

"Yeah, you own or rent?"

"We own it."

"We? Are you married?" Of course, I already knew the answer to that question.

"Married? Hell no, why would I do that to myself? I live with my mother. It's her house, but it's a great deal for me."

"How's that?"

"Well, first, I inherit the house when the old bag kicks the bucket, and it's already paid off. Next, I'm living rent free which leaves me plenty of money to spend on the babes."

"Doesn't living with your mother cramp your style?" Actually I was wondering just what, if any, style Burkett had.

"Hell no. She lives upstairs in her bedroom and turns off her hearing aid. Sometimes I got a babe in the living room just friggin' howling and no one even knows my mother's there, and she don't hear a thing. It's great. I pick these bitches up at a club downtown, bring them home for a great night, next morning drop their asses back downtown. The only way to go."

"Sounds great, JB," I said trying hard not to picture what was in Burkett's mind when he talked about making a girl howl.

"You're single, right, Gary?"

"Yeah. I'm only 24. I think I got a little time."

"Maybe we'll head down to the clubs together one night. Babes usually travel with friends anyway. May make it easier for us to score a little pussy. Whatta ya think?"

"Okay, maybe we'll do that sometime." I don't think I could've been any less committal.

I then gave Burkett the rest of the directions to my home and thanked him several times for the ride, deliberately avoiding saying anything to indicate I wanted to pursue a close friendship with him. I knew why he picked me up from the hospital; I got his message. I got Thompson's message too. Now I wanted to be left alone with my own thoughts.

Absorbing the emptiness of my apartment, I stood in the doorway for a moment, then threw my gym bag down on the floor, not feeling any need to unpack it. I felt like calling my mom just to talk. I just couldn't bring myself to do that. My brown cloth couch that I bought at the Goodwill store for $50 was inviting as I sat down and turned on the television The pain was not severe and the hospital gave me a few painkillers just in case. Knowing there was no legitimate reason to feel too sorry for myself, I somehow still found a way to do so. I fell asleep.

Chapter 4

Jim Burkett was already thinking about ending his shift and going home. But he hadn't even started work yet. Driving to roll call at the Third Precinct, which was in an isolated lot across from a shopping plaza on a four lane main street, he passed through the lower middle class neighborhood of Franklin. Looking at the small, single-family ranch houses, town homes and some federally funded, low-income, residential projects which were spotted throughout the neighborhood, he wondered which one would have a domestic dispute tonight: usually some drunken guy beating up his wife or kids, or both. Then looking out the opposite window at the shops in the strip malls, fast food restaurants, gas stations and liquor stores, he wondered who might get robbed that night.

Fast food restaurant and convenience store robberies weren't uncommon, but they were usually finished long before the cops arrived, unlike the last one Burkett responded to. He was glad that he finally got his transfer to the Third Precinct a year ago; he had served in four other precincts, always hoping that somehow a new environment would give him a fresh chance to jump-start his reputation and get a better shot at detective.

Stopping his car, Burkett punched in his pass code at the security gate in the back of the precinct, which was newly built. After 14 years on the job, Burkett noticed the number of changes from the old precinct buildings. The City Board had finally approved erecting a security fence around the rear of the precinct where the police cars were parked; they had refused for a long time, saying that it gave the precinct too much of a military appearance. They wanted to maintain good community relations. But, one night, two police cars wrecked because someone had snuck on to the lot and loosened the lug nuts on those cars' tires. That happened in August of 2001.

After September 11th, the police department did not need much more ammunition for their argument to get the fence. Not that anybody really considered Westland Park a likely terrorist target, but at that moment in history, paranoia was a strong motivator. Also new at the precinct was the bulletproof glass that protected the receptionist at the front desk. Historically, the City Board had resisted these barriers, insisting on the personal touch, but times were changing.

Burkett thought the appearance out front was too nice, lacking a tough, police aura. The building was all brick with a glass front door that had the police department insignia etched in the center of the glass. Small gardens on each side of the walkway leading to the entrance from the visitor parking lot emanated a warm, soft environment.

*****

I wouldn't have noticed any difference in the way things looked. Growing up on the outskirts of St. Louis, I was never in Westland Park before applying for this job. The closest I got was when my parents took me to the Plaza in Kansas City to watch the lighting ceremony on Thanksgiving night. I think that may have been what cost me the job with the Kansas City Police Department. During my interview I joked about how boring I remembered that ceremony being. That fell flat. Kansas Citians loved lighting up the Plaza. I kept driving west and found my place in Westland Park.

Leaving town was my escape from being dumped by Melissa, the girl I thought I would marry. She and I, and my two best friends with their girls, were together all the time. Then, I was odd man out. Once things changed like that, they never come back, especially when Melissa started showing up with her new boyfriend so soon. Everyone knew that she must've been seeing the guy behind my back. Everyone except me. That was too painful to imagine. I was the jealous type. I wasn't that far away from St. Louis — about a four hour drive — but far enough for me to feel that I was starting life anew.

This was my first night back since the shooting. Putting a dab of gel in my hair and slapping on a little aftershave, I was trying to look a little more alive than my stoic face appeared. Somehow, my six foot, thin stature looked shorter and wider than before the shooting. I probably could have stayed out a little longer, but the wounds on my leg had healed pretty well and I was ready physically, and mentally, at least according to the department shrink. I also knew that Thompson was going to stay out till the shift started next week. This would give me a chance to ride with someone else, which was something I knew I needed.

In the locker room, for no particular reason, Sergeant Hughes caught my attention as I watched him staring into the mirror fixing his tie, a little to the left, a little to the right, then he had it perfect. He then used a little cloth he carried in his pocket to brighten up his badge and the gold three striped sergeant pins on his collar. At 45, he had to fluff his hair a bit to cover his thinning spots. Ducking into the toilet stall, he ripped off a piece of toilet paper to clean his reading glasses that he then delicately put in his left breast pocket, which sported a gold pen and pencil set, each with the police seal on the clip. Looking down, he checked the shine on his shoes one more time, then headed to roll call, always the first one there, always at least 10 minutes early.

I saw Burkett finish getting ready, rubbing his shoes on the back of the opposite pant leg. He was the next one to head into the roll call room, which was set up pretty much like a classroom — chairs with little desks attached and the big desk for the sergeant in front, with a blackboard behind it. On one wall was a bulletin board where messages for the squad were posted if they got a call when they were off. Otherwise the call was broadcast over the radio. On another wall were the pictures of the city's "Ten Most Wanted." One was wanted for a murder that occurred three years earlier. Two were wanted for burglary, but most were wanted for petty thefts or other misdemeanors. Next to the sergeant's desk was a box with folders — one for each patrol sector. In the folders were warrants for people living in those sectors. Before heading out on patrol, the officer was supposed to take the warrants and serve at least one during the shift.

Between the time to book somebody and handle the normal calls, there really wasn't time to serve more than one warrant.

We rarely served warrants during the midnight shift. It just was not our policy to pull people out of their houses late at night for a misdemeanor. Those warrants were served during the day or early evening shift. In reality, most warrants wound up being served when someone got stopped for a traffic violation and the cop ran their names through the National Crime Information Center, or what was known as NCIC. For the more serious felonies, the detectives usually kept those warrants locked in their desks so they could go out and make the arrests. That made sense; most felonies were not worked by the street cops who took the report anyway. They were referred to the Detective Bureau — their case, their arrest.

Following Burkett, I took a seat on the opposite side of the room, but saying "hi" as I walked by. Burkett was carefully watching the squad file into the roll call room one by one. I had a feeling he was checking to see if Thompson was coming back tonight. My guess was that Burkett enjoyed the first few nights with Thompson out. This was the first night of our four day, 10 hour shift. It was Monday and was probably going to be an ordinary night.

Did I hope for another shooting, so maybe this time I could pull my gun and plug someone, or was I hoping never to face that again? I was not sure. I knew that I, and probably everyone else on the squad, was looking forward to having the weekend off. After our break, we would return on a Sunday night, so I wondered what plans Burkett had for the weekend, and what stories he would have, real or imagined, when we got back.

"All right, let's get started," Hughes called out as everyone took his or her seat.

"First, welcome back to Officer Hollings. We are all glad to see you."

A small round of applause broke out briefly.

"Thompson will be back with us next shift. He's doing fine."

Hearing that, I glanced over to Burkett.

"The Internal Affairs Shooting Review Board will be here in the next week or two taking statements from anyone who was there," Hughes continued. "Obviously, Thompson, Hollings and Burkett will be called in and that'll be intense, I'm sure. For the rest of you who were at the scene afterwards, just be prepared to tell them whatever you remember. Any questions?"

There was an uneasy silence, but no questions.

"Okay then," Hughes continued. He read off the description of cars and their license plates that were reported stolen the day before. Then he read from the daily crime reports. Three business burglaries occurred last night. There had been a string of those in the past few weeks.

"We've gotta start shaking a few more doors at night. The commander told me that burglaries are up throughout the city. I've been looking through your reports to see if you've been conducting suspicious person stops and doing field interviews, and I haven't seen any. We should be questioning suspicious people, rattling doors and shaking things up a little out there. The Detective Bureau is starting to wonder what we do all night."

Reading reports? I wondered. Wouldn't the sergeant know what we were doing just by listening to the radio, or maybe coming out on the street every once in a while?

"Hey, Sarge, everybody who lives in Franklin and Woodbury, in fact, the whole damn Third Precinct, is suspicious. If we get too aggressive, we'll be accused of racial profiling or harassment or something like that," Stryker responded.

"Look, I know what you are saying and those things can be real problems. I know that. But we can't let that stop us from doing good police work. If you're out there honestly stopping shady characters and checking things out, you'll be okay as long as you're not letting race or prejudice drive you. I don't think anyone on this squad, or even this department, is like that. So let's get a little more aggressive out there."

The sergeant started reading off the squad's patrol sector assignments and call signals. It was usually the same each night. Once in a while, assignments would change, depending on who was off that night. I knew I'd be riding with someone else — would it be Liz Fiero? If so, what would happen? That thought stirred my imagination.

Then came my assignment. No Liz tonight.

"Gillis, you're a training officer tonight," Hughes called out.

"Uh, Sarge, can this wait for some other shift? There are a couple of things I wanted to take care of tonight."

"You go ahead and take care of them, and while you do, teach young Mr. Hollings here how to be a great cop like you." Then the squad broke out in a healthy laugh.

"Well," Hughes continued, "just teach him to be a good cop, and we'll leave it at that."

I was partnered with Mike Gillis. Our call signal was 319 Baker. Gillis seemed like a quiet but confident guy. He did not speak up at roll call very much and he was not big on the locker room banter. When I thought about it, Thompson and Stryker were the only two guys I ever saw Gillis really have a conversation with. He had completely shaved his head and had a thick, gray moustache. A little taller than me, he was just over 6 feet, and as a former marine, was in pretty good shape. You certainly did not mind when he came to back you up.

As roll call broke up I went over to talk to Gillis. He waved me off, holding up his index finger, telling me to give him one minute as he huddled together with Stryker. He seemed to be in control of the conversation, his hands moving in many directions, almost like a quarterback calling the play. Then he walked over towards me.

"Okay, young man..." he started out, with a baritone voice, as he handed me the keys to the car. Then his cell phone rang.

"Let me get this. Why don't you check the warrant box? And if there's a warrant for a guy named Dixon, grab it. Then get the car ready and I'll be there in a minute."

"Yes, sir," I replied back.

"Yeah, listen, I don't want to hear any of that sir shit. You don't see any damn stripes on my arm, do you? My name is Mike."

"You got it."

So, we were going to serve a warrant tonight. That would be the first time I saw that done on this shift. I pulled the car up to the precinct rear door and picked Gillis up.

"So, do you know how to get to sector 319?"

Then I realized that I did not know how to get there and once again wondered just where I planned on driving to. It would have been smart to pull out the map and check before I picked Gillis up.

"Actually, I don't," I answered hesitantly, but honestly.

"That's all right," Gillis said with a small laugh. "I know you're new, but in time, you really got to get to know the whole precinct. When you're out there on your own and one of us calls for back-up, you have to have a pretty good idea of where we all are. And when you call for back-up, you'll appreciate them knowing how to get to you quickly without taking time to check the map."

Gillis gave me directions down to the sector. First thing we did was to get a cup of coffee. Gillis walked by the counter with a dollar in his hand. The clerk waved to him and let him go. I did the same. Thompson and I always got a free cup of coffee at the convenience mart in our sector, but I didn't take anything for granted. Besides, I didn't know Gillis. There was no way I was going to do anything stupid in front of him. Like Thompson, he was a senior cop; anything he said about me would go right to my reputation in the department.

We got back in the car and Gillis had me just drive around the sector as he pointed out some of the trouble spots. He knew his beat pretty well. He then had me head to a neighborhood called Ashburn.

"This is your typical white trash around here. The only thing we lack is a trailer park. Actually, we got one of those in the next patrol district east of here. You got bikers, wannabe bikers and just general punks. They like to drink, fight and beat their girlfriends. When they're not doing that, they're stealing cars or pushing meth. A lot of this is spillover from Kansas City."

"Why is that? Why would they come here?"

"Simple. The KCPD got a whole lot more manpower than we do to handle this crap. Then, when you add on all those federal task forces they got going on with the FBI, DEA, ATF, there are so many swinging dicks over there carrying a badge, there are more cops than criminals. These maggots know that and don't need so many cops up their ass."

"So they cross the border and come here, thinking a smaller city police department can't handle it, huh?" I asked to show I was following his thoughts.

"You got it. All the scum of the earth has to do is just cross the city line over to us where we have less than half the number of cops and we spend most of our time handling petty fights and vandalisms. Maybe one day, we'll start taking this street crime stuff a little more seriously than we do now and we'll push all this shit back over to KC. But if the chief keeps putting all this priority on quality community service, we won't get shit done out here." Gillis stopped to take a breath, and then continued.

"I know you didn't want to hear all that. That's just how I get sometimes. Let's get out of here for now; I'm sure we'll be back a little later for some bullshit."

Gillis sounded pretty much like he looked — aggressive and serious about crime. He did not come off like he was big on community relations or handling routine service calls. He wanted to fight crime right out there in the streets or at least just fight. He looked tough and I bet he was. *Yeah*, I thought, *now maybe that's more the kind of cop I want to be.*

"So how long have you been on this squad?" I asked him. Apparently, he was not going to ask any questions about me; he had absolutely no interest.

"About five years. I worked in the First Precinct my first few years on the department. But I got a transfer out here when I bought a house out in a subdivision in Mattison. This precinct was a lot closer. Then, I was on the day shift for a while, but that started too early for me, and I didn't like all the traffic accidents we had to handle, so I put in for this shift. Midnights aren't too bad. Not perfect, but not too bad."

"I was having a little trouble keeping my eyes open past midnight, but I'm getting better," I told him.

"Yeah, that happens. But a young, smart kid like you won't be on patrol very long. Keep out of trouble and you'll move up the ranks real fast. Just watch out for those three B's."

"Three bees?"

"Yeah, booze, broads and bucks. If you get into a bind in any one of those, you get all fucked up. Almost any time a cop's career got ruined, it was over one of those things."

I thought about that for a moment, a very long moment. It made complete sense. I could see that any one of those problems would probably lead to the other two. Flattered by his confidence in me being able to move up the ranks, I couldn't help but remember that Thompson told me the same thing. Was I really that impressive, or did these guys just like feeding my ego for some other reason?

"Circle around that block again," he directed me, as if giving a military order.

"Why? Did I miss something?"

"Do you think you did?"

"Well, um, no, I, um, don't think so," not being quite sure what to say.

So I circled back around and looked closely for what I missed. I didn't see anything. I didn't know what to say or do. After driving down the whole block again I was waiting for some instruction from Gillis. He didn't say anything, so I had to ask.

"I hate to say this, but I didn't see what I was supposed to see. Should I go back again?"

"No, because there wasn't anything you were supposed to see. But there are two lessons to be learned here."

"Okay, I'm ready," I told him.

"First, you weren't sure if you missed something, right?"

"Right."

"Is that possibly because you were just driving without really looking for anything or at anything? You couldn't remember one thing you saw. Could you?"

I had to stop and think about that for a second; I guess I really had my head up my ass.

"No, you're right. I was just driving. I wasn't looking around; I didn't take notice of anything, or, um, anybody. Especially, after what the sergeant just said, I guess I should have been more alert."

'Well, don't beat yourself up. You're new. You're here to learn, which brings us to our next lesson."

"What's that?" I asked anxiously, in anticipation of hearing my other screw up.

"You gotta circle back every now and then and be unpredictable. The maggots out there are watching you. They see you coming and may just be waiting for you to pass by before they do whatever it is they were going to do. If you circle back unexpectedly, you may just catch something in progress. But you will be better off if you know what things looked like before you circle back. See what I'm getting at?"

I did. That was some good advice. I'm sure it was nothing Thompson didn't already know, but he didn't think of telling me. There's a lot an experienced cop can teach a young rookie, and then there's a lot you can learn only by doing. Cruising around a little more, we made small talk which seemed as aimless as our patrolling, but I was trying to stay alert to my surroundings, and pay attention to the radio. We drove through the neighborhood of Heaven Hills. It was a predominantly black neighborhood, which did not appreciate Westland Park's mostly white police department. Gillis checked his watch as he had already done two times earlier tonight.

"Drive to the Full Moon convenience store on the corner of Pimmit and Route 7. I want to check on something. You know where it is?"

I looked at him with a look that clearly showed I didn't. Gillis gave me directions to the convenience store, which was only a few blocks away.

"Now, there will be a lot of guys hanging around out front. When we drive by, drive real slow. Make our presence obvious. You keep your eyes on the road and I'll give them the stare. Got it?"

"Got it." I wasn't sure what Gillis had in mind, but it sounded interesting and I was about to learn another lesson.

We drove by slowly, as Gillis directed me. He stared. I watched the group of men, who were in a small crowd of about four or five standing under the light of the store's awning, quickly separate and just stare back at us as we drove by. I didn't know what the men were doing, though it was probably illegal since they scattered the way they did. I wasn't sure what we accomplished, other than maybe just to show our presence.

"All right, just turn the corner now and drive up that hill and follow it around the bend till it ends in the parking lot for those apartments," Gillis told me as he pointed in the direction he wanted me to go. So I did.

"Now, park behind that building," Gillis said, this time pointing to one of the three story buildings in this small complex.

We parked, and when Gillis asked, I told him that there was no warrant for anyone named Dixon. Gillis called in Dixon's name on the radio for an NCIC check. There was always the possibility another department had a warrant for him. The dispatcher radioed back that there were no outstanding warrants for Willie Dixon.

"Too bad. Now would be a good time to pick him up on one, but I think we may get to do so anyway."

Gillis grabbed a pair of binoculars out of his bag and we walked to the side of the building, which by now I had figured out overlooked the Full Moon store. Gillis started focusing in.

"Okay," he said to me, "look down there at the store. The crowd is back. You should be able to see one guy off to the left and the crowd off to the right. Now watch and tell me what you see," as he handed me the binoculars with his left hand while still keeping watch on the Full Moon.

With my right hand, I took the binoculars and fumbled with them, taking a few seconds to find the target. Then I started watching. For the first few moments, I didn't see anything unusual. Then a car drove up. Somebody got out of the car and walked over to the man on the left. The guy from the car picked up something from the ground very quickly, and then furtively handed something to the man on the left. It was so furtive, it was obvious. I told Gillis what I saw.

"Do you know what you just observed?"

"No." I had to honestly admit it, because I simply had no idea other than one guy handing something to someone else.

"The guy on the left is Willie Dixon. That's why I wanted to know if there was a warrant on him. What he's doing is selling crack. He's got mostly eight-balls out there. He leaves it on the ground, so if cops do approach him, he just says it's there on the street. It's not his, and he can't get arrested. He knows that we'll grab the crack though, so he won't put more than maybe a grand worth of it out there at any one time."

"That's still a lot of money."

"Not really. Whatever he loses, he just sucks up and puts more out there. It's all just a fuck'n game. And here's our game plan. Ready?"

"Ready."

"We're gonna cruise down the hill to get a little closer with our lights off. As soon as we get to the back of the store, we come to the front from opposite sides. If you catch anybody who just picked up something, or gave something to Dixon, grab him. I put the habeas grabass on Dixon."

"What if we don't see any transactions?"

"I'm grabbing Dixon anyway. We saw him taking money from guys who took the crap off the ground. That's probable cause of drug trafficking as far as I'm concerned. We'll sweep up the dope, seize his money and let the prosecutor and defense attorney duke it out. We just testify to what we saw. Make sense?"

"Yeah, sounds great. There's a number of fuckers down there. Want me to call in for some back-up?"

"No, no back-up," Gillis almost snapped at me. "I don't like too many people knowing what I'm up to. Either something will leak out or somebody will cruise by to see what's happening and ruin everything. In some cases, less is more. Besides, I'm gonna get Stryke on the side channel to help out."

"Okay." I responded with a quiver in my voice. Asking for back-up hit a raw nerve with him.

Cruising down the hill with our headlights off, we stopped the car on the side of the road that was out of view of the front of Full Moon. We were in a single family home area of the neighborhood next to someone's backyard surrounded by a rusted chain link fence. An old swing set was creaking as the swing was pushed by the light winter breeze, which made it feel just a little colder than it already was. Some toys and a tricycle were lying around, partially covered in snow. The upstairs window reflected the dim light of a television set. It was a dismal view of life. Gillis switched the dial on the radio console to the side channel, which transmitted car-to-car and did not go through the dispatcher.

"Stryke, I got Dixon at the Full Moon. You gonna come in from the west?"

"You got it, buddy." Stryker did not ask any questions. He seemed prepared for this. Next thing I heard on the radio was Stryker calling in to dispatch.

"I'll be out with 319 on suspicious activity at the Full Moon." And the dispatcher acknowledged.

As I got ready to get out of the car, Gillis held his hand out to stop me.

"Hold up, turn off the overhead light so it doesn't go on when you open the door. And when you close the door, do it quietly. Then turn down your handheld radio. Last thing we need is for them to hear us coming." Those were three things, although obvious after he said them, I know I would not have thought of.

We walked quietly down the block to the back of Full Moon unnoticed. Our approach did not get anybody's attention, though we both had to pay attention to the jingling sound made by all the things hanging off our utility belts. We went to opposite sides of the back of the building. On Gillis' cue, we circled the store. As we turned the corner of the store, the guys facing Dixon saw Gillis and ran my way, right past me. I didn't see anybody touch anything so I just let them go. Dixon turned around and ran right into Gillis' waiting hands. Gillis spun him around and pushed him up against the wall so fast, I didn't even see it happen. Dixon's left cheek was pressed hard against the cold brick wall.

Of course, it wasn't much of a contest. Dixon stood at maybe 135 pounds and 5' 8" at best in those black cowboy boots he was wearing. A boyish face with a stubbly beard, he was light skinned and had a noticeable twitch in his right eye, while his left eye and whole left side of his face was hugging Full Moon's brick wall, via the forceful push of Gillis' left hand. Dixon didn't have the look of a drug dealer. Then again, what should a small time drug dealer look like? I didn't know. He wore a long black leather coat with deep pockets. Gillis moved slowly and cautiously while searching him. Dixon was handcuffed, so Gillis wasn't as worried about Dixon grabbing a weapon as he was about the possibility of getting stuck from a needle. That I had learned in the academy.

"Grab the dope," Gillis yelled to me.

I bent down and picked up the packets of tin foil off the ground and put them in my pocket.

"Check around a little more for any stray packets that may have gotten kicked around. We don't wanna leave any crack on the streets here."

I turned my attention back to the ground and started an almost grid-like search, the way we learned to search for evidence at the academy. I did not find any more drugs.

"That shit ain't mine," Dixon hollered out. "You ain't got nothing."

"And you ain't got no crack anymore," Gillis retorted, giving Dixon a light tap to the back of his head.

"Go ahead and help Stryker. He's on the west side with some dickhead he stopped trying to run away," Gillis instructed me.

I must have missed it; I didn't hear Stryker call on the radio and say where he was or ask for help. Just like Gillis was trying to tell me — I had to learn to take in everything that was going on around me. I ran to the side of the building where Stryker was frisking down some poor slob in a flannel shirt and dirty, oil stained, torn jeans. Not saying anything to distract him, I just walked over to Stryker. I knew he would tell me if there was something he wanted me to do.

"Okay, turn around, asshole." Stryker barked out his order as he grabbed the guy by his shoulders and spun him around, just as Gillis did to Dixon.

"You live in Kansas City and you're hanging out here. Why don't you just stay home and sling your dope there? You got lucky now, but I don't want to see your ass ugly face around here again. Got it?"

"Yes, Officer," were his words as he turned and walked away, up the hill Gillis and I had just descended. As he got about 20 yards away he stopped and looked back. He looked at Stryker, then me with an almost imperceptible shake of his head, as if he disapproved of what we had done. He almost looked as if his feelings were hurt. I couldn't figure it out. Stryker hadn't roughed him up, didn't arrest him; all Stryker did was pat him down. So what?

"Keep moving, douche bag," Stryker said only loud enough for me to hear. Then Stryker laughed to himself. He turned away and lightly slapped my shoulder, indicating that I should follow him. We walked back over to Gillis just as he closed the back door on Dixon, handcuffed and strapped in the rear seat.

"Any weapons?" Stryker asked.

"Nah, he knows better than that. Didn't want to buy himself any more time in jail than necessary," Gillis replied.

"You got the dope, rookie?" Gillis turned to me sporting a self-satisfied type of grin.

"Yeah, right here," I answered him as I patted on my left front pocket.

"How much?" Stryker asked.

"Looked like 10 or 12 eight-balls," Gillis answered him, probably knowing that I had no idea.

"Phew. Nice bust." Stryker seemed impressed.

"All right, I guess we gotta head downtown with Mr. Dixon here," Gillis announced.

"We have to call the Sarge down to the scene when we seize dope like that. Don't we?"

"Yeah, if you're a by-the-book guy you do. Hughes ain't like that. He's kind of a hands-off manager, but I'll call him if it'll make you feel better."

Gillis picked up the radio already tuned to the side channel.

"319 Baker to Car 300."

"This is 300. Go," Hughes responded.

"We just picked up Willie Dixon with some dope. Gonna book him and drop everything in the evidence vault. You wanna respond here first?"

"No, that's all right. Just take care of it. Nice bust."

Sergeant Hughes was in the precinct, probably rereading some of the squad's reports from the shift last week. He liked correcting spelling and grammar. He kept notes on how many reports each officer wrote and the quality of the report. He was judicious about checking everyone's monthly stats for tickets and arrests. He spent a lot of time in the precinct working on these administrative matters. How else could he fairly assess the work of his officers? Why were the other sergeants spending so much time on the streets? That's what the patrol officers were supposed to do — patrol. Sergeants supervised; they didn't work the streets.

"10-4, Sarge. Thanks."

"See that? Everything's okay," Gillis reassured me.

It took about another two hours to get Dixon booked. He did not talk much and was very compliant. I guess most criminals know when it's worth fighting and when it's not. Gillis showed me how to handle the evidence. We weighed the drugs and sealed the package. We both signed the chain of custody form and then deposited the drugs in the evidence vault.

"That seemed a little too easy. Can you pull that off every night? Have you done it before?" I had to know.

"Yeah, I pull this off every once in a while, but only when I have some good information comin' in. Now this is what I was talking about. To me, this is the real police work: getting drug dealers off the streets. But you gotta be careful and not let them predict what you're gonna do or when you're gonna do it. Otherwise, they just move elsewhere or put lookouts out on the street and you walk right into a trap."

"So, does that mean Dixon will be on the lookout for you now on?"

"Maybe. A snitch of mine told me that Dixon was back in town, so I figured he'd be there. But Mr. Dixon will be on vacation for a little bit. His supplier will move the operation somewhere else, so not much will happen at Full Moon for a while. It was a good bust, but it may be a little while before I get another one like that. It's a little luck, a little timing and a little information."

We had about an hour left to the shift. I kind of liked Gillis. He wasn't like Thompson and he certainly wasn't like Burkett. Maybe he was the kind of cop I should model myself after. He seemed like a good, straight-shooting cop. He said what he meant, meant what he said. I wanted to get his insight about the folks on our squad.

"So, any good rumors going around the squad that I should know about?" I asked, thinking he may start talking about Thompson or Burkett.

"Like what?"

"Oh, I don't know. Just stuff."

"Lemme guess. You want to hear about Liz Fiero, right?"

That caught me off guard. What about Liz Fiero should I know? So I asked.

"Well, I hadn't heard anything about Liz, but now you got me wondering, wassup?"

"Word has it she's screwed a few of the boys while on patrol. I never hear who, when or where. It could all just be talk. I mean, she's been in the department for about 10 years and that's all I hear, so I tend to think there's something to it." Then he hesitated for a moment. Gillis started looking at me with an impish smile.

"You looking to get a piece of that?"

Did he suspect something? I was pretty sure that nobody other than Thompson had seen that kiss at the hospital. And Thompson was at home. I couldn't imagine that a tough cop like him had nothing better to do than to gossip and start some stupid rumor about Liz and me.

"Hey, I just wanna do a good job now and get cut loose from this rookie stuff. I ain't looking to do nobody at work. I keep my personal life at home."

"Good thought. You say that now, but we'll see what happens.

You got a lot of years ahead of you and a lot of things you ain't been exposed to yet. Has Thompson taken you to see Bullet Brenda yet?"

"Bullet Brenda... who's that?"

"I'm gonna leave that to Thompson."

I really wanted to know who Bullet Brenda was, but I already knew Gillis was not giving it up. He was leaving that to Thompson, just as he said. Gillis was right. I had a lot to learn.

"So any advice for me when Internal Affairs comes around? I'm a little nervous."

"Just don't fuck with Internal Affairs. All you do is tell the truth. Besides, you got nothing to worry about. All you did was get shot. Thompson's covered. He shot the bastard right in the ass; you can't beat that. Now Burkett, he may have to do a little tap dancing. It was his call and he let you walk right into an ambush. That ain't good. That's why you guys weren't ready and still had your weapons holstered when you took those rounds. Unless, of course, you guys somehow fucked up. Then you got some explaining to do. The only thing Burkett has to show for this is a shot-out exit sign. I don't know. It'll be interesting to see how it shakes out."

"Well, you know ..."

"Nope, don't say any more," Gillis interrupted me. "We're not supposed to be talking about this at all. It's an open investigation," he continued. "You don't want to give IA any reason to think you manufactured your story by talking to me or anyone else. Just give 'em the facts."

Those were some interesting thoughts Gillis had. And he was right. I had been warned not to discuss the shooting until after the Review Board hearings. But it certainly did seem that Gillis wanted to throw in a few pointers. I didn't imagine that Burkett would really have to be concerned with the way things worked out, but after hearing Gillis, I was not so sure. Clearly, there was a lot riding on this IA investigation, for all of us. Thompson's little lecture to me in the hospital was still ringing in my ears, and now Gillis was throwing a few not so subtle hints my way. I realized that I was going to have to choose my words carefully.

"It's been a good night, partner," Gillis said to me. "How 'bout you buy me a cup of coffee to finish the night off?"

"That sounds good."

Chapter 5

Finally, it was Friday night and I was off. That was the night for single people to go downtown to the nightclubs and get a date for the next weekend. No girl will go out with you the next night, even though you both don't have dates; she'll look too desperate by going out last minute on a Saturday night. I've been playing the nightclub game since getting dumped, and not all that successfully. Each time out, I was getting better at it, though there were still guys a lot smoother and more polished than I. Asking a girl to dance was becoming a little bit easier; the "no's" weren't as hard to swallow. Now that I was a cop, I was hoping that I'd have a little more self-confidence. And now, I would have a lot more exciting things to talk about. I'd been shot during an armed robbery. Thompson planned on turning that into some kinda pussy magnet, so why shouldn't I? Could not leave for a nightclub without a mirror check. Turning to the side, I assured myself that I'd work off a little of the weight I gained while in the hospital. No signs of the hairline receding yet; thinning hair ran in the family. My short brown hair and clean shaven face of innocence just wreaked of being a cop.

Burkett asked me to meet him there at the Warehouse Night Club. It was appropriately named, as it was a renovated warehouse with a long L-shaped bar that was on the perimeter of a huge dance floor. Dark with flashing lights and loud music, it was probably not much different than the discos I'd heard about from Jimmy, the oldest of my brothers; though I am sure the music had changed. From what I saw of his photos, so had the clothing, thankfully. Jimmy was killed fighting in Iraq. I look at his photos now and then. I still look up to him.

I remember once in the schoolyard handball court, Joey G, a neighborhood tough, surrounded by four friends, threw a soda can at Jimmy, just for the hell of it. Jimmy stopped playing, and calmly told him, "Pick up that fuck'n can or I'll ram it down your throat." Joey G looked at his friends, smiling, as if Jimmy was going to back down. He didn't. Joey G picked up the can and walked away, threatening Jimmy. It was an empty, face-saving threat, and everybody knew it. That story got around school fast.

Going out with Burkett did not seem like a wise thing to do, but then I figured what the hell? I had no other plans. Not getting too close to Burkett on a social basis was my concern. Talking about the shooting and the Review Board was something he was going to try to fit in; I knew where he was going with that. Having a fun night out was my only goal. Besides, this was supposedly the hottest nightclub in town. I heard it said that if you couldn't score there, you couldn't score anywhere. I didn't really want to test myself against those criteria, not wanting to be disappointed.

"Hey, buddy," I heard with a loud slap on the back from Burkett. The place was pretty crowded. I was surprised he found me.

Saying "hi" in return, I noticed his dress; he looked very out of place in khaki pants and a dark green plaid sports jacket. He was wearing a weapon on his belt, so I was assuming and hoping that he planned on keeping that jacket on all night. My weapon was tightly wrapped around my left ankle. The gun was part necessity, part pain in the ass. Wearing it off-duty was optional. But should something break loose, you were expected to react accordingly. If you weren't prepared to act, it would look bad. Yet, if something did happen and that gun got away from you, things would be even worse. If that weapon managed to spring loose while you were dancing — let's just say it would not be a pleasant situation.

Wearing a plain white, long sleeve shirt and casual blue pants with my dress black shoes, I was hardly a fashion statement myself. I wore my clothes slightly on the tight side. I was thin with a muscular physique, so I would show off what I could. On the outside, I looked more confident with women than I really was. A lot of young guys there knew how to dress the part and most likely knew how to play this game much better than I. I had one advantage — standing next to Burkett should have made me come off as movie star.

We stood around for a while, watching the crowd, sipping our beers. We engaged in the normal man talk of two off-duty cops who were looking, but not brave enough to act — "What an ass. I should be sucking on those tits right now. Come here, baby. I'll frisk you down and you can rub my nightstick." They were just fantasy opening lines to keep each other amused: nothing we would ever have the nerve to say. While forcing our laughter to appear as if we were really having fun, we each quietly contemplated our first move. Burkett spoke out first.

"Just walk over to the bar with me. Stay on my right, while I try to get next to that blonde in the pink top. You see her?"

"Yeah, okay, I can do that."

So I followed Burkett over to the bar, the music becoming louder as we got closer. Burkett managed to get himself next to his target.

"So, how are things on patrol going for you, partner?" he said rather loudly, catching me off guard.

"Uh, I guess okay." I didn't really know what to say.

"Whadda ya drinking?" he asked me.

"Another light beer sounds good."

"A light beer and a black Russian," he called out to the bartender. Then turning to the blonde, he said, "and whatever this young lady likes."

It took her a moment to realize what he was doing. She was talking to her friends on her left. She looked up at him, kind of checked him over and said, "Oh, that's okay."

"No, please," Burkett went on. "That's why we come here, to buy pretty girls drinks. What do you want?"

She stared at him, thinking for a moment and finally said, "How about a vodka sour?"

"A vodka sour it is," Burkett said, turning to the bartender and laying his money down on the bar.

I was able to overhear only a little bit of the conversation that followed as Burkett turned completely in her direction and tried to move in a little closer. Between his big frame, the loud music and all the one liners being slung around the bar, I couldn't hear much, although I was quite curious as to how Burkett's lines, which I'm sure were well-rehearsed, were coming off. I picked up on him telling her that he was a cop. Somehow, that did not surprise me. The bartender served them their drinks and I moved to the other side of them, so I could observe a little more carefully. I felt like a voyeur. Fascinated watching Burkett in action, I noticed that his face showed more determination here than I had ever seen while we were out on the street. He was intense, yet she seemed distracted; she kept turning back to her friends. Burkett looked like he was trying so hard that he was not picking up on her body language.

After a few minutes I thought I should take the opportunity and talk to her friends. Maybe I would meet somebody, playing off Burkett's offensive move. As I made my way over to them, I heard the blonde say to Burkett, "Well, my friends want to get going now. It was really nice meeting you. I'll probably run into you later." She grabbed her drink and walked off with her crew of two brunettes and a red head. Burkett watched them walk off and I watched Burkett. He just stared at them with that same smile he always seemed to force upon himself. I felt bad for him.

"They seemed a little too stuck up for guys like us," I said to Burkett, trying to soften the blow.

"Definitely," he replied.

"Well, maybe you shouldn't be so quick to buy them a drink. You can go broke doing that before you hit upon the right one."

"Nah, that's what money's for. And that's how the game is played. I don't mind spending a few bucks buying a girl a drink. If it works, it works. Loosen up a bit," he came back at me, still with that smile on his face.

Maybe I was wrong. Maybe Burkett was okay with the way people responded to him and he took his lumps. Maybe that smile wasn't as forced as it appeared. Maybe I could learn something from Burkett. I thought about that. Then I looked at him closely. I looked at that smile again; it had an almost clownish quality. It was just a façade that masked his sadness. His dress, his weight and how he talked about living at home with his mother helping his sex life — no,

I didn't think I had anything to learn from Burkett. Burkett did not have a good picture of himself or how others saw him. Did he believe the things he said or did he just live in a fantasy world that he built for himself?

We spent the next 15 minutes or so just drinking our drinks. We talked a little more about the pretty girls at the nightclub; we talked some bull about the job and the squad. Burkett tried to regale me with some stories of the women he had met in this club, and the action he got out in the parking lot or in his car or when he got the girl home. Nothing rang true. But in the meantime, I was still sitting there with Burkett. At least he had made one attempt. I had done nothing but critique him.

"Hey, you see that one over there?" he said, pointing to a large crowd of guys and girls hanging around on the other side of the dance floor.

"I think you need to be a little more specific, JB."

"The one with long black hair, white top. She's sipping a drink right now."

"Yeah, I see her. She looks cute from here. Kinda bopping around a bit over there."

"That's her. She looks like she wants to dance. I'm gonna go over and ask her."

"Go for it, my man."

Burkett strut over to his target. Surprisingly, he walked with a certain air of confidence. I didn't want to see him get rejected again. He made it over to her. They engaged in some conversation. From what I could tell, she seemed a little hesitant, but Burkett persisted, with that same smile on his face. Then she turned to her friend and gave her friend the drink she had been sipping. That could only mean one thing. Yes, they were walking out on the dance floor together. Watching Burkett move on the dance floor was amusing — he wasn't half bad, especially for a guy his size. On the dance floor, he seemed to shed some of his awkwardness.

I watched for a little while and after only a minute or two, I noticed his dance partner started looking away. Was she just checking on her friends? I started to walk over in that direction. Once again, maybe I could meet one of her friends based on Burkett's moves. I couldn't help but notice that constant turning of her head. What, or who, was she looking at? As I got closer, I saw. She was looking at a tall, very well-dressed man, with thick black hair. They were exchanging glances. Soon they were smiling at each other, all while she was dancing with Burkett. I didn't like what I was seeing. All of a sudden she got up close to Burkett to say something to him. I don't know what it was, but I could imagine.

Quickly, she turned around and walked off the dance floor headed for the SOB she was smiling at. She was quickly in a deep, flirtatious conversation with him while Burkett was still on the dance floor, by himself, clearly a little stunned by that unexpected turn of events, but still smiling. Burkett made that long, lonely walk off the dance floor, trying to appear unmoved.

"Hey," I said, simply trying not to react to what had happened, though he knew I saw him left standing there on the dance floor.

"Hey, listen. I'm a little tired tonight. I'm gonna get going, all right?"

"Okay, JB. I'll see you at work in a couple of days."

Feeling bad for him, I watched Burkett walk to the door and out he went, to the coldness of the winter night from the coldness of this social scene. That must've been very embarrassing for Burkett to be left out on the dance floor like that. I thought about the cruelty of the dating game. While men are usually vilified for their lying and scheming just to meet women, women can be just as mean. The desire to meet a mate who has the appearance and attributes that we think we deserve must be so strong, it brings out some of our own worst traits. Is that really so much different than the motivation of those whom I arrest?

They steal something to which they feel they are entitled, but are being denied for reasons beyond their control. At what point do we decide that our own desires justify disregard for the rest of humanity? Whether we steal their possessions, damage their property or assault their hearts and souls, where do we cross the line from sin to criminality? How far will I go to get what I want? Who am I willing to hurt?

Burkett was probably worried that I would use this night as fodder for jokes about him during locker room banter. That was Thompson's style, not mine. I wasn't sure how much longer I wanted to stay at the nightclub myself. But I was there, and should at least make some efforts to meet a girl.

I hadn't had many dates since Melissa. I was starting to get a little lonely. Scanning the crowd filled with good-looking women, I was trying to see if my gut would help me identify someone who was sweet and kind, and more importantly, would be interested in talking to me. Sipping my now warm beer a couple of times, my eyes homed in on someone who really caught my attention. Her short black hair and smile were comforting. I walked over to her without hesitation.

"I think you should dance with me," I said quite boldly, standing behind her.

She turned around and looked me over. "Oh, should I?"

"Yeah, or else."

"Or else, what? I get arrested?"

"Arrested and whatever else goes along with that."

"Well then, Officer, I guess I have no choice."

We both smiled. She grabbed my hand and led me through the crowd out to the dance floor.

This saved me a trip back to the hospital. A chance meeting wasn't a date, but a great start to get to know Nurse Janie. She looked great. Her sleek black dress hugged her slim body and showed off her nice thin legs. She still was a little light in the chest department, but I already knew that, and overall, she met my needs.

We finished dancing and she accepted my invitation to walk to the bar and have a drink. She didn't fall back on the standard line of having to stay with her friends, so I took that as a good sign.

"You didn't strike me as the nightclub type" was her opening line.

"I can certainly say the same to you."

"Really, why is that?"

"Oh, I don't know. Something about being a nurse just spells innocence and sincerity, not the sexy babe playing the singles scene that I see now."

"Oh, that nurse thing again. What you really mean is the image it conjures up: that old male fantasy of conquering the innocent virgin."

While she was right, I just sat there speechless for a moment. Hearing it put so bluntly, from her, caught me off guard.

"Well, if we're being so honest, uh, yes, I guess that's it."

"Of course, and you being a cop just makes you a typical male 10 times over."

"Really, why do you say that?"

"Oh, I've known enough cops and dated probably more of them than I should have. I've gotten a pretty good idea of what makes you guys tick."

"So, you've dated cops before. I'm afraid to ask how many."

"Don't ask, don't tell. Besides, you know that cop nurse thing."

"Yeah, I do. Is there a little room for you to try dating one more cop?"

"Maybe. What about that girl on your squad? Are you seeing her?"

"What girl?"

"The one who gave you that big kiss when they all came to visit you."

"Oh, that girl." I really didn't know what she had been talking about. Probably because I couldn't imagine how she had seen that. "How did you...?"

"Don't forget, I work overnight shifts just like you. I just got in and was about to come by and say 'hi.' But then I saw you sucking on her tongue, so I figured I wouldn't walk in and interrupt."

"No, you got that all wrong. That's just how she is. It was only a friendly kiss. Nothing else, really."

Janie looked at me skeptically. I didn't blame her. I didn't know what to believe myself.

"So, I'm real glad we ran into each other," I told her to keep the conversation going.

"Well, then why did you leave it to chance? Why didn't you ask me out in the hospital?"

"I don't know. Maybe I thought you were a bit smitten with my tall, blonde, dashing roommate. He always seems to get the girls' attention."

"Oh, I don't know. I found your plain brown hair, brown eyes, pale skin and little more than average height quite attractive."

"That's what I like: a girl with low standards. And I guess that I was not the married one didn't hurt either, huh?"

Without responding, she just smiled. Probably just as well. We spoke for about another hour. We talked about our careers, our friends and our families. And yes, I threw in the fact that I lost my oldest brother, whom I idolized, while he defended our freedom. That brought a sympathetic touch of the arm from Janie. My brother was looking down upon me with approval — anything to get the girl. We had a great time just doing the "getting to know you" talk and she accepted my offer to go out on a date. She wrote her phone number on a damp napkin sitting on the bar, which I quickly folded up and put in my pocket. Then, I walked her out to her car, passing the burly bouncers at the door, outside where a light snowfall had begun. There was something attractive about the small white snowflakes getting caught in her dark black hair. She stood at the driver door, looked at me shyly and said good night. Then we hit that awkward moment. I thought if Burkett could put himself out on the dance floor, I could go for a good night kiss. The kiss good night turned into another kiss, then another kiss and then long, long kisses.

"Should we take this into your car, or maybe back to my place?" I asked without trying to sound too aggressive, yet surprised at myself for being that aggressive at all.

"Whoa, slow down. I told you, I know how you cops work. That style is not going to work with me. If you're in a rush, then just forget it," she said to me while she gently, playfully pressed her index finger against my lips.

"No, no. No rush, I'm sorry. It's just..." she interrupted my pathetic attempt to explain myself.

"Just call me during the week. We'll have a real date next

weekend."

She gave me a quick kiss on the lips and got into her car without a word. I hated to admit it, but I had Burkett to thank for this. As for Burkett, he went home to his mother's house.

Chapter 6

"All right, Mom, I'm leaving now."

"But it's so early. Don't you still have a few more hours? What about dinner?"

"I'll be fine. I'll grab something to eat later. I've got to be interviewed by the Shooting Review Board. I wanna make sure I'm on time. It's not a good idea to leave Internal Affairs waiting."

"Okay, I'm sure everything will be fine. They will see what a hero you are. You'll probably get promoted. You'll see. I love you."

"Yeah, Mom. Love you too."

Burkett went through his standard routine he did four times a week of walking to his patrol car and driving off to work. A few things were a little different today. He had taken his uniform to the cleaners to be pressed. He polished his black shoes and black leather belt. He shined the silver badges on his uniform and his hat. He had gotten a haircut the day before. Today, his mind was not on what awaited him on patrol, but what awaited him at the Shooting Review Board. All cops fear Internal Affairs. After all, they earn their hash marks by finding fault with a cop — after the fact.

Of course, everyone in Internal Affairs started on patrol like every other police officer, so they did have some point of reference when making decisions. But they could not have experienced every matter over which they must pass judgment. Taking time to think and second-guess a decision a cop made in nanoseconds, with lives on the line, was easy in comparison. They were not there and they did not experience what the officer appearing before them did. Sometimes, a cop is clearly in the wrong. Beating a prisoner, no matter what the motivation, is and always will be wrong. Taking money for doing or not doing your job is wrong. Seeking sexual favors for not writing a ticket or making an arrest is wrong. Allegations such as those were not common in the Westland Park Police Department.

Burkett knew the problem he was facing. Two cops were shot; it probably didn't have to turn out that way. It was his call. It was his responsibility. Someone was going to be held at fault; he knew that. That's just the way things worked. Some things, no matter how tragic, are unavoidable. This probably was not one of them; maybe getting two cops shot could have been avoided if he had just done things a little differently. Burkett played the events over and over in his mind. What could he have done differently? He did not know. How could he have stopped Thompson and Hollings from getting shot? He did not know the answer to that either. He was talking to the clerk, trying to figure out what was going on; he wasn't watching Thompson and Hollings. Was it their fault? Did they do something wrong? Again, he did not know.

At least the clerk didn't get shot. If only Burkett had hit the robber and not the exit sign, he might have come out of this looking better. Most cops do not hit their target during a shoot-out; everybody knows that. Yet, Thompson hit his target. Just lucky, Burkett was sure. That won't matter. What should he say to IA? He didn't know what they would ask, but he could guess. He had never been through this before. *How about just telling the truth?* he thought. That possibility gave him no comfort.

Burkett arrived at the Westland Park Police Department Headquarters, which was just one part of the County Office Building, which housed the County Court and the District Attorney's Office. It was a huge, modern complex of brick and glass. The hallway at the entrance was adorned with works of art and sculptures. Burkett parked up front in the police only parking. He was in uniform so he was able to bypass the security and metal detectors. He stood for a few moments watching the floor numbers light up as one of the three elevators made its way down to him. He heard the bell ring as the elevator hit the ground floor. He took the elevator up to the fifth floor to the Internal Affairs Division and signed in with the receptionist.

"They will be with you shortly, Officer Burkett," was her short, matter-of-fact welcome.

Burkett took a seat. There were no magazines to read. He just stared at the pictures of previous IA commanders lined up on the wall.

A tall, thin man, bald on top with graying hair on the sides of his head and wearing gold-rimmed bifocals, approached Burkett. He was dressed in a starched white shirt with a shiny gold badge and two gold bars on each collar. His shoes were shined brighter than Burkett's. His uniform and appearance were impeccable.

"Good afternoon, Officer Burkett. I am Commander Tim Jensen of Internal Affairs," he introduced himself with a deep voice and extended his hand to shake with Burkett.

Burkett, who had been somewhat transfixed on the commander's intimidating, official appearance, stood up and shook hands with him. Burkett was caught off guard by the strength of Jensen's grip.

"Thank you for coming in, today," Jensen said in a slow, polite, deep voice.

Burkett just smiled in return. There was really nothing for Burkett to say in response to that nicety. He knew he had no choice but to be there, as the commander knew as well.

"Please come with me."

"Yes, sir," Burkett replied, again knowing that a response was unnecessary, but not wanting to remain completely silent. He wished he had stopped at the men's room before arriving. Jensen led Burkett into the conference room.

"Please take a seat," Jensen said, pointing to the one chair facing the long oak wood table where two men in uniform and two in civilian clothing sat in high backed leather chairs. Behind them were full length windows with white translucent drapes drawn closed, blocking a view of the Westland Park woods. The sun peeked in through the narrow opening where the two ends of the drapes met. Jensen then sat in the center chair, which had been left unoccupied for him. He reached over to the tape recorder on the desk and hit the record button.

"Officer Burkett, I have turned on this tape recording machine so that all of this Review Board's questions, your answers and all discussions related to this inquiry will be recorded. Do you understand that?"

"Yes," he responded.

"Let me introduce the panel, though I am sure you know everybody here. On my far left is Captain Johnson, head of our Detective Bureau. On my immediate left, of course, is our deputy chief, D.C. Harrington. On my far right is Jay McManus. He is a retired police commander from Kansas City who sits on these boards. On my right is Major Sharpe, the western zone commander."

Burkett politely exchanged nods with each man as they were introduced. There were a lot of years of experience sitting at that table. Burkett felt both respect and fear towards these men.

"And you know Sergeant Hughes, who as your immediate supervisor will be an observer only, to these proceedings." Commander Jensen pointed off to his left where Hughes was sitting quietly in a row of chairs lined up against the wall, on which hung pictures of each chief of police since the department's formation. Burkett had not even noticed Hughes sitting there.

"What we hope to accomplish through these hearings, Officer Burkett, is to establish all the facts leading up to the shooting in the convenience store. Our job is to determine if proper police protocol was followed at all stages of this incident, and if all officers involved used appropriate judgment and responded according to the training they have received, and to the policies and high professional standards of the Westland Park Police Department. Do you understand that?"

"Yes, sir, I do," Burkett responded to Commander Jensen with a lump now forming in his throat.

"Good, we will interview you and all officers who were involved or were in a position to make any observations. I will ask most of the questions, but any member of the Review Board may interject at any moment, and you are directed to answer their questions as well. We will also review the forensic evidence as collected by our Evidence Response Team, interviews of the clerk and his wife and any other information that comes into our possession. This is an administrative hearing, not a criminal investigation; therefore the rules of evidence and criminal procedure do not apply. If at any time this does become a criminal investigation, you will be so advised. At that time, you will be entitled to an attorney and all the laws and rules of a criminal investigation will apply. Based upon our review, we will report our findings to the chief with any recommendations, if appropriate. Do you understand all that I have just explained to you and your rights, as they apply to an administrative inquiry as opposed to a criminal investigation?"

"Yes, sir," Burkett responded again, the lump growing, sweat beads forming at the top of his forehead. The austere tone of Commander Jensen's voice was extremely discomfiting and began to worry Burkett.

"Do you have any questions before we begin?"

"No, sir, I do not."

"Okay then, let's get started."

First, Commander Jensen stated the date and time for the recording. He repeated the name of each person present and the purpose of the hearing. He cut no corners. He was a "by the book" type of guy.

"Officer Burkett, can you please tell us how you responded to the call, up to but not including the actual shooting?"

"Yes, sir. Upon hearing of a possible robbery in progress, I responded with my emergency lights activated, but not my siren. I was fairly close and did not want to risk a hostage or barricade situation. I approached from the side street, having turned off all my lights a few hundred yards before approaching the gas station lot and the store. I called in my arrival and waited for back-up."

"Yes, Officer Burkett. The radio dispatch log confirms your arrival within two minutes of receiving the call. Go on, please."

"When Officer Thompson arrived with his rookie, Officer Hollings, I asked Thompson to cover the rear while Hollings and I approached the front. I told Hollings that we would look in as safely as we could to see if there was any activity in the store."

"And what, if anything, did you see?"

"At first, we didn't see any activity."

"Did you find that suspicious?"

"Not by itself, no. There are times when the clerk goes to the bathroom or does some stocking or inventory late at night when there aren't any customers. But the door was locked. I did find that a little suspicious."

"Did you broadcast to Thompson on the side band or to dispatch that the door was locked?"

"No, sir. But that had already been broadcast as the complainant had reported the locked door."

"Okay, but did you confirm that finding over the radio?"

Burkett hesitated. That was a question he was not expecting. While he came to this hearing with all the facts clear in his head, now, all of a sudden, his recall was getting fuzzy. He could not afford that. He knew from court testimony that not remembering or being unsure comes off as dishonesty. He was trying to think quickly, but time seemed to be moving slowly now.

"Sir, I cannot recall if I did or did not broadcast that confirmation."

"Okay, Officer, the dispatch logs do not indicate any such broadcast. Please continue."

Burkett took a moment to remember where he left off. He was only minutes into the interview and he was already becoming rattled. Subconsciously rubbing his twitching left eye brow, he thought to himself, *Okay, the door was locked. What did I do then? Think, think.*

"When I discovered the door was locked I told Hollings to stand off to the side. I was going to knock on the door and announce my presence to see if I could get the clerk to open the door."

"Did you ask dispatch to telephone into the convenience store to see if we could get the clerk on the phone without exposing yourself that way?"

"No, sir, I didn't. It just didn't seem necessary at the time." He licked his now dry lips and took a swallow. He saw the deputy chief and Captain Johnson exchange a quick glance. Was that a sign of their mutual disapproval?

"Go on, Officer."

"Well, then, I, um, I saw the clerk come out of a back room. He, he came and, um, he opened the door."

"But the door was locked from the inside, correct?"

"Yes, sir, it was and the clerk opened it. And then..."

Commander Jensen interrupted him in mid-sentence. "Did you notice anything unusual or suspicious at that moment?"

Burkett hesitated; actually he stopped dead cold and just stared. That was not really a question. Jensen was getting at something specific. *What is it? What's he getting at? Think, think.* Burkett's mind was racing. What seemed like an hour to him was only a second or two, but then it hit him. *Wow, Jensen really did his homework.*

"Yes, sir. I noticed the clerk fumble a little bit getting the door unlocked."

"Did that indicate anything to you, Officer?"

"I did take notice of that, sir. It made me a little suspicious. But it was late at night. He could have just been tired or nervous about seeing us. I didn't think that it indicated a robbery in progress, no sir."

"Did you say anything to Officer Hollings to indicate what you thought was going on?"

Burkett stopped again. Jensen knew just about everything. Burkett didn't think Hollings or Thompson had been before this board yet. How did Jensen have so much detail?

"Yes, sir. I made a joke that maybe he was getting a little in the back."

"You mean you thought he was having sex, not getting robbed?"

"Well, I was only kidding. I didn't know for sure what was happening."

"No, obviously you didn't. Go on, please."

"Well, I spoke to the clerk and he said that he was just taking inventory in the back and locked up while he was doing it. Then I asked Hollings to call Thompson on the radio and ask him to respond to the front of the store." Burkett hesitated to see if there were any questions. There weren't. He continued, the lump in his throat now accompanied by a knot in his stomach.

"When Thompson came in, I got him and Hollings off to the side.

I told them that the clerk was acting nervous and that they should check things out while I continued to talk to the clerk to try to get more information."

At that moment, the deputy chief broke in, the first time anyone other than Jensen had spoken. That flustered Burkett; he wasn't even sure who was speaking at first.

"Officer Burkett, when Thompson arrived, did you explain to him that the door was locked? That the clerk had some trouble opening the door?"

"Uh, sir, I uh, I cannot recall if I did or did not tell that to Thompson. Hollings may have told him."

"Officer Burkett," the deputy chief continued, "we are asking you about what you did or did not do. Please do not give us speculation about what someone else may or may not have done." The deputy chief's voice was soft and polite, but those words came off like a scolding.

"Yes, sir. I am sorry, sir." Burkett began to squirm a bit in his seat. The beads of sweat on his forehead had now become full blown perspiration trickling down the sides of his face. He began to rub his sweaty palms together. He felt the wetness in his armpits.

The deputy chief did not respond verbally, but held up his hand signifying that he wanted Burkett to stop the apology. Jensen began the questioning again.

"So Officer Burkett, clearly you had at least some concern that something may be wrong. How did you relate that to Officer Thompson?"

"Well, sir, just as I said, I told him that I felt the clerk was acting nervously, even though he was saying everything was okay. I asked them to check the store just to be sure. I thought that was the best course of action."

A silence overtook the room for a moment. Jay McManus stood up from his chair and walked over to Jensen and started whispering in his ear. Jensen nodded and whispered something back. McManus then went back to his seat.

"Okay, Officer Burkett," Jensen started again, "you suspected something, but you're not sure exactly how you related that. Did you specifically tell Thompson and Hollings to check the store and to be prepared for a possible robbery in progress?"

"Um, well, sir, no, not exactly. I mean Thompson is an experienced officer. If I say something is suspicious, he should react accordingly and take proper precautions. I can't..." The deputy chief interrupted again. Burkett's speech was getting faster and faster.

"Officer, please let me remind you, you can only speak for yourself and what you know, you saw or you heard. Do not try to guess or presume what was in someone else's mind, please."

"Yes, sir." This time Burkett offered no apology. His fear was turning to anger, but he knew better than to let that anger show. While he may have lacked some social skills, 14 years in the department did teach him something, and going head to head with the deputy chief and commanders was not a winning proposition.

Burkett was about to speak again, but decided to wait for the next question. Jensen picked up the questioning again.

"Okay, Officer. You told the other officers to check the store. You were not sure if a robbery was taking place or not. Did you take the clerk out of the store to talk to him?"

"No, I spoke to him right there in the store."

"In the store, where there was possibly an armed robber hiding out?"

"Well, at that point, I had not really determined that a robbery was in progress. I was still trying to sort things out."

McManus now spoke up. "Officer, I am troubled that you say you suspected something, but you didn't give Officers Thompson and Hollings sufficient notice. Then you failed to remove a citizen from a potentially dangerous situation. Do you see some inadequacy in your response?"

"Sir, with all due respect, given what I knew and what I observed at that moment, I believe I responded appropriately."

"But two officers were shot; it sounds like you were all taken by surprise."

"We were, sir. We didn't know there was someone hiding in the back. That's what I was trying to determine."

"Yes, but standing in the store with the clerk, while there is someone possibly pointing a gun at his head, doesn't sound like the best way to find things out."

"Sir, nine times out of 10 these calls are false alarms. I was..."

McManus interrupted, "Yes, but it is that one time that gets an officer killed as it almost did here. We never let our guard down."

Burkett did not have time to think of a response before Jensen started again. Probably just as well.

"Now, Officer Burkett, after you heard the first shot go off, what did you do?"

"I pushed the clerk to the ground to assure his safety."

"And that is commendable."

Burkett couldn't believe he had heard those words from Jensen. Was the tone of this review about to change? Were things beginning to look up?

"But," Jensen continued, "what was your next response?"

"I fired at the gunman, sir."

"Firing at the gunman while he was fleeing, isn't that correct?"

"Yes, sir. Our shooting policy allows us to shoot someone fleeing the scene of a violent felony like that." Burkett rushed to get that line in to head off any possible accusation of violating the department's use of deadly force policy.

"I'm aware of our shooting policy, Officer. What I'm concerned about is that you firing your weapon may have provoked return fire that could have put the clerk in danger. Is that not correct?"

"Sir, I stepped away from the clerk by a few yards. If I had drawn return fire, it would have been directed at me. The clerk would not have been in the line of fire."

"That's assuming, of course, the robber was a good shot. Even a good shot can miss by a wide margin when fighting for his life. Would you agree, Officer? After all, your scores on the range are consistently high. But in this confrontation, you missed your target by a significant distance. Isn't that right?"

"Yes, you are correct, sir."

"Okay." Jensen turned to the rest of the board. "Are there any other questions for Officer Burkett?"

Burkett sat quietly praying there were none. His prayer was answered.

"Do you have anything you would like to say to the board, Officer?"

"Yes, sir, I do," Burkett, uncharacteristically mindful of his manners and conduct, stood up to address the board.

"I have been a dedicated officer of this department for 14 years now. I have a spotless record. I can see that in reviewing my actions, there may have been things that I could have done better. But I did not just walk away when the clerk told me that everything was okay. I did suspect something and that is why I told Officers Thompson and Hollings to search the store. I am so sorry they got shot. I wish it had been me instead. But I did the best I could at the moment, with the information I had. I ask that I be judged based on the circumstances of the moment. Thank you."

Jensen was thinking that Burkett made a rather articulate closing statement. He was impressed. But the Shooting Review Board had a lot more to think about than the quality of Burkett's closing remarks.

Drying his sweat soaked hands by wiping them on his pants, Burkett shook hands with each member of the board. About to leave, he remembered that Sergeant Hughes was in the room and went over to the sergeant and shook his hand as well. He wanted to ask the sergeant how he felt it went, but he knew he couldn't do that. Hughes saw the look of concern on Burkett's face, but he too did not know how to respond. Giving Burkett a nod, he said, "Okay, I'll see you at work tonight." Burkett quietly walked out. He knew he did not express himself well; he rarely did. Yet, he hoped the truth would prevail, knowing that hope had failed him many times.

The board excused Sergeant Hughes, who was to wait outside, while they wrote down some notes and discussed the interview. The next interview, which was Thompson, was scheduled to begin in 20 minutes. Pacing the halls, Hughes was overcome by a discomforting feeling that his future was not looking bright. Not this shooting, but something was lurking out there; call it cop instinct, but Hughes was so sure of it, he became weak in the knees and moved rapidly to the closest chair he could find.

Thompson showed up right on time: not early, not late, but just on time. His uniform was neat and clean, but he had not taken the care and preparation that Burkett had regarding his appearance. Thompson walked into the conference room with a confident gait and smiled broadly as he was introduced to each member of the Shooting Review Team. Thompson made no observations about the conference room; he didn't care. But he did notice Hughes right away. He turned and said, "Hi, Sarge" in a booming voice that seemed to surprise everyone in the room.

Commander Jensen went through the same formalities with Thompson as he did with Burkett. The questions leading up to the shooting remained the same and Thompson's answers were fairly consistent with Burkett's. But eventually, that began to change. Jensen, as before, led the questioning.

"Officer Thompson, when you were called to the front of the store by Officer Hollings, what were you told about the situation?"

"Upon my initial arrival at the front of the store, Officer Hollings advised me that Officer Burkett was of the opinion that the clerk was probably just getting a little, excuse my French, sirs, in the back room and he didn't seem very concerned."

"Did you challenge or question Office Burkett about that opinion?"

"No, sir. Officer Burkett knows his beat pretty well. If he thought that's what was going on, he probably based it upon his years of experience. As a fellow officer, I trusted his judgment completely."

"Officer, did there come a time after you entered the store that you spoke to Burkett directly?"

"Yes, sir." Though Thompson knew there was more expected of his answer, he left it like that without expounding. That's what cops learned about courtroom testimony. Answer only the question asked, with as few words as possible.

"And what did he say?"

"He said that the clerk thought everything was all right and there was nothing to worry about."

"Then what did you do?"

"I suggested to him that perhaps Hollings and I just do a quick sweep of the store to be sure. I thought that would be a good experience for Hollings, to see what it means to go the extra step in these kinds of calls."

"Okay. At that point, did you draw your weapon?"

"We didn't draw our weapons, sir, until after we were shot."

"Why not?"

"Well, sir, we did have our hands on our weapons as a precaution. But, based upon Officer Burkett's assessment, I really believed that all we might wind up doing is scaring the hell out of a half-naked woman when we hit the back of the store. I was trying to set a good example for my rookie partner. When that robber came flying out of the back, we were completely taken by surprise."

Jensen paused and rested his chin in his left hand. Then his forefinger slowly began rubbing his lips. He brought his hand back down. He was pensive, staring straight at Thompson. Thompson did not flinch. He maintained his composure and confidence.

"Officer Thompson, are you sure that Officer Burkett did not express any concern to you over the suspicious behavior of the clerk?"

"No, sir, other than the fact he thought he was possibly having sex in the back room."

"He said that to you?"

"No sir, Hollings told me that."

"Did Burkett mention the trouble the clerk had opening the door?"

"Trouble opening the door? This is the first I am hearing of that, sir."

"Officer Hollings didn't mention that to you?"

"No, sir, he's just a rookie. He probably didn't notice a lot of important things. But all in all, he's doing really well. I think he will develop into a fine officer."

"That's fine, but let's try to stay on the subject here."

Then there was an uneasy silence in the room, but it did not seem uneasy to Thompson.

"So you are saying that Burkett expressed no concerns that anything seemed strange. You are also saying that it was you who suggested that you and Hollings check the store out."

Thompson was about to answer when Jensen began speaking again.

"And," Jensen continued, "you had no reason to believe that there was a robbery in progress, which is why you did not draw your weapon. Is that correct?"

Thompson paused for a moment, acting as if he was reviewing all parts of that complex question.

"Yes to all of that, sir" was Thompson's answer.

"You fired two rounds. One missed and the other one hit the guy square in the ass. Considering you were wounded, that was pretty good shooting."

"Thank you, sir. I think it was just luck and some good training. I was in a lot of pain. I'm not sure I knew exactly what I was doing — I just did it. I'm really more satisfied that I was able to stop this guy before he hurt anybody else. And if I may say so, I think Officer Burkett did a fine job running after him and making the arrest. It was a real team effort."

"Yes, it was. Does anyone from the board have any questions for Officer Thompson?" There was silence.

"Do you have any closing statements you wish to make, Officer?"

"No, sir. I just thank the board for its time in reviewing this important matter."

"Very well, you're excused."

Thompson stood up and went over to shake hands with each member of the board. Thompson did not have to dry his hands off. He never broke a sweat. He said good-bye to Hughes last and then left. Hughes was getting ready to leave as before, to give the panel some time to talk, when Commander Jensen called him over. As Hughes approached, Jensen put his arm around Hughes' shoulder and walked him over to the corner of the room.

"Dave, those questions about what Burkett said to Hollings when they were knocking on the door, and then again when Thompson joined them in the store, were based on what you told me you picked up in locker room banter," Jensen whispered.

"Yes, it was," Hughes whispered back.

"You didn't tell him that we would be asking those specific questions. Did you?"

"Sir, of course not," Hughes answered indignantly. "Besides, I wouldn't want my men to know that I was reporting back what I heard them say to IA. That would ruin whatever reputation I have left, not to mention making my job impossible."

Closing the door behind him, Hughes left the board to discuss Thompson's testimony.

"Well, we have two completely different versions of what happened. Thompson answered much more quickly; he was more prepared and more confident than Burkett. Wouldn't you say?" Jensen expressed his concerns.

"Yes, I noticed that too. But then again, Thompson is much more self-confident than Burkett and he's an excellent cop," Sharpe answered.

Jensen looked at the rest of the board. "Did anybody else find something disingenuous about Thompson's statements, or is it just me?"

The deputy chief was the first to address that question. "He did seem a little too sure of himself, but maybe we are comparing him to Burkett's piss poor performance just before this. What Thompson said did make sense. And it is fairly consistent with what Hughes said he was picking up from the locker room chatter."

"Yeah, and what about that? Hughes reporting information he overheard back to IA? That seems unusual in itself. He's been so withdrawn for the last couple of years. Ever since that shooting of his, he hasn't been the same. Now, he's spying on his own squad. It's, well, it's something..." Jensen replied.

"I think he's just trying to suck up to you, Tim. He knows that lieutenant spot is opening up soon. Maybe he is finally looking to come off the street and get behind the desk like he should have done years ago," Captain Johnson offered.

"I don't know," Jensen said, sounding a little frustrated. "Let's break for a few minutes."

Jensen walked to the doors. He opened them and turned, and approached Hughes as he walked back up the stairs after going outside the building to grab a quick smoke.

"Dave, come here a second," Jensen directed him.

Hughes stopped and walked down the corridor with Jensen.

"Dave, listen, we've been friends for a long time. I shouldn't be talking out of school like this, but I gotta tell ya, something stinks. I don't know what it is, but it's there."

"Okay, but why did you come after me just to tell me that?"

"Because, Dave, somehow you're gonna get sucked up in this. I don't know what Thompson is up to, but I think he's fucking with you somehow. That wouldn't have happened years ago when you were on top of your game, commanding a SWAT team. Dave, you know you haven't been the same. You're not in charge of things like you used to be. You know?"

"I know, Tim. I appreciate your candor. But what's done is done."

"Nothing is done just yet. I don't know how this inquiry is going to turn out, but I am a little worried. There is something about Thompson that sets my warning lights off. Just take control of things. You're the sergeant. Are we communicating?"

"Yes, I understand. Thanks."

"Sorry about that," Jensen starting saying to the others as he re-entered the conference room, I was just..."

"Okay," the deputy chief interjected, not wanting Jensen to continue, "we still got Hollings coming in. He's just a rookie. He shouldn't even know how to throw us a line of shit. Let's see what he says. But right now, I'm inclined to go along with Thompson. Look at Burkett; he can barely remember what he said or did. Thompson looks like a sharp cop. But we'll see."

Hughes made his way back to the conference room where he sat. Now he was a little nervous. He and Jensen were old friends, but that friendly advice seemed to come off more as an ominous warning.

Hughes was not clear on what the warning was. Thompson had confided in Hughes, off the record, that he thought Burkett screwed up, but he didn't want to say anything to IA. Then Hughes heard from Stryker, also off the record, that Thompson was concerned for Burkett, hoping that Burkett saying that he didn't think anything was wrong in the store wouldn't come up in the Review Board questioning. That would hurt Burkett. Hughes knew the rules — there was no off the record. If he heard something about an officer's conduct, he was required to report it to IA, and that's what he did. What Hughes wasn't thinking about was that Thompson and Stryker were senior officers. They knew the rules too. They knew that Hughes could not just sit on that information.

*****

About one half hour later, I showed up for my interview. My state of nervousness probably fell somewhere between Thompson's and Burkett's. I picked up a number of pointers on how to handle this kind of inquiry, just by listening to my colleagues. I knew what was at stake for me, Thompson and Burkett, and that was pretty much the order of my priorities. I also knew that as a rookie, there would be limited expectations of me. I had rehearsed this. I knew what I wanted to say. And, I rehearsed how to make my statements not sound rehearsed. But I also knew I was up against some pretty experienced cops.

Once again, Jensen went through the introductions and formalities. The questioning began and I related the facts leading up to the response to the gas station. Jensen took the lead for the third and final time today.

"Officer Hollings, when you and Officer Burkett approached the front door to the convenience store, what did you see inside?"

"Actually, sir, we didn't see anything."

"Did Officer Burkett say anything to you about what he thought might be happening inside the store?"

"Yes, sir. He said that he thought the clerk was just having sex in the back room."

"Did you question that at all?"

"With all due respect, sir, I was barely out of the academy. I would not question the judgment of a senior officer."

"Okay, I understand that. Do you remember when Officer Thompson responded to the front of the store?"

"Yes, sir, I do. I was the one who called him on the radio and asked him to come in."

"And you did that based on Officer Burkett's directions, correct?"

"Yes, that's correct, sir."

"When Officer Thompson came in, did you, Thompson and Burkett have a conversation about what Burkett thought about what the clerk was saying?"

"Yes, sir, but the conversation was mostly between Thompson and Burkett."

"You weren't included in that conversation?" Jensen asked curiously.

"Well, sir, they didn't specifically exclude me. But while they were talking, I thought I'd keep an eye on the clerk. I guess I was just trying to do something a little more productive than just stand there like a helpless rookie."

"That's very admirable," Jensen said with a small hint of sarcasm.

"So," he continued, "did you notice anything about the clerk that was suspicious or gave you reason to believe something was going on?"

"Not really, sir. I kinda thought that Burkett probably knew what was going on, so I didn't really think anything was up; I was just watching the clerk."

"You thought the clerk was doing nothing more than having sex. What exactly were you watching him for?"

"Well, sir, I remembered the role playing we did in the academy, especially the ones about domestic disputes. As soon as you took your eyes off one of them, you would get attacked. So, I just figured that while Thompson and Burkett were talking, I would keep an eye on the clerk. I didn't really expect him to do anything, but I really learned my lesson from those role playing exercises." That evoked a few snickers from the board.

"So you didn't really hear what Officers Thompson and Burkett said to each other?"

"No, sir, I didn't."

"Whose decision was it to search the store?"

"I don't know, sir. But when they finished their conversation, Thompson told me we were going to check the store."

"Did he say why you were going to check the store?"

I feigned a pensive pause. Then I slowly started answering.

"Sir, I'm sorry. I just can't remember. Since the shooting, I've been giving everything a lot of thought and I realize I just can't clearly remember every little thing that happened right before the shooting started."

"You didn't have your gun drawn. Is that correct?"

"Yes, that's correct."

"Why is that?"

"Again sir, with all due respect, I was just following Thompson's lead. He is my training officer."

Now, Jensen gave a pensive pause and found himself staring at me, probably the same way he stared at Thompson. We were two very different personalities, but Jensen sensed that there was something awfully similar in the way we answered the questions.

"Okay, Officer Hollings, is there anything you can remember that can help us get a better understanding of what led up to the shooting?"

"Well, sir, all I know is that some guy came at us shooting and Thompson was able to plug him right in the ass before he got away. I'm glad Thompson was there. I realize I'm too new to really understand what good police work is, but I think I learned a lesson from what Thompson did that night."

"Just like the lesson you learned from role playing in the academy?" Jensen's sarcasm was not lost on the board, which tried not to laugh, at least not too obviously.

"Do any of the board members have questions for Officer Hollings?" There were none.

"Do you have any closing remarks for the board, Officer Hollings?"

"No, sir, thank you."

"Thank you. You're excused."

I quickly walked out without looking back at anybody. Out of the corner of my eye, I saw Hughes sitting in the corner. Initially, I started to turn in his direction and acknowledge him, but something told me to just keep walking and not to stop till I was out that door and back in my car.

Jensen turned to Sergeant Hughes. "Sergeant, anything you want to say to the board before we start deliberating?" Hughes thought for a moment, wanting to give some input, but couldn't think of one thing to say.

"No, sir, I have nothing. I think my officers explained their positions the best they could, given the gravity of the circumstances." He left, this time knowing to shut the door behind him without being asked.

Jensen turned to the board. "He's a slick one for a rookie, this Hollings kid. Isn't he?"

"Yeah, he is Tim," the deputy chief said. McManus and Williams nodded in agreement.

"So what do we make of all this? Something just isn't sitting right."

"I don't know, Tim," Deputy Chief Harrington chimed in. "Thompson's clearly one arrogant guy and it has rubbed off on his rookie. But I think the story is pretty clear. Burkett didn't assess the situation correctly and two cops got shot."

"I don't know. I have some doubts. What do you guys think?" Jensen turned to McManus and Williams.

They went over all the statements, the evidence and their own gut feelings. They spent two hours discussing their final decisions and recommendations to the chief. The deputy chief made a proposal. The vote was unanimous.

Chapter 7

I had been on my own for several weeks, enjoying patrolling by myself and handling things my way. Best of all, I didn't have to listen to Thompson every minute, though I did not mind meeting him for a meal or pulling up and talking window to window. After just a few shifts, I felt that I was starting to get a pretty good feel for how to handle most calls, but I knew I still had a lot to learn. Thompson, Burkett and I were still waiting for the findings and recommendations from the Shooting Review Board to make it to the chief and for his final decision to come down. There was no public hue and cry on this one; no one was demanding an immediate response from the department. After the story appeared in the press the next day, it faded into history rather quickly. Only an armed robber got shot, not an innocent kid and there were no racial overtones. That was not great fodder for the media. Without external pressure for an answer, I guess the board and the chief weren't in a rush.

Actually, I wasn't too worried. As a rookie, I knew I was not going to be found at fault for improper procedures. We responded to an armed robbery in progress and no innocent people were hurt, so how much fault could be found in all that? Thompson didn't seem that worried either. Those proceedings were supposed to be confidential. But juicy news in the department always leaked out early.

Word was going around that Burkett crashed and burned during the hearings and that he was going to take a hit. Thompson and I were going to be found to have acted according to policy and protocol. The rumors were affecting Burkett. His concern and worry were obvious in his appearance — his usually forced smile had disappeared. He was a little more sloppy than usual. He moved with lethargy even out of character for Burkett. Though Burkett was hard to define, he clearly was not himself.

The winter was tapering off and I was glad the weather was

getting a little warmer, though it was still in the low 40s with a slight breeze. I was able to rid myself of that heavy winter jacket and moved to just wearing my uniform with two warm undershirts underneath.

Janie and I were dating fairly regularly, though we did not often have the same days and nights off. I think that worked for her and me as well. Janie definitely wanted things to move slowly. She took relationships seriously. It was obvious that she had dated some cop who broke her heart. On the one hand, I wanted to know who it was, and on the other I didn't want to know. Anyway, it could've been any cop from any one of the local departments. It didn't matter. She never talked about it directly, but her little comments and innuendos about cops told the story, at least her side of the story. But, we were having fun; that was the bottom line. She was two years older than I. I didn't mind and it didn't seem to bother her. Janie seemed to take life fairly seriously, which was something I tended to do, but was trying to get away from. I wanted my perspective on life to be somewhere between Janie's and Thompson's.

I remember when my perspective started to change. It was about three or four weeks after I got out of the academy. Thompson and I responded to a fatal wreck. While the accident investigators took over the scene because it was a fatality, we drove over to the hospital. We had to go into the morgue to confirm the body's identity. The only dead body I had ever seen was my brother's at his funeral. My family rationalized his death by reminding themselves that he was a soldier and he died following his dream and defending freedom. If he had to die, at least he died a hero in a cause worth dying for. I did not know if anyone really believed that, but it helped numb the pain; it helped justify the unjustifiable death of a young man.

I walked into the morgue and saw rows of feet sticking out from under blankets with toe tags on them. Then I saw a tiny, little pair of feet and just imagined the anguish of some parents who I would never know. I could not imagine there was any rationalization for that death that could numb their pain. That's when I began to understand about living for the moment.

Now, I was on another routine call, just watching, as a car was getting towed away from an accident on a residential block in a neighborhood known as the Heights. It was not a serious wreck, only minor injuries. I always remembered that fatality and whenever I responded to a car accident, I almost always wrote someone a ticket. Accidents usually happened because someone did something they shouldn't have. People die so unnecessary. Tonight, I wrote one driver three tickets at once. One was for failing to yield the right of way. That's why there was an accident. He deserved that ticket. The second ticket was for defective equipment — his rear tail light was out — and the third was for not having his insurance card. Normally, I wouldn't write such petty tickets, but the guy was being such an asshole about the accident, I enjoyed writing them. Besides, that would help my statistics as the month was coming to a close and Hughes would be tallying up those numbers.

The Heights had become my beat. I was learning the streets pretty well and was starting to recognize some of the regular troublemakers and trouble spots. The Heights was mostly low-income apartment complexes where the tenants liked to hang around the parking lots drinking and getting mildly rowdy. Most of the complexes had only one way to drive in, so it was only a matter of moments after I entered the complex before everyone knew I was there. I was driving over to the Camden Gardens apartment complex, just to take a drive through — let them know I was there. There were at least two calls per shift over there. Usually a fight, a domestic dispute or someone breaking into someone else's apartment. I don't think my visibility really served a deterrent effect, but you never know. That's what I was paid to do.

As I took a drive through, a group of white men, mostly in their 30s, hid their beer cans and liquor bottles behind their backs as they stood up by the cars they were sitting on. They knew how to play the game. We were glad they did. Nobody wanted to waste their time getting into a fight, trying to arrest someone for drinking in public. If I didn't see it, it didn't happen. I rolled down my window and called out to them, "How's it going tonight?"

"Just fine, Officer" was the response I got.

I drove deeper into the complex. There I found a group of black men, about the same ages, acting pretty much the same way. We exchanged the same salutations. These weren't gangs and they weren't claiming their turf, but the racial tension and the concept of who belonged where was fairly evident. Nothing really seemed to be happening — at least nothing I was going to discover by driving around. I headed out of the complex onto Westland Boulevard. I was thinking of driving over to the gas station convenience store on Westland and 7th. They had some of the best-flavored coffee.

I heard that momentary static on the radio and knew a broadcast was about to come. My only thought was just hoping it wasn't another car wreck assigned to me.

"All units, 10-3," the dispatcher called out. By now, I had learned that the 10-3 call meant to remain off the radio and expect an emergency call. The call could be for anybody, and there would most likely be a call for back-up, so you wanted to be ready. I pulled over and stood by.

"318 Baker, 318 Baker," the dispatcher called. That was Burkett.

"318 Baker, go."

"318 Baker, rape just occurred. Called in by the victim at 674 South Washington Street in the Belmont Apartments, apartment 1C."

"10-4, 318 Baker en route. ETA 1."

"321 Baker, proceed for back-up."

I knew I was going to be called for back-up once I heard the address. I had backed up Burkett there a number of times on calls.

"321 Baker en route. ETA 2."

It was a good feeling to know how to get to a call quickly without having to stop and look at that damn street map. I was starting to feel like a real cop.

Flipping on those switches turned on my lights and siren, which I had only done twice since the robbery. One was to a barroom brawl that Gillis was handling; the crowd started to turn on him and he yelled for back-up. The other wound up being a false alarm of an auto theft in progress — some guy had just locked himself out of his car.

Making my way into the Belmont Apartments, another low income complex of five four-story apartment buildings, I had to use the car's spotlight to find the correct building, as only a few of them had their addresses showing. I did not want to be that distracted while I was trying to watch for anybody who looked like he might be fleeing from the scene of the rape. The only description broadcast was a white male in dark clothing. While I was looking, the tenants hanging around the parking lot were watching me closely and carefully, part curious, part nervous. I couldn't find the address, but I saw Burkett's car parked at the building at the end of a long driveway with speed bumps painted in yellow. Burkett was waiting for me in the lobby and then we walked over to the apartment together. After knocking on the door and announcing ourselves, we saw the peephole open up and Burkett moved back so that his badge and uniform were in sight.

Meekly answering the door was a young lady, about my age, with lips quivering and hunched over, almost afraid to look at us. Wearing a loosely tied, pink terry cloth bathrobe, she was trying to hold it together at the neck with one hand. Her shoulder length brown hair was disheveled, tears rolling from her eyes and an obvious look of shock and despair had come over what appeared to be a pretty face. She was a small girl, maybe 5' 2" and not much more than 100 pounds. She could not have possibly fought off the attacker. Burkett having the lead on this call was a bit of a relief to me. I had not yet handled this type of situation and was not sure what to do. A rape was one of those calls where almost anything you say or do could be misinterpreted and end up disastrous. We talked about it in the academy, but reality is another story. Burkett spoke in a soft voice and introduced us by name. Before we entered the house, Burkett asked if there was anyone else in the house with her right now. She answered no.

"The person who attacked you has left. Is that correct?"

"Yes," she replied.

Once again, Burkett surprised me. I just learned a couple of things. First, Burkett asked if anyone was in the house. I would not have thought of that. I assumed the rapist fled. After walking into an armed robbery and getting shot, I would've guessed that I had learned my lesson. Clearly, I had not. I also noticed how Burkett spoke softly and carefully chose his words. He said attacked, not raped. I saw the importance of that. Burkett then asked her if she was well enough to talk to us for a few moments. She was. He led her into the living room, passing a small narrow kitchen with just enough room for a sink, a counter and a refrigerator. She sat on the white, vinyl couch, which was really more of a love seat; it would only fit two people.

There were some pictures of her family hanging on the wall above her. The rest of the walls were bare. Obviously not wanting to look us in the eye, she kept her head down as she crossed her legs and nervously tapped her dangling foot against the edge of the oval table in front of her, which looked liked it was made of pine wood with a walnut stain. Burkett took a seat beside her on the only chair in the living room, which was also made of wood, with thin, curvy legs and had a bamboo-like seat. My first thought was that the chair could not support Burkett, and he'd fall right through. I stood on her opposite side, near the pole lamp that barely lit the small square room, as most of the light was absorbed by the dark brown shag carpet. From where I was standing, her robe was open wide enough that I had a full view of her breast. As wrong as that was, especially in this situation, I knew I was staring, and probably would not stop, so I walked away to avoid any further temptation to look, and I took a position near Burkett.

"He must've pried open my sliding glass door. I heard some noise. I started to get up and the next thing I knew, this guy was on top of me. He held a knife to my throat and grabbed my hair with his other hand." Then she stopped. Burkett was waiting for her to gather her thoughts. We didn't want to rush her, but we wanted to get as much information as possible so we could broadcast a lookout.

"Ma'am, I have to ask you to describe him the best you can."

She paused and thought for a moment. Then with a soft voice, almost a whisper, she started to speak.

"Well, I know he was at least seven or eight inches taller than me. He made me stand to get undressed and I was right in front of the mirror, so I could see him, behind me, in the reflection."

"Can you tell me more about what he looked like?"

"He was wearing all black. He had a mask, like a ski mask, over his face. Then he had a sweatshirt with a hood that was tied real tight around his head. It was pretty dark in here. I couldn't see much."

"Could you tell if he was black or white?"

"Oh, he was white. I could tell that much from his hands, or really more from his wrists. He wore gloves, but the skin between the gloves and his shirt was white. I could also see from around his lips."

"Was he thin or heavyset? Could you tell?"

"He seemed a little heavy."

Burkett stood up. I wasn't sure why.

"I'm 220 pounds, and close to the same height. Would you say he was thinner or heavier than me?"

She stared at him for a moment.

"I don't know. He may have been a bit thinner than you. I'm just not sure. It's pretty close." She started to cry.

Burkett looked at me with a nod. We knew that was all the important information we were going to get for the moment. In reality, the rapist was not going to get caught tonight, but we had to try. I went into the kitchen and telephoned in the information. I gave the rapist's description within a range of a possible height and weight, which was then broadcast over the radio. We knew that a victim's description, under those circumstances, could only be partially accurate and not very useful. Then I came back to the living room where Burkett was still interviewing the victim.

"Did he say anything?"

"Yes, he told me to take everything off and if I made a sound he would cut my throat. So I did what he said."

"Okay, then what?"

"He just stared into the mirror for a few minutes looking at me in the mirror. Then he pushed me down face first onto the bed." She stopped, and started to cry. "Then he..."

"That's okay, I understand." Burkett stopped her. There was no need to make her revisit the rape in such explicit detail. Burkett knew that.

"Ma'am, I'm going to have to ask you some questions now that are fairly personal regarding what happened. I don't want to embarrass you or make you feel uncomfortable, but there is information that we need to help us catch the man who attacked you, okay?"

She nodded that she understood. "You don't have to call me ma'am. Nina is fine."

The questions were awkward to ask, and probably even more awkward to answer. Burkett had to know if she had showered or washed herself off at all. That would be important for evidence gathering. That question set her off.

"Of course I washed myself off. He came all over me. It was disgusting." Her lips trembled and she looked as if she was going to vomit.

Burkett and I knew the significance of that comment. Withdrawing before climax and potential DNA were important facts for the investigation. In asking the next questions, Burkett's choice of words was critical. He made a tactical move.

"Ma'am, he…" and Burkett hesitated, hoping she would fill in the blank. And she did.

"Yes, he came on me. But, he had a towel or something with him and he wiped it off. I don't care. Nothing is gonna make me feel clean enough." Now she was yelling, angry that we were forcing her to talk about such a traumatic and humiliating experience, especially to two men she did not know.

Burkett and I looked at each other in disbelief. Was the rapist that prepared?

Burkett knew that he had to go through the specific movements of the attacker in search for fingerprints, hair or other bits of himself that he may have left behind. Then the doorbell rang. The poor girl almost jumped out of her skin.

"That's just one of our officers. He's bringing over some evidence collection equipment. After I take you to the hospital, officers will remain here and dust for fingerprints and collect evidence. Is that okay?" Again she nodded in agreement as she pushed back her hair that had been covering her face. Wiping her tiny nose with the back of one hand, her other hand clasped the small gold cross hanging around her neck. Then she cupped both hands over her eyes, trying hard to maintain her composure. I went over and let Gillis in, with the evidence collection equipment. Then I went back to join Burkett.

"Nina, what I would like to ask you to do now is to go into your room, and get dressed in some comfortable clothing. Please do not touch anything you were wearing during the attack and try to stay away from anywhere the attacker was, the best you can. The best thing to do, if you don't mind, is to let Officer Hollings here escort you into the bedroom so you can get the clothes you want. Maybe get dressed in the bathroom, just so we don't accidentally destroy any evidence. Then you can call someone to meet you at the hospital if you want. Is that all right?" Again, she simply nodded yes without saying a word, but fighting back the tears.

We got her clothes and she went into the bathroom to get dressed. Burkett asked Gillis and me if we could stay back and process the scene for evidence while he drove the victim to the hospital.

"No problem, JB," Gillis answered, "but did you ask her if she wanted a female officer to escort her instead?"

"Uh, no. I think I established a pretty good rapport with her. We were communicating real well. I thought it might upset her if we changed on her now. I'm just going to get her into the sex crime exam room at the hospital. We should be okay."

"C'mon, JB, don't be stupid. You know the rules. When a girl gets raped, you're supposed to ask her if she wants a female officer. That's standard," Gillis insisted.

"Okay, I didn't know that was policy. I thought we did it only if we thought it was necessary, and it just didn't seem necessary. I'll call Fiero."

"JB, don't call Fiero," Gillis came back at him.

"Why not? She's the closest female unit."

"This poor girl just got raped. You want her dealing with

someone like Fiero who spreads her legs as a hobby? She'll probably say something really stupid. How about calling Mac? She's a good cop and a real lady. I think she'll be much better for the victim."

Burkett looked quite annoyed. It was obvious he wanted to handle this himself. Burkett looked at me.

"Do me a favor, please. Get Hughes on the phone, not over the radio. Tell him we'd like Carol MacKenzie to escort this girl to the hospital. If he asks why not Fiero, just tell him Gillis and I thought it was a better personality fit and leave it at that. But I don't think he'll even ask."

"You got it." I wasn't sure why Burkett couldn't make that call himself.

Burkett was right. Hughes didn't ask why or anything else; he rarely questioned things, anyway. Mac showed up and escorted the victim to the hospital. It was not unusual for a rape victim to want a female officer. More personal questions had to be asked, such as whether he made her do any unusual acts; and whether she recently had sex prior to the rape. Pictures would be taken of her vaginal area. The investigation was almost like being raped again. But this was all necessary to put together a focused investigation and hopefully an arrest, followed by a successful prosecution. When a woman was raped she was victimized again, well after the assault occurred.

Burkett and I stayed back to do some initial review for evidence processing. That was an important part of the Police Academy curriculum. We dusted for fingerprints around the sliding door where the rapist broke in, which led right into the bedroom. Even though the rapist wore gloves, you never knew what you would find. He may have had them off at a particular moment. Part of the gloves may have torn off. We took some photographs of the apartment and we looked for any other physical evidence to point out to the sex crime investigators when they arrived. We would turn all that evidence over to the detectives. They would do the more intricate search of the bedroom looking for hairs, semen samples and things most patrol officers would not be alert for. The department also had a Crime Scene Unit. They were called if the scene required more evidence collection than usual: if there were footprints to lift, blood to collect or anything more than a patrol officer or a detective could handle. Shootings, murders, and fatal car wrecks were automatic call-outs for the Crime Scene Unit.

We were working fairly diligently for a little while before Burkett broke the silence.

"Man, she was a good looking honey. Wasn't she?" Burkett asked me.

"Yeah, she was kinda cute," I answered him.

"Did you get a look at those tits every time she bent over? They were nice, very nice."

I couldn't admit to Burkett that I did sneak a peek. But at least I walked away.

"No, JB, I wasn't looking at her like that. After all, the poor girl was just raped."

"Well, I thought she was pretty fine. I wish I had gotten a piece of that instead of some fuck'n weirdo who has to rape women for a little action. Life just ain't fair. Here I am working my balls off as a cop and some scumbag is running around tapping that fine piece of ass."

I realized that we were alone, and we talked about women like this all the time, but right after a rape? That just didn't seem right. Maybe I was still too much of a rookie and had to loosen up a bit.

"That's the problem with girls living on these ground floor apartments, with sliding doors. They're just begging for this kind of trouble," Burkett went on.

"Ya know, JB, I'm sure they would live elsewhere if they could afford it. They do the best they can and just hope nothing like this happens."

"That's why she needs a cop like me to come around every once in a while to make sure she's okay... just in case this asshole plans on trying this again."

I wasn't really sure what Burkett meant or what he was getting at. Do rapists usually attack the same woman more than once?

"She'll figure out what to do and how to help herself. There's a lot of potential victims out there, JB; we can't protect them all."

"I know, but a good looking bitch like her, she's gotta be a prime target. Besides, if she wanted a little, I'd be right here to give it to her. Oh, yeah."

Burkett sounded more stupid each time he spoke. I felt bad for this girl, but she was hardly the first rape victim in Westland Park. Why Burkett was getting so focused on her escaped me. Just when I thought he couldn't say anything more idiotic, he went on.

"When she was talking about standing in front of the mirror like that, naked, I thought my dick was gonna burst right through my pants like a fuck'n rocket."

"Hey, JB, I'm not interested in your dick and I think you're getting off the mark here. Let's just finish up what we're doing. The Sex Crimes Unit will be here in a few minutes."

They wouldn't get there fast enough for me. Watching Burkett handle the rape victim made me think that he was a pretty good cop. Listening to him afterwards made me think he was just plain fucked up.

We didn't talk for the next few minutes and finished what we were doing. JB walked back into the bedroom.

"I think we're done in there, JB. Whatta ya doing?"

"Uh, nothing. Just checking out the crime scene, seeing if I can come up with something good for Sex Crimes. Still got hopes of making detective one day, you know."

"Whatever."

The Sex Crime Unit from headquarters showed up a few minutes later and started collecting the evidence in the bedroom. The detectives who worked major crimes — murder, rapes, narcotics and armed robberies — worked out of headquarters in the Detective Bureau. The detectives stationed out of the precincts worked the thefts, burglaries, assaults, frauds and other general investigations and were appropriately called precinct detectives.

"Anything special we need to know?" Detective Patelli asked.

"He came in through the sliding glass door here. We processed that. The rape occurred in the bedroom, on the bed. The rapist forced her down face first," Burkett told the detectives, trying to speak boldly and decisively. "He hid his face pretty well, with a ski cap and hood and was armed with a knife. He was prepared, definitely not new at this. I bet a quick review of the recent prison releases will give us a good suspect. I'll get us started on a neighborhood canvass to try finding any witnesses. Then I'll come back tomorrow night and next week at the same time of the rape and look for additional witnesses." Burkett wasn't telling the detectives anything new or anything they didn't already know. But his attempts to impress them were transparent and didn't seem to be scoring him any points.

"Thanks, Officers."

"You got it. Listen, I've been working this sector for a long time. If there's anything I can do to help, give me a call," Burkett said to Patelli. Patelli did not answer; he just gave Burkett a polite nod and smile. Burkett was not the first patrol officer to try to schmooze his way into a detective slot. Patelli probably got there the same way.

Burkett and I started knocking on doors looking for witnesses. We never said a rape occurred, only that there was a break-in and an assault. We were trying to protect the victim's privacy, as per policy, but the story always got out anyway. As expected, nobody saw anything.

"You know, Hollings, I'm gonna do some follow-up on this thing. No little fucker is gonna go around my beat raping women and getting away with it. I'll dig up something," Burkett said with bravado that I found almost funny.

As patrolmen, we were allowed to do some basic follow-up on crimes that occurred during our shift, as long as it did not interfere with the detectives and we reported everything we found to them. If they wanted us to back off, we did. The investigations were their cases.

I was going to ask JB about his newfound enthusiasm. I decided to let it go. Besides it was well past two in the morning. I was supposed to meet Liz behind an office park in her sector at three o'clock. On one hand, I was kind of glad when Gillis recommended that Mac take the girl to the hospital. But, I was not quite sure how I felt about what he said about Liz. Maybe she was a little flirtatious, but spreading her legs as a hobby? That seemed a little brutal. I got back in the car, hoping that neither Liz nor I got a call.

It was three o'clock on the button. I cruised around to the back of the office park with my lights off. There was Liz sitting in her patrol car. We both got out.

"So what's up, hot stuff?" Liz asked me.

"Not much. Just finished up working a rape with Burkett. He's a piece of work, isn't he?"

"We're not here to talk about Burkett, and as for that rape thing, that sounds a little exciting right now." Liz held up a set of keys and started jiggling them. Giving me a "come and get me" look, Liz started walking to the back wall of the building. My instinct told me to follow. Opening the door to what appeared to be a maintenance shop, she looked back at me again with a devilish smile and walked in, once again playfully jiggling the keys over her shoulder. Reaching up and pulling the string dangling from the ceiling, she turned on the single bare bulb sitting in the socket on the ceiling.

"How did you get the keys to this place?" I asked her.

"Hey, this has been my beat for over two years now. I get to know the right people."

We walked farther into the small room with tools and equipment sitting on gray metal shelves. There was a mop in a bucket sitting in the corner. In the center of the room of dark cinder block walls was a plywood worktable straddling two workhorses, with a few hand tools resting on top. There was a smell of motor oil and a different foul odor coming from the silver trash can in the far corner. Looking around at my environs, I partially slipped on a grease spot on the concrete floor. Liz sat up on the table and waved her finger signaling for me to come over. Turning the knob a couple of extra times, I made sure the door was locked. She put her arms around my neck as I walked over to her and simultaneously rested my hands on her hips, just above her police belt.

"You know, you're one helluva rookie," she said in a soft voice.

"Is that so? Maybe I can be rookie of the year."

"Oh, you will be tonight."

Grasping me behind my collar with the energy of a mugger

roughing me up, Liz pulled me closer. No hesitation from either one of us. We started kissing, really getting into some long wet, tongue action. She began to breathe pretty heavily and was even moaning a little. My hands just went right for her tits, but her bulletproof vest stopped that. At that point, I realized that we were both wearing a lot of equipment. Liz stood up and started unsnapping my police belt. I reciprocated. It took a few more minutes than it would in civilian clothes, but soon, there we were — shirts on, pants and underwear down, hanging over our boots which were still on our feet. Our belts with our guns holstered were laid out on the floor, beyond our reach, and the radios crackled with static. We kissed a little more and then she turned around and leaned up against the worktable. I looked at that beautiful, round, milky white, soft skinned ass of hers with one little dark freckle on her left cheek. I moved forward, shuffling my feet.

The two of us having sex during patrol was not a smart move. I was being a lot less cautious than I ever thought I would be. This is something Thompson would do. But she looked too good. This was an opportunity that I was not passing up. She enjoyed making out, but nothing like what was happening now. She was excited; she was so wet that I slid into her like I was on a ride in a water park. She moaned, she groaned and soon she was almost screaming. The noise was starting to worry me. I knew we were in a locked room in an empty building in the middle of the night, but getting caught was just not an option. I moved fast. The faster I moved, the more she screamed. The more I tried to bring this to climax, the more it seemed to elude me. I was running out of steam; she was not. Finally, it happened. I leaned over, on top of her back and tried to catch my breath. She was breathing heavy as well. Then, as fast as it began, it was over.

"Wow, that was great," she said with me still leaning on top of her.

"Yeah," was all I could come up with.

Partially resting, partially in disbelief, I just stayed down, hunched over her.

"I think you'd better get up now. Time to get back to work," she told me in a very matter of fact tone.

I moved off her and we started getting our uniforms back on without saying a further word. Was that all there was to it? Did Liz just want a quick one, and I just happened to be her man of choice for the night? We started to walk out and I got to the door first, unlocking it. Liz grabbed my elbow and gave me a tug. I turned around.

"Hey, you really are something else."

"Well, so are you."

"Listen," she said, "no one else has to know about this. And despite what you hear, I don't go around doing stuff like this."

Though I didn't respond, my blank stare and motionless, half-opened mouth spoke for me.

"No, I don't. There was just something about you. I thought we had a good connection," she continued. Then she got up on her toes and gave me a quick kiss on the lips.

Liz sounded sincere; maybe she wasn't what everyone was saying she was. Maybe she just had a couple of indiscretions, like tonight — what woman hasn't? And then whomever she was with opened his big mouth. That's how guys are, especially cops. But, I wasn't going to do that. With no more words between us, we got back in our patrol cars and went back to work, knowing that we would both act as if nothing had ever happened. I tried to get back to my sector quickly, before I got a call.

Sex is a funny thing, affecting everybody differently. I really enjoyed what just happened. It was spontaneous with no thought or discussion about what it meant or anything else. It just was; I was living for the moment. I thought about the rape that occurred earlier tonight and how sex affected that poor girl. I thought about Janie and wondered how this sex would affect her. Then I realized, it wouldn't affect her at all. She would never know.

Chapter 8

Summertime brought sunshine and a warm, pleasant breeze that could make almost anything look nicer than it really was. Now, with summer in full bloom, the Heights looked much less drab, more lively, and less likely to have as much crime as it usually did. Ironically, summer was the busy season for patrol. More people were out on the streets, kids were out of school just looking for something to do, and stress from the heat built up fast — especially for the unemployed or underpaid who could not afford air conditioning. It was a volatile mixture.

"Let's get started," Hughes called out to begin roll call, snapping me out of my daydream of spending the summer on the beach.

After reviewing all the regular information, Hughes focused on one particular issue.

"Listen up; the Detective Bureau has issued a warning notice. Three different precincts have reported rapes, and they all match the same description of the perp. As a matter of fact, it sounds like the same guy from the rape that Burkett handled a few weeks back. We're not getting much more than a white male in dark clothing, who wears a hood tightly closed over his face and a ski mask. He's from 5' 10" to maybe 6' and 180 to 200 plus pounds, which is the normal range of descriptions we get for any one perp. But, he also used a knife, similar to the one used on Burkett's call."

"Anything else about his M.O., Sarge?" MacKenzie asked.

"Let's see. He's either broken into ground floor apartments or attacked a girl on the jogging trail in the Fourth Precinct's area. There's not much to go on. There have been no witnesses, and the rapist is careful not to leave any DNA samples behind. We won't expound upon that. Keep your eyes open. It's pretty warm out there now. Maybe if you see a white guy in a black hooded sweatshirt and ski mask running around your beat, you may want to give him a little field interview."

That got a chuckle from the squad, somewhat unexpected from the usually dry Hughes.

"Just be alert," were his last words for the roll call.

We tossed around a few stupid jokes for a minute or two and then Hughes told us to hit the streets. Roll call broke up and we all headed for our patrol cars. On the way out to the parking lot, Burkett walked up next to me and put his hand on my shoulder. He spoke in a soft voice, not quite a whisper, but he obviously did not want to be overheard.

"Looks like our boy is getting a lot of pussy out there, huh, partner?"

What the hell was he talking about, and what was that partner bullshit?

"Huh, JB, who's our boy? Whatta ya talking about?"

"You know, the hooded wonder. The guy who did our girl in the Belmont apartments. Just like the Sarge was talking about."

In a matter of a couple of sentences, Burkett went from calling me partner to calling the rape victim "our girl." Where he was going with this one, I could not imagine.

"Yeah, well, I know we don't have much on him now, but he'll screw up. We'll catch him. Unfortunately, he'll probably get away with a few more rapes before we do, but he'll get his," I said to Burkett, aware that what I just said was neither reassuring to Burkett nor insightful in any respect.

"In the meantime he's getting a lot of action, and I bet he's picking some good looking babes." Burkett was sporting that ridiculous smile on his face once again.

Not only should Burkett have realized how stupid and unprofessional that comment was, but he sounded as if he was in admiration of the rapist. Burkett sure was a strange one. As long as he did his job, and left me alone, I could handle it. We worked together and that was it. Though we had not spoken much since the night at the Warehouse Night Club, and he had been more withdrawn since rumors of the Shooting Review Board started floating around, he did seem talkative when it came to the rapist. I was hoping this conversation was not an indication that he wanted to get friendly with me. I didn't want to be mean, but I was going to keep my distance the best I could. Too many conversations over a cup of coffee would send the wrong message that I saw a friendship developing between us.

"Yeah, right. I'll see you out there." I had no idea how to respond to him. I just walked off and got into my car.

The summer uniform was much more comfortable. Wearing a lightweight, short sleeved shirt, open at the collar, was easier on the neck than those starchy collars from the winter uniforms. We did not have to wear ties during the summertime and the cars were well air-conditioned. Driving around the Heights with nothing particular on my mind, I decided to take a drive through Camden Gardens. The two gardens that bordered the entrance to the complex were blooming with beautiful flowers of gold, pink and violet, though I could not name one flower. That almost gave the name Camden Gardens some meaning, and they sort of looked like the gardens at the entrance to our precinct. Beer cans, liquor bottles and trash that were strewn in and around the gardens certainly ruined what could have been an attractive entrance. But those small remnants of long, lost evenings brought the scene back to reality.

As I did my drive around the complex, Burkett drove over to the Belmont apartments. He called in his location over the radio and advised that he would be out on a follow-up.

A follow-up at Belmont? There must've been something else that happened there. Maybe a break-in or a theft that I didn't know about. There was no way he was following-up on that rape, I thought to myself, not knowing what to think. Actually, this was not really any of my business; that's why we had sergeants.

*****

Burkett walked up to the door and knocked gently, again walking back far enough so his badge and uniform could be seen through the peep hole.

The door opened, but with a chain strung across the door and the young lady answered, "Well, hi, Officer Burkett. I'm surprised to see you again."

"Hi Nina, how you doing?"

"I'm doing all right, I guess. Um, is there something to report on my rape?"

"Oh no, I'm just checking in on you, making sure you're okay."

"Really, I'm okay," she responded. Then there was silence. Burkett broke the silence.

"Can I come in for a minute just to talk to you and kinda assure myself that you are all right?" he said, trying to come off in a light-hearted, but caring manner. Nina did not say anything and took a moment to respond. She looked back into the apartment as if someone was there and then quickly turned back to Burkett. She closed the door to unlock the chain and let him in. She had changed out of her work clothes and was wearing a white undershirt and blue shorts and white socks. She led Burkett to the living room, while Burkett noticed how cute she looked with her hair pulled back in a ponytail. She sat on the couch and Burkett in the chair, the same setup as when Burkett first responded there after the rape.

"This is your second visit to me since I was attacked. Do all rape victims get such special attention?"

"Not all. But I think you deserve it. Have things been okay for you at work? Have you been able to get back into the swing of things?"

"Oh yeah, just like I told you last time you stopped by, everyone at work has been very supportive. They're letting me ease back slowly. I'm really doing well."

"Good. That's good. You know, the guy who attacked you, we believe has attacked other women in the county."

"Oh no, that's terrible. I hope you guys catch him soon."

"We will, but in the meantime, I just want to make sure you're safe."

Worry and bewilderment spread across Nina's face.

"Why do you think I'm not safe? Has someone been watching me or something? What do you know? What's going on?" Her voice became high pitched and excited.

"Oh, no, no. Nothing is going on. I didn't mean to scare you like that. I'm just concerned that he may come back, you know, since he knows that you live alone and everything. I just don't want to take any unnecessary risks."

"So, what should I do?"

"Well, do you have a boyfriend who could stay over or something like that?"

"Officer, that's a little personal, but no, I don't have any man in my life who sleeps over now." Nina, looked at Burkett askance, and curiously waited to see what Burkett was going to say. Unaware of her movements, she started to slowly slide over to the other side of the couch to put a little more distance between herself and Burkett.

"Okay, and you keep that sliding door locked at night, right?"

"Oh yes, I had a new lock put on that right away."

"Do you want me to take a look at it? Make sure it's a good lock?" Burkett started to get out of his seat.

"No," Nina exclaimed." That's okay. I had a real good locksmith do it. It's good, but thank you."

Burkett walked over to the lock anyway and took a look. He really had no knowledge of locks, but feigned that he was giving it a quality inspection. He then nodded as if approving of the new lock.

"Hmm. I guess I could drive by a little more, just in case he does start to scope you out. That way he'll know that we're keeping an eye on you."

"I appreciate that, Officer, but I don't think you really need to do this. And I am afraid if my neighbors keep seeing you coming over, they may suspect something is really wrong. So, I'm grateful, but I think any special attention may not be a good idea."

"Okay. I won't come to the door, but I will keep an eye on you. Listen, here's my card. Actually, I'll write my home number on the back if you need anything. Now, I never give my home number out, but for you... Just please don't give it to anybody."

"Oh, I won't. Well, I really appreciate it and I'm sure you're pretty busy out there, so I don't want to tie you up."

Standing up from the chair, Nina started walking to the door displaying the old, non-verbal communication that said, "Please leave." This type of personal involvement was making Nina uncomfortable, even from a cop. She did not sense a physical danger, but she had been around enough men to know when something was not right.

"So, thanks for coming," she continued as she opened the door.

Burkett was a little slow taking the hint and getting to the door.

"Okay, and really, call me anytime," he said as she was closing the door. He didn't hear, or at least didn't notice, how loudly she clicked the lock on the door. That was one message that went over his head.

As Burkett got back into his car, he heard the radio traffic of a call that was assigned to Fiero. Burkett had turned off the radio on his belt while he talked to Nina, so he didn't hear what was going on. That was not proper police procedure. Burkett listened, trying to figure out what had happened.

*****

Fiero and I were responding as back-up to Gillis and Stryker. It sounded like Gillis had rolled up on another crack deal and, with Stryker, busted it up. It turned bad and there was a fight going on. Gillis and Stryker together, calling for back-up, sounded like some shit had really broken loose. I kicked it into high gear, heading for the back of the Maplewood Office Park, just about five minutes out of the Heights.

The office park was situated at the end of a cul-de-sac. This time of night and Gillis knew some guys would be dealing crack back there behind some building? He must have had some good informant. Patrolmen just didn't make drug arrests like that, except by chance, and rarely.

I remembered the night we busted Willie Dixon. Gillis kept looking at his watch. He had to have had a pretty good idea of when Dixon was going to be there. That kind of information was hard to come by. Now that I thought about it, I remembered him getting a call on his cell phone right before we hit the street. That had to be his informant calling in. I've made a number of arrests while I've been out there, mostly for assaults, drunks and shoplifters. A couple of the drunk drivers had some baggies of marijuana in their car. That was the best drug bust I had made. I did not know anyone else on the squad doing any different or any better. I had no idea of how to get an informant like the one Gillis had.

"318 Baker, I have an ETA of 2 and can respond as back-up," Burkett called on the radio. There was no possible way Burkett estimated his time of arrival was only two minutes. He just wanted a chance to jump into the fray. I didn't blame him. We were cops for a reason — we enjoyed that stuff.

"Negative 381 Baker, 315 and 321 Baker are en route. Maintain position in your sector till further advised," was the dispatcher's staccato response.

I could only imagine the look of disappointment on Burkett's face. But I knew what he was going to do. He was going to head in that direction just in case there was a call for more back-up.

I saw Liz pull into the front parking lot, which was dark and barren, without slowing down and I pulled my car in right behind her. She called in our arrival on the radio while still driving. I hadn't thought about that: another one of those procedural things that I was still not doing by instinct. The reflection of the red blinking lights was like a lighthouse leading us to Gillis and Stryker's patrol cars. Something about those red lights was very reassuring to a cop whose back was against the wall. Speeding to their location down the narrow alley, with the building on our left side and a brick wall with a fence on top of it on the right side, Liz and I deftly maneuvered our cars to come to the aid of our brothers. We saw Gillis and Stryker in action as we rounded our cars to the left. We swung our cars around almost in perfect unison and came to screeching stops. Jumping out of our cars quickly, leaving the engines running and the doors open, we moved with a real sense of urgency — we were pumped.

We saw Gillis sitting on one guy, pushed up against the back wall of the building. His gun was out, pointing at the two other guys who were trying to circle Stryker. That made my heart race. I could not be sure what he was going to do. Was I about to be in the middle of another shooting? I looked over to Stryker. He had one hand over his weapon, still in the holster while holding off the two guys, waving his nightstick. I figured out what he was doing. Stryker knew if he pulled his weapon out, he might lose it during a scuffle. That's every cop's concern. Gillis knew that too; that's why he was ready with his weapon. Stryker was just holding these two pukes off until back-up arrived.

Liz took the lead right away and jumped on the bigger of the two guys surrounding Stryker. Actually, it was more of an NFL tackle. She went right for the knees. That was one good move; she never would have been able to take him over just with upper body strength. The swiftness of her response, and her lack of hesitation, took me by surprise. The one moment I took to think about what I should have done could have been one critical moment too long.

My attack was not as tactical. I jumped the other guy at the head and neck and got him into a headlock. That was not a good position to be in; I had to protect my weapon from being grabbed. The more I leaned over to wrestle him to the ground, the closer my face came to the top of his head. The stench of his hair reminded me of the hospital hallway. It was nauseating. I had no peripheral vision. How were my partners doing? Not knowing what was happening around me set me off into a little bit of a panic; I could feel myself breaking out in a sweat, on my forehead, under my arms and all over my body under my bulletproof vest. I couldn't hold my grip much longer, but I did not want to let go and start over again, giving him another shot at overtaking me. This was not meant to be a fair fight — I had to win. Some of the same feelings from the shooting came back to me. Once again, nothing seemed real; time seemed to be moving slowly, very slowly. What I did not know was just how fast things had moved.

Liz's perp had tried to get up from the tackle as Liz held onto his legs, both of them struggling and twisting around on the ground. Eventually, brute strength won out. In a matter of seconds, Liz was kicked off her assailant and he was getting up. If it came to a one-on-one fist fight, Liz would have no choice — her weapon would be coming out. It did not get that far. Stryker ran over and whacked the nightstick across the back of his head and just about knocked him out. Even in the midst of my struggle, I heard the sharp crack of nightstick meeting skull.

Then, Stryker ran over to help me and rather artfully kicked the bastard's legs right out from under him. Falling straight to the ground face first made it pretty easy for me to get on top and cuff him. I picked up his head by his greasy hair with my now sweaty palms. He was bleeding from his nose and mouth, where his face struck the ground. I didn't say anything, but I was glad to see it. The anger I felt was overwhelming. Stryker patted me on the shoulder as a sign; I understood. He was telling me to handle this myself now and he took off to help Gillis.

Now in control, at least of my immediate situation, I was less fearful but more angry. I was afraid for what might have happened. A strong temptation to ram his face into the ground one more time overcame me. Scanning the area quickly, looking over each shoulder, I could see that my partners were all engaged with their own problems. They would not see one extra shove, nor would they care. For a long second, I sat there, holding his slimy hair, grabbing harder and pulling back, waiting to hear him at least groan in pain. Then I took his head and gently pushed it back down. Close, but I just was not ready to cross that line. I hoped I never would cross that line. "Fuck you," under my breath, was all I could say.

Looking over towards Gillis and Stryker, I watched them take control of their prisoner. Standing him up and patting him down, they did it with some pretty rough handling, with an extra push or two against the wall. They pulled some stuff out of his pocket and looked it over. Then they looked at each other and simultaneously smiled. Obviously, they had found the drugs. At that moment, all the activity must have caught up to Stryker. Standing erect and motionless for a moment, he walked a few feet away from Gillis and leaned against the brick wall. He then leaned over and rested his hands on his knees, trying to catch his breath. He certainly earned his pay in those few minutes. Never one to try to come off as super tough or oozing with macho, tonight Stryker showed what was he was made of. Maybe that was what made someone a real cop — not how much he talked about what he did, or how many guys she was screwing, but what they did when the shit hit the fan. Liz and Stryker proved their mettle tonight. Were they the kind of cops I wanted to be? Who knows?

All three drug dealing pukes were in custody, lying on the ground, face down with their hands cuffed behind their backs. Most importantly and probably amazingly, we were all safe. Gillis walked over to Liz and me and thanked us for the assistance. I was sure Burkett was somewhere close by just waiting to get called in. Edmonds was driving the wagon tonight; he came and was able to take the three prisoners at once down to the jail. Stryker and Gillis would go down to the jail for processing — fingerprinting and photographing, swearing out arrest warrants, storing the evidence and interviewing these guys, hoping for a confession that rarely came — all the things that went along with a good drug bust. The car would have to be towed and impounded. Stryker called ahead to have a medic standing by for the dumb shit who took the baton to the head.

"Hey, I'll wait for the tow truck, so you guys can get to work," I offered, trying to be a team player.

A strange silence came over Stryker and Gillis and they looked at each other with awkward smiles, yet clear discomfort.

"No, that's okay, Hollings. We need to do some clean up here. We'll wait. Thanks."

Gillis' response was devoid of a true thank you. I wasn't sure why they wouldn't take me up on an offer to handle a bullshit duty like that, but nobody on the squad would challenge Gillis.

"Okay." That seemed like the best response.

Walking to my car, Liz walked up next to me and said softly, "Meet me at the gas station across the street; let's get a cup."

A cup of coffee seemed innocent enough. While driving over to meet Liz something told me to just stop and give Janie a call, and say hello. My hand started to scramble around the driver area when I could not find my cell phone attached to my belt. The department did not like us losing their equipment. Picking up the radio, I switched to the side channel.

"Liz, I'll be there in one minute. Stand by."

After the panic of possibly losing some equipment settled down, I realized that I must've dropped the cell phone during the scuffle. I wanted to get back there quickly before it got lost or someone drove over it, so I turned the car around to the back of the building where I knew Gillis and Stryker were finishing up. As my headlights tilted towards where they were, I saw a figure dash into the bushes. Nervously I slammed on the brakes, put my hand over my weapon and sat motionless, trying to figure out what might be going on. Within one second, I heard the slamming of a trunk, then another trunk. Turning in the direction of the noise, I saw Stryker, who had just slammed shut the car they were getting ready to impound. Then I saw Gillis over the trunk of his police car, which he had just shut. They both had their weapons drawn and trained their sights in on me.

"What the fuck?" I whispered to myself.

Giving them a few moments to recognize me and see that they had just drawn down on a marked police car, I opened my window and shouted.

"It's me, Hollings. I just came back 'cause I dropped my phone."

Slowly, and with deliberate and exaggerated motion, I got out of the car and began walking with my body in the defensive, bladed position, moving forward with the side of my body. They looked at each other and put their guns back into their holsters.

"What the fuck, Hollings! You scared the piss out of us," Gillis called out.

"Yeah, Hollings, what the fuck are you doing?" Stryker added.

"Well, it's just that, I, uh, came back to get my phone. Then I saw someone running away and I heard the trunks slam. Next thing you know I'm looking down the barrel of your fuck'n weapons. What the fuck is going on here?"

"Well, shit, Hollings. We're cleaning up the mess of a friggin' drug deal and you come screeching around the corner. We didn't know who was coming. It could've been one of their drug dealing cronies coming to get back at us. You should've radioed us just to let us know it was you."

"Okay, I guess. But who was running away?"

"Someone running away? I think you're seeing shadows. That happens to rookies sometimes, you know." Gillis looked at Stryker; then they both started laughing.

"I saw something, and it didn't look like no shadow. Then I heard the trunks slam and you guys were sitting there staring at me, ready to blow my fuck'n brains out. Everything's okay? You sure?"

"Yeah, we're sure. But are you okay? You're acting pretty weird."

Without even responding, I turned and pointed my flashlight around where I had been in my scuffle. There sat my phone. I quickly picked it up and walked back to my car.

Something was very fucked up. *That was a lot of paranoia from two experienced cops* was all I could think. I drove off to meet Liz.

"Hey, great work. I saw that tackle. Very nice," was my greeting to Liz in the gas station's convenience store, where she was sipping a cup of coffee.

"You sound surprised."

"Uh, no, just nice police work." I was too obvious, but I could not admit that I was surprised how she jumped in there. She was pretty tough and held her own when the time came. She slithered over to me to whisper into my ear.

"So, you can't believe that I'm more than just a good fuck, huh?"

"I never said that." I could not help smiling, though I tried not to.

She knew what I was thinking — I was busted. Or, at least, she knew what I suspected before tonight. I was not sure what to think; but right then and there, she had shown herself to be a good cop. That was all that mattered. There was still no doubt about it; she was right about one thing — she was a good fuck. I wanted to ask her if she had experienced the same fear I had during that fight, just like I would ask any other cop. But, given that we had shared a private moment of intimacy, she was not just another cop. Not that secure in myself, I did not ask. I also wanted to get her opinion of what just happened with Stryker and Gillis. I decided not to ask that either.

I drove off and started heading back to my sector calling in on the radio that I was clear. As soon as I did, Burkett got me on the side band. "Hey, Gary, meet me at the Triple 7, 10-4?"

"Yeah, okay," I responded hesitantly. The Triple 7 was a 24-hour convenience store with stores all over the city: actually, all over the country. They seemed omnipresent. The name for this particular Triple 7 was quite appropriate. Coincidentally, it sat on the border of three patrol districts. It had never gotten robbed. Yes, it gave free coffee to cops. There was usually a cop in there any time during the day or night. I got there first and grabbed a cup. I waited for Burkett. He showed up, got a cup and then we drove to the parking lot across the street and pulled up window to window.

"So how did Gillis' arrest go? Sounded like you guys had some good action, huh?" Burkett wanted to know what he had missed.

"Eh, it was all right. Gillis had one guy down and Stryker was holding off the other two from springing their buddy loose. They weren't armed, but they were certainly ready to fight."

"You guys put a whoopin' on 'em?"

"We did okay. I tell you, Fiero jumped right in there. I was impressed."

"Well, I just wish I coulda been there. They would've felt a little nightstick action right up their ass."

"I'm sure you'll have plenty more chances, JB. Hang in there. I heard you were at Belmont earlier. Anything special going on there?"

"No, I was just following-up on that rape. You know, now that it looks like a serial rapist, I thought it'd be a good idea to stay in touch with the victim. She may start remembering something, or he may even try to come back and attack her again."

"Don't you think you should leave that to the detectives, JB? It's their case now."

"I know, but I think I got a real good relationship with her. She's opening up to me. That's all."

"Maybe so, but I'd be careful with that, a rape victim and all. I don't know."

"Don't worry, rookie. I got it covered."

I thought carefully about what happened tonight. It worked out okay. We all walked away without getting hurt. But Gillis and Stryker really had their backs to the wall, both literally and figuratively. Should just the two of them have taken this on? Why didn't Gillis call for more back-up in advance? He could have asked in roll call. Did he even tell the sergeant that this would be going down? Was grabbing some two-bit dope dealer and a little crack really worth that kind of risk? I didn't think so. I also didn't think I should be questioning a senior cop's judgment, but I was getting a pretty good feel of what good police work was. While I thought highly of Gillis — he seemed to be one solid cop — I just didn't have a good feeling about the way he was doing these drug arrests. But then again, who was I to question it? That's why we had sergeants.

Chapter 9

"Okay, everybody, summertime will be winding to a close soon. As you all know I will have my yearly Labor Day barbeque at my house. You and your families are all invited. The day works out well this year. It will be the last day of the shift. So you go home, get some sleep — actually very little sleep — and start rolling into my house anytime past noon. As always, we'll have plenty of good food and good family fun and games. My beautiful wife, Melinda, and I are really looking forward to it."

Hughes was happy to be announcing his party. He had one every year since he had been reassigned from SWAT to a squad sergeant. I was excited about it. Meeting everyone's spouse, boyfriend or girlfriend would probably prove interesting and maybe even a little revealing. You can tell a lot about somebody by the partner he or she chooses. I would be bringing Janie. I liked showing her off. She was no model, but she was cute, intelligent, and had a good sense of humor despite her serious nature.

"Okay, if there is nothing else, let's hit it," Hughes said to end the roll call and get the night started.

We all got up and headed out. Hughes called Burkett over, waving his fingers, but looking down at his desk. I knew what that was about. So did everyone else. Burkett had a pretty good idea of what was in store for him and walked over to the sergeant's desk. Hughes closed the door and came back to where Burkett was standing. That was the last glimpse I had of them.

*****

In the roll call room, behind the closed door, they both sat and talked for a few minutes. Then, Hughes picked up an envelope off his desk and handed it to Burkett. Burkett took the envelope in his right hand and tapped it against his left hand, in between the thumb and index finger, several times. Hughes had told him what it was going to say, but he just didn't want to read it. Hearing about it is one thing; seeing it in black and white was another. Burkett scratched his forehead three or four times. Finally he opened the envelope. He read the letter without emotion.

The letter, signed by the chief, on his personal letterhead, first congratulated Burkett for arresting the armed robber. That was done within the first two sentences. However, in the rest of the one page letter, the chief reprimanded him for not adequately assessing the risk when responding to the scene. He did not exercise adequate care and caution and he did not fully explain what he had observed to his fellow officers. Consequently, they were not prepared and were shot. He was receiving a three day suspension without pay.

Deep inside, Burkett was devastated as he fought from allowing the tightness in his chest, and needles being stuck into his heart, to overcome him. He had played the events of the shooting in his mind over and over again since the day it happened. It was his suspicion that led to discovering the robbery in the first place, and he did tell Thompson and Hollings his concerns. They chose not to take him seriously; they decided not to draw their weapons. How was that his fault?

Slumping over slightly, right hand on his chest, Hughes began to get out of his chair, afraid that Burkett was having a heart attack. Then Burkett spoke.

"I want to appeal this," he told Hughes, in a weak, scratchy voice.

"That's certainly your right, JB. You have 10 days to get that appeal to me and I'll forward it to IA. I hope things work out for you."

"Yeah, me too."

"Are you okay working tonight? Do you want to take the night off?"

"No, it's not like I hadn't heard the rumors and seen it coming. I'll be okay. I'll see you later, Sarge."

Stoic and robotic, Burkett walked out to his car and started his patrol for the night. The word on Thompson and me had not come out yet, at least not publicly. Hughes knew what it was, but he was waiting for the right moment.

*****

I was just cruising around thinking about Janie and what she might wear to Hughes' barbeque: how she would look. Then I heard the radio broadcast.

"321 Baker, we have a domestic dispute called in. Complainant heard a woman's screams coming from an apartment. Complainant was anonymous."

Of course, these complainants were always anonymous. Memorizing the address, I headed to the Gardens and knew exactly how to get there and where to go. Burkett got right on the radio.

"318 Baker, I'm close. I'll back him up."

Yep, I was not going to shake off Burkett tonight. He'd back me up and then he would want to talk over a cup of coffee.

I got to the apartment building and waited for Burkett. He showed up quickly. We walked up one flight of stairs to the second level in the dimly-lit staircase, our shoes sticking to the dirt and grime on the floor. The odor of urine was sickening. We didn't even want to touch the banister as we climbed the stairs. We reached the apartment from where the screaming had been heard. It was quiet now. We knocked on the brown metal door and a big, big biker guy opened the door.

He must've been 6' 3" and 300 pounds, with black wavy hair and a goatee, dressed in a white sleeveless undershirt and dirty blue jeans. His nostrils flared, he grunted and then went to slam the door shut, but I had already learned about that. My nightstick was ready in my hand and I held it in the doorframe. He tried slamming the door two more times before he realized the door was not going to close. He stepped back.

Burkett and I walked into the apartment with gold colored carpeting, a black leather couch and a few chairs. Pictures from biker rallies adorned the walls. A slight aroma of marijuana wafted by us. I told him that there had been a report of a woman screaming coming from this apartment. He said there was no screaming. We were in the wrong place and he wanted us to leave. We weren't quite ready to leave. I told him I was going to look around, just to make sure everything was all right.

"Where's your warrant?" was his first question; it always was from someone who had been arrested enough times to think he knew the law.

"I don't have one. I'm doing an illegal search, so you just stand right there and you have nothing to worry about, right? As a matter of fact, why don't you make yourself comfortable and take a seat over there?" I said, pointing to one of the metallic legged chairs with a cushion covered in plastic.

"I don't wanna take a fuck'n seat and I don't think the two of you cop motherfuckers are gonna be able to make me." He stood his ground, arms crossed, a strong, unblinking glare, just hoping for a good fight.

"You know, you're right," I answered him. "You are a big dude, and I don't think the two of us can put you down." He looked a little satisfied with himself for the moment. "But, if you don't sit down, I'm gonna get on this radio and call over three more cops. One of them is going to Taser your ass. Then when you're done shaking and go down to the floor writhing in pain, we're gonna gag you, shove a nightstick up your ass and hog tie you until we finish up here. Your choice."

He looked at me for a moment waiting to see who would blink first. He did. He sat down, and glared at us, but now, with a touch of humility. Sometimes a good bluff works. I walked over to the bedroom and stood by the doorway, partially behind the wall, where I could see a young woman sitting on the bed, her back towards me. She knew I was there, but she was not turning around. That made me nervous. I got back behind the wall a little more, just sort of peeking around the doorframe and asked her to turn around. She got off the bed, stood up and turned around to me. She was wiping tears from her face and holding her head back to keep any more blood from pouring out of her nose. The running black mascara blended with some of the dried blood.

"What happened, ma'am?" though I knew the answer.

"I get nosebleeds sometimes; that's all."

I looked at her face carefully. Yes, her nose was bleeding. But I also saw a small bruise on the side of her right eye that, by tomorrow, would be a full blown shiner. The sadness in those big brown eyes, her scrunching dark eyebrows and the trembling lower lip spoke volumes. This was not the first time he had beaten her. It was probably not the first time that some man in her life had beaten her. And I would suspect that it would not be the last.

"Miss, I know what happened. I really don't think protecting him is a good idea. It's only gonna get worse. Press charges now. We'll lock him up and give you a chance to get out of this mess. That's the best advice. Actually, it's the only advice I can give you."

"I get nosebleeds."

"Okay. If I am not back here later tonight, I'll be back another, with the ambulance right behind me so the medics can peel you off the floor. If that's what you want for yourself, fine. Have a good night."

I saw the blood. I had probable cause that a felony occurred and could've arrested the biker even without the woman's statement. What was the point? She wouldn't testify and then charges would be dropped. I had been through this so many times before in my short career. I knew that there was a whole psychology behind women who allowed themselves to be abused like that, but I was no social worker.

This guy would not go down without a fight. It would have taken at least three of us with nightsticks to beat him down. Maybe we would have used a Taser. No problem — he would've deserved it. Then she would jump in. There would be a whole lot of injuries. She wouldn't press charges. It just wasn't worth it.

Walking out of the bedroom, I tapped Burkett on the shoulder, about to announce that we were leaving. Then I stopped, turned around and walked back into the room.

"Ma'am, please. I understand that you're afraid. But if you leave with me now, I will get you to a women's shelter. You don't even have to press charges. Just get yourself out of this situation. I'm telling you, I've seen this a hundred times before. He's going to hurt you again. Please, walk out with me now."

She stared at me for a moment. "I get nosebleeds."

No response came to mind. I walked out again. I went over to our biker friend wanting to really get in his face, but common sense told me not to get within his reach.

"Okay, dipshit, a big motherfucker like you beats up that little woman of yours. If I get called back here, I'm not even asking questions. We're just coming right in and taking you down. You got it?"

"Yes, Officer," was his sarcastic answer. He knew what he was getting away with. And he knew he would get away with it again.

The rest of the night held nothing special. Surprisingly, I didn't get called back to the biker's apartment. I thought about Burkett's rape victim — and that's what she was, a victim. Then I thought about the beat-up biker girl; was she a victim too? I guess that depends upon who you ask. Janie would certainly say yes. Me, I was not so sure. We were there; we offered to help. She had a way out and didn't take it. At what point do we stop blaming everyone else and accept responsibility for our own choices? Sometimes we get what we deserve.

Towards the end of the shift I heard Gillis call in, clearing from some call he had been handling. I got on the side channel and asked to meet up with him. He agreed.

As I was driving over to talk to him, I thought again about the danger he had put us in — was it worth it? Just like this domestic dispute tonight, I didn't think getting into this big fight when the victim wouldn't press charges anyway was worth it. Police work was a dangerous job and we had to take risks. But did we have to take every risk we were confronted with, no matter what? Was that our job? Some risks were worth taking. Some weren't. I hoped I would always know the difference.

Maybe I just think too much. That's probably what Janie and I have in common. *Lighten up*, I thought to myself. *If I agonize over every domestic dispute call like this, I will have one long miserable career ahead of me.* Besides, I wanted to clear my mind before I spoke to Gillis. There was something I wanted to bring up to him. He was a senior cop and I didn't want to piss him off. I had to handle it just right. I pulled up to him and rolled down my window.

"How's it going, young man?" he said to me.

"Everything is all right. How you doing?"

"Good. I hope you plan on making it to Hughes' party. We all have a pretty good time."

"Oh yeah, I'll be there."

"You bringing somebody?"

"Yes, I am. As a matter of fact, I'm bringing my girlfriend Janie. She was my nurse when I was in the hospital after the shooting."

"Cool. Funny how things can work out."

"How 'bout you? You're not married, are you?"

"No, not now. Getting off marriage number three," Gillis answered. "But I've been dating this babe for about six months now. I'm gonna bring her. She'll enjoy meeting everybody."

"Sounds great."

"Ya know, I haven't had a chance to talk to you since that drug arrest you and Stryker made a few weeks ago."

"Well, you did a great job. I hope I thanked you for helping me out like that."

"No, no, it was nothing, and you did thank me. I wanted to congratulate you on another good drug bust. You the man."

"It's all about having good information, like I told you."

"I know. I got the message. But, ya know, I thought Fiero did a pretty good job out there. I mean she jumped that big dude's ass without blinking an eye. Whatta ya think?"

"Yeah, she did. It was a good job. And I'll thank her again when we get back at the end of the shift if you don't think I already did. She deserves the credit."

"No, it's not that. You thanked us both. I'm sure she's not concerned about that."

"Then what's up?"

I hesitated before I spoke, unsure how this would come off.

"Well, remember what you said about her six or seven weeks ago, when we were at that rape Burkett was handling?"

"Hey, I can't remember back that far. I barely remember last night. Tell me again. What did I say?"

"Well, we were gonna call Fiero to escort the victim to the hospital and you said no, to call Mac because Fiero wasn't a lady. She made a hobby out of spreading her legs. Remember that?"

Gillis grinned. Then he laughed. "That sounds like something I would say."

"Well, after the way she helped you out like that, do you still think that's a fair statement to make?"

"Hey, buddy, I just call it like I see it. That's her rep and she doesn't seem to try to dispel any of that. Reputation is everything in this business. That's what I think. She spreads 'em easy. Why? You wanna try to get a piece of that? Go for it. She ain't a bad looking bitch."

"No, that's, uh, not quite where I was going with this."

"So, where are you going with this? What's your point?"

"It's just that you talked about her like she's some kinda whore. Then she goes and does a really good job taking someone down, just as good as anyone else on the squad would. Now, that doesn't really seem like a fair thing to say. Does it?"

"Hey, I never said she wasn't a good cop. Did I?"

"No, I guess you never did say that."

Chapter 10

Oh shit, not now. Just a half hour before the damn shift is over. Some jerk wrecked his car and I had to respond to the southern tip of my sector. I really wanted to get off duty on time this morning. Hughes' barbeque was later today and I was hoping to get some sleep before we went. I also had to pick up Janie. She lived about 30 minutes out of the way. Maybe I should ask her to meet me at my place. Yeah, why not? She's a big girl; she can drive and save me some time.

Arriving at the scene of the wreck, I could only think one thought — what the hell happened here? This car went right into the lamppost. The road was dry. The sun was first rising from behind the car; there was no other traffic on this residential street. How did this guy manage to pull this off? I saw the medics standing around the driver's side of the car. That impact must've put a hurting on the driver. Watching the activity of the medics, there appeared a lack of urgency; it didn't seem to be a fatality. I called it in on the radio and walked over to the car. The medics put the final touches on some bandages and helped the driver stand up. I walked over to one of the medics first.

"She's gonna be okay. Got some facial bruising, but no broken nose. Nothing else. She's pretty lucky. This could've been a lot worse," the medic told me.

"All right, buddy. Thanks." I patted him on the shoulder as I went past him.

I walked over to the driver. She was a woman in her late 30s, stood around 5' 6" and was thin, very thin. She looked so thin, almost as if she had been sick. Her long brown hair, hanging straight down, framed her gaunt face. She had a white bandage across her still intact nose and bruising and scrapes around her mouth. Her speech pattern was a bit discursive, but she was still coherent.

"Ma'am, I'm glad you're okay. I know you're a little shaken up now, but I do have to ask you a few questions."

She answered yes, her voice cracking. Going through the normal procedures, she handed over her license, registration and insurance card.

"So what happened?" I asked her.

"I don't know. I was just driving and lost control. I don't know how it happened."

"Where were you heading?"

"Oh, I was, uh, I was, I don't know. Oh, I'm sorry. I was on my way to work, downtown."

"They must have quite a casual dress code," was my inappropriate response, but she was in a blue sweat suit; it just didn't seem like business clothes for downtown.

She didn't say anything. She started crying.

"Look, it's okay. Just be happy you weren't seriously hurt. This could've been a lot worse. Where do you live?"

"About a half mile down the road."

Staring at me, looking as if she had more to say, yet she didn't say anything. Just at that moment another patrol car pulled up. I looked over and Stryker got out of the car. I wasn't quite sure why he was there, though I knew his patrol sector started just a few blocks away.

"Hey, Gary, everything okay?"

"Yeah, we're fine, Stryke. What brings you up here?"

"I was just a couple of blocks away at the Triple 7 and heard the call. I thought I'd stop by and see if you needed any help."

"I appreciate it." And I did. It was getting to the end of the shift and it was nice of him to come by just to help. "It's a little strange," I continued. "This car went right into the lamppost. I can't figure out why. Weather's clear. Road condition's good. The driver is crying. She couldn't explain what happened."

Stryker slowly walked over to the car, a small gray Honda with the front grill still wrapped around the lamppost, cracked windshield and leaking fluid.

"What did the driver say?" Stryker asked me.

"Not much. Just that she was driving to work and lost control."

Stryker walked around the car, obviously making mental notes. He walked over to the driver who was now sitting on the curb, her head in her hands with her elbows resting on her knees.

"How are you, ma'am?"

"Fine, thank you, Officer."

"Okay, listen. This officer will drive you home and I'll arrange to get your car towed, okay?"

She nodded. Then Stryker continued. "And also, think about this accident and what happened. Maybe you will want to talk to someone about it. Maybe just release some of the stress. You know what I mean?" He stared at her. She stared back for a few moments with a look of awe on her face, like Stryker had hit some nerve. Then she looked away and did not respond.

Something just happened that I didn't catch on to. Stryker came and sort of took over my call. I appreciated his help, but didn't think he needed to do that. I had it under control. He tapped me on the arm and indicated I should follow him. We walked off to the side where he spoke softly.

"Listen, Gary, would you mind if I make a suggestion to you?"

"Of course not," I told him.

"Look, I've been doing this a long time. This is no car wreck."

"Whatta ya mean no car wreck?"

"Look at this, Gary. You said it yourself. There was no reason for her to go off the road like that. She's not claiming anything went wrong with the car or some dog or something jumped out in front of her. And look, there are no skid marks, so she didn't try to brake suddenly. But given her limited injuries, I do suspect she slowed down and had second thoughts."

"Had second thoughts?" I was beginning to understand what he was getting at, maybe.

"Yeah, Gary, this was no accident. This was a suicide attempt. Look at her. See that gaunt face? She looks like she hasn't eaten in a week or two. She's sad, but she's not worried about her car; and she's not asking about insurance or anything like that. She didn't even ask where we were towing her damn car to.

"I hate to admit this, but that didn't even occur to me."

"That's fine. It all comes in time. Why don't you drive her home and see what you can get out of her without pushing? In the meantime, I'll wait for the tow truck so we can get out of here almost on time and get to Hughes' party not too exhausted."

"Sounds good, Stryke. Thanks."

I helped the young lady into my patrol car. As was protocol, I radioed in the time and the mileage on my odometer. When I arrived at her home, I would radio in the same information. Police officers routinely did this to guard against false allegations that the female was driven elsewhere and sexually assaulted. With times and mileage recorded, we would at least be able to defend ourselves by accounting for our whereabouts. That was one of the sad realties of our job.

"So, how are you feeling about everything now?"

"I think I'll be okay," she said in a soft voice, looking over at me with a shy smile and her head tilted down.

"Is there anything you'd like to ask me or talk to me about?"

"No, I'm fine."

"Okay. You know, looking over the scene, I couldn't really figure out what caused you to wreck. I've seen a lot of car accidents out here and this one had me a bit baffled. I don't see what caused it. Can you think of anything that may help us figure this out? 'Cause, uh, you know, I gotta write a report, and right now, I have no idea about what to write."

"I'll guess I'll have to think more about it."

"Well, I don't want to push the issue with you, but is it possible that maybe you didn't really lose control of the car?"

"Officer, what are you getting at?"

"Oh, you know, sometimes we do things we wouldn't normally do, maybe because we're upset about something or life deals us a bad blow. You know what I mean?"

"I'll think it over, Officer, and let you know if I come up with anything."

That was it. I had obviously reached the limit of what I was going to get her to say. We pulled up at her door. It was a nice apartment building that was renovated about a year ago and turned condo. A circular driveway brought us to the front glass doors under a white awning with the apartment's name prominently written in black letters on the front of the awning. There was no doorman, but at least the doors remained locked. She fumbled with her keys for a little bit, so I stayed parked there until I was sure she was in the building. These condos were a little more expensive than most other housing around the Third Precinct, probably because it was only a few blocks away from our border with the Fourth Precinct, which had more affluent neighborhoods than the Third. She must've had a decent job, so I was probably right about not wearing sweats to work.

Stryker must've been right about the suicide attempt. That was some good police work. I hoped I learned how to do that — how to know what was happening without even thinking about it.

I honked my horn to get her attention before she got in the building. I ran over and I handed her my card.

"Please call me if you can think of anything that might help explain what happened."

"I will," she said politely.

"And also, if there is anything I can help you with, feel free to call."

"I will, Officer." Before she went to the elevator, she turned around to face me through the glass window, waved and mouthed the words, "Thank you."

I waved back and smiled, and then drove off. I wasn't starting that accident report tonight. I was getting home and going to sleep. Then, I had to laugh. That was probably the first time I had handed a girl my card without the intent of trying to get a date. I actually had police work on my mind.

Those few hours of nap went by fast. I heard my doorbell ring. I lived in an apartment building in the Fourth Precinct, but I certainly couldn't afford the condos I dropped the young lady off at last night. It was a small, one bedroom, one bath apartment. No pictures hung on the wall. In front of my couch was an oval wood table that I took from my grandmother's house when she died. I also took the dresser and night tables in my bedroom as well as the four-chair dining room set. I did buy myself a new bed with a comforter designed with red and black geometric shapes. My bedroom window overlooked the complex's parking lot and trash bins. At least I was five stories up.

I opened the door without looking through the peephole first; I was expecting it to be Janie. Not good cop instinct. If a girl had gotten raped because she opened the door without knowing who was there, we'd all say that she was so stupid, she almost deserved it. That's how cops were. They were always criticizing everyone, sinners and victims the same. When I realized what I was doing, I almost slammed the door shut. I didn't. Just as well; it was Janie. She had no make-up on, but her plain style and naturally attractive face with those bright blue eyes didn't need make-up. She was wearing dark pink and white plaid Bermuda shorts and a solid white tank top that would have revealed a cleavage if she had one. But, all in all, she did have some sex appeal.

"Hey, you look like crap," she greeted me with a kiss on the lips.

"Thanks," I said, reaching down and giving her ass a squeeze with both hands.

"You want me to make some coffee?" she offered.

"That would be great."

She walked into my small kitchen and I sat in the dining room at the table.

"You know," she said, "every time I look at those table and chairs of yours, I think of when I was about eight years old and was at my grandmother's house. Where did you get these anyway?"

After that, I couldn't admit the truth. "So, I take it, you don't like my dining room set?"

"Well, I know that home décor is not your forte, but maybe one day, you can splurge and buy something a little more appropriate for a young single man like yourself. Didn't any of your old girlfriends ever mention your taste in furniture to you?"

I wasn't falling into that trap. We all have curiosity about our companion's previous love life. I learned as early as my first year in college, you're better off staying away from that subject. When I found the girls I dated got laid more in high school than I did, I started avoiding the whole subject. That was how the saying went, "Don't ask questions, if you really don't want the answer."

"I don't know. You're the first one I ever had over."

"Oh, here comes that old cop line of bull again."

Almost everything she commented on with me referred to her distrust of cops, at least on the personal level. No doubt, it had to do with her old flame. It was starting to get a little old. But, I didn't feel like taking it on, at least not now.

We finished up and got ready to start the drive to Hughes' house. I grabbed the directions and my cell phone. I had already programmed Hughes' home telephone number in for when I got lost.

"Oh wait, I forgot something." She ran back to her car.

My car started and with the engine rumbling, Janie got in carrying a gift-wrapped box.

"What's that?"

"It's a gift for your sergeant and his wife, mostly his wife."

"We weren't supposed to bring anything. Hughes said they had everything covered."

"Yes, I'm sure they do, but you still bring them a gift just for hosting the party. It's a little thing called manners."

"Wow, I never would've thought about that."

"I know you wouldn't. That's why I'm here, right?"

"Right."

She was right. I found little, thoughtful things like that very attractive in a woman. Those were the kind of "heart of gold" qualities I would look for in a potential wife. Then I started thinking: Did I just say that? I can't be thinking about that now, can I? Maybe she was thinking like that. It had never come up, though. I'd leave well enough alone for now.

We pulled off the highway at Exit 53, just like the directions said, turned left and drove west bound along the winding narrow road lined with large elm and oak trees, at least according to Janie. I couldn't tell the difference between oak and elm. Wooden log fences separated large tracts of property from the road. It was a quiet, peaceful residential area of medium size houses of brick or brightly painted siding with green lawns and well-kept landscaping.

Hughes lived in Fairmont County, about 40 miles outside of Westland Park. You couldn't find this much property in this kind of quiet, almost farm-like community anywhere in Westland Park, especially on a cop's salary. If you wanted some land, you had to get out of Westland Park. Hughes' ride to work had to be close to an hour. Everything has a trade-off.

After about 10 minutes of driving down this scenic road, we found Hughes' street. I didn't think we'd be able to do that without calling him — not every street had a sign. We drove close to a mile, only passing two homes, one on each side of the road, before reaching Hughes' house. We pulled up into his long driveway lined with evergreens about four feet high, where several cars were already parked along the opposite side. There was one Jaguar — which one of us could afford that? Off to the right of his house we could see the big backyard with the wooded area in the back that demarcated his property line. There was a volley ball net up. Three little kids were playing horseshoes and there was blue smoke being blown across the yard from the other side of the house. When we got out of my car I had already forgotten about the gift that Janie had brought. She went to get it out of the back seat, but I had already locked the doors. She stood there at the car's back door just looking at me. I couldn't figure out what she was doing.

"The gift," she said to me in a curt manner, showing her annoyance with my inability to remember these little details. Except, they weren't little details to her.

"Oh yeah, sorry." I immediately unlocked the car so she could reach in and grab the present. As she bent over, I looked at her and thought again about what a nice, thin ass she had. I never liked too much meat back there.

As we walked into the backyard to join the party, Janie grabbed my hand. Hughes was at the barbeque in the midst of the smoke while his wife was bringing out some more burgers and franks. It was a fancy barbeque pit surrounded by brick on the three sides. Hughes waved to us. Stryker was the first to come over and say hello. He introduced himself to Janie and then introduced his wife, Nancy. She was a tall blonde, about an inch taller than Stryker. With her fair skin and emerald eyes she certainly appeared to be a Norwegian beauty. She was the first of the wives and girlfriends that I would try to assess by looking at how they dressed. To me, how a woman dressed said a lot about her. She wore dark shorts and a light colored, button down shirt. She wasn't showing anything off, but she looked good. Then their two kids came over, one boy and one girl. Each had mom's blonde hair and light skin. Then I thought, yes, she was dressing like a mom should dress. But when she was younger, I bet it was different. The kids looked nothing like Stryker, who had dark hair.

Then Nancy introduced her children to us by name. I tried to say something cute and funny to his kids, but I was not good at that. I was not around kids too often. Nancy told the kids to go back to playing and gave each one a kiss on the head. Stryker did not. He barely acknowledged their existence. We engaged in normal introductory remarks and within a minute or two, Hughes and his wife, Melinda, came over to greet us. Hughes was very friendly, and so was she. She wore a tight, light blue sleeveless shirt with a low cut neck. Even with a bra, she showed off those round, hard, almost perfect breasts that they both seemed so proud of. Her blue cotton shorts were not as tight, but still highlighted her slim and shapely thighs. I was sure Thompson would take notice of it all, probably in much more detail, once he arrived.

"So you must be the new girlfriend I've heard about. Aren't you the nurse he met in the hospital after the shooting?" Melinda said to Janie.

Looking a little surprised, Janie responded, "As a matter of fact, I am." Then she gave me a funny look with a little smile. There was an awkward silent moment.

"Oh, I guess I shouldn't have asked that. I probably should've checked first. That could have been embarrassing," Melinda then said with a smile and fake laugh, covering her mouth with both hands.

Yes, it could have been. But, I've been pretty open about my relationship with Janie. And I did tell some of the guys on the squad that I would be bringing her. Thompson knew all about it. I was starting to realize that once Thompson knew something, everyone else knew shortly thereafter. Gossiping was not above senior, crusty cops.

"That's all right, Mrs. Hughes. She's my girl, as long as she continues to behave herself, of course."

"Mrs. Hughes!" Melinda exclaimed. "Please call me Melinda. I don't think I'm more than a few years older than you. Save the Mrs. for your mom's friends."

Not quite; while she was much younger than Hughes, she was still about ten years older than me. Since I sort of saw Hughes in a father figure light; calling her Mrs. didn't seem that strange. Hughes was still Sarge; I wasn't comfortable calling him by his first name, even at an off-duty barbeque at his house.

Then Janie handed the gift to Melinda. Janie made sure to give the gift directly to her and politely thanked her for hosting the party. I am sure that we were the only ones to bring a gift. That was Janie; she had more refined social skills than the rest of us.

"Oh, thank you. That really wasn't necessary. We do this every year as a tradition."

"It's our pleasure," Janie said, "just to celebrate our first of what we hope will be many more happy barbeques."

"Oh, you're such a dear," Melinda said, reaching over to hug Janie.

While hugging her, Melinda looked at me and said, "If I were you, I'd hold on to this one."

"I plan to."

Janie then gave me that "I told you so" look and she seemed happy, or actually more like satisfied with herself.

"Behave myself, huh?" she joked with me, grabbing hands and swinging them as we walked over to Thompson, who was arriving with his wife and daughter. Janie was happy that I had told everyone on the squad about her. That, I guess, was official confirmation that she was in fact my girlfriend, and she let me know she planned on sticking around and coming back with me next year.

"Hey, I think I like those hot sexy shorts more than your hospital garb," was Thompson's opening remark to Janie.

Not particularly liking that remark, I looked over at Janie to see her reaction; a polite smile led me to believe that Janie didn't like it either. I could not imagine that his wife appreciated it. Thompson went over and gave Janie a big hug, lifting her off the ground. Obviously, he knew her from the hospital, but he certainly did not know her that well. Lifting her with his left hand, his right hand was dangling free and I watched closely to see if he was going to try a little grab-ass, not quite sure how I would react. He didn't, and when he put Janie down I waved hello to his little daughter, remembering what she looked like when he was at the hospital. Today, she was wearing blue denim shorts.

"Oh, how adorable she is," Janie said and bent down to make some kid talk with her, knowing that I was not going to try that again.

"Nice to see you again," I politely said to his wife, devoid of any familiarity. Even though we had met at the hospital, I certainly was not going to comment on whether she looked sexy or not, and even more certainly, I was not going to hug her and pick her up. She was dressed modestly; like Nancy Stryker, she dressed as a mom should probably dress — at least according to the way I saw things.

We all walked over to where Stryker and his wife were sitting with Gillis and his girlfriend. Gillis' girlfriend looked like a tough broad with short hair and broad shoulders. She wore a black tank top that showed off some pretty stocky arms, which looked like they should have sported the same big tattoo that was on Gillis' arm. Her black shorts displayed the same kind of legs. If I hadn't seen her with Gillis, I would have thought "dyke." I could not imagine that was the message she wanted to give off, but if she was trying to tell everyone to back off, that message came through.

Paul Edmonds and his wife were also there. They personified the all American Midwest, Bible Belt type of family. Paul often spoke of his deep religious convictions and his wife seemed to share those beliefs simply by her appearance and dress. Her shorts were down almost to her knees and her shirt collar was snug around her neck. No skin showing there. Probably just as well. Thompson talked his little girl into running off with some of the other little kids.

Then MacKenzie walked over with her boyfriend; at least I assumed it was her boyfriend. That seemed unusual. Nobody knew MacKenzie even had a boyfriend. Mac was always careful to keep her personal life out of the squad room. She was a mildly attractive girl, a little lacking of sexuality. We never talked about her the way we talked about Liz; Mac was more like one of the guys. That was probably how she wanted it: known as a good cop and well-respected for the work she did. Mac was sure to mention that her boyfriend was an investment banker. Now I knew who had the Jag. I wondered how he was going to handle the level of conversation with this group of blue collar cops. In that this was a family event, we'd probably be much better behaved than normal, I hoped.

We all grabbed some lawn chairs and arranged ourselves in a circle. Hughes and his wife came over handing out bottles of beer. All hands grabbed for one. When we each had a beer and started drinking, Hughes and his wife sat down.

"I have some announcements to make, but I want to wait till the rest of the squad gets here," Hughes called out. We were still waiting on Fiero and Burkett. I wasn't sure if I wanted Liz to show up or not. I wanted her to see me with my girlfriend, but I didn't want any clues of that night slipping out.

While we all made small talk, Burkett appeared with a fairly decent looking young lady. She was tall, a little heavy, but not too bad, with shoulder length light brown hair. She was very modestly dressed in loose fitting beige shorts with a striped, short-sleeved shirt. No cleavage showed on her, though she clearly had some to show off. Watching them as they walked up the driveway, I thought I espied Burkett reach to hold her hand followed by her quickly moving her hand to her face to push back her eyeglasses; it was quick and subtle, but I saw it. Was there anything of significance to that? Burkett looked like Burkett. He was the only one of us who wore long pants. He had on a denim shirt with short sleeves that hung past his elbows and over his forearms; the shirt was not tucked in and fit loosely; that was probably a good fit for him.

Fiero then showed up. She was dressed the way everyone expected her to dress. Her dark shorts were really short — right up to her crotch with her ass hanging out just a little, and just enough to get a second look from not just the guys, but the wives, and Janie, I was sure. With her ankle high socks, Fiero was showing a lot of leg. With a tight white undershirt, her tits were noticeable enough, but at least she had the sense to wear a bra to a family picnic. She looked good, and I wanted to take her into Hughes' house and play two cops in the maintenance closet again.

She came walking up the driveway holding hands with some guy nobody knew. I guessed Liz kept some of her personal life out of the locker room as well. Certainly, I was going to have to get to know this man in her life, though I was not sure why. The squad was all together now, the latecomers standing in the back. Looking happy and proud, Hughes stood up and began speaking.

"First of all, this is the third year in a row where the entire squad has shown up for our end of summer barbeque." We all gave a playful cheer.

"But let us never forget our good friend JJ who we lost last year in the line of duty. He was a great cop and we miss him."

There was a moment of silence, which came upon us naturally. I had heard about JJ in the academy. He had been chasing some guy who was suspected of shoplifting a leather coat out of a clothing store in one of the malls. JJ wrecked when he tried to make a quick exit off the highway while in a high-speed pursuit. He lost control, spun around and slammed into a barricade. That was one of those in-the-line-of-duty deaths that seemed so unnecessary. I started thinking again about the risks worth taking and not worth taking. Then I stopped. This was a fun event. I was going to have fun and not think about the socio-psychology of police work; I was getting like Janie — taking life way too seriously. After a moment, Hughes continued on.

"We welcome the wives, girlfriends, boyfriends of our squad mates to our home. And now let me share some really exciting news for this squad. That's why I am glad everyone is here. We should share this together. First, Officer Gillis, would you please come up here?"

He slowly got up, handing his beer to Patty and joined Hughes in front of their guests.

"As most of you know," Hughes continued, "Gillis has one of the highest, if not *the* highest, drug arrest rates for any patrol officer in the Westland Park Police Department. Accordingly, the chief has decided that Officer Gillis is now Detective Gillis, assigned to Narcotics in the Detective Bureau."

We broke out into a small cheer. Gillis pumped his fist and ran back to Patty. He appeared uncomfortable in the spotlight. Patty leaned over and kissed him on the cheek. Gillis seemed more interested in getting his beer back from her. I was not surprised by Gillis making detective; probably none of us were. I had seen him in action and didn't know how he did it, but he did it. Hughes continued.

"Now, even more exciting — Mr. Hollings, please step up here."

That caught me by surprise. It took me a second to realize he was talking to me. Janie and I exchanged a glance and a smile, and I stood up and walked over to where Hughes was standing.

"Mr. Hollings, though you are rapidly losing your rookie status, at a time when you were clearly nothing more than a baby cop, still wet behind the ears, you were confronted with a very dangerous situation. And we all know what I'm talking about. You were at an armed robbery and took two rounds in the leg. With very little street experience, you were able to hold it together. You didn't panic and you returned to duty as soon as possible, doing a bang-up job since. Because of that, the chief has decided to award you a Bronze Medal of Valor. Those don't come easy. In a few weeks, the chief will host a public ceremony and officially present the award to you there. Congratulations."

Everybody started applauding. I couldn't believe it — mostly, I couldn't believe that I hadn't heard about it. Word usually travels fast. I could not get the smile off my face.

"Okay, okay. We have one more thing to take care of before we start having real fun. Mr. Thompson, come up here, please."

Thompson stood up with no sign of surprise and all the confidence he always seemed to possess. He strutted up to Hughes.

"Mr. Thompson, at that same robbery, you were no rookie, but you did okay yourself. As a matter of fact, after getting shot in the shoulder, you managed to draw your weapon and shoot the bastard right in the ass — the perfect shot. Because of that, the chief has decided to award you the highly coveted Silver Medal of Valor, also to be awarded by the chief at the ceremony. Congratulations."

Thompson held up both fists in the air and started pumping his arms. No humility there. Thompson slowly walked back to his chair, amongst the squad's applause, to his wife who rewarded him with a big hug and kiss.

"There's plenty of food at the barbeque and let's get a good volleyball game going," Hughes said to everybody.

The group started to break up and walk over to the barbeque or the volleyball net. As they did, it occurred to me, only after the excitement wore off a little, that Burkett got no recognition whatsoever. His name wasn't even mentioned. We all heard about his suspension although no one ever mentioned it in front of him. What was going through Burkett's mind? How was he feeling in front of this new girlfriend of his? Was anybody thinking about Burkett? I wanted to look into his face, just to see if I could gauge what was going on inside his head. I couldn't look at him directly, but glanced over while trying not to look like I was looking.

He was sitting down on a lawn chair talking to his girlfriend. He had that smile on his face. Then, surprisingly, he got up and walked over to the volleyball court. I knew he was hurting, but he wouldn't show it. He couldn't show it. None of us would. As much as I thought Burkett was strange and I didn't really want to be friends with him, I couldn't help but feel for him. On the other hand, I couldn't allow that to spoil my achievement. I was going to be awarded the Bronze Medal of Valor. This was my moment and I wanted to enjoy it.

"You playing volleyball, hotshot?" Janie asked me, looking with raised eyebrows and a small grin. Coming from behind her, I saw Thompson walking over to me pointing his finger; I knew he wanted to talk to me.

"I don't know. Maybe a little later. You go ahead. Let me talk to Mark for a second."

Thompson put his arm on my shoulder and with a little bit of a push, started walking me towards the back of the yard.

"Nice going, rookie. Guys go their entire careers and never get recognition like that. Ride that baby. You know what I mean. I expect to see you make at least deputy chief one day. You hear me?"

"We'll see. I can't believe that I hadn't heard any rumors about it. I was really surprised."

"I gotta tell ya, it wasn't easy for me to keep it from you for the past two weeks."

"Two weeks? How the fuck did you know about it two weeks ago, and why didn't you tell me?"

"Hey, hey, it was all unofficial. We were out to dinner with Hughes and Melinda and he let it slip. He swore me to secrecy because he wanted to announce it here. You know me. I keep my secrets."

"Yeah, I do know you." But something more interesting than the medals just came to light.

"By the way, since when do you and the Sarge double date?"

"Ever since the shooting, we just started getting friendly, probably 'cause we both know what it's like to shoot somebody, ya know?"

"Huh" was all I could say in disbelief.

"He's a pretty good guy."

"Yeah, Mark, he is."

So Thompson and Hughes had been out socializing together. Hughes was not Thompson's kind of buddy. Thompson had to be playing an angle — he was up to something.

"Hey, how do you think Liz looks in those shorts?" he asked me with a big smile.

"She looks pretty good. Great set of legs and just enough ass showing to get the imagination stirred up," I answered him trying not to give any hint of our rendezvous.

"You know it. And I'll tell you this, and I ain't leaving this to the imagination... if you picked up those shorts just a little more, you'd see the cutest little freckle on her left cheek."

"Huh, what?" He caught me off guard with that remark. "How do you know that?"

Thompson looked at me as if I had asked the stupidest question imaginable. I obviously did.

"C'mon, buddy. It's Liz, Officer Catch Me, Fuck Me Fiero. I think she got all hot and bothered over us getting shot. One night, when we were working, she took me to some small maintenance room in some building somewhere and let me nail her deep and hard. It was pretty cool."

"Well, good for you." I didn't know what to say.

"And now that you're a Medal of Valor holder I guess it's time to introduce you to Bullet Brenda," Thompson told me.

"I think I've heard about her. I forgot who mentioned her to me. What's she all about?"

"Oh, you'll find out, my friend."

I didn't know for sure, but it wasn't tough to guess what it had to do with.

"I don't know, Mark. I know you don't want me preaching to you, and I'm not trying to do that. But do you think that maybe you push your luck just a little too far sometimes? I mean, your wife..."

"Hey, stop right there and listen to me. We don't get paid a lot of money, we work fucked-up hours and the public shits on us. Other than a pension, there ain't a whole lot of benefits we get from this job. But getting a lot of pussy is one of them. Don't we deserve any benefits for what we do? I mean you gotta enjoy life a little. Loosen up, my friend. You have a long career ahead of you."

He didn't give me a chance to respond and he kept looking back over his shoulder. Then he continued, "Well, I don't know about you, but I'm gonna go and play some volleyball."

I guess Thompson was making the most of my philosophy of living for the moment. So, he stuck it to Liz, too. I was hoping that he did her after I did. The thought of taking his sloppy seconds was a bit disturbing.

Up until now, I thought all the talk about Liz was nothing more than rumor. I actually thought there was something about me that really attracted her. There was so much I did not understand. What I did know was that for one quick encounter, she was on my mind way too much; I needed to forget it. I was sure Liz had.

Thompson ran off to the volleyball court where some of the squad was hitting the ball around. He took over and quickly organized a game. Somehow Melinda Hughes wound up on his team, standing right next to him. Hughes was on the other team. I looked for Janie. She was sitting off to the side of the court on the grass talking to Mac, Stryker's wife and Burkett's girlfriend. She was smiling and seemed deeply engaged in chick talk and I did not want to interrupt. She was sipping some iced tea from a straw; there was something sexy about that. I was glad that she was not having any more beers because she would be driving home. Playing volleyball did not sound appealing to me at that moment. With nothing else to occupy my thoughts, I walked over to talk to Gillis and his girlfriend.

"Congratulations, Mike. Nobody deserves making detective more than you."

"Oh, thanks. And congrats to you. That's some award to get. Hey, you've met my girlfriend Patty, haven't you?"

"Yeah, we met earlier. So what do you do, Patty?"

"I'm a DEA agent."

"Ah, the Drug Enforcement Agency... so, you're a federal narc. Well then, I guess that makes you doubly proud of Mike making it to Narcotics, huh?"

"Yep, he'll be great."

"I'm sure. So, uh, how did you two narcs meet?"

Gillis spoke up, "A friend of mine on Kansas City PD works on the federal drug task force with Patty. He introduced us."

"Wow, that's great."

I did not have much to say to the two of them and the conversation dragged for a bit. There was not much interaction between them either, other than shallow conversation. They seemed as if they were more business partners than dating.

Politely excusing myself, I went and introduced myself to Liz's boyfriend. His name was John and he sold real estate. He sounded intelligent and seemed like he was making a pretty good buck. Of all things Liz may have been, stupid was not one of them. Screw around with the cops, but go out with the guys who make the money. I guess Liz and Mac had one thing in common after all.

"How long have you been dating Liz?" I asked.

"Six months," he told me.

"Oh, sounds like it might be getting serious, huh?"

"I hope so," he said to me with what appeared to be sincere feelings.

Poor guy, he's getting serious with her and she's doing who knows what to whom. Can he not see through her, or does he just not want to? Like they say, I guess we are all blind to things that we just do not want to see. I had to wonder what his reaction would be if he found out that two of the cops, right there at the party, had slipped it to his little girlfriend. More importantly, what would Janie's reaction be if she knew I did Liz? Would she really care as much as she hinted that she would? Should I even concern myself with that? Who knows what she does when we are not together? Stories of doctors and nurses screwing each other all the time were nothing new. Maybe she liked living for the moment too.

I watched the volleyball game for a little bit. There was Thompson — loud, animated and running the show. Then, when Melinda Hughes made a good hit and scored a point, Thompson ran over to her, picked her up by the waist and spun her around. From where I was watching, it looked like his face was planted deep in her cleavage as they did a quick twirl. Was this a family barbeque or a bachelor party? Was I the only one noticing this? Did Hughes notice, or even care? Once again, this really was none of my business.

The party went on past sundown. At that point most of us were sitting on the lawn chairs making small talk. It started getting chilly out and was becoming a little uncomfortable, considering our summer attire. We were all exhausted and it was obviously time to start heading home. Everyone on the squad let their partner drive; we were all too tired to drive, having gotten only a couple of hours of sleep, not to mention downing a few beers.

As we got to the cars, I was a little surprised as Mac and her boyfriend walked past the Jag. Maybe it was Fiero's boyfriend's car. Then I saw Gillis and Patty get in the Jag and drive off. Gillis looked back, watching me watching him.

"So did you enjoy yourself?" I asked Janie as she pulled the car out onto the road.

"Oh yeah, I learned quite a bit by talking to the ladies."

"Really, what did you learn?"

"Well, the first thing they wanted to talk about was Liz Fiero. I heard all about her and that she gets around, a lot."

"Ah, I don't know about that. It's probably just talk and rumor."

"I wouldn't be so sure. According to the ladies, she's screwed a lot of guys in the department. And looking at those shorts she was wearing, I don't doubt it. I told them about that kiss I saw her give you in the hospital. Let me tell you, I'd better not find out you're screwing her too. You know where I stand on that kind of stuff. You cops are the worst."

There she goes again with that cop thing, I thought to myself. I hoped this had a life span that would come to an end soon. I didn't want to make an issue of it, but it was beginning to annoy the piss out of me.

"C'mon, not all cops are the same. I've known a couple of wild nurses in my time. They tend to like uniforms — cops, firemen, even doctors in those stupid gowns. Are you all the same?"

"No, of course not. I know there are some wild nurses out there. I've seen it. But we are nothing like you cops. And that buddy of yours, Thompson. I heard he's quite the player. I bet he even screwed Liz. What do you think?"

"I don't know and I don't really care. Besides, he's not my buddy.

He was my field training officer. That's it."

How she figured out that he did Liz beat the hell out of me. One of those woman things, I guess. I impressed myself by not reacting.

"Well, I don't like what I heard. I don't trust him," Janie continued on.

"So what else did you learn? What did you think of Burkett's girlfriend? I'm curious about any girl who would date Burkett."

"Oh, now that's a good question, because she is not his girlfriend."

"No? What then, just casually dating? Friends with privileges?"

"No, not even that. They're old friends. She seemed anxious to make that point."

That probably explained the hand holding thing I saw. Poor Burkett.

"And your friend Stryker, this is his third marriage."

"Third? I didn't know that." Of course, there's no reason I would know that. He and I never really discussed personal issues. So that made two guys on the squad, both with three marriages. I didn't know what to think about that, or if I should think about it at all.

"Yes, his third. She almost didn't marry him because of that and he almost didn't marry her because she had two kids."

"Oh, well that explains why those kids look nothing like him."

"Yep, and from what his wife was saying, I don't think he's the greatest stepdad in the world to those kids."

"You got all this just from talking to a couple of the girls for a little while?"

"Oh yeah, we like talking about you guys."

"Hmm, anything else interesting?"

"Well, I did mention how proud I was of you getting the award. It was a way of bragging without really bragging."

"Very good. I'm glad all the ladies got along so well."

"That's not completely true."

"Whatta ya mean?"

"I mean that the wives would like to see Liz transferred somewhere else. I'm just letting you know..."

"Okay, okay. I got it. Look, I hardly talk to her anyway, but besides that, you know Gillis, right, the one who got promoted to Narcotics?"

"What about him?"

"His girlfriend's a DEA agent. Isn't that kinda funny?"

"DEA? They're the drug cops, right?"

"Yep. They're the feds. Here Gillis makes these great drug arrests and he's dating a drug agent. I don't know why... it just seems a little, I don't know, a little something."

"I really didn't get to talk to her at all. They didn't seem that social. Anyway, what are you suggesting? I don't get it," Janie asked me.

"I don't know," I answered, not quite sure myself of what I was getting at.

"Oh, and by the way, it didn't get past me how you changed the subject when we were talking about Liz."

"C'mon, please let's stop talking about Liz. In the meantime she looked like she was really into that boyfriend of hers. I'm sure it's all just rumor. Let it go."

Those were my last words for the drive home. I fell asleep. Or so I thought.

"Wake up."

"Huh, what's going on? We there?" Janie woke me up from a deep sleep.

"Where are we?" I asked again.

Janie had pulled off at some rest stop that was completely deserted and drove into a dark corner where she parked, kind of like what we do on midnight patrol.

"Jump into the back seat."

"What?"

"Just do it."

So I did. Then, she climbed over the front seat right after me.

"We're going to play a little game now," she said.

"And what game is that?"

"You're gonna be the lonely patrolman, and I'm going to be Officer Liz Fiero."

"Okay, then what?"

"Oh, well, I'm just a horny little bitch and I want you to fuck my brains out, right here and right now, before the sergeant catches us."

Did Janie really say that? I'd never seen her act this way. I hadn't done this in the back seat for quite a while. In a two-door, it was a little difficult to get the clothes off, but certainly easier than with all the police equipment on. I did as she asked. As she crawled on top of me, she was hot, breathing heavy and this was turning her on. I slipped into her just like I did Liz, and that was what I was thinking about — pounding away at Liz in that little maintenance room. Not good.

We got back in the front seats and started wiping the condensation off the windows. Then she asked, "Will that take care of your little police fantasies for a while?"

"Yeah, I guess so." I imagined her motivation had something to do with her worrying about me having my eye on doing Liz. I didn't really care what her drive was. I was seeing a whole new side to her. And I liked it. As we drove off, I fell back to sleep.

Chapter 11

The warmth of the summertime would soon be a distant memory. With fall approaching I was back into my long sleeved uniform shirt and jacket; the temperature was dropping at least 10 degrees by nighttime. I had gotten together with the squad only once socially since Hughes' barbeque. Stryker hosted a card game at his house. Me, Thompson, Burkett and Hughes came. We had a pretty good time playing poker and Texas Hold 'Em. I lost 10 bucks. Hughes was the big winner, winning 15 dollars. We only bet quarters. Edmonds never came; he didn't believe in gambling. Gillis was off to something new, now in the Detective Bureau. Mac and Fiero were invited, but they knew that was just a courtesy. This was a guy thing.

The ceremony for the Medals of Valor was a week away, but it seemed that the glory of my Bronze Medal of Valor had already faded. The robbery, the shooting and everything about that night was long forgotten, by everybody, though maybe not Burkett. His appeal of his suspension was going to be heard soon. Once again, the department was just not in a rush; it had been months since he submitted the appeal to Hughes. I was getting very comfortable out there on patrol. I began to feel as if I actually knew what I was doing.

Stryker was breaking in a new rookie, Matt Bergman. Bergman was from New York City, with a strong New York accent and a real sarcastic personality. What was he doing in Kansas City? The guys did not know what to make of him and they were not warming up to him. Bergman rarely gave a straight answer and had no patience for questions that he thought were stupid. He seemed like a sharp guy to me; he had those city street smarts. Word had it that he graduated at the top of his academy class. He wore a small but shiny gold Star of David around his neck. Nobody was used to seeing Jewish guys on the police department. The way Stryker and Thompson talked, you would think they had never even met anyone Jewish before Bergman came. As I thought about it, maybe they hadn't.

One day, Thompson saw a dime on the floor of the locker room. He yelled out, "Ooh look, a dime. Lemme grab it before the cheap Jew sees it." Thompson reached down, grabbed the dime, laughing, obviously thinking he was funny. Some of the other guys, mostly just his buddy Stryker, gave an uncomfortable laugh. Bergman walked right over to Thompson, put out his hand, palm up.

"You're right. I want that fuck'n dime. Let me have it."

"But I found it. I guess it's mine," Thompson retorted.

"Then I guess you're the cheap motherfucker who needs to scavenge a dime off the floor, huh?"

Frozen, jaw slightly open, Thompson obviously did not expect that from a rookie. The look of shock all over his face was comical, at least to me.

"Listen, rookie, you're not calling me a cheap motherfucker, are you?" he said, in a tone that he thought would intimidate Bergman.

"Well, let's see. You just called me a cheap Jew, but you're the one who grabbed the dime. You tell me, asshole."

Bergman stood there, unflinching, his hands loosely at his waist; it was not quite a fighting stance, but one that sent a clear message. Thompson stood still, trying to intimidate Bergman with nothing more than a stare. Thompson blinked.

"Okay, then, here's the dime for the faggot Jew boy," and Thompson gave him the dime.

Bergman grabbed the dime out of Thompson's hand and pocketed it. He then said, "Thank you, but next time you say something disparaging about my religion, you may find this dime shoved up your ass. Are we clear?" I wasn't sure Thompson even knew what disparaging meant.

The locker room became dead silent. Bergman was taking quite a chance, as a rookie threatening a senior, popular officer like Thompson. However, Thompson was on very shaky ground. Joke or no joke, the police department would never tolerate that kind of talk; they would not back him up. Thompson knew that, but he had to save face in front of the squad. Thompson turned around, walked to his locker and laid down the police utility belt he was about to don, on the bench. Then he turned back around, started walking slowly, very slowly back over to Bergman. Thompson had an "I'm gonna kick your ass" look on his face, though it seemed rather artificial to me.

Bergman did not move; he did not flinch. He looked as if he welcomed a confrontation. Stryker and Burkett got in the middle and sort of redirected Thompson back to his locker, probably as Thompson expected, maybe even hoped. No further words were said. *Man*, I thought, *this Bergman guy had one big set of balls, especially for a rookie. Or, was he just stupid?*

In the days that followed, Edmonds took any chance he had to corner Bergman in the locker room to discuss the flaws of the Old Testament and how Bergman could find truth in the New Testament. Bergman, while not overly religious, was pretty well-grounded and educated in Judaism. He did not like those conversations and tried hard to avoid Edmonds. Bergman believed what he believed and was not inclined to discuss or defend it. He did not question anyone else's beliefs and did not want anyone challenging his. As for me, Bergman was the rookie now, relieving me of that title. That's all I cared about.

Over the next two weeks, I tried to talk to Bergman in the locker room or after a call if he was there as well. Bergman struck me as a real interesting person, probably someone I could become friends with. I would've liked to talk to him a little more, but he had to stay attached to Stryker's hip. Once he was cut loose I would try to get together with him: give him the rookie-to-rookie perspective, at least from my point of view. Given that strong New York personality, I was interested in his perspective as well. I liked that arrogance of his, which tended to piss off the other guys. Maybe it was the fact that it pissed them off that I liked.

We had all just finished up our two and a half day break between the shifts. I was not ready to return. A few more days was all I needed, but that always seemed to be true. Roll call was about to break up.

"Okay, Thompson said he's got to leave about two hours early.

Stryker, you and Bergman cover his sector till the end of the shift, 10-4?" Hughes called out.

"No problem, Sarge," Stryker responded.

*****

After I left, a familiar scene played out when Sergeant Hughes called Burkett back in the room. Burkett was probably just going to get an update on his appeal. Once again Burkett walked over to the sergeant's desk and Hughes went to close the door. I was curious, but there was nothing for me to see or hear at that point.

Hughes did not sit down this time. Neither did Burkett.

"Listen, JB, I got a call the other night from a woman named Nina Wilkes. That name sound familiar?"

"Well, yeah, she's the rape victim I handled a while ago. I've been in touch with her trying to help her out."

"Well, as far as you helping her out, I don't think she sees things exactly the way you're seeing things, JB. She told me that you've been there twice already and the other night called her up for a date."

"Oh, I don't believe this. It wasn't a date. I merely suggested getting together for a cup of coffee or something, just to see how she's doing. I'm only following-up. I'm concerned that she might get targeted again."

"That's fine, but she's getting a different message and she wants you to stop calling her and coming by. So, can we do that?"

"I don't get it. We had a good rapport. I wonder what happened. I don't know why she would turn on me like this. I was only trying to help."

"Look JB, she's a rape victim. Nothing more, nothing less. Leave her alone and let it go. Sex Crimes is handling it. It's not your case. Stay out if it. Got it?"

"Got it. But I should at least go over or call just to apologize. I didn't mean to do anything to upset her."

"JB, what are you not hearing? No, you do not go over there. You do not call. I am ordering you to stay away from her." Hughes began to bark at JB — rather uncharacteristic for him.

Hughes looked at Burkett's childish, sad face. "Look, JB, you've got your IA appeal coming up. All you need is some citizen complaint, especially from a rape victim, hanging over your head. Don't be stupid. Stay away from her completely. Am I perfectly clear?"

"Yes, sir, that is clear. Anything else, sir?"

"No, you're dismissed. Get on the streets now."

*****

I was heading out of the locker room with my gear when I ran into Burkett on his way in. He looked angry. His fat, round face was red, his head down staring at the floor and he was murmuring to himself, something about a stupid bitch. I did not ask.

Bergman walked by me on our way to the patrol cars.

"Hey, Bregman, how about when you get cut loose from Stryker, we meet up for a meal? Talk rookie to rookie," I asked him.

"Well first, it's Bergman, not Bregman. That sounds like a good idea. It should only be a couple of more shifts now. I appreciate it."

I started to head out to the Heights. Ever since the barbeque, I wanted to call Liz on the side channel and ask her to meet me for a cup of coffee and to find out about her boyfriend. I wasn't really sure what I wanted to know, but was still curious. I didn't want her to think I was trying for another quickie in the maintenance shop, though I thought about that often, almost obsessively. Of course, I should've thanked Liz for some of Janie's new-found spontaneity. Maybe a little jealousy and mistrust was a good thing.

Tonight was not very busy. I handled one minor domestic dispute, a car accident and wrote a couple of tickets. I was trying to catch up on all my paperwork when Thompson got me on the side channel.

"Hey buddy, you busy?"

"A little, but nothing I can't do later. Wassup?"

"Meet me at the Triple 7 on 9th and River Bend Road. You know it?"

"I'll find it." That intersection was not familiar to me. I had to whip out my street map once again. It took me a few moments and then I finally located it. That was in Stryker's patrol sector. Why would he want to meet me there? Usually we met somewhere in the middle.

I drove over and Thompson was waiting for me.

"Hey man, how's it going these days?" I asked.

"Okay, I guess."

"Everything all right at home?" I asked him.

"Yeah, why do you ask?" he responded in a defensive tone that caught me off guard.

"Hey, it's that you've been leaving early from your shift a lot. You never do that. Just wanted to make sure that everything was okay. What's with the attitude?"

"Ah, it's nothing. I'm sorry. Just have to handle a few things. That's all. Anyway, are you ready?"

"Ready for what?"

"See that clerk inside the store?" he pointed to inside the Triple 7.

"Yeah, she looks cute, at least from here. What about her?"

"That's Brenda."

I thought for a second. That name sounded familiar. Only a few seconds were needed to figure this out. "Is that the famous Bullet Brenda?"

"Sure is. I know it's been a little while, but you didn't think I'd forget, did ya? Go in there and let her see you have a box of bullets in your hand and that's it."

"That's what?"

"She takes you to the back room and you give her the box."

"Then what?"

"Shit, why do I have to spell this out for you? You give her the bullets and she gives you a fuck'n BJ that you won't forget. Trust me."

"A box of bullets for a blow job. Sounds fair, but how do I get an extra box of bullets?"

"You are still a rookie, I guess. Just open your glove compartment or look in your trunk. There should be about six or seven extra boxes of ammo in there. Ever since that shootout in Atlanta where the feds ran out of ammo, we've stocked our cars up, like a lot of departments did. Next time you're at Firearms, pick up an extra box or two or six. Nobody counts that crap. You could buy plenty of BJs."

"I don't know, Mark. Is this cool?"

"Hey bud, this is your indoctrination into becoming a real cop; no more rookie status bullshit for you. It's a squad tradition. C'mon, man, you can't break years of tradition. Now get in there. I'll listen up on the radio for you. Don't take too long. Shoot your wad and get back to patrol."

This did not seem like a good idea. Getting a BJ for some bullets? But a little spontaneity, a little action with no talk or obligation, and of course, the taboo. I knew I liked that. What guy didn't? I hoped this wasn't some sort of practical joke — Thompson setting me up for something. But I had heard about Bullet Brenda before. *Do it, don't do it.* Both thoughts raced through my mind with equal weight and equal rationalization.

"C'mon, we don't have all night. Go, enjoy yourself. Don't be such a pussy."

I was fairly surprised when I found myself walking in to the Triple 7 with my palm wrapped around a box of bullets. I walked around the store for a few minutes, just staking things out, a little unsure, a little paranoid. Everything seemed okay. Putting the box in my front pants' pocket gave my baggy pants a pretty noticeable bulge. I grabbed a cup of coffee. I went to the counter to pay for it, for a reason. Brenda looked up at me with wide brown eyes and I focused on her full red lips. She was short and thin and wore her black hair pulled back in a tight ponytail. She was wearing the white jacket all Triple 7 employees wore, with the emblem on the breast pocket. She was kind of cute with smooth olive skin and she had a look of innocence that belied what was about to happen.

"Let me get my money." I reached into my pocket as if I was fumbling.

"Damn, my pockets are full." I struggled to take out the bulky box of bullets and then rested it on the counter top.

"Let me just get the change out of my pocket..." and then Brenda picked up the box and started walking to the back room. I stood there at first and then she glanced back at me. Her look clearly told me to follow her. I did.

We got to the back room standing amongst the cardboard boxes of supplies and fast foods ready to fill the shelves. She closed the door behind us and backed me up against it. She took off her jacket and then her shirt, slowly pulling it up over her head. She stood there in her bra, looking at me with an impish smile. Then she reached up and slowly unhooked her bra. It came down to reveal her average sized, but attractive breasts with dark, hard nipples. She grabbed my left hand and put it on her breast. I was getting very hard. Then she knelt down. I was still a little nervous and kept my hand on my weapon as she undid my belt and pants. She moved quickly and was obviously experienced in undressing a police officer in full uniform. Then she began. I tried hard to not make a noise and to listen for any surprises. I was getting close. Then I heard the radio.

"All Units, 10-3."

I just knew that the emergency call was going to be for me.

"319 Baker, 319 Baker," the radio called.

I reached down and grabbed the radio to respond, my voice first cracking in a high tone pitch.

"319 Baker, rape just occurred. 5601 Stanton in the Clearview Apartments, apartment 106. Complainant called it in. Description is a white male in black hooded sweatshirt covering his face. No further at this time."

I knew that sounded like the rapist Burkett handled and whom we thought had now become the county's serial rapist. I moved right away to get myself together.

"315 Baker, respond for back-up."

I ran out and got into my car. Thompson pointed out that my fly was wide open. I kind of knew where the Clearview Apartments were, but not how to get there from where we were. I checked the map and saw it was close to the northern tip of my sector. I was just past the southern tip, out of my assigned area. I pulled away and headed for the highway going through a few residential streets. As I entered into my sector, I realized I was in the same area as that car accident which Stryker thought was a suicide.

Then I thought to myself, didn't Stryker say he was at the Triple 7 when he arrived at the wreck? He did. I did not want to jump to conclusions, but something told me Stryker had just come from a visit with Bullet Brenda. How many things were going on with this squad that I didn't know about? Was there a whole other side to police work that I hadn't learned yet? It sure was beginning to seem that way.

Knowing that I was a few minutes farther away from the rape scene than I was supposed to be really bothered me. Reporting that I was out of my sector was not really an option since I was getting a BJ while on duty. We were not supposed to leave our sector without first notifying dispatch; and we required a good reason for that — this did not qualify. Even Hughes, as detached as he was, would not have tolerated a trip to Bullet Brenda. I called in an ETA of three. I knew it was more than five. I didn't like putting myself in that position. What if a cop was in trouble? Those extra two minutes could have made a difference. Someone could've gotten hurt because I was too busy getting a blow job. On the other hand, the odds that those two minutes would have ever made a difference were astronomical. It was only a blow job; no harm, no foul.

Fiero beat me to the scene of the rape. By the time I got there, Liz had gone to the see the victim by herself. There were no rules against that, but we usually went in pairs, just in case the perp was still on the scene or so the victim, in her trauma, didn't make any accusations against one of the cops. With a female officer, that was much less likely.

"Shit, Hollings, what took you so fuck'n long?" Fiero whispered to me as she met me at the door.

"I was on the other side of my sector. It took a little time. Whatta we got?"

"We got a black female, 28 years of age, raped by a male, probably white, wearing a ski mask and a black hooded sweat shirt. Approximately the same height and weight as the guy good for all the other rapes we've been hearing about. He got in through the bedroom window — broke the glass and opened the lock. It was pretty easy for him to crawl in. By the time she woke up and figured out what was happening, he was on top of her."

"Let me guess... with a knife."

"Yep, with a knife, right at her throat. Ripped open her pajama top, made her pull off her bottoms, then turned her around and raped her. Edmonds is on the way with the crime scene equipment."

We switched off each shift as to who was responsible for crime scene work. It was a good process and everybody took a turn at preliminary fingerprinting and collecting evidence.

"Sex Crimes is about 20 minutes away. I'm gonna go back and interview the victim a little more. C'mon," Fiero directed me.

Walking back to the bedroom with Fiero to talk to the victim, I couldn't help but notice the window the rapist came in through. The breeze was blowing the opaque white drapes against the wall on the right and, on the left, against the three-drawer dresser on which she had an assortment of photographs and some trophies. I walked over and saw that she had won several track meets in high school. If only she'd had the chance to run away this time. Dressed in blue jeans and a button-down denim shirt, her hair was damp and unkempt, appearing as if she had just wiped it off with a towel. With socks and sneakers on, she looked like was ready to go somewhere. Not crying, speaking slowly and coherently, she seemed to have regained her composure.

"Ma'am, I have to ask you a few more questions about what happened and what the man did, okay?" She nodded. "But first I have to ask you a different question. You look like you may have just showered. Did you shower after you were attacked?" Fiero asked.

The woman hesitated and stared harshly at Fiero. "Yes, of course I showered. I had to get his filth off me, didn't I? Did you expect me to sit here with any part of him still on my body?" Her eyes glared at us with anger, her voice got deep and coarse. She waved her fingers in a way that I knew from the first rape I handled, what the rapist had done.

Fiero and I knew what a problem taking a shower posed for the investigation. After a rape, there was a lot of evidence that the rapist left behind on the victim. A shower washed all that evidence away. Fiero and I knew not to show any disappointment, or worse, disapproval, at what she did. It was a very natural and understandable reaction.

"Ma'am, I understand that. I am sure I would feel the same way," Fiero went on.

"How do you know? Have you been raped, Officer?"

"No ma'am, I haven't."

"Then don't even pretend to know how I feel, because you don't know." Her voice was filled with rage that she was now directing at Fiero.

The female to female rapport that sometimes helped in rape cases was not working here; actually it seemed to be making matters worse.

"Ma'am, I understand your anger. I really do. Any woman can feel for another woman who has been through what you've been through. Please trust me. But in order for us to help you, you have to help us. There are some personal questions I need to ask you and then we are going to do a crime scene search of your apartment to collect evidence to help us catch the man who did this to you." Fiero was almost pleading for some cooperation.

"Oh sure, you're all gonna drop everything else to catch some white man who raped a black woman. I don't think so. Since when did white cops ever care about what happens to us here in the Heights?"

That really bothered me; that was an unfair question. None of us treated the black community any differently than we treated the white community, Hispanic community or any other minorities. At least, we didn't see it that way. We had black police officers in the Westland Park Police Department, though not many and only a few were assigned to the Third Precinct.

"Ma'am, I understand your concerns. Please, just work with us and give us a chance to prove to you what we can and will be doing for you, and every other woman out there who may be targeted by this man. Please, we need your help. Will you do that? Will you give us a chance? Please." She nodded to Fiero reflecting a rather unenthusiastic yes.

"Great, thank you," Fiero responded. "Why don't you and I sit here in the living room and talk for a little bit?"

At that moment the doorbell rang, startling the victim, which was not uncommon. Fiero explained to the victim named Faith Newman that it was only another police officer bringing in some crime scene equipment. Fiero tilted her head towards the door indicating for me to answer it. Actually, this was my call and I should have been in charge. But Fiero got there first, because I was too busy getting my dick sucked, while on duty. Besides, I thought Fiero was handling this better than I could. So, I let it go. I opened the door expecting to see Edmonds with his gold rimmed eyeglasses, his thin blonde hair neatly parted on the left side with a schoolboy smile. I didn't see Edmonds. I saw Burkett — quite a contrast.

"JB, what are you doing here? Are you crime scene tonight? I thought it was Edmonds."

"It is Edmonds. I was close by and wanted to help out. This sounds like my boy from a few months ago. I knew he would strike again around here. That's why I was so worried and was trying to follow-up more. Can I get a little info on the M.O.?"

"All right," I said hesitantly. We walked over to Fiero and the victim.

"Ms. Newman," I addressed the victim, "this is Officer Burkett. He is working on a case similar to this where we may be looking for the same person. He's going to stick around a little bit to see if there are any consistencies he can tie to the other attack, if that's okay with you."

She waved her hand indicating for us to continue: that was not really a big concern to her at the moment. I could tell from the look on Fiero's face that she neither understood nor appreciated Burkett's presence. Fiero pulled me over to the side.

"Why is that fat fuck here?" she asked with near exasperation.

"He's just doing follow-up on the rape he handled. You know, trying to do a little detective work. I'll keep an eye on him. It'll be fine. You just take care of the victim."

"Follow-up? What is he, a fuck'n detective now? This is bullshit."

I looked at Fiero with no response.

Okay," she went on, "but if he fucks anything up or says something stupid, I'll cut your fuck'n balls off."

"Okay, Liz, chill please."

We walked over to the victim who was left sitting by herself rather uncomfortably.

"Oh, and there will be another knock at the door. Don't worry. It's just going to be another one of our officers," I told Faith.

I took Burkett into the bedroom where the rape occurred and showed him the window the perp broke in through. He looked at the broken window carefully, as if he expected to find a particular piece of evidence. I explained to him how the attack occurred with the knife and then he made her turn around.

"Yep, sounds like my guy," Burkett said. "Same thing: single female, living alone in a ground floor apartment. He does his homework. That's why I'm worried he'll be attacking the same women more than once. Sooner or later he's got to run out of potential victims. Don't you think?"

"I don't know, JB. There's a lot of women and a lot of territory out there to cover. He may go outside of Westland Park. He may already have hit anywhere from here to the other side of St. Louis, and all points in between. Who the fuck knows?"

"Well, we need to be doing more. Let me just hit the head for a second. I gotta take a whiz."

"JB, can't it wait? She showered in there. Sex Crimes is probably gonna want to look through there. I don't think they want to pick up your urine samples."

"I know. Don't worry, junior. I got good aim. I won't touch anything and I won't mess anything up."

I found it strange that JB had to go to the bathroom at that moment. I also knew that he understood the importance of crime scene integrity, so I didn't know what to think. I heard him turning the doorknob to open it and then he stopped. Then I heard the toilet flush, and he came out. Everything about Burkett was weird to the max.

I went over to Fiero where she was sitting with the victim on the black leather couch pushed up against a bare white wall on beige carpeting. Faith seemed to be calming down a bit, her anger subsiding, at least the anger directed at us. Liz was explaining that she would drive Faith to the hospital where a special room was set up for these kinds of incidents and she would be afforded great privacy.

The doorbell rang again.

"I'll get it," I told Fiero, as this time I knew it would be Edmonds.

But once again, I was surprised. A young black lady was in the doorway and started to walk in without telling me who she was or why she was there. I stopped her to an angry yell of "Take your hands off me, Casper."

'Well, ma'am, who are you? You're not just walking in here."

"It's okay," Faith yelled out. "It's Charisse, my sister. Let her in."

At that point, I put my arm down and let Charisse pass. I didn't know what harm there would have been if she had simply introduced herself. Charisse walked by, but not without giving me a nasty glare. Did I deserve that? I was only trying to protect her sister. Fiero stood up with Faith and told her sister that they would be driving to the hospital.

"No, I'll drive her," the sister said defiantly.

"Yeah, I'd rather do that" was Faith's answer.

Fiero responded quickly. "I understand why you want to drive with your sister and we appreciate her offer. But it is really important that you drive with me. There are still a few more things you and I need to talk about in the car. In the meantime, your sister probably has some information that can be important, so I'd like her to stay and talk to Officer Hollings here, okay?"

Nobody was responding. There was that uncomfortable silence. I broke the silence. I didn't want to give Charisse a chance to influence Faith.

"Okay," I said. "That's perfect." I clapped my hands once and then led Fiero and Faith to the door, almost herding them out. Before Charisse could say anything, I told her, "Charisse, you may really be in a position to help your sister. Why don't you and I sit down and talk a while? Officer Fiero will make sure that your sister gets the proper medical care she needs. How does that sound?"

Even Charisse seemed unable to counter that argument. Boy, I was getting good. Every day on patrol taught me something new about human nature and how to work around it. I also realized how well Fiero took over this matter. She was a good cop and had another side to her besides having a problem keeping her legs closed. Unfortunately, Gillis was right about her; reputation was everything, and no matter how well she did as a cop, she would never be seen as anything other than an easy screw. Janie would argue that guys like Thompson and me are no worse when we go out and stick it to her, but life wasn't fair. When it came to sex, men and women were judged on a different scale — that's just how it went.

The doorbell rang again. I signaled for Burkett to get it as he wasn't doing anything useful at the moment. At least this time, it was Edmonds.

"What the fu... I mean, heck took you so long?" Burkett whispered to Edmonds, knowing how Edmonds felt about the "f" word.

"Hey, we had a smash and grab up at Dalton's Diamonds and I just finished processing that scene. I got here as quickly as I could. Two major crime scenes in one hour. Anything else happens tonight, we'll have to call for help from another precinct or have the Headquarters Crime Scene Unit head out. Is Sex Crimes on the way?"

"Yeah, they are. The rape occurred in the bedroom on the bed and then she took a shower," Burkett told Edmonds.

"She took a shower?"

"I know. Not great for collecting evidence."

"Well, that's how some girls react. I guess you can't blame them," Edmonds noted with a sympathetic tone.

"So what are we looking at?" Edmonds asked so he would know where to start collecting evidence and what to leave for Sex Crimes.

"Over there, we have the window where he broke in. It's in the bedroom, but we can dust for prints and pick up some broken glass samples. She said he left through the window too, so maybe he cut himself on the glass. Be careful to look for blood. I didn't see any footprints, but I guess we can try. I would stay away from the bed and the bathroom, and leave that for Sex Crimes with all their fancy ultra violet lights and shit like that. 10-4?"

"Got it. What's Hollings doing?" Edmonds asked Burkett.

"He's interviewing the sister. You know, asking about old boyfriends, guys at work who may have been hitting on her, the usual suspects."

"You wanna stick around and help me a bit, JB?"

"I'll stay for a few minutes, but with Hollings tied up and Fiero at the hospital, we're a little light out there on the street. I'd better mark clear soon. I'll start processing at the window."

"Okay, whatever."

I was engaged in conversation with Charisse, asking just the questions Edmonds and Burkett knew I would be asking. They had both handled rapes many times before. While this sounded like the serial rapist acting randomly, the possibility of some connection between him and his victims could still exist. Publicly, the department had acknowledged that there had been a disproportionate number of rapes lately, but evaded the question of whether there was a serial rapist running around. We warned the community about the dangers of ground floor apartments in general, but we didn't want to give away the little information we had on the rapist or his M.O. — we needed him to keep his pattern. Somewhere at some time, he would leave a vital clue. This kind of case fueled my desire to make detective as early as possible.

The door bell rang and Burkett jumped up to answer it. He knew who was there and wanted to greet the Sex Crimes detectives.

"Hey, Detective Patelli, Jim Burkett. We met a couple of months ago at the Nina Wilkes rape. Remember?" He held out his hand for a handshake.

"Yes, Burkett, I do remember. I think you know Detective Leslie Lake."

"Hi, Detective." Burkett held his hand out to Lake and she replied with a limp handshake. "Let me show you something in here," and he led them to the bedroom.

"Look, these drapes were closed and you can't see through them. So, apparently this guy knew exactly what he was doing. He knew that she was in there alone. Just like the Wilkes rape I handled. Whoever he is, he watches his victim for a while, and knows exactly when and where to strike."

"Yes, Officer, I think we can all agree on that," Patelli answered.

"Right, but what concerns me is that he is so cautious. Do you think he will attack the same girl more than once, because he knows the territory and he may feel more bold and confident?" Burkett said, once again trying to impress the detectives.

"Well, Officer, repeat rapes are not common, but they have been known to happen on occasion. All of this is so unpredictable. We will have to set up a strategy to attack this problem. We can't allow ourselves to remain in a reactive mode. We'll have to get proactive. If you have any ideas, please call the Detective Bureau and let us know. We welcome fresh perspectives."

"I'll do that," Burkett said. "I gotta tell you, though; my guess is he is gonna strike again in our precinct — maybe the same apartment or even the same girl again."

"And why do you say that, Officer?"

"Well, you know, I read a lot of the forensic psychology books and stuff, and I can tell. It looks like he's sticking to familiar territory: places he knows, maybe even people he knows. That's all."

"Maybe, but that kind of speculation may be a bit premature. Unfortunately, we will see soon enough. Thank you, Officer."

"Well, I'd better get back to patrol now."

I was a little surprised to see Burkett rush off like that. I'd thought he would have stuck around and have done a little more sucking up.

I checked in with Edmonds and the Sex Crimes detectives. They didn't need me anymore. I took off to the hospital to catch up with Fiero. I had Charisse follow me, to take Faith back home when all was finished. I went to the hospital's Sex Crimes treatment room where Fiero was in with the victim and the hospital staff specially trained to handle rapes, and I waited outside. The doctors and nurses would collect the evidence and hand it directly to the officer — in this case, Fiero. There was also a female social worker available. Knowing what was happening, the pictures, the swabbing of the vagina and all the personal procedures going on, suggested that a male officer walking in was not proper protocol.

Charisse wanted to go in. I got Fiero on the radio to see if Faith had asked for her sister. She had not. I told Charisse to have a seat with me and wait. Relatives meant well, but their presence more often than not was disruptive. They questioned and challenged everything we did. Before long, they destroyed any rapport or relationship that had been built between the cop and the victim, and they stopped cooperating. Cooperation was the key to solving these cases. After about an hour of waiting, Faith came out with Fiero who had all the evidence, bagged and tagged. Faith left with her sister.

"Hey, it was your call. I was just back-up. It's all yours," Fiero said, holding out the bag of evidence.

"You did a great job. I don't think I would've gotten that kind of cooperation. Nice work," I told her as I grabbed the evidence.

I thought again about how Gillis didn't want Fiero handling that rape a while back because he didn't consider Fiero a lady. He was wrong. She was very much a lady in the way she handled this rape. Her sex life was not my business, but maybe she would be well advised to keep it out of the department. It certainly wasn't my place to tell her or to judge her. Besides, I was sure she would not appreciate my advice. I would like to look at her as just another cop, but that night in the maintenance shop was indelibly burned into my memory, and when I saw her or heard her name, that experience was first and foremost in my mind, and I wanted to relive it. That was not about to change. As for Fiero, that night in the maintenance shop was nowhere near being on her mind.

The shift ended and I made my way back to the precinct. While putting my reports in the sergeant's in-box, I happened to notice a message with my name on it posted on the message board. That was unusual. I rarely had a message. It must've come in during the shift tonight, as the sergeant usually grabbed all the messages and handed them out during roll call. It was a message from Amy Barkley. Amy was the woman who was in that unexplained car accident, when Stryker came and helped me. It was now 7 a. m., probably not too early to call on a workday morning, so I did. I got her on the phone and introduced myself.

"Officer, I just wanted to thank you for your help."

"I appreciate that, but it was no big deal. We handle accidents all the time. That's our job and I didn't mind driving you home. It's okay."

"No, it's not that. I got what you were saying to me and you were right. That was no accident."

"What do you mean?" I asked, a bit stunned, yet knowing where she was heading.

"I was trying to kill myself, and you knew that."

"But why? Why would you want to do that?"

"Oh, my husband just left me out of the blue and I didn't know how to handle it. I was very depressed."

"I'm really sorry to hear that. I wish I was in a position to give you some advice, but that's nothing I'm really good at. The only thing I would strongly suggest is that you get some help: find a professional to talk to. Someone who can give you real advice to keep you from thinking about doing something like that again."

"I already have. But if you didn't make me admit that to myself, I may have tried again. I guess what I'm saying is, thank you for saving my life."

"That's quite all right. I wish you lots of luck, and if you ever need anything, feel free to call."

I hung up the phone feeling pretty good about myself. Maybe I actually saved a life. I knew it was really Stryker's observation that it was probably a suicide and not an accident, but I followed-up on it and obviously got through to her. Maybe Stryker deserved the credit, but the way it worked out, it was mine to claim, if only to myself. I would tell Janie. *She'd be impressed*, I thought.

Chapter 12

"You're two hours late."

"Huh, two hours late for what?"

"I thought you get off at seven."

"Uh, I do. What are you doing here?"

'What? You're not happy to see me?'

"No, no, it's great to see you. I'm just surprised. I wasn't expecting you." I reached down to give Janie a hug and kiss. I didn't expect to find her waiting for me at my door. We hadn't made any plans. It was a nice surprise, just unexpected. It was also the first time one of us showed up at the other's place unannounced. That sounds like a major step forward in the dating game as you never know what you might find when you get there. She had a McDonald's breakfast for us, which was now cold.

"Why so late? One of the cop parties after work? A little drinking, a little fooling around?"

"It's seven in the morning. I don't think we would be doing any drinking, and I don't know what fooling around we'd be doing." That was only half true.

We have had some beer drinking parties after work. While seven in the morning sounds early, it was only a drink after work for us, like many people had. One time, we went over to Stryker's place and watched some porn while we drank. Nothing more than a little tension releaser. It was all harmless. Of course, Edmonds didn't go; neither did Fiero or Mac.

"Well, first of all, it's not seven, it's nine. And who knows, maybe Miss Liz was getting a little frisky after a long night at work and wanted to party a little."

"Yes, it is nine. I had a last minute arrest. It kept me late. But at least I got a few hours of overtime. And listen, I didn't want to bring this up, but you're going to have to get over this cop thing and Liz issue. I don't know what your last boyfriend did to you, and I never asked. If you want to get it on the table we can discuss it. But it's not fair for you to take out all that on me. Let's just enjoy what we have and see how it goes, okay?"

Janie seemed a bit surprised at my response. I certainly was. A silent, stress filled moment followed. Did I just lay down the gauntlet? Was I drawing a line for Janie not to cross? This could have been the defining moment, or ending moment, of our relationship.

"Well, okay then. I'm sorry. How about some cold McDonald's?" She sounded a bit contrite as well as annoyed at my response. I didn't know what else to say and she didn't leave. It must've been the right response.

We went into my apartment and had breakfast, yet Janie didn't seem all that satisfied with my answer. I wasn't sure what was bothering her. I hadn't done anything that should upset her. At least, nothing that she knew about.

"What time is your shift tonight?" I asked her.

"Well, I told them I might be a little late so I could go to the awards ceremony, and then go out with you and the guys afterwards. It sounds like fun."

"That's great. Thanks. I've got to get a little sleep in, so I don't fall asleep during the chief's speech. I need to stay awake. I'm beat. Could I interest you in taking a nap with me?"

"Sounds good."

Janie went into the bathroom to do whatever she needed to do. I stripped down to my underwear and threw my clothes on the floor — my normal procedure before going to bed. What I didn't know was that Janie was washing up and taking off her clothes, folding them neatly and placing them on top of my dresser as she walked into my bedroom. She slithered into bed completely naked, obviously in the mood and ready for sex. That would've been great, but for one problem. I had already fallen fast asleep. I only had about three hours to sleep before I had to get over to the ceremony that afternoon to officially and formally receive my Bronze Medal of Valor.

I had a restless sleep, tossing and turning a lot. I don't know if it was the excitement of the awards ceremony coming up or all the things that had been happening the last several weeks. Barroom brawls were one thing. A girl letting her boyfriend beat her up was another. Girls getting raped and one trying to commit suicide over a broken marriage were just a little more. Life can really deal some sad blows to anyone; it hardly seemed fair. In the past three weeks I handled a battered infant, a store clerk who was hit with the butt of a gun after giving up all the money and a 50-year old man who hung himself in his home. I could come to the scene of any crime or crisis after the fact and try to help, but could I really stop anything?

I had been wondering how much I had really added to the safety of our community. Even the armed robbery... maybe if Burkett, Thompson and I hadn't arrived, the robber may have just taken some money and left. Then nobody would've gotten shot. But, everyone says that we saved the clerk and his wife's life. I don't know if that's true or not, but I'll take the credit, and my medal. I woke up in a sweat, to find my blanket on the floor and my sheets half off the mattress. When I woke up, one thing was missing — that was Janie.

I never had a girl walk out while I was sleeping and leave a note. Wasn't that a guy thing to do? I read the note. Nothing serious. She said that I seemed tired and noticed what a tough time I had sleeping, so she left to let me get some rest for my big day. The words were innocuous enough, but there was something about the tone. I didn't know what was bothering her.

Grabbing a small snack of tuna fish, I ate it right out of the can. Not exciting, but I didn't want my stomach grumbling during the ceremony.

The last time my rumbling stomach embarrassed me was when I handled a call with Stryker one night. We had to go over to the home of a family and return some personal items of their 16-year old son, who had been killed in a car accident. While talking to the parents, my stomach grumbled loudly. There was no ignoring it. The father, who was fairly composed, offered us some food. I almost jumped right up and accepted, but Stryker declined. Only two minutes later, my stomach was grumbling again, even louder.

"Please, Officers, people have been bringing us food for the last two days; we have more than we know what to do with. Let us offer you something to eat."

I started to stand up to accept the food. I thought it was the polite thing to do.

Stryker stood up first. He held his arm out, partially restraining me from walking towards the kitchen. "We really appreciate the offer. We just want to return these items and offer our condolences. Feel free to call us if there is anything else we can do." He then directed me to the door.

"Can we get something to eat now?" was my first question as we left the house.

Stryker was laughing. "You young punks. Probably can't control your dick any more than your stomach. The poor family is in mourning and you want to eat their food."

"Well, they offered twice. I was only being polite."

"Whatever. C'mon, I'll treat you to some real food at the Blue Valley Pancake House."

They wound up being pretty good pancakes.

Bringing my thoughts back to the present, I shined my shoes one more time and unwrapped my uniform from the plastic covering of the dry cleaner. I polished all my brass, including the twelve bullets lined up on my belt. Standing in front of the mirror, I went through the routine Sergeant Hughes went through daily. Fortunately, though, I didn't yet have reading glasses to clean. I drove over to Westland Park where the ceremony was to be held. I was certainly hoping I wouldn't pass a car accident or anybody expecting me to stop and help. It was a sunny, mild day, so an outdoor event would be perfect. Otherwise, we'd be indoors at the civic center. That wasn't a bad place, but parking was a little tough there. There was something about the outdoors that gave this event an aura of happiness.

Pulling up to the police parking area, I found that Thompson and I had been saved a parking spot right next to the chief. That was almost an honor by itself. Four other cops were being recognized today: no others from our precinct. One cop pulled a woman out of a car on fire. Another cop negotiated a man out of his own bathroom while holding a gun to his wife's head. One cop arrested a bank robber while she was off-duty. She happened to be standing in line when the jerk robbed the bank. The fourth cop was working plain clothes and he caught someone about to break into a ground floor apartment. The department got excited with that arrest, thinking the serial rapist may have been caught, but it was just a burglar. These four cops were all getting commendations, while Thompson and I were getting the medals. In reality, I knew that what those four cops did was probably much more heroic, much better police work than what I had done. But I got shot, and that's the politics of police work.

We went up on the podium and took our seats. I looked at the front row. The entire squad showed up, including Burkett. Burkett was emotionless. No stupid smile, just a stoic visage. But he was there and I was impressed. If I were him, I would have found reason or rationalization not to go. Sergeant Hughes looked proud. The squads for the other officers and their sergeants were all there as well; additional squads were brought in and paid overtime to cover for those squads that were scheduled to work. Few cops turned down overtime.

A sense of pride and brotherhood overtook me as I saw four rows of about 30 police officers in uniform, there to honor their brother and sister officers. Their presence sent a message of camaraderie, or even more than that — a sense of family. I looked in the crowd for Janie, but could not find her. We were going out for lunch afterwards with the entire squad. I would find her later.

The ceremony went on schedule. The wooden podium at the center of the raised platform prominently displayed the department's seal. Each side of the podium was adorned with a flag. The United States flag was on the right and the State flag on the left. The metal chairs in the audience, with the uncomfortable low backs facing the podium, were staring straight into the sun that was hanging above Police Headquarters. Headquarters served as an appropriate backdrop for the ceremony, which was held in the park's parking lot.

Inside the park were jogging paths that runners and bicyclists used often in the warm weather.

The ceremony opened with the police honor guard marching down the center aisle and then everyone singing the national anthem. The police chaplain gave his invocation to the Heavenly Father. The chief then made his opening remarks and paid respect to the officers who had fallen in the line of duty, naming each one. He did that every year at the awards ceremony. The surviving spouse was always afforded a seat on the podium as a guest of honor. Fortunately, we had experienced only a handful of line-of-duty deaths, considering the size of our department.

Chief Lee Harper handled these presentations with the appropriate sense of solemn respect; he was an impressive public speaker with a deep voice that reverberated at just the right moments. Then he went on to the granting of the awards. He gave a short but emotional rendition of each story leading up to the award. Each officer receiving the commendations stepped forward to accept the honor, shook hands with the chief and then had his photograph taken. As Thompson and I were being given the highest awards, we were last. The chief called my name first and I slowly stood up. I walked over to him cautiously, fearful of tripping over a wire or even just my own two feet. He read a short statement of how, as a rookie in training, I responded to a robbery in progress and kept my composure after being shot. That was really all he could say. I didn't do anything else.

As I lowered my head and the chief strung that medal around my neck I heard thunderous applause. I knew who was in the audience cheering for me — cops with years and years of experience; cops who had probably done things so much more valuable to society than just taking a bullet in the leg. I was humbled and I was proud. Yet, there was still a feeling of emptiness inside me, as I knew there was something disingenuous about me getting this medal. If I had let myself, a tear or two may have made their way out of my eyes. After the chief gave me the medal, he shook my hand, a photograph was taken and he pointed me back to my seat. I was relieved that the moment had ended.

Then it was time to present Thompson with his Silver Medal of Valor. When his name was called, he showed none of the hesitation I displayed. He stood up at his chair and stopped for a moment, almost as if he was posing for the crowd. The chief spoke of Thompson's actions.

"And after being shot in the shoulder, Officer Thompson still returned fire. But what was truly exemplary was that he returned fire in such a way that there is one felon out there who won't be showing off his battle scars." And to that the chief received a response of laughter and applause.

The chief then put the medal over Thompson's head and Thompson stood up straight and absorbed the applause. In no rush to get back to his seat, he slithered closer to the chief and whispered something to him. The chief's head popped up and looked at Thompson; he was obviously surprised by whatever Thompson said. Then the chief nodded yes. Thompson did not return to his seat. He walked over to the podium and adjusted the microphone. I couldn't imagine what he was going to say. Surely he wasn't going to expound upon the chief's remark about shooting the guy in the ass. I think that message was played out. And even Thompson was beyond trying to toot his own horn even more, I hoped. His opening words were surprising to me, as I am sure to many others as well. He thanked the squad, he thanked his wife for her love and support and then he thanked me for standing by him in the face of danger. It was certainly a nice thing to do.

Then, I was waiting, but it didn't come... he didn't even mention Burkett. Why would he not take the opportunity to give Burkett at least some credit? It would've been so simple. Right then and there, at least for Burkett and me, who knew how the shooting really unfolded, the truth about Thompson was rubbed in our face, especially Burkett's. Thompson really was a self-absorbed prick, but more than that though, he was mean, and he was a bully. He knew what he was doing to Burkett: someone who did not have the inner strength that Thompson had and could not fight back. Being tough on the street is easy when you stand there in uniform with a baton, a gun and a whole squad of cops just a radio call away. Thompson was just a punk with a badge.

The chief quickly came to the podium, thanked Thompson for that little speech, ushered him back to his seat and then thanked the audience for coming. I looked over at Burkett. He sighed heavily and his eyebrows furled. But he held it together.

At the end of the ceremony, as we walked off the stage, the squad stood in line to congratulate us with Sergeant Hughes at the head of the line. I followed Thompson, as to be expected. Everybody gave us a firm handshake and a friendly, professional embrace. Burkett shook hands with Thompson, but he did it with a limp hand and didn't even look Thompson in the face. I didn't blame him. I wondered what the rest of the squad was thinking. Once again, I didn't think anyone ever considered what Burkett was feeling. Then I got to Burkett. He was a little more responsive to me.

"Congratulations, Gary. That really was a good job, especially for a rookie."

"Thanks, JB. And listen, I'm sorry for the way things played out. I know what a good job you did out there. You deserved some recognition too. And I think the squad knows that. Ya know, I hear people talking. They know."

His face lit up a bit. "Really?"

"Yeah, JB. People know. Thanks for coming. It meant a lot to me."

Actually, I had not heard anybody talking. Nobody was giving Burkett the credit he deserved. But what did telling him a little white lie like that hurt anyway? At least it lifted his spirits a bit.

I thought I smelled alcohol on his breath. Fortunately, he was not on his way to patrol. But he was in uniform and anything could happen. I really couldn't be sure that he had been drinking and someone else on this squad of experienced cops would have noticed. Sergeant Hughes was there; it was his responsibility. Then I got to Liz. I hesitated. She threw both arms around me and gave me a hug. Then she pulled back. I expected her to let go, but then she planted a kiss right on the lips and hugged me again. We were in uniform.

That could not have been appropriate in any sense. I looked around to see who was watching. Nobody was really paying any attention except Thompson. He smiled and gave me the thumbs up. Then, I waited at the front of the podium for Janie. It was not like her to be late. I called her cell phone several times, getting no answer. Finally, she answered.

"Where are you? Did you miss the ceremony?" I asked.

"No, look to your left in the back. I'm here."

Scanning the area which was thinning out, I saw this small, lone figure standing behind the last row of seats near the few cars that were still parked in the lot.

"Then what are you doing? Why are you back there, and why didn't you answer your phone?"

"Because I was thinking of leaving."

"Leaving? What are you talking about? We're all going out for lunch, remember?"

"Well, it looks like you and Liz want a little private time, so I thought I'd go home."

Then I knew that she saw that kiss. I should have guessed that. Just like in the hospital, Janie always seemed to be around at the most inopportune times.

"What are you talking about?" I said, feigning ignorance.

"I saw that kiss. I don't know what's going on with you two, but I'm not here to get in the middle of it."

"Oh, c'mon. It was just a friendly congratulation. Please, let's not go there now. Look, if you don't want to go out with the squad, let's just you and me go out to lunch and get through this once and for all. There is nothing for you to be concerned about, okay?"

There was a pause. I got worried. Was she was going to leave?

"Okay, drive to my car and I'll follow you, but I don't want to go anywhere near your cop buddies. Got it?"

"Okay."

"Hey, Mark," I called out. The guys were waiting for me to get off my cell phone. "Listen, you guys, go ahead. I think Janie and I are going to go out alone."

"Oh, those little lover quarrels. They're so cute," Thompson said with a laugh.

I looked over to Liz. She had a self-satisfying smirk on her face. I did not like it. More importantly, I was not going to do anything about it.

Janie and I sat down to lunch at a local diner. Because I was in uniform, everybody watched me as we walked towards our table. We each slid into the opposite sides of the booth with red leather seats. The diner had a '50s motif with the sound track of *Grease* playing in the background. She started toying with the salt shaker: just rolling it around in little circles. I didn't say anything and wanted to let her speak first. When she did, she got right down to business. That was good. Small talk would've been a waste of time at that point. I needed to know what her problem was. We needed to get past it. She laid it out to me.

"Two years ago, I was dating a detective from Kansas City. I thought it was getting pretty serious. I thought we were heading for an engagement," she told me. Then she paused and started to catch her breath, which sounded like it was running short.

"Okay, so it didn't work out. That happens. Was there something about the break-up that makes you so suspicious of everything I do?"

"Well, yes. It wasn't just things not working out. He and his partner were working vice and they both wound up getting fired." Her voice now started to quiver, her lip trembling slightly.

"Wow, what were they doing? Ripping off drug dealers or something?"

"No. They were screwing the prostitutes who they were supposed to be arresting. Not only did I have to deal with the fact that I was dating a slime ball, but I spent months getting tested for all sorts of sexually transmitted diseases. For all I knew, I could've gotten AIDS." Now her voice went into a soft yell. There was anger. She wiped a tear dripping from the corner of her left eye.

Despite my attempt not to react to that, she saw the selfish look of concern on my face. I guess that kind of worry would be hard to hide.

"Don't worry. I've been tested for everything at least twice. I'm completely clean. I wouldn't have slept with you if I wasn't. I'm no whore." Her voice got even angrier.

Whether it was because of that experience or because she saw I got nervous when she said AIDS, I was not sure. But who could blame me for reacting to that?

"Janie, I'm sorry. I had no idea. Now I understand where you're coming from. I wish I had known. Why didn't you tell me earlier?"

"I told you when I was ready to tell you. Today, especially today, seemed like the right moment. I hope you're being honest about really understanding, because I am not willing to go through that kind of pain and humiliation again. And if you're gonna be taken in by tramps like your friend Liz, let's just drop things now."

I had not had many serious relationships in my life. This was definitely the heaviest issue I'd had to deal with.

"No, no, I don't want to drop things." I almost fell into the trap and said "I love you," but I caught myself. "Okay, but look. I can't control how Liz acts and I've got to work with her. But I promise I will keep my distance from her. I won't give you any reason to get upset or to worry. You're my girl, my one and only, and I hope, and I plan, on keeping it that way. Whatta ya say?"

Not sure how she was going to respond, I felt myself trembling a bit. She was angry at what happened to her, and she was sad. But was she still hurting from a broken heart? I loved her and wanted things to work, but I was not going to compete with the memory of an old boyfriend. I was also going to protect myself. If she pulled a Melissa move on me, I was not going to be the deer staring at the headlights; I would be ready to move on.

Saying nothing, she grabbed my hand and smiled, though it was a bit forced. I felt a little relief, and I then put my other hand on top of hers. I realized at that moment how much I really cared for her.

"This can work," I told her. "But you, no we... we have got to put the past in the past. I've had my heart broken too, but we all do at some time in our life. Let's forget about that and move on, together, okay?"

Janie nodded yes with a bigger, more natural smile and began to cry. Those were happy tears and I wiped them from her face. I also knew the kind of promise I was making. I didn't know if I could live up to it. I was young. I was horny. I was a cop. As Thompson put it, there were certain fringe benefits to the job. But right now, I wanted to keep Janie. I couldn't imagine hurting her like she was hurt before. I'd worry about those other issues if and when they arose.

We finished lunch and our conversation and I got home about three in the afternoon, hoping to get at least a couple more hours of sleep before the shift started. I felt like taking the night off. The ceremony had drained me a bit and Janie really zapped my mental strength. I did not have a lot of personal leave built up yet; I was trying to save what I had so maybe Janie and I could take a small vacation sometime. After our talk at the diner, a few days away together alone might be a good test of our relationship.

Before I knew it, I was back in roll call.

"The serial rapist issue is starting to become a public relations problem. The chief may be forming a task force. Some cops from each precinct are gonna be pulled to help out the detectives." That was news from the sergeant that got my attention.

A task force sounded like a good assignment. Probably would be some cop's first step to becoming a detective. I kinda fantasized about that opportunity. Becoming the department's youngest detective was an aspiration that I didn't verbalize, yet my senior fellow officers seemed to read that just by looking at me.

Thinking that Janie and I were now on a good path, I was enjoying the moment. That was until about four in the morning. Another domestic dispute was called in by an anonymous neighbor and I recognized the address. It was my biker friend from months ago. This time, I would have to follow through on my threat from last time. If there was any sign of a felonious assault, I had to lock him up, whether that stupid bitch girlfriend of his was going to press charges or not. As a cop, you can't get caught in a bluff. Just make the arrest and let the district attorney worry about making the case. Stryker was called to give me back-up. I asked for two more units for additional back up; it would take more than two of us if we had to take this bastard down.

Burkett and Bergman were dispatched. Bergman had been on his own for a while now and had established himself as a good, reliable cop. We got to the apartment and as we approached, we heard the girl screaming. I didn't knock on the door. I didn't expect the biker to answer it this time. Turning the doorknob and getting lucky, it was unlocked. I opened the door and walked in, my partners behind me in single file. We all had our batons out, across our chests, resting in the other hand. That was the non-verbal cue that we were ready. I yelled out our presence and that big fucker walked out of the bedroom. He was not expecting that show of force and he hesitated for a moment. It was more like an assessment of the situation. He did not look afraid.

"What the fuck do you guys want now?" he said as he walked towards the dining room, which was only a few steps away. We walked in lockstep with him. With a nod, I signaled to Burkett. He understood.

Burkett went into the bedroom to check on the girl. I couldn't hear him real well, but he sounded like he was giving the same pitch I gave last time. She marched to the doorway and took a few steps towards us with Burkett following her. I held my hand up, directing her to stop there and Burkett knew she was getting too close to us. He swung himself in front of her, held up both hands — a clue to calm down — and as he started to talk to her, she yelled at him.

"Fuck you. Why don't you mind your own fuck'n business, you ugly, fat piece of shit?" At that moment, sporting a bruised, swollen eye, with both hands, she grabbed Burkett's flab, hanging over his belt and gave it a quick, strong tug. That was funny. The biker, Bergman and Stryker broke out into a short laugh. Burkett, stunned and unsure of what to do, just turned red.

"Hey, keep that shit up and we'll lock your ass up too," I yelled, to get us back to the problem at hand.

Actually, I did want to lock her up. We'd all been through this before — the uncooperative, abused girlfriend. Most cops saw them as sucking us into their own problems; we had just stopped caring about them.

"So you beat up your girlfriend pretty good I see? That's all the probable cause I need to throw your ass in jail. What did I tell you last time, asshole?" I said to him.

"And what did I tell you, motherfucker?" was his response, as he picked up a chair and swung it right at my face. Reaction is usually not as fast as action. He had the jump on me and I couldn't stop that attack, though I managed to partially block it with my flailing arm. The chair struck me across the left eye. I saw stars for a moment and felt the wetness of the blood. Staggering for a moment, I fell against the sofa, trying to regain my composure, so as not to lose consciousness altogether. Stryker immediately pulled his weapon and ordered the biker to drop the chair. Burkett also had his weapon pulled and aimed at the biker. Shaken, I just watched, not quite steady enough to pull my weapon out. Bergman didn't pull his weapon, but that seemed rather deliberate, not a failure of reflexes. He slowly walked closer to the biker, but not that close. The biker held his ground and lifted the chair a little higher.

"Put that chair down, or you're gonna be eating that fuck'n thing," Bergman told him in a very confident, matter-of-fact tone.

"I don't think so, cocksucker," he said.

Bergman laughed a little.

"You know, I don't like being called a cocksucker, especially by a faggot piece of shit like you."

"Oh really?"

"Oh, absofuck'nlutely," Bergman answered him back, slightly tilting his head, but maintaining an aggressive stare and unyielding stance.

Bergman held his hand up to us, trying to warn us he was about to do something — in other words, don't shoot. Casually walking closer to the biker, Bergman went to strike him over the head with his baton in what appeared to be a rather slow attempt; that worried me. The biker easily blocked Bergman's strike with the chair. Within a second, Bergman kicked the biker once in the shin and once in the knee. The sound of a knee snapping was distinctive. The biker went stumbling back against the wall and then bounced off it, right back in Bergman's direction. Bergman swiftly moved around to get behind him and whacked that baton right across the back of the biker's head.

Crashing down to the floor, face first on top of the chair, he almost did eat it. That must've hurt. Bergman jumped on him and Burkett and Stryker jumped in. Somewhat back to normal, I pulled my weapon and stood guard, watching for the girlfriend; it would not be the first time the victim became the attacker. The biker was so stunned, we had no problem pulling back his huge arms and handcuffing him. Seeing his nose bleeding now really had the air of poetic justice.

Screaming and cursing, the girlfriend was threatening to call her lawyer and we'd all be sued and thrown in jail. Nothing we hadn't heard a million times. We were not worried. Cops are not as intimidated by lawyers as people think they are. That's just television. I was hoping she would do something stupid, besides pulling on Burkett's flab, to give us reason to arrest her too, but she didn't. Bergman and I started our retreat into the hallway with our handcuffed and bloodied prisoner. Stryker and Burkett stayed back to interview and photograph the girl. She was gonna cooperate whether she wanted to or not.

"I'll book this fucker for you so you can go to the hospital and get that head of yours checked out. It's pretty black and blue and swelling up fast. You're gonna need some stitches. You gonna be able to drive?" Bergman asked me.

"I should be. I'm okay..."

"If your girl Janie is there, maybe you'll get some extra special treatment."

"Oh, just wait till I start the sympathy thing going with her. I'll get some of that extra special treatment, if you get my drift."

"I got it. You the man."

"Hey, that was great work, Matt. Thanks."

"No problem."

Pushing the big biker's head down, Bergman got him into the back of his patrol car. He was still a little dazed from that whoopin'

Bergman put on him.

"Black belt, I assume," I called out to Bergman as he got into his car.

"Fuck'n A," he said in his deep New York accent, and drove off.

Now I was sure. Bergman really would have shoved that dime up Thompson's ass. I would've loved to have seen it happen.

Chapter 13

Preparing for trial, we had taken pictures of my big black eye, with the bruises and stitches I had from the fight with the biker, and given them to the D.A.'s office to hold as evidence, in case my bruises healed by the time the trial rolled around. His girlfriend, of course, did not press charges no matter how much we cajoled or threatened her. We charged him with assaulting a police officer, so it was not a complete waste of time. It took a few weeks just to get it to trial, but we got a conviction, and he got three months in jail; it would have been less, but he had a record. Assaulting a cop usually did not bring a long sentence. Many judges saw getting assaulted as an occupational hazard for cops; they didn't get too worked up over it. But show a judge what he thinks is a display of disrespect towards him and your ass is sitting in jail in no time. It didn't work out too badly though; the judge tacked on another two years for probation violation. Sometimes the system worked, even if not by design.

No longer needed as evidence, the D.A.'s office sent back the pictures of my bruised face to the precinct. The pictures found themselves in the bottom of the urinals in the locker room. I certainly was not reaching in to remove them; Thompson's fingerprints were all over this one. That was cop humor; you learned to live with it. The bruising on my face had all but disappeared, but not the bruising of my ego. That was sloppy police work. I knew this biker meant business. I should have been more careful. I almost deserved what I got.

The politics of the squad were certainly changing. Bergman came in with a strong personality that made him a few friends, but just a few. Most of the cops kept their distance. While we still all worked hard to help each other out there on the streets, there were clear personal preferences. I kept a cool, but not a cold, shoulder towards Fiero. She got the message and mostly all of our conversations remained professional. We would still grab a cup of coffee together after handling a call and she may or may not ask about Janie. I would ask about her boyfriend; she was on about her fourth one since the one I met at the barbeque. I was wondering who she would bring to the next one, which wasn't so far off.

Without Gillis around, Thompson and Stryker usually hooked up for their meals or coffee breaks. They often huddled together right after roll call as if planning something that nobody else was to know about. Bergman and I started to become good friends. We had not gotten together socially outside of work, but I liked his style; he went his own way and did not seem to care what anybody thought. Even Sergeant Hughes seemed unsure of how to relate to him. While Bergman was always respectful of Hughes' authority, and liked him personally, I could tell that he was uncomfortable with Hughes' weak style of leadership. Hughes was, at least what I saw, a laid back, hands-off kind of sergeant. It took me a little while to understand what drove Hughes, but by now I could see that it was not a conscious style of management. It was more like a fear of confrontation. For a cop who once shot and killed someone while on a SWAT operation, that just was kind of strange; if anything that should have made him more self-assured or more cocky like Thompson. Even though the shooting was justified, killing a man who was not out to hurt you could not have been easy to live with.

Thompson and Stryker were constantly bad mouthing Bergman behind his back, usually making old and worn out Jewish jokes. On the outside, Thompson acted as if he had gotten over the incident in the locker room, or maybe I just presumed he did, but the little stupid remarks of his made me think not. I was hoping that the next transfer on to the squad would be a black officer. I would be curious as to how freely Thompson would use the words "niggers" and "spooks" if that happened.

Edmonds would meet up with me and Bergman once in a while. We just had to keep him from discussing religion. Mac generally stayed to herself, but would meet for a meal if offered. She never suggested it, though. Burkett was becoming more isolated. He didn't seek me out anymore for a cup of coffee. He tried to strike up a friendship with Bergman as soon as he was cut loose from Stryker. Bergman told me that he couldn't put his finger on it, but there was something wrong with Burkett deep inside. That whole idea of living with his mother really bothered Bergman and he tried to resist developing any personal friendship with Burkett.

Roll call was starting and I could see by who was sitting next to whom how the squad was dividing itself up. Thompson was going to be late again. That was about the fourth or fifth time he was either late getting in or leaving early. Something was going on. It didn't seem to bother Hughes. It bothered the squad though, because we had to cover Thompson's sector.

About halfway through the shift things were fairly normal. No calls out of the ordinary so far. I was about to reach Bergman on the side channel to meet up for a cup of coffee, but as usually happens at that moment, an emergency radio call was broadcast. It was for Burkett who was busy on a traffic stop. A rape had just occurred and Burkett cleared from his stop to respond. The dispatcher gave the address and the name of the victim, Nina Wilkes. Burkett got on the radio.

"318 Baker, relay to Car 300, please."

"Go, 318 Baker," Sergeant Hughes responded.

"Sarge, that's the victim of the last rape I handled. How do you want me to proceed?" Burkett was thinking about the warning from the sergeant not to go near Nina again. Only he and the sergeant knew about that. Hughes respected Burkett's privacy and Burkett certainly was not going to let on about another rejection.

"Dispatch, assign this to 321 Baker and have 309 back him up. All units, be advised this is a repeat rape victim, probably the serial rapist. 318 and 314 Baker respond to the area to search for the subject," Hughes directed.

I did not think about why the call was being reassigned to me. It was Burkett's area and he knew the victim from a previous call, but I focused on getting over there as quickly as I could. Bergman was going to back me up while Burkett and Edmonds would search the area. We had to catch this fucker this time; I kicked it into high gear to get over there as fast as possible.

Bergman and I went over to Nina's apartment. Nina appeared more distressed than last time. She was crying more visibly and loudly, her body trembling, her hands slightly clasped around her neck. I asked Bergman to call Mac over; she had handled this with Nina last time. Waiting for Mac, we had to calm her and sit her down just to be able to get some basic information from her. I asked her if she remembered me. She did. I think that helped. It still took a little while for her to regain her composure. I told Nina that Officer MacKenzie, who escorted her to the hospital last time, was on her way. She appeared a little relieved by that. I now had a better idea of how to approach interviewing a rape suspect and getting the important details. When the moment seemed right, I began to ask her questions, in a low, soft tone of voice. Unbelievably, I had learned something from Burkett.

"Nina, was it the same man?"

"I think so, but can't be sure."

"Okay, what makes you think so?"

"Well, he kinda went through the same things he did before. He stood me in front of the mirror and then pushed me face down on the bed. But he was worse this time."

"What do you mean?"

"Well, this time he started to strangle me and was cursing me while he did it. I really thought he was going to kill me."

That was about the time Mac showed up. Mac instinctively sat down on that small couch next to Nina.

"Was there anything else different this time that you can think of?" I continued to ask for more information.

"I'm not sure, but his voice seemed a little lower, like he was trying to disguise it or something. He was dressed the same, and made me do the same things again. He just seemed really, really angry."

With that she started to weep. Just thinking about the actual rape and what she was forced to do would drive any woman to tears. Mac knew what to do. She moved closer to Nina, put her arm around her and placed her hand over Nina's hand. That clearly comforted Nina as she moved in closer to Mac. That sort of physical contact could only come from a female officer. I could try, and sincerely be professional with no sexual connotations, but how could a victim of rape be comforted by the embrace of a man she did not know? A husband, a father, maybe. But a young male cop, who she knew would be checking her out any other day of the week? I knew better. Once she was a little calmer, I started asking more questions.

"Anything else that you can tell us that might help?"

"One thing really scared me."

"What's that?"

"I think this time he called me by my name. I don't think he did that last time. Has he been watching me? Is he gonna keep coming after me?" Now she started getting hysterical.

"Let's focus on taking care of you now. Do you have anyone you want to call, maybe someone you can stay with while we investigate this?" I asked her.

"Yes, my friend Carol. Is it okay if I call her?"

She called Carol who came over within about 15 minutes. Then we heard the radio crackle.

"318 Baker, I have a possible suspect. I'm behind 678 South Washington in the parking lot. What's the clothing description?"

I got on the radio and told Burkett it was the same as last time. The perp was dressed in all black with the black hood sweatshirt tied tightly around his face.

"Okay, I got a possible. Start back-up this way. I'm gonna approach him. He's heading to the park area behind the lot."

Stryker was still in his car and started in Burkett's direction.

"Mac, Bergman and I are gonna run out and help Burkett. You got it covered?"

"Yes, go, go," she commanded. She then told Nina that we were trying to catch the guy who attacked her.

Nina was emotionless. Bergman and I ran out and tried to catch up to Burkett. Burkett got on the radio, out of breath.

"I'm on foot, in pursuit of possible rape suspect in the park area behind 678 South Washington. Have units head to Belmont Avenue where I think this park backs up to."

Stryker was in his car and headed that way. Bergman and I kept running. We got to the wooded area at the end of the parking lot and didn't see Burkett. I called him on the radio. There was no answer. Bergman and I looked at each other. No answer was never a good sign. We ran towards the tree-lined footpaths by the park and called on the radio again, a little panicked. Liking or not liking Burkett was irrelevant at that moment. He was a brother cop who may have been in trouble. Finally, Burkett answered the radio, completely out of breath.

"I lost him here in the pathways. You guys come on in, but he could've gone anywhere. It's too dark back here. I can't see anything."

"JB, come on out. We can't find you in there. It's not safe to be in there alone," I radioed to him on the side channel.

"All right, stand by."

Bergman and I stood there waiting. It took about five minutes for Burkett to make it out. He was panting and sweating and as soon as he got to us he sat down on the curb. Stryker called in on the radio and said that he had found nothing cruising up and down Belmont Avenue. After a few minutes of patrol units calling in nothing suspicious, Hughes then got on the radio and told all units to discontinue. There does come a point at which a manhunt becomes unproductive.

"Hey, good work, JB. We didn't get him, but you probably scared the living shit out of him. Crime scene can go through the woods in the morning; maybe he dropped something while running from you," I said to Burkett with a congratulatory tone.

"Maybe. If I was a few pounds lighter and a few years younger, I would've nabbed his felon ass." Burkett looked as though he was happy with himself.

"What was he doing when you saw him, JB?" Bergman asked him.

"I don't know. He was just kinda hanging out there at the end of the parking lot."

"Really, just standing there?" I asked.

JB stopped and thought for a second. "Yeah. That does seem a little odd. Doesn't it?"

It was strange that a rape subject would just be hanging around near the scene of the crime. Especially a serial rapist who was striking the same victim a second time; he must've known how we worked, that units would be around the area looking for him. Maybe he was getting a little bold. Getting bold was good. That meant mistakes would be made.

"Where's your car, JB?"

"I parked a few blocks away on the other side of the building. I thought I had a better chance of seeing something if I snuck in on foot. Guess I was right."

"I guess so," Bergman said.

"Well, listen, I have to catch up to Mac at the hospital and finish off the rape report. I need one of you guys to go back to the apartment and wait for Sex Crimes to show up and coordinate with them," I told them.

"I'll handle it, JB. You can take a break," Bergman told Burkett.

"No, I think I should go and just let them know what I saw," Burkett answered promptly.

"He's right. That would make the most sense," I said in agreement.

"The victim is at the hospital now. Right, Gary?" Burkett asked.

"Maybe not yet, but she is on her way."

At the time, I didn't realize that Burkett was making sure that he wouldn't be running into the victim.

"Okay, let me get going. Thanks for your help, guys." Burkett took off in a hurry to get back to his car.

Burkett called Mac on the radio to ask if the door was open. Mac had locked it.

"Call the superintendent. I told him one of us would be calling him to get in," she told Burkett.

"10-4. Thanks."

Burkett made his way into the apartment looking around and waiting for the Sex Crime investigators to show up. Now, he had something to talk to them about.

Outside, Bergman and I were discussing the odds of a repeat rape and whether the rapist was maybe getting sloppy, giving us a better chance of catching him.

"Hey," Bergman said to me, then stopped.

"What?" I asked.

"Ah, nothing. You get to the hospital. I'll get with you later."

"Okay, buddy. Later."

Within about 15 minutes, the Sex Crime investigators were at the apartment and I was pulling into the hospital parking lot into the "Police Only" parking area.

*****

Detective Patelli showed up and Burkett re-introduced himself. Patelli certainly remembered him.

"And you remember Detective Lake, I'm sure."

They nodded at each other with a polite smile.

"Don't know if you heard, but I had the perp in sight. I lost him during a foot pursuit. He must've had a jump on me of at least 20 yards. I couldn't catch up so I didn't get a better description or anything."

"I was monitoring your frequency. I heard. Nice job, Officer."

"Thanks, Detective. Maybe you can put in a good word for me when they get that task force off the ground. I'd like to get on it."

"The task force, huh? Well, that's still in the planning stage. This department tends to talk first and act later, much later. We'll see. Anything unusual in the apartment here that we should know about?" Patelli asked him.

"Ah, I don't know. I just got here and the victim is probably at the hospital by now."

"Well then, thanks, Officer. We'll take it from here and let you get back to work."

"If you don't mind, can I stick around and watch? Maybe pick up some pointers? I'm hoping to make detective one day. Maybe I can help you guys out."

"Sure, we can use the help, as long as your sergeant doesn't mind you being off the street."

"Nah, he's cool. You know, I had been trying to do some follow-up on this case. Do you remember that last time I told you I thought the perp might rape this victim again?"

"Yes, I do remember that. And what made you think that?" Patelli was fairly curious.

"I don't know. I tried to think what he was thinking. Here was a young single girl, living alone on a ground floor apartment. He already knew how to get in. He already had an escape route planned. It worked once. Why wouldn't it work again? That's just kinda what I was thinking."

"Well, looks like that was some pretty good thinking. Maybe you will make detective sometime," Patelli told Burkett.

That certainly put a smile on Burkett's face. Burkett walked around the apartment watching the detectives — what they were looking for, where they were looking and how they were looking. He knew they focused in on key areas: the point of entry, the path to the first contact with the victim, where and how the assault occurred and then what happened after — what the perp did and where he went and what the victim did. They looked any place that the perp could have left physical evidence or DNA, with the bed or site of the rape the most obvious. Clothes and undergarments had to be collected and packaged. Some rapists have been stupid enough to drop their wallets on the way out. You cannot overlook any possibility.

They started looking around the bedroom slowly and carefully. Again, the actual rape occurred on the bed. Burkett looked around the bedroom carefully. He was absorbing the scene; he noticed little things lying around such as jewelry and scraps of paper.

"Look at this," Patelli said as he lifted up the bed's blanket.

Lake and Burkett walked over on each side of him and looked at several strands of pubic hair grouped together.

"That's a little odd. Isn't it?" Lake asked.

"Yeah, it is," Patelli answered. "The way it's just sitting there. Doesn't really look random. Does it?"

He looked at Burkett and told him, "Usually, if we find pubic hair, it's one or two isolated hairs. This looks like... I don't know, just different."

Lake carefully collected the sample and placed it in an evidence bag.

"Just like he was hanging out in the parking lot when I saw him, maybe he's just getting weird, doing stupid things. Whatta ya think?" Burkett asked anxiously.

Patelli just shrugged his shoulders and didn't really answer. They spent the next hour picking up bits of evidence, their hands covered in those white latex gloves, using tweezers from sterile containers so they would not contaminate the evidence, taking photographs and measurements and sketching out the crime scene. Burkett observed every move they made and took copious mental notes.

The next night at roll call, the repeat rape of Nina Wilkes dominated the conversation. Sergeant Hughes complimented Burkett for his foot pursuit and attempted apprehension of the suspect. For some reason Thompson could not come up with some sarcastic remark to put down Burkett. That seemed to be just what Burkett needed; he finally showed some sign of coming back to life. Now, he spoke a little more and had that stupid smile back on his face. Maybe his near arrest would raise his spirits that had plunged since his suspension and especially since the awards ceremony. As we headed out to the street I saw Burkett waiting for everyone to leave the roll call room. As the room emptied out, he approached Hughes. I did not know what he wanted to talk to Hughes about, but I presumed it was an "I told you so."

*****

"Hey Sarge, you got a minute?" Burkett said in a soft voice.

"Sure, JB, what's up?"

"I don't mean to sound disrespectful, sir, but remember how you got on me for following-up on the Nina Wilkes rape?"

"Hold on, JB. Let's get this straight. I didn't get on you for following-up on the rape. I told you that Ms. Wilkes didn't want you to contact her anymore. You were making her very uncomfortable. We can't be doing that to rape victims, or to any citizen. I told you to stay away from her. That's it."

"Okay, but if you remember, I told you that I was worried that the rapist might strike her again, and I was just trying to make sure she was safe the next time, right?"

"Yes, JB. And the way it worked out, it was a good call on your part. But that doesn't change you contacting her. I am still ordering you not to go near her."

"No, no, sir, I got that. It's just that since I did figure out what was gonna happen and because I followed-up, I almost caught the bastard. I was wondering if that would help with my appeal. And that Detective Patelli thought this might help me get on that task force they're forming. Maybe if the chief or deputy chief knows what I did, he may not want to suspend me after all."

"Ah, I don't know about that, JB. But I tell you what, I'll call the D.C. and let him know what a good job you did last night with this whole thing and see what he says. To be honest with you, I wouldn't count on it helping. They have your appeal and they should be ruling on it soon. It's already taken much too long. But I will make this call."

"Yes, sir, thank you."

Burkett walked out to join the rest of us on patrol, knowing his chances of slipping out of that three day suspension were thin.

There had been at least one rape in each precinct, in the last month, believed to have been committed by the serial rapist. There was no pattern as to the days, times and location of the rapes, no solid leads and no suspects. I was concerned about Janie. No particular reason she would be targeted, but no reason she wouldn't be either. To make matters worse, she lived in a ground floor apartment. Maybe I should have her move in with me for a while, at least till this bastard got caught. I would have to think about making that offer. If she said yes, I wasn't sure how that would go; if she said no, I wasn't sure what that would mean.

Chapter 14

If time kept moving this fast, I would need to start planning my retirement. Hughes' end of summer party was approaching. So much had happened since the last one and it seemed to have occurred in the blink of an eye. I certainly was no longer a rookie. Bergman and I were car to car drinking coffee across from a Triple 7 and just shooting the breeze.

"So, how are things with you and your girl Janie going?"

"Pretty good. Looks like it's getting serious."

"Is that good or bad?"

"Good question." I had to laugh. "She's a great girl. And I do think I love her. But I am still kinda young. I don't know if marriage is really what I want right now."

"Has she said she wants to marry you?"

I had to think about that question for a moment.

"Well, actually, no. She has not mentioned anything about us getting married. It's more just about a serious, monogamous relationship, that kind of stuff. I was just assuming..."

"Well, then don't assume. Just chill, and don't be so presumptuous. Maybe she's not sure if she wants to marry you. Could be that she's just trying to make the most of it for whatever life expectancy it has."

Hmm, I never really thought of it that way. Janie seemed too serious; I couldn't imagine that she was getting into this relationship without a long term plan, but who knew? Bergman could be right. Not that he knew Janie, but he came off as having an unemotional, realistic view of life.

"Maybe you're right, Berg, and not to sound too arrogant, but when a girl starts talking about all that serious shit, and she's a couple of years older than me, I'm thinking... that she's thinking... that probably that's where this is heading."

"Just wait and see and enjoy the ride, my friend."

"Hey, why don't we all go out one night? You got anyone steady you're seeing?"

"Nah, I haven't hooked up with anything like that yet. Had a few good dates. Getting some good pussy here and there, but nothing I'd want to double date with yet. We'll do it sometime. It'd be fun. I've been going to that Warehouse Night Club you told me about. Maybe I'll get as lucky as you did with Janie, without getting shot, of course."

"Of course. You know, since we're on the subject of pussy, there is apparently a tradition to celebrate a rookie's initiation to non-rookie status that you may have heard about." I told him.

"No, I haven't heard."

"That's probably because Thompson's the one who usually sets it up and I guess you and he aren't on great terms."

"I don't really talk to him much. I mean, whenever he's been my back-up, he did what he had to do. And I've done the same for him. He's a good cop. But he's also a pompous asshole. I've never seen a guy so wrapped up in himself."

"I can't argue that."

"And what's up with him lately anyway? He's either late or leaving early two days of each shift and we gotta cover for him. What's that about?"

"I don't know. Good question. I asked him once if everything was okay at home, and he nearly bit my head off," I told Bergman.

"You'd think Hughes would tell him to cut the crap, but I don't think Hughes would say anything to him. I think Hughes is afraid of the senior guys for some reason."

"You may be right, Matt. He certainly doesn't have Thompson under control."

"How the fuck did you spend six weeks riding with Thompson without shooting the bastard?"

'Well, you know, when you're a rookie, you just take it. But, I don't get the impression you were too intimidated as a rookie. You stood up to his bullshit that night in the locker room."

"You learn that early in life in New York City. Once someone makes you eat a little shit, they don't stop and they keep shoving it down your throat. It's a whole lot easier if you give the message up front — throw shit at me and I'll ram it down your motherfuck'n throat. That usually works."

Maybe that worked for him better than it did for others. I thought I was fairly tough and brave, but Bergman definitely had a big set of balls on him. I admired that. I wish I had stood up, not just to Thompson, but to a number of other guys just like him during my school years. I guess we all have those stories. It's a good thing we grow up and forget about it. Well, we grow up, but do we really forget? Maybe those who don't forget become either serial murderers or cops. That was a discomfiting thought.

"So anyway, tell me about my traditional initiation," Bergman brought back the subject.

"Have you heard about Bullet Brenda?"

"No, I haven't. But I guess I'm about to."

I explained just what Bullet Brenda was all about. Bergman's face reflected no reaction.

"Sounds like you got a little piece of that yourself, huh?"

I didn't answer that question, sensing his disapproval of this initiation rite.

"I think I'll pass," Bergman continued, realizing I was taking the fifth.

"I'll get my BJs the old fashioned way, buying girls drinks at nightclubs, hoping to get lucky. Besides, why the hell would I take a chance like that? Some tramp gets arrested for something, and then she starts spilling the beans that she's been sucking off cops and getting bullets in return. Who the fuck knows what she's doing with those bullets? That's just plain fuck'n dangerous, Gary. I don't want to be your mother, but my advice to you is to stay the hell away from anything like that. Especially if it comes from Thompson, it's gotta be stupid." Bergman was not wavering on that decision.

That made me stop and think. Here's Bergman with less time on the streets than me and he certainly was displaying much better street sense and judgment than I had. I never thought about what might happen if Bullet Brenda started talking. How would the department handle that? It wouldn't be pretty. Bergman had some smarts. I wondered what he was gonna do when Liz started hitting on him, which I was sure she would. She already seemed taken by his brash and outspoken personality.

"309 Baker," the dispatcher called.

"309 Baker, go," Bergman answered.

"309 Baker, you have a two car accident, possible injuries, exit 3 on the northbound interstate. Medics en route."

Bergman finished his coffee and started to head out.

"Buddy, if you need help, call Thompson. I'm tired," I told him.

Bergman smiled, flashed me the finger and drove off. I headed back to the apartment complex where Faith Newman got raped a while back. If the rapist was bold enough to rape Nina Wilkes twice, why wouldn't he strike Faith again? Maybe that was his M.O. He could be getting off on raping a girl over and over, really feeling powerful. I'd like to catch him breaking into some girl's apartment. He wouldn't feel so powerful with my boot up his ass. It was pretty quiet in the apartments. I stopped to talk to some of the men hanging out on the front stoop of one of their buildings. They knew I wasn't looking for their beer cans or liquor bottles.

"Hey, guys. What's going on tonight?"

"Not much, Officer. How about you?"

"Nothing really. You guys know that there's been a lot of rapes in the city lately? Have you heard anything?"

"No, just some white guy that you all can't catch. Ain't none of us, as you can probably see, Officer." That drew some laughs.

"I know that. But I tell you what, if you do see a white guy walking around in black clothes with a hooded sweatshirt, why don't you give us a call? I don't want you doing anything. He may be someone completely innocent, but just call us and let us check it out. Would that be okay?"

"Sure thing, Officer. I tell you what, though. We'd call anyway if we saw any white guy walking around here, except a police officer, of course." That got even more laughs. Actually, I had to laugh too.

While they were being polite and friendly, it wasn't like I didn't know that they were trying to get rid of me. And it also wasn't like I didn't know there was little chance of them cooperating. But, for a rapist, I thought they might. They had wives and daughters they worried about. I wanted to be real careful with my words. I didn't want them attacking the first white guy they saw in dark clothing and then saying I told them to do that.

Driving around aimlessly, I made my way back onto the boulevard. Then I heard Stryker getting called on the side channel. I couldn't recognize the voice at first, but then I got it. It was Gillis trying to meet up with Stryker. I couldn't imagine that Gillis was out this late at night just to pay Stryker a social call. Something was up. And it wasn't hard to figure out. Gillis was a Narcotics detective now. He had one of his deals going down. They were meeting across from the Triple 7 where Bullet Brenda worked. I knew where that was. I decided to start heading in that direction, once again leaving my sector when I knew I shouldn't. If there was going to be any action, I wanted to be close by and be a part of it. Parking a few blocks away where I was able to see them, I felt strange; basically I was conducting surveillance on two cops. They talked for a while. Then I watched them drive off, Stryker following Gillis' unmarked car.

I sat around for almost half an hour doing nothing. I kept moving my position so some citizen wouldn't see me just sitting there. I didn't like what I was doing. Anything could've been happening in the Heights, but I certainly wasn't going to find it by sitting around. Like last time I was here, if there was a call, I'd be late getting to it. Sometimes you gotta follow your gut. I pulled in to the Triple 7. Thankfully, Bullet Brenda wasn't working that night. I got a cup of coffee and headed back to my car.

Before I could open the door, I heard what I thought was a gun shot. I stopped — I was not sure, or maybe I was sure, but just in disbelief. Then I heard another exchange of gunfire. Three, four, maybe even more rounds. I knew the direction, but did not know exactly where those shots came from. Stunned, I dropped my coffee, which splattered all over my pant leg as I rushed into the car to radio it in. Before I could, Gillis was on the radio.

"Officer down." I heard Gillis' voice full of air, almost like a loud whisper. Like every other cop listening on that frequency, I froze and chills went through my body, never really expecting to ever hear that call.

"And I've taken a hit," he continued, sounding like he was having trouble talking, even breathing. "Subjects are in a black pick-up last seen heading north on Lamont towards Highway 10. Send medics and back-up ASAP. We're at the Westland Park Motel on Lamont and 7th. We..." And then the transmission ended.

I knew I was close, but I had to get my map out anyway. After hearing those shots, my hands were unsteady and I fumbled with the map. Unable to catch my breath, I did not even try to get on the radio to say that I was en route. I was only six blocks away and headed there not knowing what to expect or what I was going to do. The red glow of the motel's few lights that weren't already burnt out, was visible when I was about two blocks away. The motel was a two story brick building painted white in a U-shape, with three sides. I was the first one on the scene — no surprise; I had just about been stalking them. I knew where they were by the red revolving lights of Stryker's car on the west side of the motel and went over to it.

Gillis was on the front seat holding the radio with one hand, holding onto the steering wheel with the other, trying not to fall out of the car. He had been hit in the leg and shoulder; it looked like it was close to the heart. He was bleeding but luckily, he was strong enough to get back to the car and get on the radio to call it in.

"Where the fuck is Stryker?" I yelled at him in anger and frustration.

"He's on the other side of the motel. It's bad. It's real bad."

Running to the other side, I stopped, almost in shock at the sight of Stryker lying on the ground in this dimly-lit parking lot with beer cans and trash strewn about him. The breeze had blown newspaper out of the open big green trash bin, up against his body. I bent over and removed the newspaper. It made no difference, but it was just too demeaning to see a wounded officer covered in trash. He had taken a shot in the head. The bleeding was profuse and he was lying in the middle of this pool of his own blood. He was alive, gasping for air, unable to talk.

"Don't move, Strkye. Help is on the way."

I got on my portable radio, screaming in terror and desperation; I was nearly incoherent.

"321 Baker, Stryker is shot. It's bad. Have the medics step it up. Gillis has been hit twice, move it, move it." I was yelling and there was no disguising my panic.

That was not great police jargon, but I got the message out. My voice was crackling with fear. There were tears swelling in my eyes. Of course the ambulance was moving as fast as it could, but I just had to do or say something. Finally, I heard the sirens approaching. I knew they would go first to the patrol cars with the red lights revolving.

"Stryke, I'm just going to meet up with the medics and bring them back here. I'm not leaving you. Hang in there."

He couldn't answer me; he did not move or make any expression. The hole just above his left eye continued to ooze blood. Stryker's eyes were wide open, but they just stared straight into the night sky. I could not even be sure he was able to hear me, but I felt he did. It was only from hearing those gurgling gasps of breath that I knew he was alive. I wanted him to know he was not just being left there. By the time I ran back to my car, the ambulance was there. It was a short run, but I could hardly breathe. Just having seen Stryker lying there sent me into a cold sweat. I was shaking uncontrollably. You would have thought I had been shot. Gillis waved me over.

"Get his phone," he told me.

"What?" I half yelled in disbelief.

"Get his phone and give it to me later. It's important. Just do it."

"Okay."

I was directing the medics back to get Stryker, trying to free myself of talking to Gillis, especially after such a strange request at a critical moment. Running back with the medics, I saw the red lights flashing in the distance and I heard the sirens of the other units coming to help. Unfortunately, there was not much that they would be able to do. As Stryker was carefully lifted and put into the ambulance, I had almost forgotten what Gillis asked. Pretending to lay a comforting hand on Stryker, I quickly and without being noticed slipped Stryker's cell phone off his belt and into my pocket. Stryker was rushed off.

Gillis' wounds were serious, but not life threatening. I didn't want the ambulance to leave with Gillis before I could get a good description of the perps. Gillis was still alert and coherent. He gave me a very good description — he already had been dealing with them in an undercover role. He knew only their first names, but was able to remember the license plate.

"Did you get his phone?" he asked me.

"No, I didn't see it. I'll go back and look for it. But first let's get you taken care of."

"Okay, but when you find it, you call me. Just some personal stuff of his I want to protect, like with his wife and all, ya know?"

"I got it. I'll call you."

Gillis was a strange one, and a poor actor. He and his friend were just shot and he was worrying about a phone. Something stunk. Something usually did stink during a Gillis operation. Ramming my fist down his throat before they rolled him into the ambulance would have been quite cathartic.

Sergeant Hughes arrived. This was the first time in a while that I had seen him out on the street. He called dispatch and asked them to request the Kansas City Police Department to get their helicopter heading in the direction of the fleeing vehicle. They did it within minutes. Our zone commander redirected about 10 units to start the search for the vehicle. The SWAT team was mobilized to make the arrest once these two were found. And they would be found. You cannot shoot two cops and get that far. An all points bulletin was broadcast and every neighboring police department was looking for them. It was just a matter of time.

Internal Affairs would, eventually, be interviewing Gillis and hopefully, Stryker would survive to be interviewed. I did not see anything, but I knew exactly what happened. It was another one of Gillis' reckless arrests. I just didn't get it. He was on Narcotics now. Surely, they had a more organized method of conducting undercover deals and making arrests. Gillis probably tried to pull the same stunt here that he did when we arrested Willie Dixon, and probably the same thing when Fiero and I had to get him and Stryker out of that jam. Why was he allowed to work like that?

The Crime Scene Unit, in their big van, arrived and started their processing of the scene with all that fancy equipment, just like the last time I saw them. They were impressive to watch. The chief was getting briefed by Sergeant Hughes and the zone commander. Within 20 minutes, the media started to arrive; they routinely monitored the police frequencies with their scanners looking for this kind of action. The chief knew once again he would have to hold a press conference. I remembered my shooting clearly and the fear I felt. I thought that was bad, but it was nothing like what I just saw Stryker going through. I wondered if he was even able to feel pain, or did he even know just how bad things looked?

By now, the entire squad was at the scene, except for Stryker's buddy Thompson. He had taken a few hours of personal leave and left early, again. Just like Thompson: not there for a friend in crisis. Unfortunately, there was nothing for anyone to do. Hughes got back to us and gathered us in a group. There was not much he could tell us other than it was an undercover drug deal that went bad — very bad.

Yeah, no shit, was all I could say to myself.

Hughes asked that we all pray for Stryker. Edmonds, of course, offered to lead us in that prayer. That was probably not what Hughes had in mind, but what the hell? We needed something spiritual. However, we still had a few hours left to the shift and we had to continue to work, as difficult as that was. The business of police work could not stop. Other police departments faced these kinds of crises more often than we did and they worked through it. Hughes sent Mac to pick up Stryker's wife and kids and stay with them at the hospital. Hughes, a thoughtful and caring man, told us that we would switch off and never leave Stryker's wife and kids without our presence until his condition improved.

"Okay now, we need to get back to patrol," Hughes told us in a voice that was cracking.

We all just stood there, motionless and staring at each other, as if nobody wanted to be the first one to move.

"Back to patrol. Now, please," he said again.

That was the most assertive I could remember ever seeing Hughes act. Bergman was the first to move and then we all followed. I headed back into the Heights. I drove around with my mind on anything other than patrol. There probably could have been an armed robbery happening right in front of my eyes and I would not have seen it. I was hoping I would not get a call. I did not know how I would handle it. I imagined everyone else felt the same way. Yet, we all knew that we could not stop. We had to keep working: all of us.

About an hour and a half later, the dispatcher came on the radio.

"All units, 10-3. All units, 10-3."

Pulling over and getting my pen ready to write if it was my call, I waited for the emergency broadcast.

"All units, Chief Harper advises that two subjects wanted in connection with the shooting of Officer Paul Stryker have been arrested without incident. More information will be disseminated at roll calls. Everyone is reminded that contact with the media is prohibited."

That was good news, though I was sure most of us would have preferred that the two were not taken without incident: that they decided to go out in a blaze of glory like some do, and gave us a chance to blow the shit out of them. Now there would be a trial — a fair trial. That meant the possibility of them getting away with it.

About another hour passed with nothing else unusual happening during this fucked-up night until the dispatcher got on the radio again.

"All units, 10-3. All units, 10-3."

Once again I pulled over to await the emergency broadcast.

"Attention all units. Attention all units. Chief Harper regrets to inform you that as of 5:27 a.m. today, Officer Paul Stryker died from injuries sustained in the line of duty."

Chapter 15

It was noon and the sun shone directly above us, making us a little warm in our dress uniforms. But there would be no unbuttoning of collars or cuffs and hats stayed on the head. Police funerals were always held with the utmost respect and dignity. The police honor guard moved in an exact and deliberate cadence with military precision. The flag-draped casket was carried by white-gloved police officers perfectly attired, who also walked in a well-rehearsed and coordinated gait. The bagpipes played Amazing Grace in the background. Gillis, one hand using a walking cane and his other arm in a sling, was escorting the sobbing widow on one side. He was avoiding eye contact with almost everybody. Certainly, he must have been carrying around an awful amount of guilt. He would carry that with him for a long time, if not forever. Thompson escorted Stryker's widow on the other side. As for Thompson, he was in pain and he was grieving. He had lost a friend and knew that he was not there when his friend needed him. But even at a funeral, you could see in his face that by escorting the widow, he enjoyed being at the center of attention.

There were cops from all over the country. They stood grouped together by department in a circle surrounding the casket. The mosaic formed by the differing colors of their uniforms gave some sense of beauty to the solemn, morose ceremony. The chief from each neighboring police department within a 50-mile radius was also there standing in front of his or her officers. There were quite a few female chiefs in our area, which surprised me. Just the sheer number of police officers present somehow gave meaning to Stryker's life and his truly unnecessary death. The District Attorney, the Mayor and the Governor made their presence known. Not that they did not sincerely feel for the death of a police officer, but they also knew the political cost of not being at the funeral of an officer killed so violently in the line of duty. Edmonds asked to read a prayer over the casket and Stryker's wife agreed. Though a short prayer, Edmonds could not make it through without hesitating to fight back the tears.

The emotions of the funeral were enough to make jaded cops cry — and they did. As the police officer handed Stryker's wife the folded flag, she broke down, one more time. Her eyes shielded by dark sunglasses, she rubbed her red, running nose. With her young children standing patiently at her side, with innocent, blank stares, unaware of the tragedy that had beset their young lives, she nearly fell out of her chair trying to embrace them. She reached into her handbag and motioned for a glass of water to help down the pills she was about to take.

Sergeant Hughes began to wipe the tears from his eyes. Watching the sergeant cry made my eyes swell with tears, though I would not allow myself to cry. Finding myself staring at Gillis I wondered if I felt bad for him — sympathetic that he was shot or that he got his friend shot — or was I more angry by what I thought was rogue police work by an out-of-control cop?

A cop was dead and life went on. Nothing changed.

The IA Shooting Review Board interviewed me not too long after the funeral. I was not involved in the shooting, so they did not give me the same time to re-compose myself as last time.

"Did you know about this arrest that Gillis was about to do?"

"Of course not. How would I know?" I answered, angered at the suggestion. Didn't they know that nobody ever seemed to know what Gillis was up to? Somehow I failed to mention that I suspected something was up when I heard Gillis call Stryker on the side channel. Was I lying? Yeah, I guess by omission.

"We understand that you and Officer Fiero once had to respond to the scene of an arrest Officers Gillis and Stryker were attempting."

"Yes, that's correct."

"And what happened?"

"When we arrived we found Officer Gillis restraining one subject. Officer Stryker was trying to fend off two other subjects."

"Did you find this to be a particularly dangerous situation?"

"Yes, sir, I did. Officer Gillis had secured his subject and had his weapon drawn. That left Stryker outnumbered two to one. I believe that if Officer Fiero and I had not arrived when we did, Officer Stryker may have been overpowered or would have been forced to shoot."

"What do you think happened that led to that situation?"

"Sir, I did not see what led to this situation. I only know that when I got there I considered the situation very dangerous."

"We understand that at one time you affected a narcotics arrest with Officer Gillis. Is that correct?"

"Yes, sir, I did."

"Did you call for back-up or notify your sergeant before the arrest?"

"No, sir."

"Why not?"

"Sir, with all due respect, I was just a rookie in training, at the time, riding with Gillis. I followed his lead."

"Okay, fair enough. Anything else, Officer?"

"No, sir, just that Officer Gillis told me that he didn't like to let anyone know about a drug arrest. He was worried that someone may leak it out or drive by and ruin the deal."

"Okay Officer, we will be in touch."

Surprisingly, they did not ask where I responded from, as I was the first one on the scene. IA seemed to know something about Gillis, though. I hoped I said what I really wanted to say, without actually saying it. Gillis was out of control; he was dangerous. To say that outright was to blame him for Stryker's death. That was more than I was willing to do, at least while on record.

The summer was one of pain and misery for our squad. For the first time, Hughes canceled his barbeque. There was just no mood of festivity. Roll calls lacked any levity. We spoke only about business; I was surprised that I actually missed the stupid jokes that I usually found so sophomoric. Thompson was finally keeping his mouth shut. Bergman toned down what was referred to as his New York personality. We were making more arrests for drinking in public and disorderly conduct than usual. I imagined that we had all become so angry and frustrated — looking for a way to vent — that we now had no tolerance for even the minor crimes that we previously found ourselves too busy to handle.

There were other concerns and rumors going around our squad and the department. There were a lot of questions as to whether Sergeant Hughes was going to be found at fault. Certainly IA and the chief would want to know how such a mess occurred under his watch. Why did Stryker think he could go and pull off a drug deal without notifying his sergeant? I guess for the same reason Gillis always had — and gotten away with it. The question was, did Hughes have any control over his squad? Hughes must have been thinking about that himself. Sergeant Ladd of Narcotics was also being investigated and he must've been asking himself the same questions as Hughes.

Why was Gillis out late at night without the rest of the Narcotics team? Why didn't Ladd know what was going on? Was he in control of his detectives? Then there was Gillis. His arrest got a cop killed. What fault were they going to find with him? He and Stryker were friends and experienced cops who had worked together before; why would they take such a stupid risk? There were a lot of questions that IA was going to have to answer. Everybody knew that heads would have to roll, but whose heads was the question. The shooting was played out in the press in a way that made the department look terrible. Why not? What happened was indefensible. It was bad police work. That was the sad truth. The chief was going to hold somebody accountable.

After several more weeks, we were almost getting back to normal on the squad. Even grief managed to pass with time. There was a little more light-hearted banter. A new officer would have to be assigned to us soon to replace Stryker and the team always wondered how a new person would affect the social balance on the squad. The IA investigation was complete. Nobody was supposed to know that, but we all did. Sergeant Hughes had his meeting with the chief coming up sometime next week; we were not supposed to know that either. Knowing a resolution was soon seemed to be good for Hughes; he was loosening up a bit. Sometimes in life, the wait is worse than the results. Hughes, like everybody else, heard he was going to take a hit. He just did not know how bad it was going to be. On patrol, we had not heard what was going to happen back in the Detective Bureau, and that really was not our concern.

My cell phone rang as I pulled into the precinct parking lot.

"Hey buddy, it's JB."

"Hey JB, what's up? Why you calling on my cell? Aren't I going to see you in roll call in a few minutes?"

"No, I won't be in. That's why I'm calling you."

"You want me to tell the Sarge you're out sick or something?"

"No, he knows. I just wanted to tell you that I got two days suspended. I'm starting tonight."

"Oh, I'm sorry to hear that."

"No, that's actually good news. It was supposed to be three days, but they gave me some credit for almost nabbing the rapist that night. Cool, huh?"

"I guess. See you next shift."

That was probably a bit terse and rude of me, but I did not know what else to do; it was so awkward. Seeing through Burkett was not difficult. He wanted me to spread the word that his near arrest was recognized and awarded. That would take the bite out of the suspension. Being disciplined like that was a professional insult, almost a humiliation.

Bergman and I decided to meet for an early dinner. That would be around 10:30 p.m. We went to a local greasy spoon which was built like a box car, sitting on a side road. You had to know it was there. You certainly couldn't see it off any highway or main street. It had a dirt parking lot, with a gas station right next to it. On the other side was some vacant land that was always home to abandoned tires, glass bottles and general trash. The ambience wasn't great, but they served the absolute best omelets. They served them 24/7. And, they were cheap. That's a cop's kind of place. The city paid us enough to live comfortably, but we still had to count our pennies every now and then.

"So, can you talk about your IA interview or are you sworn to secrecy?" Bergman asked me.

"I'm sworn to secrecy. That's how IA works."

There was some silence as we put the cream and sugar in our respective coffees and started stirring with slightly stained spoons. Then Bergman looked up at me with an impish grin.

"So, what did you tell them?"

With my own impish grin, I answered him.

"I told them the truth, which really wasn't much. I didn't see what happened; I just saw the results. Then they asked me about a couple of other Gillis' things I got involved with."

"And?"

"And, I told them that Gillis had told me he didn't like telling too many people about his drug arrests. He worried that either someone would leak it out or fuck it up somehow."

"Then that's that. You told them what you know."

I gave a heavy exhale of breath and looked down at my coffee. Bergman looked at me, just knowing there was something more that I was going to say.

"Hey Matt, I gotta tell you something."

"I'm here."

Bergman looked at me, when he saw I was hesitating.

"Gary, if there's something going on, you gotta give it up."

"No, there's nothing going on. It's just that I've always known what a dangerous cop Gillis was. I just never said anything to anybody. You've heard me bitch about the way he does things. It was almost like he was on a path to get one of us killed and I sat by and watched. I probably should have told Hughes what I thought."

"What good would that have done? We've talked about that. Hughes sits in the precinct correcting the grammar on our reports and charting out our stats. He doesn't know what the fuck is going on out there. That's probably what IA is gonna find out from their investigation of this cluster fuck."

"Well, then instead of Hughes, I should've gone to IA. But, I didn't. I didn't even tell them now how dangerous I think he is. I only hinted at it."

"Gary, to be honest with you, you should've told them what you thought. I guess if you weren't my only friend on the squad I'd be a little annoyed with you for not doing so, but, which one of us is perfect? I'm..."

"Somehow you don't seem to make these fuck-ups," I interrupted him, finding myself almost angry with Bergman for not screwing up like the rest of us.

"No, I just don't admit it when I do."

"Fuck, this ain't good, Matt. I'm not doing my job. I need to be a better cop. Maybe if I had said something back when, Stryker would be alive now."

"Whoa, hold up, pal. You are not responsible for Stryker's death. Don't even go there. That was Gillis' fuck up, not yours. Let him live with it. I'll tell you something else that nobody is saying, but they should be. Now, I don't mean to talk shit about Stryker after he gets killed, but let's face it, he was an experienced cop. He knew what he was doing. He should have never gone on those arrests with Gillis. It was his own fuck'n fault. I know that sounds harsh, but it's the truth."

"But they were friends; he probably trusted him and didn't want to let him down."

"Listen, Gary, you're my closest friend in this department and I trust you. But if you ask me to go do something that I think is unsafe, I ain't doing it. And if I found out you were a dirty cop I would call you into IA in a New York fuck'n minute. I expect you would do the same thing if it were me. We're cops first, friends second."

"You're right, Matt. So what do I do now?"

"Nothing, there's nothing to do. Calling IA just to get your opinion off your chest will make you look stupid and won't help anything. Let's see what happens from the IA investigation first. But just remember, you're not a rookie anymore. If there is something you don't like, handle it. That's what you're paid for."

"So, how is it that you have all the right answers?"

"Only for everyone else, my friend, never for myself. Like I said, I just learned to hide my screw-ups."

I thought about what I wanted to say next. Bergman looked at me.

"Something else, Gary?"

"No. That's it.

We slopped up every last morsel of egg off our plate with our toast. That was one good meal. It would only be two or three more hours before I would need something else to eat. Then we headed out back to patrol. The next few hours were uneventful. I locked up one drunk driver. Fiero made a traffic stop and caught a guy with an outstanding warrant for robbery, wanted by the Kansas City Police Department. Then the emergency broadcast came over the air.

"321 Baker, 321 Baker, armed robbery in progress at the Triple 7." The dispatcher gave me the location and I knew it right away. Like most cops, it didn't take long to know the location of most of the Triple 7s. Edmonds was backing me up. It had been about two years now, but I had not forgotten anything about getting shot at the armed robbery of a convenience store. That was not happening to me again.

Heading directly to the Triple 7, I came down a street that left me right in front of it, about two blocks down. Turning off my headlights and pulling off the road, like we all did approaching these kinds of calls, I moved slowly and cautiously. Reaching into my bag, I found my binoculars quickly and started to scope out the Triple 7. It was well-lit from the inside, which made my observations easy. I saw the clerk at the counter and a customer or two walking around. One went to the counter to pay for something, then left. The other was perusing some magazines. This did not appear to be a robbery in progress, but I was not going to live through that again. Edmonds got on the radio and said he was only a few seconds away. Transmitting my location, I asked him to meet me there. When he arrived, I gave him the binoculars and had him take a look. He held them up to his eyes and studied the Triple 7 for quite a few minutes.

"What does it look like to you?" I asked him.

"Not much. Certainly don't look like no robbery in progress."

"Yeah, but as you know, I've been through this before. I've learned a lesson about things not looking like they really are."

We discussed this a little more and agreed on a plan. I pulled up about a block away off to the side. Edmonds maintained surveillance with the binoculars. I asked dispatch to find a phone number and call in to the clerk, asking him if he could walk out and talk to me. Dispatch did call in and gave the clerk those instructions.

"I see him on the phone now. Nothing suspicious" was Edmonds' broadcast.

"Good, let me know when he gets outside the store."

"He should be out about riiight... now."

I walked up to the side of the store and called to the clerk. He saw me standing there in full uniform, so he responded when I waved for him to come over. Asking him what was happening inside the store, I listened as he responded relaxed and nonchalantly. He told me nothing was happening and sounded quite sincere, surprised by my question. I told him that we had received a call about a robbery in progress.

"Officer," he said laughing, "there is no robbery. Business is pretty quiet as it usually is this time of night. Just look for yourself."

Calm and composed, he was convincing. The only thing that was suspicious now was the telephone call claiming there was a robbery. I was not letting it go that easy. I called for one more back-up unit.

Mac responded. At that point there was only one person, besides the clerk, in the store. We had him come out. We identified him and ran him for warrants; he was clean. Mac stayed with that man and the clerk outside the Triple 7 while Edmonds and I did a complete search, with our guns drawn. We found nothing. There was no sign of a robbery in progress. Edmonds saw my hesitation to accept that fact.

"Gary, I understand what you're thinking. I really do. But you know, we get hoax calls now and then. This is probably just one of them. There's no robbery going on here."

"Let's call it." Reluctantly and very nervous that I was making the wrong call, I agreed with Edmonds. There was no way one of these calls was going to do to me what it did to Burkett.

I radioed it in as a hoax call, but I went back to my first spot two blocks down and watched the store for another 15 minutes. Then I drove off. Ten minutes later I drove back. Everything looked the same. I would have probably stayed and watched even a little longer at that point if I hadn't gotten another call on the radio.

"321 Baker, rape just occurred, called in by victim named Vicki Cordero." The dispatcher then gave me the address. The information sounded familiar, very familiar. Yes, it was the girlfriend of the biker who whacked me in the face with the chair. Did she get raped by a stranger, maybe the serial rapist, or did her biker boyfriend have something to do with this? That would not be the first time for a domestic violence rape. I would not mind another chance to lock his ass up. That was unlikely; he should still be in jail. This time I would be more careful and not need Bergman to fight my battles.

"10-4. ETA 3. Please determine if this sounds like the same serial rapist."

"That's 10-4, 321 Baker. Subject was described as a heavyset white male, wearing dark clothes and a hooded sweatshirt tied tightly over his face. Also wearing ski mask. He left through the front door of the victim's apartment, unknown direction. Sex Crimes is en route."

"Car 300 to dispatch, send 320 as back-up and have 310 and 312 respond to the scene. I'll meet them out there and we'll coordinate a search for the subject," Hughes directed over the radio.

Hughes was coming out on the street to take control. I guess things had changed since Stryker's death. Poor Burkett, he was home on suspension. He'd be out there looking hard for the suspect. He wanted to make that arrest. He saw that as his ticket to making detective.

When we got to the apartment building, I remembered that particular stench in the hallway; that had not changed. I could not put aside my frustration with our new rape victim for not pressing charges against that asshole biker boyfriend of hers and then me having to come back to get my face smashed in.

She answered the door and from her reaction I could tell that she recognized me immediately.

"Come in, Officers," she said politely.

"Ma'am, are you alone?" I asked.

"Yes, he flew out of here about 10 minutes ago."

She had one hand resting on top of her black straggly hair and was walking around in circles. Her oversized plaid shirt hung down to her knees; that was all she seemed to be wearing. Her sad, dark brown eyes looked the same as the last time I saw her. She was not crying. Her lip was bleeding and was beginning to bruise, the same way her eye bruised last time we were there. She seemed bewildered, in disbelief.

"Okay, and your boyfriend Rob, where is he?"

"Where is he? Whatta ya kidding? He's in jail. You should know that. You're the one who put him there."

"Yes, I know. I'm just checking."

"Yeah, and I'm sorry, by the way, for the way he whacked you in your face that night."

"Well, let's forget that now. Let's focus on what just happened to you."

She was worried that I would not treat her well given the fight I had with her boyfriend, though I tried to send a much different message. In reality, I had to really concentrate on looking at her as any other victim. I was pissed over what had happened. But I did my job professionally, and put those sentiments behind me.

"Let's sit down. What we first need to do is for you to tell us exactly what you can about his description. We have officers out there looking for him right now. What can you tell me?"

"I was sleeping. I think I woke up 'cause I heard like a thud. Then I saw the door to the balcony open up and this big fuck'n thing dressed in black came running right at me. I was starting to sit up and he jumped on top of me and just started punching me. Finally, he knocked me so hard I just stopped resisting. Then he put some kind of knife right to my throat."

I was able to see some small nicks on her neck where he had placed the knife.

"Can you describe him?"

"Not really. He was wearing one of those masks, like you see on TV when someone robs a bank. And he had a hood over that. I'm pretty sure he was a white guy. I didn't see his hands 'cause he was wearing gloves, but between his gloves and sleeves, I saw white skin. And he looked dumpy, you know, kinda fat."

"What did he say to you?"

"He spoke in a real low voice. He told me to do what he said and he wouldn't hurt me anymore. Then he pulled my hair back, put the knife at the neck and forced me to get out of bed. Then he told me to get undressed."

"Okay, I have to ask, what were you wearing?"

"Just this."

"You mean the shirt you have on now?"

"Yeah, I put it back on."

"I'm sorry to have to ask you this, but were you wearing any underwear or bra or anything underneath?"

"No, this is how I sleep." She was fairly calm and apparently not offended by such questions.

"Then what?"

"Well, he pushed me back down on the bed face first. Then he kinda ran his knife along my neck and then, you know..."

That was her first sign of emotion. Actually saying what happened was not easy. As she choked up, I became more sympathetic to her plight and less focused on what had happened the last time I was there.

"Is there anything else you can tell me?"

"He seemed to be having trouble getting his own pants down, kinda like he was fumbling. I pressed my legs together, but then he pressed the knife a little harder and did his thing. He was cursing under his breath, and he seemed really angry."

"Angry?"

"Yeah, just... I don't know, angry. When he was done he told me not to move or turn around. I think he was trying to get his pants back on. Then he went out, right back through the sliding glass door."

She did not think it was necessary for us to call a female officer and agreed to let Thompson drive her to the hospital after she got dressed and called a friend to meet her there.

"Let me tell you something," she said walking out the door, "whoever this guy is better hope you catch him before Big Rob gets out of jail. He'll tear the motherfucker apart piece by piece."

She wasn't kidding either. I would not want to be on the receiving end of a beating from that guy again, especially without a badge, gun and squad of cops behind me. Rob was a big dude. And he was mean.

We knew we had to go through the normal process now of identifying the evidence and coordinating with the Sex Crimes investigators. I radioed to Sergeant Hughes to let him know that we did not get a whole lot of useful information. The rest of the squad saw nothing on the street. At four in the morning, there were no witnesses. I stayed back and waited for Sex Crimes to show up. Detectives Patelli and Lake came out again.

"We're making a lot of overtime in this precinct, you know," Patelli told me.

"I thought this guy was hitting all over the city."

"He was, but recently, he's been hitting the Third Precinct the most. Something about you guys he seems to like."

"We working any strong leads?" I asked.

"No, but things are getting a little strange. First he hits the same victim a second time. That's unusual by itself. Now he hits someone on the second floor. Up until now, he either grabbed someone off the path in Meadow Woods Park, like he did last week in the Fifth Precinct, or broke into a ground floor apartment. Listen, we're gonna look around the apartment for a little bit and then try to find out how he got in here in the first place."

Starting in the bedroom, Patelli and Lake began their search for evidence.

After they did a quick scan, we walked out the sliding glass door in the bedroom that led to the balcony. The door had been unlocked. The apartment was on the second floor, so it was not unusual that the door was not locked; who would expect someone to come charging through? We looked around to find the method of entry onto the balcony. There was one apparent way. The side of the balcony had rusty iron fencing that reached from the balcony's banister right up to the roof of the building. The design of the fence, while arguably decorative with horizontal and vertical bars meeting at right angles, was almost a staircase that allowed someone to easily climb down from the roof onto the balcony. That was quite a design flaw, at least from the perspective of security.

"Something is very fucked up," Patelli said, looking at Lake. They looked at me and I knew it was time for me to leave the crime scene.

Chapter 16

Bergman probably gave me good advice. I should've listened. Having something on my mind was difficult for me. I needed to get things in the open.

Janie and I decided to meet for dinner. She had the night off, but I had to get to work after dinner. We met at 7:30 at a nice steakhouse just on the outskirts of downtown. She ordered a T-bone and I ordered my favorite dish — a full rack of ribs. Of course, no drinking before going to work. The restaurant had the mid-west ambience appropriate for a steak house.

"So, you guys are having a hard time with the serial rapist. I've been reading a lot about it in the paper," Janie said to me.

"Between that and Stryker's shooting, we're not looking too good lately. We're usually considered a model police department. We're in a bad slump. But we'll catch the bastard and we'll be looking good again. Speaking of looking good, you look exceptionally beautiful tonight."

Janie had been leaning forward with her elbow on the table. Upon hearing that, her back straightened out and she smiled with happiness and a bit of wonder.

"Wow, thank you. Not that I don't appreciate the compliment..."

"I hear a 'but' coming," I said before allowing her to continue.

"Yes, there is. I was about to say, but that doesn't sound like you. Is there something I should know?"

I was a little nervous. I found myself more nervous than when I had been in dangerous situations on the job. Maybe that's because in those situations, I have some control. Now, as soon as I pose my question, Janie would have complete control.

"Well... yes, there is something I've wanted to talk to you about."

Now Janie looked a little concerned. "What about, Gary?"

After I hesitated and took a breath I told her, "You know I love you, right?"

"Not really, Gary, because that's the first time you've told me that, at least in a serious tone, so I guess I know now."

"Then let me say it seriously. I love you."

With a big smile on her face Janie responded in kind, "And I love you, yet I am sensing another 'but' coming."

"Well, there is something on my mind and I want to be honest with you."

Now Janie really looked concerned, like she was about to cry. I love you followed by a "but," even an implied one, was never a good sign in a relationship. Obviously, she suspected the "let's be friends" speech was about to be unloaded on her.

"Gary, go ahead and be honest. Let me hear it."

"Whew, I just want you to know that I do love you, but at this point in my life, I can't promise you that we're going to get married."

"That's it? That's the big honesty thing you had to get off your chest? Well, if it makes you feel any better keep this in mind — I've never asked you to promise you were going to marry me. Did I?"

"No, you didn't, but I just wanted to get that out in the open," I told her.

"Gary, I understand what you're saying, but I don't like that for some reason you felt the need to bring this up now. Something must be driving that. If you want out of this relationship, just say so. Don't use this marriage thing as an excuse, please."

Her eyes were swelling with tears now. I saw that and answered immediately as this was not going the way I had intended.

"Wait, wait, this is going south real fast. I don't want out, hardly. I want to ask you something, but I just wanted to have everything out on the table."

"Then go ahead already and ask." Janie rushed me to get to the point. I couldn't blame her; I was making a mess of this thing.

"Well, I was wondering if, without a real promise of marriage right now, maybe you wanted to live together. That's it."

"Live together?"

Janie was surprised and slapped both hands down on the table, and turned her head to one side and then the other. She was not really looking for anything or anybody. She had been so sure this was leading to a break-up. Her smile came back. She answered quickly.

"Yes, I do want us to live together. You could have done this without the marriage speech, you know. What brought this up, though? It sorta came out of nowhere."

"I know. It is kind of sudden. But, after Stryker's death, I realized how fleeting life is. Right now, I want you in my life as much as possible. So, I thought this was the best way to go."

Janie reached over the table with her lips puckered and I met her halfway for a kiss.

"I do have one condition, and it's non-negotiable," she told me boldly.

"Okay, let me have it. What bad habit do I have to give up?"

"No, it's not a habit, though there are probably some we should work on. It's your apartment. I'm not moving into that place, with that furniture, or lack thereof. And your bathroom, forget it. You could not sanitize that enough for me to live in the same apartment. You move into my place."

"Deal," I told her. My furniture did suck, but I didn't think my bathroom was all that dirty, especially after having shared a bathroom with Thompson in the hospital.

"Then let's celebrate."

"Doesn't this great steak dinner qualify as a celebration?"

"No, because we started before we had come to a formal agreement. An official celebration can only begin after the deal is signed," Janie playfully told me with a big smile on her face.

"You come over after work and I'll make you a world class breakfast. How about that?"

"Deal again," I told her.

That was two good deals I just made and the rest of the meal was quite enjoyable, just talking about stuff. I was worried how that married thing would go over. But like Bergman told me, I never did hear her demand that I promise to marry her. This could not have worked out any better. Leaving for work in a great mood, I was living for the moment and maybe a little in the future, careful not to look down the road too far. Then as Janie headed to her car, she called me. When I looked over to her, she held up her keys telling me that she would make me some copies. The way she playfully jiggled them was very reminiscent of my night with Liz. I was going to have to forget that night.

When I got to the precinct, I found myself taking a little extra time getting ready, polishing my belt and shoes and just trying to have my appearance reflect my mood. I was a little exuberant and Bergman picked up on my excitement. He walked over to my locker.

"What's up, big guy? You look happy about something," he asked me.

"Janie and I agreed to live together."

"Hey man, that's great. Congratulations."

Bergman gave me a friendly slap on the shoulder.

I was the first one into the roll call room. After everybody was in, Sergeant Hughes began roll call. After the regular stuff, he brought up some interesting information.

"You all may remember the Kansas City detective who got shot last year during an undercover drug operation."

We did remember that. You do not forget when a cop gets killed so close to home. Same with Stryker; all the departments in the area were affected. It could have just as easily been them.

Hughes continued, "Well, ballistics showed that the gun used to shoot that detective was the same weapon used to shoot Stryker. When Homicide did a search warrant on the homes of the subjects, they recovered a few weapons and several boxes of ammo. Problem is these guys were Middle Easterners. The triggerman on the KC shooting was a white guy, so we have the weapons, not the perp. Keep this all under your hat. The chief doesn't want any of this information going public yet."

If the chief wanted everything quiet, he should not have given the information out to be read at roll call. Someone will say something to someone, who will say something to someone and before you know it, the story is in the press. Of course, when one of your own gets killed, you want to share as much information as you can. It was the least you could do for the troops.

As for these cocksuckers who shot Stryker, being involved in two police shootings is not a good position to be in. You can get off easy with hitting a cop in the face with a chair, but shooting and killing is a whole other story.

I hit the streets still in a good mood. But, this serial rapist was on my mind as it was probably on the mind of every other cop in the department. Catching him would certainly be quite an accomplishment. If I could do that on the heels of my Medal of Valor, I was sure that I would become the department's youngest detective ever. There were probably 799 other cops thinking some similar thoughts. Yeah, we're not in this business for the money. We do it to help society and all that other self-righteous stuff. After all, we are just human. We all want our moments of fame; we all want to be heroes. I knew I did.

There was little chance of any patrolman catching this rapist in the act. He was a psycho rapist, but that did not mean that he was stupid. He was not going to get caught walking around the street in that black hooded sweatshirt and ski cap. He was scoping out his victims; he knew when they were alone. With that last hoax robbery call, I can only guess that it was him, trying to lure me away from the scene of the crime. Was he that slick? He hadn't done that before. Or maybe he had. I really didn't know. And, I didn't know if anyone else knew. It didn't even occur to me to mention it to Detective Patelli at the last rape. I thought I'd call him just to tell him. That would give me a little suck up time.

If I had any chance of catching this guy in the act, I was going to have to be more aggressive on patrol. Maybe a little more driving around and less coffee drinking. Maybe I could develop an informant or two, like Gillis must have done. But, I didn't know how to do that. Not that I wanted to model myself after Gillis. Not anymore. That was a complete turnaround from that first time I drove with him. I remembered how impressed I was with Gillis. He was a tough talking, action taking type of cop; I wanted to be a cop just like him. Boy, how things changed.

The rapist was hitting ground floor apartments up until the last rape. Why would he change and do something a little more difficult? Maybe the rapist was a rival biker who knew that Big Rob was in jail and that was a good chance for revenge. Or maybe it was a fellow biker who took advantage of an opportunity. As we always say, there is no honor amongst thieves. Whoever he was, he liked hitting in the Third Precinct more than the other precincts. Did he live here, work here, or just know the territory better? These were all great thoughts, but how was I going to make them work for me?

The night started off with me backing up Mac at a fight at the Hollywood Apartments in Mac's sector. I had been there several times before to help her out with drunk and disorderly conduct calls. I knew exactly how to get there. Each night out on patrol, as I gained more street experience, I was becoming tremendously more confident. I knew the radio codes, and how to find my way around. I knew how to handle most calls. The nervous heartthrob that came with each radio call was gone. I met Mac at the apartments. The buildings surrounded a park in the center of the complex. We saw a crowd and heard some noise that sounded like something was going on. We started our approach to the park when someone yelled out "5-0." Everybody started running in different directions — every direction except towards us. I started to run towards the park after them.

"Hey, Hollings, what are you doing?" Mac called at me.

I stopped in my tracks, turned around and said, "They're running."

"Yeah, I know what they're doing. But, what are you doing?"

"I'm running after them, to see what's going on."

"And when you get there and see an empty park and nothing but asses and elbows heading in different directions, what are you going to do then?"

I stopped. I knew there had to be a good answer. I thought a little longer. There was no good answer.

"I don't know what I was going to do," I admitted to her. I

thought my days of admitting rookie ignorance were over.

"Look, take it easy. You start running like that in the dark, you're gonna fall over somebody or something and get hurt for nothing."

"So what do we do? Nothing? We did get a call about a fight."

"I know. We get over there and make sure there is no dead body or something and then call it in."

"Okay, we'll do it your way." I knew her way was the right way.

We got over to the park and found just what Mac knew we would find: nothing but beer cans, liquor bottles and cigarette butts. Somebody probably had been fighting. But they weren't interested in waiting around for the cops to break it up. They probably had drugs on them or outstanding warrants or just didn't feel like seeing us. I was responding with a rookie excitement that I thought I had outgrown. Mac reacted with deliberate temperance, the sign of a truly experienced cop. We started walking away when Mac cleared us on the radio. Right away, Mac got another call. It was a burglary in progress. The complainant was on the phone with dispatch. The burglar was on the ground floor of the apartment. The complainant was calling from the upstairs bedroom. Dispatch gave us the address. Mac and I looked at each other.

"Repeat the address, please," Mac asked with a certain amount of disbelief.

We heard the address again. It was correct. We were standing right in front of the apartment. That was just too convenient. I began to think about the hoax robbery.

"Mac, I don't want to sound paranoid, but could this be some kind of setup? Seems a little too convenient. Doesn't it?"

"You're not being paranoid. That's a good call. Let's be careful."

The description of the burglar was of a short, heavyset black male. We drew our weapons and approached the door cautiously, yet also doubtful. Mac was about to check the door to see if it was open and then the door opened itself. There stood a short, heavyset black male. His shock at seeing two cops standing outside the door was only matched by our shock at having a burglar walk out right into our hands. The three of us stood there motionless for a second. If it hadn't been such a dangerous situation, it really would have been comical. The burglar's mouth opened wide and it remained open for a few seconds. His eyes also opened wide.

Mac and I pointed our weapons and yelled "freeze" in unison, though I think my voice was more of a high shrill. The burglar shook his head as if trying to wake himself from a bad dream. Then he tried to slam the door, turn and run. I surprised myself and kicked the door back open. I holstered my weapon and ran in and charged the burglar with a shoulder shrug into the wall, just enough to make him lose his footing. He stumbled a bit, and realized he was not getting away. He stopped. I stepped back and redrew my weapon. He was looking down the barrels of two guns held by cops with no door between them. He threw his hands up. We cuffed him and took him to Mac's car. We patted him down and found some jewelry and a wallet that had come from the apartment he just burglarized.

"When's the last time you were standing right in front of a place that was being burglarized?" I asked Mac.

"Well, probably a lot. But in my nine years, this is probably the first time I actually knew about it."

"Does this qualify as the easiest felony arrest you've ever been on?"

"Absolutely," she answered.

To me, more important than making the arrest was that this incident assured me that my reflexes were fast. They were instinctive; they were good; I'd rather react a little like a rookie sometimes if it meant I had what it took to make the right moves on the street.

I started my drive back to my patrol sector. About three minutes into the drive I could not help but notice a Triple 7 off to my right. A cup of coffee sounded good. Nah, let me get back to work. With my luck, I'd probably miss another rape by just a moment or two because I stopped at the Triple 7. As I drove past, I caught an interesting sight out of the corner of my eye. Perhaps I saw wrong. I pulled a U-turn and went up the block away from the Triple 7. Then, with a couple of left turns, I was looking down at the store with my binoculars in hand and car headlights off. I took a close look. I called my observation and question into dispatch. After a minute or so, they radioed back to me.

"That's 10-4, 321 Baker. There is an outstanding warrant for probation violation for one William S. Dixon."

"10-4. Please send two units for back-up, and we'll affect the arrest of Dixon."

There was a déjà-vu. I remembered that night I was riding with Gillis when we busted Dixon slinging dope and how Gillis had Dixon's head pressed against that brick wall.

Dispatch sent over Edmonds and Fiero to assist me. We came up with a game plan on how to make the arrest. It would not be too unlike the plan I did with Gillis. Only this time, there would be three experienced cops, not one rogue cop and a rookie cop who didn't know his ass from his elbow when it came to police work.

Dixon was just hanging around. He didn't have his minions with him this time. Nothing was happening to make me think that he was dealing at the moment. I walked in from behind the Triple 7 while Edmonds and Fiero came in from opposite sides. If he tried to run, we'd grab him.

I approached Dixon and while he was a little startled at the sight of a cop creeping up on him, he did not make any sudden moves. He did not resist or try to run; he was rather compliant.

"Good evening, Officer. Can I help you?"

"Good evening, sir. Can I ask you your name, please?"

"Sure, I'm Willie Dixon, but I think you already know that."

"Do you have some identification, please?"

As Dixon moved his hand to the back of his pants, I knew he was grabbing for his wallet, but we all took a step back and placed our hands over our weapons. I held out my other hand to him, as if signaling him to stop and I cautioned him.

"Move slowly, use one hand and you better be bringing out nothing but identification."

"Easy, Officer. You asked for identification, and I'm taking out my wallet to do that. You don't want to shoot me just for following your orders, now do you?"

Of course, he was right; I had asked him for identification. What else was he going to do? Although I knew who he was, I still asked for identification, just to go through the motions of assuring I was arresting the right man. Arresting the wrong man can lead to many unnecessary problems. We placed him under arrest for the outstanding warrant charging probation violation. I searched him as I would do for anyone under arrest. I found no drugs on him. Just my luck. This was probably one of the few times that he wasn't carrying any drugs. I could have gotten a good drug arrest stat. I could only assume that Dixon was out on probation from Gillis' drug arrest. I didn't know how he got out so soon. He wisely did not resist and I placed him in my car for the trip to the jail to book him. A quick arrest, and not a bad stat, even if just on a probation violation warrant. Maybe even a little easier than Mac's burglary arrest.

We started the drive and things were silent for a few minutes. Sometimes I engage in conversation with the prisoners; you never know what they may say or if they may decide to cooperate with you. I was always chasing that elusive butterfly called an informant. Surprisingly, Dixon broke the silence.

"I'm not sure what this is all about. What did I do to violate my probation, Officer?"

"I don't know, Mr. Dixon. You will have to bring that up with the judge. I'm just serving the warrant."

"Mr. Dixon? That's very polite of you, Officer. How come you just don't call me Willie, like my friends do?"

"As you said, Mr. Dixon, I'm just being polite. We're not friends."

"You seem a little different than your partner."

"Partner? What partner?"

"Officer Gillis, of course. I didn't forget you from the last time you guys arrested me."

That surprised me. I didn't think that Dixon would remember who I was. Gillis did all the work and all the talking; he was the one who testified in court. I just stayed in the background. I was confident that Dixon had been exposed to a number of cops during his lifetime.

"I didn't think you would even remember me."

"Oh, I don't forget any cop who takes my money."

I picked my head up to look in the rear view mirror to see his face. I had heard what he said, but I didn't believe I'd heard him correctly.

"What did you just say?"

"You heard me. I don't forget any officer who takes my money. What did you guys do with that two thousand dollars you took from me?"

"What are you talking about? I was there in court during the forfeiture proceedings. That two thousand went to the state, not to us. You know that. What kind of bull are you trying to throw?"

"What bull am I throwing? What are you throwing? I know where that two thousand wound up. But what about the other two thousand you and your partner took from my other pocket? Where did that go? To the state? I don't think so."

"Oh bullshit; there was no other two thousand dollars. What kinda crap is that? How the fuck do you think you have the right to accuse me of ripping you off?"

I was watching him in the mirror. He was looking straight back at me. He had a smug smile — an air of confidence that I found discomfiting. I didn't know what that indicated.

"Look, maybe your partner didn't split it with you. But I always keep money in both my pockets. Gillis knows that. This ain't the first time he locked my ass up. Surely, you know that. And this ain't the first time he took some of my money and handed the rest of it in. He ain't stupid. He knows what he's doin'. Keep a little, show a little for evidence. No one will suspect shit. If he didn't cut you in, then you must be one rookie motherfucker and he just cut your ass out of your share."

"Hey, you were in court with a lawyer. Why didn't you bring it up then, huh? That would have been a perfect time."

"Oh yeah, and say what? Your honor, I really had more money from selling crack, but the cops stole it from me. I don't think so. Shit, you really are a dumb ass rookie. You don't know what's going on. Do you?"

I didn't know what to say. I didn't like the way Gillis did things, but there was a big difference between being a hot dog and being corrupt. I couldn't believe it. Yet, it wasn't beyond the realm of possibility. Could I be a dumb ass rookie who didn't see what was going on? Maybe, but should I even be considering that based on the word of a lowlife drug dealer like Willie Dixon? Then again, that's why we need informants on the street — to tell us things that we wouldn't otherwise know. Maybe he did know something. No, he was full of shit... he had to be.

I ended the conversation by telling Dixon to shut up because I'd heard enough of his bullshit. He complied; he just smiled a little bit and stared out the car window the rest of the ride down to the jail. When we got there, I took him through the booking process without saying a word other than to tell him what to do. Of course, he had been through this so many times before, he could've booked himself without any of my help. That was kind of a neat idea: self-booking. Think of all the police man-hours that would be saved if we could do that.

I was in a bit of a tizzy the rest of the night. I couldn't imagine the thought that Gillis was dirty. Sloppy, rogue and dangerous — yes. That's bad, but being dirty is a whole other thing. Of course, that could explain the Jag he was driving; ripping off a few grand here and a few grand there can really add up. Could he have ripped off Dixon right in front of me? Even for a rookie, I would have really had to have my head up my ass for that to happen. I got a call to back-up Bergman on a domestic dispute. Quickly and randomly I pulled over a car and said I was out on a traffic stop. Dispatch sent Thompson instead. My mind was elsewhere and I didn't want to go into one of those situations without a clear head; that's just too dangerous.

The poor motorist I stopped couldn't figure out why I had stopped him. There was no legitimate reason, of course, other than me avoiding a call. After I took his license and registration I just sat in my patrol car with it for a moment. I ran a warrant check for the hell of it. As expected, he was clean. I returned the license and registration to him. He asked why I had pulled him over, being very polite but naturally curious. I told him that his car had matched the description of a car used in a robbery in Kansas City about a half hour ago, so I was just checking. He seemed satisfied with that explanation. I was sure I was not the first cop to use that line of bull simply to pull a car over for a reason we could not explain, or did not want to explain — like a good-looking babe.

Later that night I got called to the scene of a car accident. While normally I didn't like those calls, this one was welcomed. It would be a pain in the ass, but it wouldn't be dangerous. I would spend the rest of the night handling that call and doing the report just to make sure I didn't get called out to something else. That was the best accident investigation of my career. The shift couldn't end too soon for me.

"Hey, how about a little breakfast before heading out?" Bergman asked me.

"Appreciate it, but I'm supposed to go over to Janie's for a celebration breakfast. You know, celebrate the whole moving in together thing."

"Ahh, that's so cute," Bergman said in his best, teasing tone.

"Fuuuck you" was my succinct response back.

I was glad I had the excuse of not meeting for a bite after the shift. Ordinarily, I wouldn't mind. But not this morning. I didn't want to talk to anybody. I had to resist my urge to vent what was on my mind. I couldn't put a cop's reputation on the line just from the word of a puke like Dixon. But, it was possible. I didn't see a way out of this one; I would have to do something. My mind was so cluttered with thoughts that as I drove back, I instinctively drove to my apartment, not Janie's place. I could have kept driving, but didn't feel like it. She would see there was something on my mind and want me to talk. Then when I didn't want to talk, we'd wind up in an argument. Yep, maybe this was where I needed to be, so I called Janie.

"Hey, listen, I'm not gonna make it over today for that special breakfast. I've gotta get back to the precinct this afternoon and take care of something and staying here saves me some driving time back and forth. I also want to sneak in at least five hours of sleep before the next shift tonight, okay?"

My apartment was closer to the precinct than her place was, so that was only half of a lie — I could live with that.

"Is everything all right?"

"Yeah, yeah. Everything is fine. There was just some paperwork I didn't finish and I left my wallet in the locker. I want to grab that for the day before going tonight." A couple of more little lies, but no harm.

"Okay, I'll miss you."

"Miss you too, baby. Talk to you later."

"Okay. Bye." She was abrupt trying to get off the phone.

"Wait, can we do this tomorrow instead?" I was almost pleading.

"Of course. Just be here tomorrow."

"I will."

"Okay. But you'll tell me if you're having second thoughts about our living together. Won't you?"

"Yes, I'll tell you and no, that's not it. I promise."

"Okay, bye. I love you."

"Love you too, baby."

Well, at least that was no lie. We weren't even living together yet, but the white lies had started. Did that mean it only got worse from here? Or, is that just a part of life that would be present in every relationship? It's not like I had another girl in my apartment or anything like that. I only wanted to be alone with my thoughts, really more my worries. Was that so bad? Janie probably had told some white lies of her own. She must have.

There was only one thing I could think about — could Gillis be dirty? What about all the other drug arrests he'd made? Were those rip-offs? He usually had Stryker or Thompson with him. Okay, they were friends, and cops like to work with people they trust and are comfortable with, especially in dangerous situations. Could he have been pulling that off in front of them without them noticing, like he might have done with me? Or, did that mean that Stryker and Thompson were dirty too? Could that be why Stryker went into such a dangerous situation without back-up? Was he hoping for a rip-off?

If Gillis was ripping people off, no wonder he didn't tell anyone about the arrest in advance and only used one other guy. Now it made sense — he couldn't do it alone; that would be much too dangerous. But, with all those people at the arrest, there would be too many eyes watching, so he couldn't pull it off. Then what about Sergeant Hughes? Was that why he was not out there watching what these guys were doing? Was he just letting them rip people off? Was he getting a cut? Should I go to IA? What if they were dirty too? Anything seemed possible now.

No, no. I was thinking crazy thoughts. We were a great department. We were not without some problems, but widespread corruption was not one of them. Maybe Gillis was dirty, maybe not. Even if he was, that didn't mean everyone else was.

Sleep was not coming easy. I spent at least an hour staring into the dark, then walking around my apartment, which didn't provide much room for roaming. Eventually, I drifted off into a very restless sleep.

There was time for only a few hours of sleep. Given the way things worked out, I didn't lie to Janie after all. I did go to work, heading down to the jail to speak with Dixon. Weapons were not allowed within the prison facility, so even as a cop, I had to check my weapon into a locker. That was a naked feeling for a cop, but it was standard policy for a jail. If a prisoner was to get hold of the weapon, the implications were obvious. Of course, if a gun was to be smuggled in, I would hate to be unarmed, but those were the rules.

The deputy sheriffs put me in an interview room to wait for Dixon. It was a perfectly square room with four walls of white painted cinder block. One wall, of course, had the two way mirror. The front wall had the steel door with the small window for the deputy sheriffs to peek into. There was one brown desk with metallic legs, and two black metal chairs at either side. The room was not brightly lit, yet certainly not dark, with one hanging lamp as would be shown in the movies. Dixon was brought into the room. The deputies removed the handcuffs from behind his back and handcuffed one hand to a chair. That chair was bolted to the concrete slab floor.

"Why am I not surprised to see you, Officer?" Dixon asked.

"That's a good question. Why? Were you expecting me?"

"I wouldn't go that far. But I knew what I told you had you thinking and now you want to make sure I was telling you the truth. Right?"

"Maybe. But before we do this, let me get some formalities out of the way. I am not here to talk to you about your probation violation or any other criminal acts. Do you understand that?"

"Yes, Officer, I understand that."

"Good. I'm going to read you your Miranda rights. I assume you know what those are." He nodded yes and I went on to read each of his rights. This technically wasn't necessary. I was not questioning him about a crime of which he was suspected. I had no intention of using anything he told me against him in court. But, when he got his court appointed attorney to represent him for his probation violation, the attorney would throw a fit if a cop spoke to him without a lawyer present. If he voluntarily waived his rights, and we did not discuss his case, there was really nothing for the attorney to complain about.

Dixon initialed off on each of the individual rights on the Miranda Warning form. He then read and signed the statement indicating that he understood each of those rights. Now, with that in hand, should Dixon admit to a crime, I could use his statements. But that wasn't my interest and that wasn't going to happen. Dixon was too well-seasoned at this stuff.

"So, what is it you want to know about — Officer Gillis?"

"Well, you said he stole two thousand dollars from you. I don't believe it. I was standing right there and I saw him take the money out of your pocket."

"Yeah. You saw him take the money out of my right pocket and that's what he showed you. What you didn't see was when he reached into my left pocket and took the money out of there and stashed it in his own pocket."

"And you just happened to have two thousand bucks in each pocket. Why would you do that? Why wouldn't you have it all in one pocket like normal people do?"

"C'mon, how much of a rookie cop are you? First, it's just too thick. Second, I'm always reaching in and out of my pockets. I don't need anyone else to know what I'm carrying. And third, in case someone tries to rip me off, I just pull out a wad from one pocket and they think they got all my money. It's pretty simple."

"Okay. But how would Gillis know that you had that cash in your left pocket?"

"What did I tell you? He arrested me before. He asked the same questions you asking now. Man, why you having so much trouble with this? You never heard of cops ripping people off before?"

"Not in Westland Park I haven't."

"Besides, word on the street is that Gillis runs with a pretty rough crowd of feds. I heard he's got friends in DEA."

"How'd you hear that?"

"Just word on the street. Gillis is about the only uniformed cop in Westland Park that anybody worries about. Now we heard he's a narc for you guys."

"How is it you know so much about Gillis?"

"C'mon, man. Where you been? The man goes around busting up dudes just trying to make some cash with a little crack. He's all over us like stink on shit. You don't think people on the street talk?"

"All right, people are talking. Who else they talking about?"

Now Dixon was laughing. "Ohh. So now I guess you believe me and you worried. That's it, man. That's all I gotta say."

"Well, just tell me..." and he interrupted me.

"Officer, I'm done talking. If you want to talk any more you'll have to see my attorney."

That was that. He didn't want to talk. Was he just screwing with me? Or maybe he was holding back information so he could make a deal next time he was arrested. Maybe that's how he got out on probation from Gillis' arrest. Maybe he gave up other cops. What was I supposed to think now? One thing especially bothered me. When he was arrested, both times I noticed the twitch in his eye when he got nervous. His eye was not twitching now. I did not want to admit it, even to myself, but I believed him, at least about Gillis. Maybe my eye should be twitching.

That night I headed out to patrol, knowing that I could not let my concerns of Gillis and corruption consume me. This was just the word of one lowlife crack dealer. But, as I knew, those were the kind of guys who knew what was happening on the street. That's why we tried to make them informants. Bergman got me on the side channel and we met for dinner. Apparently, a poker face is something I don't have. Bergman was not one to beat around the bushes; he got right to the point.

"What's on your mind tonight, big guy?" he asked me, remembering how easy I spilled my guts, or most of them, last time we spoke. Bergman knew that he was the only one on the squad I felt close to. He also knew that I still had this high-schoolish need to talk things out.

"Eh, nothing. It's just... ahh... forget it."

"Okay, but usually when someone says forget it, they really mean, please press me to talk about it."

"Oh, I don't know, Matt. It's just that I got some information that I don't know if I can believe or not and I'm not sure what to do about it."

"What kind of information?"

I looked up at him. Without having to say it, he could see how sensitive I thought this information was, and just how hesitant I was to disclose it. I put my hand over my forehead and started staring down at the table.

"Look, Gary, I don't want to press you, but whatever it is, it's clearly upsetting you. I hope there is not an issue of trust here," Bergman said to me.

"Oh, c'mon, Matt. You know that's not it. I just don't want to be spreading rumors that are based on a rather questionable source."

"Well, that's another thing. I think you know that what we say to each other never goes anywhere. That's a given. This something good? Like maybe Fiero and Mac were doing each other in the back of a patrol car?"

"What, huh? Where did that come from? No, nothing like that, but the thought of that is rather titillating, to say the least," I continued, trying not to get caught up in that fantasy. "Shit, that would be easy compared to this."

"All right then, what could be so bad?"

"Whew, what would you do if some low-level drug dealer told you that a cop was dirty, was ripping money off people he arrests?"

"Gillis, huh? What you hear?"

I picked up my head and looked up at him with a naive look of surprise. Before I could speak, Bergman jumped in.

"Oh, Gary, please. Why do you look so friggin' surprised? You're talking about drug arrests. And ones that may have a dark side. Who the fuck else can you be talking about?"

"I know. You're right. I'm not saying he is dirty, just that I got some information. And like I said, the source is not very reliable."

"What kind of source you talking about, Gary?"

"You know that puke I picked up on that outstanding probation violation warrant last night?"

"No, I don't know him, but I heard you call it in. That was a nice bust, though."

I explained to Bergman about the arrest of Dixon that Gillis and I made and I told him what Dixon was saying about Gillis.

"I never really thought he was dirty, not like that. But in all honesty, this doesn't really surprise me, Gary. I've said it before. The guy is a rogue cop. He's dangerous."

"Okay," I interjected, interrupting him, "but that doesn't make him dirty. Does it?"

"No, it doesn't. But as far as I'm concerned, that kind of personality is prime for being dirty. He doesn't stop and think; he just loves the action. All his self-righteous talk about how we have to do the real police work by being tough on the streets and the department doesn't understand what we're up against. The community doesn't appreciate all we do for them. Maybe that's his way of justifying ripping off drug money. It makes sense to me. I believe it. Hey, you're right about one thing. This is some deep shit and you better take care of it."

"Well, at least you didn't hold back your feelings."

"Would you want me to?"

"No, I wouldn't. What would you do?"

"You kidding? You know what I would do. I told you the other night. If I thought you were dirty, I'd turn you in. Does that answer it for you?"

I did know what he would do, and I knew how he was going to answer that question. I guess I just wanted to hear it.

"But what if it's not good info? He's already got problems with IA. Why should I make things worse if it's not true?" I asked him, still hoping for a different answer that I knew was not coming.

"Figuring out if it's true or not is IA's job, not yours. You ain't the judge and jury. You're a cop. It's that fuck'n simple."

"I don't know, Matt..."

"You don't know what?" Bergman's voice nearly reaching anger pitch.

"Well, you know, it's just..."

"Hey, Gary, it's just fuck'n nuthin'. If he's dirty, let's get his ass off the street now. I'm not even sure what we're discussing."

"We're discussing a cop's reputation and his life and..."

"And fuck you. You know what to do."

Bergman stood up, holding his hand up like he was stopping traffic. Then he leaned down towards me and spoke in a firm, loud whisper, pointing his finger at me like a disapproving teacher. For a moment, I thought he was going to ram his fist in my face.

"There's nothing not to know. You got information that there's a dirty cop in our department. You don't even have a choice. The rules say you got to report it to IA. Whatta ya gonna do, Gary, sit on it till he gets someone else killed? You turn him in, or I will. Just fuck'n do it."

Throwing down a few singles in cash, Bergman walked out. I had never seen him act like that, not even while making an arrest. This was going to be one test of our friendship, if we even had one left. His sense of duty was unshakeable.

Chapter 17

Now I would have to cancel breakfast with Janie again. She was not going to like this. She was not going to believe me. She would be sure that I was getting cold feet on the moving in together issue. I couldn't come out and tell her the truth. I called her.

"Hey, baby," I started the conversation nonchalantly.

"Hey," she said all excited. "Should I start getting breakfast ready?"

"Listen, you're not going to like this, and you gotta believe me, but I really can't make it this morning."

"What? Why not? Gary, if there's something going on with you..."

"No, no. I swear there is nothing going on. I mean, there is something going on at work, and I can't talk about it, but it's nothing to do with us. I swear."

"Gary, this is just the kind of stuff I knew would happen if I started dating a cop again."

"Janie, please, don't go there again. That's not fair. Really, I just got a big problem at work that I have to take care of right away. After today, I should be done with it. I promise. Let me get this done and maybe we can meet for dinner before our shifts start. Please."

"Okay, but if there's something you should be telling me, please don't play games with me."

"No, no games. It's just work. One day, I will be able to tell you. Just not now. Trust me, please."

"Okay, call me later," she said.

"I will. I love you."

I waited to hear "I love you" from her, in return. Instead I heard that infamous click. I didn't have to be with her to know that when she hung up the phone, she was crying. That was Janie; she read more into this than what was really there. She was so afraid of being lied to, of being hurt, that she sometimes couldn't see the truth if things didn't fall perfectly into her plan. That was her, and I guess I would have to learn to deal with it if this relationship was going to work. My next telephone call was to IA.

"Detective Sanchez, may I help you?"

"Yes, Detective. This is Officer Gary Hollings from the Third Precinct. I would like to meet with you. I have some important information."

"Okay, Officer. Are you on duty now?"

"No, I do midnights. I just got off."

"Do you want to come in now?"

"I'm not gonna come in. I don't want anybody seeing me anywhere near IA. Let's meet somewhere."

"You name it."

"Take Grant Highway out to Dumont County. As soon as you cross the county line, there's a shopping center off to your left. I'll give you my cell phone number, and when you get there call me and we'll hook up. How about one hour from now?"

"Sounds good, Detective."

"Okay, Officer. I will be with my partner, Detective Fiske. We'll see you there."

I arrived there almost an hour to the minute. So did they. I still didn't imagine that IA received too many calls from patrol officers who said they had important information. In Westland Park most IA investigations were based upon citizen complaints of unprofessional conduct and a few prisoners claiming they were roughed up. There probably were not a whole lot of corruption cases. I had never heard anyone ever talk about a Westland Park cop getting busted for being dirty. One had been caught soliciting a prostitute at a nightclub in Eastport. The prostitute wound up being an undercover Kansas City cop. That was very bad luck, considering all the real prostitutes that are out there. There went a career over something really stupid.

We found each other and went to a diner to talk over a cup of coffee. Unbelievably, my hands were shaking. Never having imagined that I would be doing something like this, I had trouble getting to the point and was just making stupid small talk. They were very patient with me. After all, they had been street cops themselves at one time; they must have understood how difficult this was. While IA was considered the bane of a police officer's existence, what they did was important. We had to be able to police ourselves. Misconduct — dirty cops — was dangerous to the rest of us who followed the rules and tried to maintain the integrity of our department.

"Officer, we know you're nervous, but there is no need for that. You have information and you know that you are required to report it. So, no matter what it is, you are doing the right thing," Sanchez said, opening up the conversation and taking the lead.

"I know, but what if it's wrong? What if I ruin the reputation and career of a veteran police officer on flimsy information?"

"That's not going to happen. You have to give us a certain amount of credit and trust that we know how to do our job. Whatever you tell us, we will investigate, quietly. If there is nothing there, no harm, no foul. If there is something there, then of course, all bets are off."

"What about me? Do I get dragged into this if you do find something?"

"We do everything we can to keep your name out of it. But, if it comes down to it, and we need your testimony to make the case, then yeah. You'll be dragged into it. Let's not forget, it doesn't matter who we're looking at, you are still a cop and you've got to do your job."

"I think I've been getting that message loud and clear."

"Okay, so let's have it."

I told them what Dixon had told me. They both knew Gillis for a couple of reasons. Sanchez had worked patrol with him for a few years. Fiske went through the academy with him. And of course, they knew all about the shooting and Stryker's death. From the questions they asked and the way they asked them, I had a hunch that they already had a bad feeling about Gillis. They asked whether I had any particular reason to believe or disbelieve Dixon.

"I think I do believe him."

"And why is that?"

"Mostly, what he said and how he described what happened sounded credible. He appeared calm compared to other times I had spoken to him. And ..." Then I stopped.

"And what, Officer?" Sanchez asked me.

"And... well... Gillis is just plain dangerous. I don't like how he does things. I don't know how he goes out there and makes arrests without telling the squad or the sergeant. He uses only one other guy; he's so secretive about things. It just stinks. I don't know if that definitely means he's ripping people off, but there is enough to make you worry. But, that's for you guys to figure out, right?"

"That's right."

I was getting a little worked up. I wanted to express some frustration with Hughes for not reigning in Gillis, but there was no value in pointing the finger at another cop. I didn't know if I liked Hughes or felt sorry for him, or something in the middle. We finished up the discussion — or more appropriately, the interview — with the standard, "Thank you. You did the right thing." All that bullshit. Then I left, leaving them to pick up the tab. It was only a cup of coffee.

Another miserable morning after a long shift. All of sudden, I was not having as much fun on this job as I used to. I thrived on excitement, but this melodrama was wearing on me. I would have liked to have gone to Janie's place and just curled up in bed with her at my side. The warmth that would usually emanate from her tight hugs would be so reassuring right now. Unfortunately, I knew that was not in the cards and it would not be good timing. Resisting the urge to drive over there, I went back to my cold, unappealing, bare-walled apartment and just repeated my routine of walking around going nowhere. I was thinking a lot, yet there really wasn't much to think about. I did what I had to do. Everything was now in the hands of IA. I only managed another couple hours of sleep. That could not continue. You could not be effective on patrol if you were not well rested and alert.

Slowly and robotically, we found our way into the roll call room, with Mac sitting at the sergeant's desk. We assumed she was just trying to be funny. But, by the time we were all seated and ready to begin, she was still there and Sergeant Hughes was not in the room.

"If we can get started please," Mac called out and the low rumble of our side conversations subsided.

"Sergeant Hughes called me earlier. He had to see the deputy chief and he asked me to handle roll call."

"The D.C. is working past four o'clock? Was he able to find headquarters in the dark?" Fiero said to a few laughs, which quickly subsided.

Mac was the most senior officer on the squad there at roll. It would have been Thompson, but he was coming in late, again. There was nothing unusual about Mac handling roll call in the sergeant's absence. What was unusual was Hughes being called to headquarters at night. While Fiero was only joking, it was a half joke. The D.C. rarely worked at night. We knew something was up; we just didn't know exactly what. That's why we quickly quieted down shortly after Fiero's comment. It hit us that something ugly was on the horizon.

*****

As we all headed out to patrol, Hughes made his way to headquarters. He pulled into the mostly empty parking lot and got his security pass from his wallet out to get him into the locked glass doors, under the watchful eye of the video surveillance camera. Without looking up, he waved to the camera as a courtesy to the midnight shift clerk who was monitoring it on the other end. He headed straight for the elevators, which were already on the ground floor with the doors open. He hesitated for a second deciding whether to take the one on the left or the right. Maybe one would bring him more luck than the other. At those moments, rationality is not important. He, more than anybody, knew this late night meeting could not bode well for him.

Gillis would be reviewed for his arrest procedures, but Gillis had acted without Hughes' authorization, so surely Hughes would not be held at fault, he thought and hoped. Hughes tried to calm his nerves by talking himself into believing that the timing of this meeting was not as ominous as it appeared. If the D.C. was really mad, he would have Hughes come to see him in the morning, after a full shift. Why would the D.C. work at the convenience of Hughes? Yeah, that didn't make sense. Everything would be fine.

Hughes walked out of the elevator into a hallway that usually bustled with activity during the day. Now it was quiet. The only thing he heard was his own footsteps; he seemed to be moving slowly. He walked towards the deputy chief's office, passing the men's room on his left. Then, he stopped, turned around and went back in. He didn't need the toilet, but he did need to stop and splash cold water on his face. He checked his appearance one more time. Tie straight, and badge shiny. He brushed his hand down the sleeves of his uniform, one time on each side, and continued on his short trek to the office. Hughes stopped in the doorway, which was open, and Deputy Chief Harrington was sitting at his big mahogany desk, with the window overlooking Westland Park behind him. He apparently had nothing else to do other than to wait for Hughes. Harrington did not get up from his chair.

"Hi, Dave, please come in and have a seat." Harrington pointed to the two light brown leather chairs facing his desk at 45 degree angles, about two feet apart.

Hughes came in and pulled back the chair on his left and sat down, fidgeting for a moment trying to get comfortable.

"Dave, how are you doing tonight?"

"Well, sir, I'm doing fine."

"Good. You know, Dave, after Officer Stryker was shot and killed, we did a pretty extensive IA investigation into what happened and how it happened."

"Yes, sir, I was interviewed by IA as well."

"Dave, certainly you can understand that the chief and I were a little concerned that Detective Gillis conducted an undercover drug arrest without notifying his sergeant or anyone else."

"Yes, sir. As you stated, Gillis was a detective at the time, no longer under my command."

"I'm aware of that. But Officer Stryker was. While we, unfortunately, can't ask him now, we do wonder why he didn't call in the arrest to you and get your approval before doing something so dangerous."

"Well, sir, he certainly should have. But, he was friends with Gillis and he must have assumed this was approved by Narcotics and there was a need for secrecy. I could understand that being the case."

"I'm sure you could. But that was not the case, Dave. Gillis never notified Sergeant Ladd."

"Then I think that will need to be addressed with Sergeant Ladd."

"And it will be, Dave. That's not your issue. What concerns me is that Gillis had pulled these drug arrests off several times while he was under your command. IA determined that he never notified you in advance of his arrests and neither did the officer assisting him at the time."

"That, uh, is correct, sir. However, it was well-known that Gillis had an informant who was giving him good information on these arrests, and Gillis was probably just trying to maintain operational security by keeping it quiet."

"Operational security? Does having two cops trying to take down three drug dealers, possibly armed, at some remote location sound like operational security to you?

He knew the sad answer. "No, sir, it does not."

"What about this informant? Did you ever meet him?" Harrington asked, although he obviously knew the answer.

"No, sir, I did not."

"Why not?"

"The proper opportunity never arose."

"Never arose? What about when he paid the informant? We require another officer present during payment. Why didn't you go then?"

Hughes did not lift his head. "Sir, Gillis never requested money for his informant."

"He never asked for money for his informant? Doesn't that sound a little odd to you, Sergeant? A drug informant who never asked for money in return for his information? I don't know; it sounds very odd to me."

"With all due respect, sir, I've never worked Narcotics; I've been on patrol and SWAT my entire career. I am not really familiar with the operation of informants. So, in all honesty, that did not really attract my attention."

"Well, it should have. Just by the fact that you were his sergeant, you should have asked a few more questions. You could have called the Detective Bureau for a little advice. You're a sergeant responsible for a squad of police officers. You need to know what you don't know. You had an officer running wild on informant information and you never questioned anything."

"Sir, I don't think he was running wild. He made some pretty good drug arrests. I mean, isn't that why he got promoted to detective?"

"Sometimes stats don't tell the whole story; you have to look behind them, which we probably should have done first. Since Officer Stryker's death, we've been asking a lot of questions, and basically, we don't like the answers we've been getting."

Hughes knew that Harrington was about to tell him what those answers were. He didn't know what, if anything, he should say at the moment. He chose to remain silent.

"Let me tell you what we've found out," Harrington continued. "On at least half a dozen occasions, Gillis pulled off one of these rogue arrests with just one cop with him, sometimes two. Usually he was with his two friends, Thompson and Stryker. Gillis never told anybody, not even you, about the arrest in advance. Neither did Thompson or Stryker. Does that sound right to you, Sergeant? Your most senior officers breaking protocol over and over again?" Harrington's voice became more authoritative with a critical tone. Hughes did not miss that he was now being addressed as sergeant as opposed to Dave when the conversation started.

Hughes started to stammer. He wiped the sweat from his brow. "That, that, yes, sir, that, I believe, that would be correct." He swallowed twice.

"Did you ever pull him aside and warn him to cut the crap and let him know what proper police protocol was in these circumstances?"

"No, sir, he was a senior officer. He was making some great busts. Like I said, I didn't know anything about Narcotics. Whatever he was doing was working. I thought to leave well enough alone. I mean, why try to fix something if it ain't broken?"

For a moment, Hughes thought he'd hit upon a witty response that would break the austere tone of the conversation. He decided to look up and face the D.C. That certainly didn't help. Harrington moved his head to the left and looked at Hughes out of the corners of his eyes, squinting in apparent disapproval.

"Sergeant, it wasn't always working. I think it was broken. I understand that Officers Fiero and Hollings had to respond once to a dangerous situation brought on by one of Gillis' drug busts." Hughes was about to acknowledge that, but before he could utter a sound, Harrington went on. "Then of course, we had the most recent tragedy, which brings us here today. Whatever Gillis was doing, it clearly was not working. You should have taken control of the situation, and you didn't. Now a cop is dead."

That statement nearly broke Hughes. His lips were quivering and he fought to hold back tears. Just by being the sergeant, he felt guilty for Stryker's death, and now, the D.C. was holding him directly responsible. That was more emotional baggage than Hughes was prepared to carry. He sat there for a moment, breathing heavily and unable to speak, not even trying to formulate a response. Coherent thoughts eluded him. Hughes knew he was facing trouble.

"Sergeant, the chief and I have given this considerable thought. You have been a dedicated member of this department. You were heroic when you were forced to shoot a man who threatened the life of other officers and civilians." Hughes waited for the "but" to come. "However," Harrington continued, "you have not adequately exercised supervision over your squad, specifically the actions of Detective Gillis, when he was an officer under your command, as well as the participation of Officers Stryker and Thompson."

Hughes took a deep breath and swallowed one more time. He cupped his hands together and rested them gently on his lips. He waited.

"Therefore, Sergeant, the chief has decided to suspend you without pay for 30 days. When you return to duty you will be on probation for one year. Any more incidents that indicate you are not adequately supervising your squad, you will be immediately demoted back to patrol officer. Is that clear?"

"Yes, sir."

"Finish out this shift and begin your suspension next week. We have already arranged for Ralph Dickson to cover for you as sergeant."

Hughes stopped, lifted his head and stood at attention for a moment and then he turned to leave. He was a veteran police officer with honors and commendations. Now he was being disciplined.

"Dave, if you need to take some time off or something, let me know. You can even go home tonight if you want; we will get it covered," Harrington called out to him.

Without turning around to face Harrington, he replied, "No, sir, I want to face my squad personally and accept responsibility for what I have done."

Hughes walked back down the hall that he had just walked to get to Harrington's office. Once again, the only thing he heard were his own footsteps, only this time they were quicker. He needed to get out, right now. He headed straight to his car, knowing it could have been worse, much worse.

Yet suspension, followed by working under the threat of demotion, was a lot to swallow for a loyal and committed police sergeant. In a matter of moments, his entire career seemed to have just slipped away. He could appeal the decision, but all that would do was forestall the inevitable. The appeal panel was empowered only to make a recommendation to the chief. Hughes knew the chief was not going to change his mind. In Hughes' eyes, an appeal was not an honorable course of action and if nothing else, Hughes was a man of honor.

Hughes took a deep breath and headed right back into his patrol car, calling dispatch to advise that he was back in service. By the time he got into the Third Precinct territory, there were still a few hours left in the shift.

*****

"So much for Mac's 15 minutes of power," Bergman said to me over a cup of coffee as we sat car to car.

I had asked him to meet me, hoping to keep our friendship alive. Although I wasn't supposed to say anything, I at least hinted, strongly, that I went to IA. What was the harm? I had already shared with him the information about Gillis. Had I not gone, Bergman probably would have gone to IA himself. Then I'd be in trouble for not reporting it. Kind of ironic. Bergman would have done that without a second thought, even though I would get in trouble. Yet, that was what I liked about him. We were good friends, but as he was very clear, he was a cop first. Our friendship appeared to be back on solid footing now.

Mac had just been called to the scene of a rape on the jogging trails. The victim, Wendy Summers, had been attacked from behind, with a knife held to her throat. It sounded like the serial rapist again. Edmonds was backing her up, calling in that he was only a few minutes away. I got on the radio and said I would search for the area for the suspect.

"See ya," I said to Bergman.

"See ya, Detective," Bergman said with a smile; he knew me too well.

I was several minutes away from the scene and was waiting to hear if Hughes was going to respond to coordinate the search for the suspect. He did not. I continued on.

Before I could get into the area, Burkett got on the radio and responded that he would be out of his car on foot searching for the suspect. Fiero was on her way as well.

By the time I got close to the scene, all we had to go on was the same description and no direction of travel. I tried to think whether he was more likely on foot or in a car. I could see reasons for thinking either way. I drove around, but I knew that if the suspect had been in a car, he was long gone. Or maybe not?

Would he have pulled off somewhere to change clothes, or maybe just let things cool down before he headed out again? I spent the next half hour looking down dark alleys, behind buildings or cars suspiciously parked on quiet residential streets.

"All units, perpetrator took victim's purse with keys, driver's license, some cash and a few personal effects. The empty purse has been recovered by Officer Fiero."

So, the rapist took some of his victim's stuff. Hughes finally got on the radio and directed us to respond to Fiero's location. We formed a perimeter around the location where Fiero found the purse, and started looking for any of these items that the rapist may have dropped or left behind. After about a half hour, I came up with nothing and walked over to where Burkett was, mostly out of curiosity as to what he was up to.

"Got anything?" I seemed to have startled him as he was standing back up from reaching for something.

"Oh, no. I just dropped something."

A moment later, the search was called off.

Then I got a radio call — an argument between two neighbors back in the Heights. I could not wait to see what excitement that would hold.

The shift, as all shifts do, finally ended. We got back to the precinct, curious about Hughes though not expecting him to say anything about what had happened. We just wanted to see him; what would his face reveal? It was not much different than rubbernecking at an accident scene. You won't see much or really know what occurred, but you just want to see.

"Everyone in the roll call room," Hughes hollered over the sound of the flush as he came out of the bathroom stall. "Go get Mac and Fiero and I'll see you in five minutes."

It did not take five minutes. We were there in seconds.

Hughes stared straight at the squad, his head held erect and uncompromising. His face showed no emotion; he was stoic.

"Everyone knows that I had to see the D.C. tonight. IA completed their investigation of Stryker's death and I am being cited for failure to properly supervise."

There were a few small groans, yet nobody was really surprised. We knew the reality of his predicament. Before an uncomfortable silence set it, Hughes quickly began to talk again.

"They were right. I haven't been supervising the way a sergeant should supervise. I have been suspended for 30 days. That's probably generous. I deserve more. But that doesn't really matter now. An old friend of mine, Ralph Dickson, will cover the squad in my absence. He's a lieutenant now, in records, so he probably is looking forward to getting back on the streets for a while. He'll be good for this squad. He knows the crisis we're experiencing and he'll act accordingly. When I get back, things will be different. You'll have a sergeant you can be proud of: actually a sergeant that I can be proud of."

I was proud of Hughes. It could not have been easy for him to have accepted that kind of responsibility in front of his squad. No excuses. Now, I looked forward to his return and working for a man of honor.

The following week, our squad showed up to roll call to be greeted by the chief. That was not a common sight at roll call. He came to introduce Lieutenant Dickson.

"We know what this squad has been through lately," the chief told us. "Lieutenant Dickson will provide some much needed leadership for this squad, especially during this critical time for you." The chief sounded like he was taking a cheap shot at Hughes while he was gone.

"Thanks, Chief," Dickson responded. "Leadership is important for the success of any police squad," Dickson now was addressing us, "and I plan to give you the benefit of my many years of experience and make up for what this squad may have missed."

The silence that overtook the squad was more uncomfortable than when Hughes addressed us about his suspension. What were the chief and Dickson doing? Wasn't it enough that Hughes was suspended? Did they have to insult him to his squad, especially when he was home on suspension, unable to defend himself? There was something very cheap and sneaky about this.

Chapter 18

Janie and I finally moved in together. Eventually, she got enough seniority at work to be offered a daytime shift. She turned it down. As long as I was still working midnights, she thought she would stay on midnights too; that would give us more days off together. So far, that seemed to be working well. Time would tell. I still kept my apartment, by mutual agreement. If after a few more months we were fairly sure things were working out, I would take the plunge and give up the apartment. Then, of course, Janie would expect me to split the rent; that was only fair. Giving up my apartment was not a terribly big risk for me. If I needed a new apartment, I could always find something. I would dump what little furniture I had. We didn't need it and Janie did not want to see that crap at her place. I hadn't fanaticized about another quickie with Liz for a while. That had to be a good sign.

About three weeks after Hughes went out on suspension, I heard that Gillis made his first appearance back on Narcotics. He had finished his administrative leave, completed his physical therapy for his arm and leg, and been cleared by the department shrink to return to duty. We later found out that one bullet grazed over his rib cage, leaving only a scratch on the skin. He was lucky. I did not know how he would be able to come back to work at all. Was he not feeling a tremendous amount of guilt over his friend's death? He must realize that the IA Shooting Review Board was not going to just gloss over this. They would move more quickly than they did for my shooting investigation.

A cop had been killed, there were a grieving widow and children, and the circumstances of the shooting were questionable. Actually, the circumstances were more than just questionable. On the surface, they simply sucked. My guess was that he would not be on the streets for very long. IA would probably come down heavy on him for the bad shooting; but if they were able to substantiate any of

Dixon's allegations, it would be over for Gillis. I wondered what thoughts were going through that thick, bald head of Gillis'. Knowing myself, I would not be able to handle that kind of pressure. I still got a little nervous about the free cup of coffee. I'd better keep my nose clean. That's just who I was, and I was glad about that.

Before roll call began, Dickson called me aside. I could not imagine what it would be about; we had not said much to each other since he took over. I was sure IA did not tell him anything about my meeting with them. That's just not how it was done, or at least that was what I was hoping. We walked over to the Precinct Lieutenant's office, which was now empty.

"I think I have some good news, Hollings," Dickson told me.

"I certainly can use that, sir. Things have been kinda nuts around here lately."

"Well, apparently, the detectives working on the serial rapist were impressed by you, and given your Bronze Medal, they wanted to invite you on to a task force they're starting to investigate the rapist. You'll be assigned there temporarily for as long as the task force has to stay up. Whatta ya think?"

"No fuck'n way" were the first excited words out of my untrained mouth. Then I continued, "Uh, excuse me, sir. I'm sorry. But, I'm really excited."

"That's all right, Hollings. I've heard it before."

"This is great, sir. Just great! I don't know what to say."

What I really wanted to ask was, why me? I couldn't imagine that my one suck-up phone call to Patelli about the hoax robbery really carried that much weight. Dickson's mention of the Medal was a pretty solid hint. It was politics. But why not Thompson? He was the big dog with the Silver Medal. Sadly, I thought I knew that answer. His friendship with Gillis was probably working against him now. Hughes was not in Thompson's corner anymore, though having Hughes' support at this point was more a deficit than a benefit.

I should not have even been asking, "Why me?" It was me. That's what I'd been working towards, and now the plan was coming together. I didn't give a fuck why. I was just gonna enjoy it.

"Just say you want it."

"I want it."

"Then you got it."

"Wow, thank you. Really, I appreciate it. That's just great. Thank you so much."

"You can stop thanking me. Someone over in the Detective Bureau must've liked you. I know that Hughes gave you a strong recommendation, but I'm not sure how much that helped. He doesn't have much clout with HQ these days, ya know. He really screwed up. I am glad I was here to give your squad the leadership you deserved. Anyway, they'll be starting up maybe by the middle of next month. So, a couple more shifts with us and you're going to be struggling to adjust to normal working hours. When you report over there, just make the Third Precinct proud. We need it."

"We sure do, sir. I'll do my best."

I followed Dickson's lead and as we started walking back to the roll call room, he gave me a hard, but reassuring, pat on the back. As excited as I was, and as wrapped up in my own good fortune, I still caught the fact that Dickson had not missed another opportunity to take a shot at Hughes. Hughes was right about one thing — Dickson enjoyed being back on the streets. Hughes was wrong about another, more important thing; Dickson was not his friend.

When I walked in to the roll call room, everyone was already seated, and all eyes were on us. The buzz lowered to a hum. The curiosity of what the sergeant had to say to me was apparent on everyone's face except Thompson — he still seemed indifferent to everything, or at least things that did not affect him.

"Good evening, everyone. Let's get started. Before I get into the regular minutiae, let me share some good news with you. Our very own Officer Hollings has been selected for the serial rapist task force being formed at the Detective Bureau. Let's give him a round of applause."

The squad responded with some rather lukewarm applause. Inclined to think there was a little bit of jealousy going on, I tried not to be too disappointed by the lack of enthusiasm from my team.

Maybe it was because, except for Bergman, I was the most junior cop on the squad. I think any one of them would have liked to have been asked, especially Burkett. I was sitting right behind Burkett so I could not see his reaction. We went through the rest of roll call and Dickson realized that he had lost his audience. Everybody seemed to be elsewhere. This was not good — we were a squad of distracted cops. If that did not change, we'd be heading for another tragedy. Maybe the rumor of the chief splitting up the squad was a good one.

Dickson brought the roll call to an end, about 10 minutes earlier than usual. There was no conversation of things going on in the county or any of the normal ball-busting. We all got up from our chairs and headed to the locker room to get our gear and hit the streets. I was hit in the back by another firm, but well meant, slap.

"Nice going, buddy," Bergman congratulated me.

"Thanks, man. It really was a surprise."

"Yeah, to everybody, I'm sure. I get the feeling there are some real sour grapes out there on the squad. I know a few people who would have liked that chance."

"So do I. But that's how it goes."

"All right, my man. I'll get you on the side channel later. If we can hook up for dinner, my treat, to celebrate."

"Oh then, we're hooking up. And no fuck'n pancakes either. I want some real food."

"You sound like my date from the other night."

"Good, because you ain't getting a BJ from me either, so your record is perfect."

Bergman laughed a bit. "I bet you might get one when you tell your little sweet Janie about this. She'll be so proud of you."

"Oh, she will be, but one little thing might keep me from getting that prize."

"I'm afraid to ask."

"No, nothing like what you're thinking. It's just that she recently had the chance to go to day work and she turned it down so we could be on nights to have more time together during the days. Now, I'm gonna be on day work while she's working nights. Kind of ironic, huh?"

Bergman laughed again. "Somehow I don't think ironic is exactly how she will describe it, but good luck. I'll see you later."

Bergman was right about Janie not viewing this new schedule thing as ironic. She took our time together as one of those serious matters. We headed for our cars to start patrol.

Burkett passed right by me without a word. He had been somewhat withdrawn since returning from his two day suspension. I really wanted to talk to him, just to see how he was handling my assignment to the task force, not to rub it in his face. He must've been thinking that the department kept screwing him. This would probably make him realize that he was never going to make detective. But then again, Burkett did not always exist in the real world. One thing I noticed was he did not have on that stupid smile.

The night was moving slowly, till around four in the morning.

"321 Baker, we have a possible kidnap, assault in progress. Anonymous complainant stated that he saw two men struggle with a female and force her into a car. The car then headed to the parking lot of the Oak Hill Mall. No descriptions given and no call back number."

"321 Baker, that's 10-4. I have an ETA of 3."

We didn't get too many calls like that. When there was no complainant with a call back number, it got frustrating when you couldn't ask any further questions. Edmonds was backing me up; the mall was right next to his sector. The mall, which was a bit upscale, three stories high and built in a V-shape, brought in a lot of shoppers from Kansas City. It had two large outside parking lots and an underground parking lot, which was closed up and dark late at night. There shouldn't have been too many cars in the lot this time of night. Sometimes employees or commuters left their cars overnight. If we saw any, we would have to check each one out. Edmonds wound up getting to the scene first.

"312 Baker, I'm at the mall. I have about three cars parked in the north lot. I'll start checking them. If 321 Baker can come in from the south, we can work our way towards the underground lot."

"321 Baker, that's 10-4. I'll be there in a minute."

I came in from the south as Edmonds advised and also had a few cars scattered in the lot. I approached each one slowly. They all appeared to have been sitting there all day. The hoods were cold: no heat from a recently running engine. Like Edmonds, I called in each license plate, but didn't see anything that appeared suspicious. We met up at the underground lot, which had a gate down, blocking vehicles from coming in, or out.

"We're gonna have to go in there on foot. With this gate down, they couldn't have driven in either. Who knows? They could have dragged her in there, if there really was anything to this. I don't know. This could be a bullshit call." I had no idea what was up.

"It probably is bogus, but I don't see any other way," Edmonds acknowledged. "We certainly can't ignore it."

We took out our flashlights and radioed in that we would be on foot. We locked up our cars and ducked under the gate. Slowly and cautiously, that was the method. Even though we thought this was probably nothing, we couldn't take any chances. There were five cars parked in the underground lot. We had to approach each one, considering the possibility there was something going on inside. They would probably see us coming.

Trying to listen for anything, we did not speak to each other and turned our radios down; as well, we did not want our approach to be heard. As we moved through the lot, we could not hear the call on the radio. Unbeknownst to me, Burkett was being called to handle another rape occurring in my sector.

*****

"All units, 10-3. 318 Baker, Leslie Watson called in a rape and beating. Said she is bleeding from the head. Medics en route." The dispatcher gave Burkett the address.

"318 Baker, I'll respond. I have an ETA of 2."

"309 Baker, proceed for back-up," the dispatcher called out to Bergman.

"10-4, I'm several minutes away, but I'll step it up," Bergman replied.

Burkett got there quickly, certainly in less than two minutes. He parked about two houses down from the victim to see if he could find anybody suspicious lurking about. The house was on a block of small, one story homes with small fenced backyards. As he called in on the car radio, he slowly got out of his car, quietly closed the door and walked down to the house with his flashlight in hand. It was quiet in the neighborhood, as it should have been that time of night. The automatic light of the neighbor's house turned on as Burkett walked by, startling him. Burkett let out a small gasp and jumped to the side, grabbing the top of his weapon. He quickly realized that it was just a driveway light with a motion detector. He stopped and took a breath. He was nervous as he approached the house.

The silence of the radio was broken when Burkett, talking on his handheld radio, called in that he heard a noise in the back of the victim's house and was going to check it out. Moments later, he was back on the radio.

"I've got movement in the backyard. Someone's back there. I'm gonna check it out."

"309 Baker, I'll be there in a minute," Bergman responded.

"315 Baker, respond for additional back-up," the dispatcher directed Fiero to the scene.

"Car 300, I am en route," Lieutenant Dickson responded.

"All units, 10-3," the dispatcher directed everyone to remain off the radio until they heard from Burkett.

The radio always had an eerie silence when we waited to hear from an officer who was out on an emergency call. Burkett called in, with excitement in his voice.

"Someone jumped over the fence in the backyard and is heading towards the next street over. I don't know the name of the street, but have 309 head that way to try to cut him off."

"10-4, 318. 309, did you copy?"

"That's 10-4. I'll head towards the back, less than a minute away."

"315, I copy. ETA 2," Fiero responded.

"Car 300, ETA 2," Dickson also responded.

"10-4. All units remain 10-3," the dispatcher reminded everyone.

"318, I lost him. I couldn't get a description. I'm heading back to check the victim. Have units check the area and stop anybody they see."

The scream of the approaching sirens let Burkett know that back-up was just moments away. He went to the back door of the house, which led to the backyard where he was. The door was open and he walked in, loudly announcing himself. Within a minute, he was back on the radio.

"318, we have a possible homicide. Start medics this way ASAP."

"Car 300, I am en route to the scene. Hold the frequency, 10-3," Dickson instructed dispatch.

*****

Edmonds and I finished our search of the underground parking and all the cars in there. As we would have guessed, there was nothing to the call; it was just another hoax. I got on the radio to call in that we were finished when I was rebuked by the dispatcher.

"321 Baker, we are 10-3, possible homicide," the dispatcher yelled at me over the radio. The shrill in her voice was a little sexy.

Edmonds and I looked at each other, eyebrows raised in surprise. A homicide? That was not something we expected. Westland Park did not have many homicides. Stupidly, I almost got on the radio again to ask what the situation was. Then I pulled out my cell phone and called into dispatch. They filled me in. I told them I would be responding as it was in my patrol sector and then I told Edmonds what had happened. He looked shocked. It should not have surprised me that another rape was called in about 10 minutes after Edmonds and I started searching the parking lot. It occurred at the other end of my sector, again. This was the second time the rapist played me with a hoax call. That pissed me off; it made me look bad. Was I the only cop getting pulled away during these rapes?

*****

I drove up to the scene as fast as possible. This was one area of my sector with which I was not really that familiar. I could not remember the last time I got a call there. Patrol cars were circling the neighborhood, but we all knew it would be to no avail. The perp was long gone or hiding in some bushes somewhere watching us drive around in circles, and enjoying the show. All the police activity and red flashing lights in front of the victim's house woke what had been a neighborhood in a serene, deep sleep. Everybody on the block was buzzing about trying to find out the story. They would know soon enough as we started to interview everybody in a neighborhood canvass — a standard practice after a major crime. We were hoping that somebody heard or saw something that could help. The rapist had now upped the ante. All of a sudden he killed. That had not been his M.O. With the victim dead, we would not get any more intelligence on his actions, his words, anything that might give him away. I walked into the house.

Dickson put his hand up to stop me for a moment and cautioned me not to disturb any evidence; Crime Scene would be there momentarily.

"Let's be careful at the crime scene. That's how we do things now."

At first, I was not really sure what he meant; then I realized how he was pumping up the Dickson brand of leadership.

I went to the kitchen where this young woman in an open silk bathrobe lay on the gray linoleum floor in the pool of her blood oozing from a cut above her brow, mixing with the blood spewing from her cut throat. The rapist had finally put that knife to use.

This was not the first dead body I had seen, nor was it more gruesome than some car wreck where a body was mangled. But this was murder, cold and calculated. Somehow, that made this death more personal to me. Someone had stared into that sweet, pretty face, devoid of any human emotion, violently and painfully ending her life. He watched her gasp for her last breath. Weakness overcame my body for a moment and I could barely stand, not at the sight of blood, but at the reality of what I was unable to stop.

I wanted to cover her exposed, naked body, out of respect, but I knew I had to leave the crime scene just as it was. This was a strange one; the rape had already been called in by the victim. The perp must have left the scene and then come back to kill his victim. Why would he do that? It just seemed awfully risky and out of character for him. I stood by the lieutenant and asked what he made of the situation. Before he could answer, Burkett walked over to us.

"Fuck, if only I could have gotten here a minute or two faster, or gotten over that fence a little quicker, maybe I could've caught the prick. Maybe I could've stopped this murder. Fuck." Burkett vented to us as he swept his right hand across his forehead to wipe off some sweat. There was some blood on his uniform that he must've gotten while checking on the victim.

"Easy, JB. Nothing more you could have done. I think this fucker came back and killed her before you even got here. You did a good job, JB. Our response was a lot better than it would have been a few weeks ago. We're doing things correctly now."

"Thanks, Lieutenant. Maybe you can keep that in mind if another opening comes up in that task force," JB said, looking over at me from the corner of his eye. That was pretty bold of him, I thought. Bold good or bold bad? I was not sure.

"Ok, JB, I will certainly keep that in mind."

Our focus went back to the murder where it belonged — not on Burkett's fantasies. We set up a secure perimeter around the crime scene and directed the media to one specific spot where the chief would meet them to give a statement when he was ready. We had tight control over the ingress and egress of the victim's house. Usually cops just meandered through crime scenes out of curiosity, as I was doing, but often destroying evidence in the process. Nobody, not even command staff, was getting in or out without signing a log. Mac was handling that and she was just the right person for the job. She was not going to put up with anybody's crap. The zone commander ordered units from the other precincts to help with the neighborhood canvass. As with any crisis, we still had to keep units on the street patrolling. The business of police work could not come to a screeching halt.

About an hour before the shift was over, I headed back out to patrol. I called Janie just to talk for a moment and told her about the murder, nothing else. Bergman got me on the side band.

"Got time for that last cup of coffee?"

"Sure do. Meet me at the regular spot," I answered him and headed out to the Triple 7, which we almost always met at. It was not the one where Bullet Brenda worked.

"So what do you make of this? The rapist turning murderer all of a sudden?" I asked Bergman.

"Fuck if I know. It sure does sound strange. Something about it I just don't like."

"You're telling me. This is the second time I got called to some hoax while a rape went on. You think that's a coincidence or is this guy slick enough to get me out of the area before he attacks?"

"You think the perp is working around you? That sounds more like an Eastwood film than life in Westland Park. Don't you think?"

"I don't know, Matt; when you put it that way... Maybe there's nothing to it. What about Burkett, coming within two foot pursuits of the perp? Too bad he isn't a little lighter on his feet so he could have caught the prick."

"Hey, that would be something — Burkett, hero cop."

Then we looked at each other, laughed and in unison said, "Not."

Deep inside, I think we were both a little intimidated by the possibility that Burkett could have shown us up.

"Moving on to a more interesting subject, I've been dating this one babe, Mindy, for a few weeks now. I think it might be double date time. Wanna try it?"

"Yeah, Matt, that sounds great. I'll talk to Janie and give you a call."

"Good. Okay, now, next subject. Whatta ya think of this Dickson guy?" Bergman asked.

"I don't know. Why do you ask?"

"I'm not sure. There is just something about him. I think his name is fitting. He really is one son of a dick."

"Well, there are some things I thought were strange. Whatta you getting at?"

"It just seems that he's taking every chance he can to take a shot at Hughes and the way he did things. Not that I was a big Hughes fan.

He was far from perfect, and I think he could've taken more control of things, but he always meant well. He doesn't deserve to have some fuck from headquarters slamming him behind his back with little innuendos."

"Yeah, yeah, I know what you mean." I was getting a little excited that Bergman was seeing the same thing I was. "When he was telling me that I was going to the task force, he threw something in about Hughes not having any clout at HQ anymore. I didn't know what that was about, but I wasn't about to say anything. And then just before, at the murder, he kept saying things like we now do things better or now we do it the right way, and bragged about his leadership and bullshit like that. Like everything we did sucked before he got here. What's up with that?" Now that I knew what Bergman was getting at, I let him know what I had been thinking.

"I can only guess that he's trying to make himself look good, like we needed him to come in like a white knight and rescue us from Hughes."

"But they're supposedly friends. Why would he do that?" I asked Bergman in sincere but naive wonder.

"Because, that's how people are. They're your friend until not being your friend serves a purpose."

"What purpose could that be? He's just filling in. He's a lieutenant anyway; he's not looking for a sergeant's job."

"No, but think about it. He knows that everyone at HQ, including the chief, has turned on Hughes. Dickson makes it look like he saved this squad, like he's some fuck'n miracle worker. That's sucking right up to the chief. Then he tries to turn that into a transfer out of the Records Division, probably to Operations, all on Hughes' back."

"Whoa, that really sucks."

"Yes, it does. Hey, like I said, this guy is one son of a dick."

"Man, you would hope you wouldn't see that in police work. Aren't we above all that crap? What about all this talk about our blue blood and how we're a family?"

"Oh, you are so young and so innocent, my dear Mr. Hollings. We're a family of cops and all that bullshit, but we're just people.

Getting that badge didn't free us of our human foibles. Some of us are just worse than others."

"Well, once again, that sucks."

The shift ended and I headed home to see Janie.

First, we talked about the rape and murder for a little bit. She was genuinely upset by it. Then I sprung the good news.

"You're never going to guess what happened to me tonight."

"Okay, I give up. What happened?"

"Well, they're forming a serial rape task force and guess who got invited on to play detective?"

"You're kidding," Janie said with a big smile. "I know how much you want to do something like that."

We were sitting on the side of the bed talking. She reached over and gave me a hug and kiss.

"When do you start?"

"Not till next month."

"What are your hours?"

"Well, um, initially, regular business hours. I'll be working days."

"Gary, I just turned down a chance to work days because you were on midnights. Now what's going to happen? We won't have any time together." Her happiness for me quickly dissipated into frustration over the hours.

"Well, can you go back and tell them that you changed your mind?"

"No. They already filled that spot. I'll have to wait till someone else rotates out again. I don't know when that will be."

"Look, I'm sure this day work thing won't be that long. We're just going to start chasing leads, talking to people and trying to develop a suspect. Then, we'll be out at night trying to follow him around or something. After all, that's when he hits: early morning hours. So I'll probably be back on midnights before you know it. Things will work out. I promise."

"Okay" she said hesitantly. "Anyway, you be careful, now. This guy is a murderer. There's been too much death lately. I cannot even think about losing you. You understand me?"

I did not answer her. I didn't have to.

*****

Hughes had been back for a few shifts now and was living up to the promise he made before going on suspension. He had changed. He was on the streets more, and he was asking questions. He was making decisions. What was most startling was that he had turned a cold shoulder to Thompson. We were glad to see Dickson go back to headquarters. I was counting the days before I headed to the task force. Thompson, who barely spoke to me now, got me on the side channel and asked to meet me.

"So, what do you think of the new and improved Sergeant Hughes?" was my first question to Thompson, as I pulled up so we could sit car by car. He did not even turn in my direction.

"I don't think anything of him. He can't be anything other than what he is. He ain't shit."

"I thought you guys were friends."

"Listen, you piss ant rookie. Don't you be worrying about who my friends are. Tell me this — how the fuck did you get pulled for that task force? A little junior prick like you. Either you've been really sucking some dick down at HQ or you've been doing something else that makes somebody there happy."

"Hey, fuck you, Thompson. Maybe I got it by doing a good job. I know you think you're the man 'cause you shot some robber in the ass. But get over yourself. In the meantime, you're never around; you're always taking off early or something. You..." I stopped.

"I what, you little piece of shit?"

Thompson knew I was about to throw something about Stryker's death at him. He also knew that I did not want to go down that road.

"Nothing. Look, sorry they picked me and not you. That's how it goes."

"Well, let me tell you something. Word has it that you've been meeting with IA. Remember, there aren't many secrets in this department. I don't know what the fuck you've been telling them, but you'd better not be trying to climb up the ranks while stepping on your brother officers. Cops don't like cops who do that. Especially cops like me and Gillis. Know what I mean?"

"Oh, just fu..."

Just then we were interrupted by none other than Gillis on the side channel calling Thompson. That was strange timing, not to mention pretty nervy, given all that had happened.

"Hey, can you meet me at that place in five?" Gillis asked.

"Yeah, be right there."

Then the radio blasted with Hughes asking the dispatcher to direct his message to Thompson.

"Do not proceed to meet Detective Gillis. Remain on patrol in your sector." Hughes' directive was loud and very clear.

Thompson hesitated, probably out of shock. "10-4" was his only response.

Then Hughes directed his radio traffic to Gillis.

"Detective, do you have official business in my patrol district?"

"That's negative, Car 3."

"Then leave the district right now. If you need to return have your sergeant notify me."

"10-4."

That communication must have caused every cop on that frequency to stop and try to figure out what just happened. Did Hughes just take on two senior, hotshot cops?

"Go ahead and hitch your wagon to that faggot Hughes. Then I'll watch you follow him off the cliff," Thompson told me with a red, angry face.

He drove off, looking like he felt a little sheepish having been scolded over the radio by Hughes.

That was something and it was scary. How did Thompson know that I went to IA? Was he threatening me? Were he and Gillis really planning to come after me somehow?

The shift couldn't end soon enough for me after that encounter. I got back to Janie's place, or actually our place. Janie would be upset if I ever referred to it as her place; that showed a lack of commitment on my part.

Chapter 19

Thompson and I had not said a word to each other in the last two shifts, other than what was necessary to get the job done. Whenever he was around, I found myself looking over my shoulder, not really expecting anything, but his threats still resonated in my mind and made me uneasy. Bergman assured me that it was just tough talk from a guy who, without a gun and badge, had no balls. Thompson was always a major figure on the squad; his personality was definitely a driver of squad morale. Now, with Thompson on edge, the pressure cooker atmosphere on the squad was getting to everyone. Not only that, I was getting tired of listening to people's stupid problems. Of course, that was most of what police work was. With only a few years on patrol, I was starting to burn out. I was anxious to get to the task force and start on something new. Another few shifts and I was on my way. Thompson could kiss my plain clothes, task force ass.

Roll call ended and for some reason I sensed Thompson looking my way. Not wanting to look back and get into that staring game, I just glanced at the door window and looked at his reflection. I thought I detected a smug smirk. I ignored it. I had only driven about a mile from the precinct when my cell phone rang. That couldn't be good. Janie knew not to call while I was on patrol unless it was an emergency. I didn't like being distracted. I would call her during slow times. Struggling to get the phone out of its holder, with one hand, I flipped it open and was rather surprised.

"Hollings, meet me at the 7 on 7. Don't say anything on the radio. Just go there."

"Yes, sir," was my quick response to Hughes' very short directive. That was certainly strange — Hughes being so secretive. 7 on 7 was our lingo for a certain Triple 7.

Seeing Hughes pull into the rear parking lot, I followed him, swinging the car around so we could talk.

"What's up, Sarge?"

"Listen, I'm gonna tell you this, but you are not to repeat it to anybody, not even your buddy Bergman. Just listen and forget we had this conversation. Got it?"

Voice quivering, I could only say, "Yes."

"You brought your cruiser in for servicing last week, right?"

"Yeah, of course. I got a notice that it was due, like we always get every three months. They gave me this one to use in the meantime. It should be ready soon. Wassup?"

"Gary, did you clean the car out, before you brought it in?"

"Well, yeah, I got all my stuff, the ammo, flares, first aid kit, all that shit. Why? What's going on, Sarge?"

"Okay, listen. The guys in the garage found two thousand dollars in twenties wrapped up and stuffed under the driver's seat."

"Oh, come on. That can't be."

"Yeah, it is. They probably would've kept it if they didn't think IA was trying to set them up. You know, some integrity test or something."

"Why the fuck would I have two thousand dollars in the car?"

"Well, Gary, it's worse than just that. IA did a test. There was a heavy presence of cocaine found on the money. That ain't good. There's been rumors of cops in Westland Park ripping off drug dealers."

"Cops ripping off drug dealers? Yeah, I bet. I know who they should be looking at, and it ain't me. Look, Sarge, I didn't tell you this, but..."

Holding up his hand, Hughes stopped me. "Right, you did not tell me anything. Keep it that way."

Well, Hughes obviously knew that I had gone to IA about Gillis. Now the accuser had become the accused. Somehow Gillis, and probably Thompson too, had set me up. Eyes off them and onto me; Thompson was living up to his threat. Shallow breathing, mind racing, I was in a near panic.

"How did you know about this anyway, Sarge? Wouldn't IA be

tight lipped on something this sensitive?"

"They are. Look, my career may or may not be salvageable at this point. But, I still do have a friend or two left at HQ. Besides, nothing is really a secret in this department."

"Shit. I see that. What do I do? Should I go to them, offer to be polygraphed or something?"

"No, because you don't know about this, right?"

"Yeah, that's right. Then what do I do?"

"Just play it cool. They were thinking of canceling your transfer to the task force."

"What, no! Please, no."

"It's all right. It's going through, but not to keep you happy. They don't want to do anything that might tip you off. They're transferring you, but they're looking at you hard, Gary."

"So, what now? How am I supposed to work with this thing hanging over me? I need to straighten this out somehow."

"Don't do anything. You'll only make things worse. Just act like nothing happened. I'll try to keep up with things and let you know. Just be careful."

"Okay, Sarge. Hey, this is quite a risk you're taking for me. Why?"

"I lost one good cop. I am not losing another."

That was not the way to start off a shift. Now, I was really afraid of what could be happening to me. This wasn't just a minor violation. I could be fired. I could be prosecuted. This was some serious shit. I met Bergman for coffee about an hour before the shift ended.

"You look like shit, my friend. What's going on?"

"Berg, I can't tell you, but I got problems. Big fuck'n problems. You trust me, right? I may do some stupid things, but I'm clean. I'm a good cop. You know that, right?"

"Fuck'n A, I know that. C'mon, Gary, what's going on?"

"Really, Berg, I can't tell you. But I swear, I didn't do anything. I'm getting set up."

"All right, I understand. Let me tell you this: I know I hit you with all my self-righteous bullshit when we start talking. Sometimes I don't even know if I believe what I'm saying myself. Look, if you're getting fucked with, you let me know. I don't know how, but we'll straighten this shit out. You're a good cop, and I ain't sitting back and watching my friend go down. Got it?"

"Got it, buddy."

That made me feel better, at least a little better. I trusted Bergman. But, what could he do? He was just a young street cop like me.

*****

When the shift was finally over, we were all back in the locker room changing into our civilian clothes. We were leaving when I heard Hughes call Thompson back in. They walked over to the lieutenant's office and shut the door. Was this about the conversation I had with Hughes earlier?

"Why don't you straighten this out before it all comes falling down on you, Mark?"

"I don't know what you are talking about, Sarge."

"Don't be so cute with me. Isn't it enough you stood by while your buddy Gillis got Stryker killed?"

"Oh, we're pinning that on me, are we? Aren't you the one who just got suspended for having your head up your ass while that went down? Where were you, Dave?"

"That's Sergeant to you, Officer."

"Well, Sergeant, are we going somewhere with this? I don't hear any accusations. Is there something I can help you with, or can I go home now?"

"Look, Thompson, I let you play me. I know that now. Don't get too cocky. You're starting to make mistakes. And when you make just enough of them, I'm gonna nail your ass."

"Yeah, let's wait and see who's nailing whose ass." Thompson was almost laughing as he walked out of the office. Before leaving the precinct, he stopped at the door to use his cell phone.

"We need to talk," he told whoever was at the other end of that conversation.

Three more nights of patrol, then a break over the weekend, then I was off to the task force. I was in the final stretch — not that going over there would end my problems. IA was watching me, probably planning on how to set me up further. On the one hand, I knew I was clean. On the other hand, I still suffered from my rookie idealism and was rather naive. That made me vulnerable. I had to be careful. Although Bergman was junior to me, I found myself seeking his counsel on many things. But he wouldn't be on the task force with me; I needed to watch my own back.

Finally, tonight was my last shift before heading to the task force. It was also another shift with Thompson arriving a few hours late. Hughes was driving around the patrol sectors just checking in with us when he got a text message.

"Come home now," was all it read. He called home first; there was no answer.

"Dispatch, I have to head home for a bit."

Hughes asked Mac to cover as acting sergeant and started his trip home. He was focused on just getting there. As any of us would be, he was worried about getting a text like that while at work.

*****

Pulling off the highway, and going a little over the speed limit on that suburban road, he was now only a block away. With tunnel vision setting in, and no reason to be looking around, he did not see Gillis parked off the road, behind a tree, sitting there in the dark. Gillis started texting.

By the time Hughes pulled into his driveway, he did not even remember the drive home. He walked into his house and upstairs to the bedroom. Normally, his first step was to lock up his weapon in the safe sitting on a shelf in the bedroom closet. All cops knew that when they got home, locking up the gun was the first and smartest thing to do. Hughes was not thinking about that now; he did not take off his weapon and lock it up. It stayed right on his belt. He walked in the bedroom and stopped at the doorway. He and his wife startled each other. Their eyes locked for a moment.

Hughes did not speak, his squinting eyes fixed on Melinda. Lips quivering, he had to bite down on his upper lip to keep it still. A weakness invaded his knees, but he did not move and maintained his frozen stance. He felt a shortness of his breath, but gave no sign of his suffering. No words had to be exchanged. Right away, Melinda knew what kind of crisis had just entered her life. So did Hughes. Standing still for a long moment, simply staring and thinking about what to do with his gun, Hughes reached his right hand back and ran his fingers over the top of the gun's handle. There was a stare-off. Who would blink first? Then he removed his hand. Dropping her head, Melinda breathed a heavy sigh of relief. Hughes turned around and walked out of the house, quickly retracing his footsteps, almost reliving that ignominious walk he had taken out of Police Headquarters not too long ago.

Hughes called into dispatch that he was back in service.

*****

The shift finally ended. My time had come. But where were things heading? We all had finished getting undressed in the locker room and realized that Hughes was not back yet. The front desk receptionist got on the intercom.

"Do any of you know where Sergeant Hughes is? He has not marked in at the precinct and he hasn't called in to say that he was out on anything."

We all looked around; nobody knew where Hughes was. That was strange. First he had gone off duty to go home and then came back. He was rarely out of the precinct and he was always back before the rest of us. Thompson was the first one to show any signs of alarm.

"Hey, this isn't good. We need to find him," he said, addressing all of us in the locker room.

"I'm sure he's fine. Maybe he stopped to get a cup of coffee or something," I said.

"Yeah, why don't we just hang tight for a little bit and if we don't hear from him in about five or 10 minutes, then we'll sound the alarm? Let's not panic," was Bergman's suggestion, to which we all agreed by a nod of the heads.

"Okay, but do me a favor," Thompson said, looking at Bergman, "go get Mac and Fiero, and tell them not to leave yet. I'm going to the front desk to double-check with dispatch and make sure he didn't call something in on the phone for some reason."

Three minutes passed quietly. When another two minutes passed, Thompson made it clear that he was exercising command as the senior officer. He directed each of us to go back to our patrol sector and start a methodical search for the sergeant. Thompson notified the precinct Lieutenant, Tom Leone. Once again, we asked KCPD to send over their helicopter. A missing cop was a high priority. Fellow police departments always stood ready to help. Their helicopter was airborne within 15 minutes. Leone then authorized our helicopter to be mobilized. That would take about another hour, to get the pilot and observer mobilized. We did not use our helicopter as much as KC did.

After about half an hour, the KCPD helicopter called in a single patrol car with the engine running, idling in the parking lot of Meadow Woods Park, behind Police Headquarters. Leone immediately called in that he was responding, directed Thompson to respond and then dispatch called for Mac to back them up. The Charlie team was out on patrol already. We were not handling calls, only searching. It did not matter what dispatch had said; the entire squad rushed with lights and sirens to the lot. I was fairly close. Leone and Thompson were there in minutes. I did not know what had happened, yet I did know. Walking over to the car, I could barely see through the driver's side window and windshield. The blood and brain matter covered them both. As I moved along the hood of the car to the other side, I could see in. What was left of Hughes' head was slumped forward, resting on the steering wheel. When I got to the passenger side window, I could see the gun, still in Hughes' hand. Light-headed, I went to the curb to sit down as the rest of the squad came rushing in.

I watched Thompson. At first, he seemed composed and controlled given the circumstances. Was that his "in command" persona? How could this not shock him? But then he started to unravel. He began screaming, cursing, almost crying, but not really; something about his response did not seem real. He circled Hughes' car, looking in disbelief. Then unexpectedly, he opened the passenger door and jumped in. He grabbed Hughes' limp arm, shaking him.

"Wake up, Dave. Wake up," he screamed.

Even for a cop in shock that seemed melodramatic, more like a Hollywood version of a cop's untimely death and its impact upon his brothers in blue, especially in view of Thompson's comments to me about Hughes. Hughes was clearly dead. Leone and I jumped up and grabbed Thompson, pulling him out of the car, as if making a felony arrest. No matter what, this was a crime scene, and it had to be protected. Resting her head on Liz's shoulder, Mac was crying uncontrollably, her tears appearing more natural than Thompson's. Edmonds began to say prayers. Burkett stood there staring at the car, just staring. Leone kept his wits about him. He calmly called it in to dispatch.

He directed that the chief be notified immediately and that Crime Scene respond ASAP. He asked the zone commander to assure that the park was cordoned off so that no media could get in and take pictures of this gruesome scene. He assumed that none of us would be emotionally capable of making the notification to his wife. The deputy chief was dispatched for that heartbreaking assignment. The chief would have to field the media questions. Leone then gathered the entire squad together, almost in a team huddle.

"I know how tragic this is to all of you. Dave was a friend of mine as well. But right now, there is nothing for any of you to do. I want all of you to leave the scene and return to your homes. None of you are to report to work next shift. I have replacement units on the way from other precincts to cover. The police chaplain and our employee assistance program are available and I will direct them to reach out to each and every one of you. If you wish to seek comfort or guidance from your own clergy or doctor, I encourage you to do so. Take off as much time as you need. All of you go home, now." A second cop was now dead; this time from his own hand. This was more than any squad of cops could endure.

As to be expected, nobody moved. We just looked at each other uncomfortably. As we stood there looking at each other, this scene seemed all too familiar. Another cop on our squad was dead. How could this be?

"That's an order. All of you leave and go home now!"

One by one, we slowly peeled ourselves away from the scene and into our cars to drive home.

"I gotta talk to you, seriously," I walked past Bergman and said in a low voice.

"Now?"

"Right fuck'n now."

"Pancakes?"

"See you there."

I called Janie from the car. She broke down in tears and asked me to please come home right away. She was surprised when I told her that I had to stop and take care of something first. She would have been more surprised if she knew I was taking care of this over pancakes.

"What's up, Gary? This night is pretty fucked-up all by itself. You got something else?"

"Yeah." As I sipped my coffee, I reached into my pants' pocket and pulled out a cell phone, sliding it across the table.

"Your cell phone. So what?" Bergman wanted to know.

"Not mine."

"Okay, talk to me."

"It's Stryker's or at least it was."

"What the fuck? That was evidence. You took evidence from a crime scene? From the murder of a cop? Gary, what's going on?"

"Look, when Stryker was shot, Gillis asked me if I found his phone. The guy had two bullets in him, his friend was dying and he was worrying about some stupid phone. I knew something was up. So, I took it."

"Okay, Gary, not something I would have expected from you. So you have his phone. Why are we here talking about this 20 minutes after our sergeant blows his brains out?"

I leaned over and hit a button on the phone.

"Oh shit. Is that what I think it is?" Bergman was stunned.

"Sure looks that way."

"So you've been sitting on this. Why?"

"I didn't want this to get out; I didn't think Hughes could take it."

"Okay, I get it. But look where we are now. So, what do we do? Go to IA with this?"

"We can't go to IA, Berg."

"Why not?"

"Because they can't keep a secret themselves. Besides, how can I explain that I've been sitting with this? They'll really fuck me over now."

"All right, obviously there is something you're not telling me. Spill it."

"They set me up, Berg."

"Who? Whatta you talking about?"

"Some mechanic found two thousand bucks in 20s rolled up in my car. They called IA. IA tested the money and it was soaked in cocaine. I'm sure it was that two grand that Gillis ripped off from some dealer. Now IA is up my ass."

"How did you find this out?"

"That's my point. Hughes told me."

"Hughes told you? But how did…"

"Yeah, even Hughes had enough contacts to hear what was happening in IA. As he said, there are no secrets."

"So why did he…"

"He was trying to make things right, Berg. And look where he wound up. I think they set him up too."

"Whatta ya mean?"

"Think about it. Hughes went home for some reason, then came back to blow his brains out. Look what's on Stryke's phone. Thompson was out when Hughes killed himself. I don't know exactly how, but everything here is connected. Thompson knew how to push Hughes; he knew Hughes would freak."

"Who wouldn't? Especially a guy like Hughes whose career was unraveling."

"Yeah, exactly. This was well-planned out."

"That's a great theory, Gary. We may have some serious shit going on here. Can we prove anything?"

"I don't know. Probably not."

Then there was a silence — a frustrating silence. Bergman looked up.

"The phone," he said.

"The phone?"

"Yeah, IA is going to look at Hughes' phone and maybe there will be a text or something that points to Thompson and blows this thing open."

I thought about that possibility for a moment. Then I reflected on the scene at Hughes' car earlier tonight.

"He did it again, Berg. That son of a bitch Thompson did it again."

"Did what?"

"He did what I did to Stryker, only more theatrical."

"What are you talking about?"

I couldn't figure out that scene in the car — Thompson crying over Hughes' body. He hated Hughes at that point. Why would he be so upset? Especially a guy who cared about nobody but himself?

"And...?"

"He was almost hugging Hughes' half decapitated body. Why? Because it gave him a chance to grab Hughes' phone. He knew exactly what he was doing, Berg."

"Shit, Gary, he is good."

"Yeah, and he's gonna screw me. I know it. What do I do now?"

"We'll think of something. Can I keep this?" Bergman asked, holding up the phone.

"Yeah, I guess. Why?"

"I think it's time to get back to New York. Gotta visit my mother for a couple of days. You heard the lieutenant. Take the time we need to grieve. See you in a few days. You know, we can't talk about this to anyone, and I mean not anyone. Understood?"

"Understood. See ya."

With no idea of what Bergman had in mind; I did not want to know. But I would probably like it.

I drove to Janie's in disbelief over the series of events that had occurred. In Westland Park, this was surreal. More importantly, this was not the end of it. I knew that. Janie would want to talk things out. I used to be like that. Now, talking seemed to bring nothing but trouble.

Chapter 20

Finally, I reported to the task force. Janie had to take me shopping for a few sports coats and slacks, and forced me to buy two suits. Getting out of uniform was a nice break.

With an IA investigation looming over me and trying to keep Thompson and the squad, even Hughes, off my mind, I was not enjoying my new assignment the way I should have been. Life can be awfully unfair at times. For me, the key was to stay focused on the job and not let everything else distract me. Of course, that was easier said than done; the harder I tried not to think about things, the more I thought about the what-ifs. Even though I was deep into my own issues, I still felt for my squad mates. The squad was so much of who I was and had been for the past few years that I could not really detach myself that completely and so soon after such tragedies. It was just one crisis after the next for them. I felt that I had escaped, but did that give me the right to forget about the deaths of two fellow police officers?

The task force was such an exciting opportunity. I couldn't believe it. The IA investigation would probably clear me, or so I hoped. Being innocent wasn't always enough. I could not let myself become distracted by anything or anybody and keep me from making a name for myself in the Detective Bureau. Somehow, I would have to put the Third Precinct Baker squad out of my mind.

I made it into a meeting room at headquarters 15 minutes ahead of the scheduled start. It was just a large classroom, with a desk in front of a whiteboard and chairs lined up in rows facing forward: not much different from the roll call room, just bigger. As to be expected, things appeared a little chaotic at first. At least one patrol officer from each precinct had been selected for the task force. I saw a lot of gray hair around me. For sure, I was the youngest patrol officer selected for the task force. That had to mean something. I did not know any of the other patrol officers since I had not really met anyone outside of my own precinct. Most of the older guys seemed to know each other and were engaged in light-hearted conversation, laughing heartily.

Uncomfortably, I stood there by myself, waiting for the meeting to begin. Detective Patelli came over and greeted me. It was good to see at least one familiar face. We shook hands. His grip was firm and strong, crushing my hand, as if he were sending me a message. I did not flinch. "Okay, everybody take a seat, please," someone yelled out.

Everyone finished their conversations, and poured themselves another cup of coffee from the coffee urn that had been set up on a table off to the side of the room. They all eventually grabbed a chair and settled in.

"For those of you who don't know me, my name is Paul Moran. I am the Sex Crimes Unit sergeant. I will be in charge of this task force. Off to my left is Lieutenant Willman. He is the Detective Bureau Lieutenant. If you have any complaints about me, you go see him. But, I'll tell you this right now, we don't want to hear any complaints; we just want to catch this bastard. Ain't that right, LT?"

"Absolutely. Besides I can't imagine anybody having a complaint about you. You're such a warm, fuzzy guy." That generated some light laughter from the audience, which consisted of around a dozen guys and three women.

"All right, let's get right to it," Moran continued. "As you all know, we've had a serial rapist striking in the county for over a year now. We're getting beat up in the press because we can't solve it and the chief is starting to get pissed, especially with all the other, uh, shall I say 'issues,' he's been dealing with. The timing of this task force is pretty good. Most of you probably already heard that this fuck took his rapes a step further and killed the victim. It happened up in the Third Precinct. As a matter of fact, Officer Hollings, who is on our task force, was at the scene."

Moran said this while pointing to me. Everyone just instinctively turned to look at me. I felt rather stupid, since I had nothing to say. Moran continued with his briefing.

"Now, we've had six rapes occur in the footpaths of Meadow

Woods Park. We've been putting out the word for women not to go on those paths past dark, but some are still doing it. The last rape occurred less than a week ago in the Fourth Precinct's area. We've had five rapes occurring at the victim's residence. All have been on a ground floor apartment, except one. That was a second floor apartment where the perp climbed down from the roof. That was in the Third Precinct. Actually, all the strange stuff with this guy happened in the Third Precinct. He raped one Nina Wilkes, twice. At the scene of the second rape, detectives found pubic hair on the bed. It was a rather unusual sample, more than we usually get and just lying there almost like it was planted. That pubic hair matched hair samples taken from the victim, Faith Newman, who was raped earlier in the Third Precinct; that's when we confirmed that we had a serial rapist."

"Excuse me, Sergeant." One officer raised his hand to ask a question. "So what do you make of the fact that all the unusual patterns occurred in the Third Precinct?"

"We can only make some educated guesses right now. Clearly, the perp is much more comfortable in the Third Precinct's area, so we have to think that he lives or works there. Even his decision to murder all of a sudden occurred in the Third Precinct. Oh, and I should mention that at the murder scene, we found a small personal article belonging to a rape victim on the jogging path in the park a week or so earlier. There is something driving this guy that we can't figure out — at least not yet. Having said that, this is a good point for me to introduce Detective Marsha Peters, from the KCPD. She's been trained in profiling and goes to school for all the psychobabble stuff that the rest of us can't understand. She'll be working closely with us on this, trying to form some kind of profile that can help us narrow down the suspect pool, which by the way, we have no suspects as of yet. Thank you for joining us, Detective. Are there any other questions?"

I felt pressured to ask an intelligent question, since most of the rapes occurred in my precinct. Worse than that, two rapes were in my sector and the murder was in my sector. That couldn't look too good for my patrol skills. Given those facts, I thought maybe I should just keep quiet for the moment.

"Yes, Sergeant, I have a question." Another officer raised her hand.

"Go ahead."

"Has the rapist struck outside of Westland Park?"

"We're not sure. We've checked with Dumont and the other surrounding counties and KC. A couple of rapes have similarities but none closely match the M.O. of our guy. Anything else?"

Another detective had a question.

"Yeah, I would like to ask Detective Peters a question. What do you think of these little bits of evidence from one scene showing up at another? I know there is always the possibility of transference, but is that what you see here?"

"Thank you. That is a very good question. As you know, it is not unusual for a rapist to take things from the victim so that he can relive the events in his mind. Much like cutting out the newspaper stories of the rape. Maybe this rapist finds some fascination in connecting one rape to another. Or, it can be some totally different motivation. It's a little early to say now."

"Hey, Sarge, what similarities do we have amongst the victims? Is there some commonality that seems to be attracting the rapist?" came from another of the patrol officers.

"Another good question. We obviously picked the right people for this task force. There seems to be no physical characteristic in common. But they are all in the mid-20 to late-30 age range. The rapes on the jogging paths were clearly opportunity driven. None of them really looked enough alike or had anything in common to detect a pattern. Four of the victims were married, two were not, but since they were all by themselves at the time, that fact may be fairly useless. In the residential rapes, he definitely did his homework. Each woman lived alone. He knew how to get in and out of the residences quickly, even though on two occasions an officer from the Third Precinct did see the suspect, but lost him in a foot pursuit."

"May I add something, Sergeant?" I found my chance to offer something productive.

"Yes, please, Officer Hollings."

"In one of the rape cases, the victim, Vicky Cordero, lived with a biker. But I had arrested him for assault and he was still locked up when the rapist attacked, which was good for the rapist. That biker was a pretty big dude." I got a few chuckles, then I continued. "So the point is that the perp is really scoping his victim out, making sure she is alone."

"Very good point. I should have mentioned that. That shows how closely he is watching his victims. This will be tough. What we're going to start out doing is re-interviewing the victims. Now that they have had a little time to recuperate and hopefully, some of the shock has subsided, they may remember something. We want to know about ex-husbands, old boyfriends, even guys they turned down for dates or any guy who was acting weird with them. I know that doesn't sound like a good beginning point for a serial rapist, but we've got to start somewhere. You will be assigned to the interviews in your precinct. And of course, we'll still be doing forensics hoping to come up with something.

"Okay, each patrol officer is going to be partnered up with a detective from some branch of the Detective Bureau. Detective Patelli will coordinate logistics. He'll be calling out the teams and handing out a package with the interviews and other leads we want covered. As you develop new leads while you're out on the street working, be sure to call them in first to Patelli."

"Oh and if may offer one more thing," I asked.

"Certainly."

"I think everyone should know that before two of the rapes I was pulled away on a hoax call. So that just shows how well this guy is planning it out." I guess I did have something important to offer after all.

"That is significant. We might have some police buff who listens to scanners and knows how we respond to calls. Something else to keep in mind. Okay, everybody, good luck."

I got partnered up with Detective Keith Mannings, a senior

detective about 45 years old. He had done his 20 years and could retire at any time, but he loved what he was doing. Retirement was not in his plans any time soon. As an African-American, he was probably one of very few black officers when he came into the department. I saw only one other black officer in this task force. There was no doubt about it; we were not a very diverse group. Surely, it was not easy for Mannings to make it to detective. But, he did. That probably said a lot about him. His regular assignment was homicide and robberies. There weren't enough homicides in Westland Park for full-time homicide detectives. Our interviews were what I expected. We had to go back and re-interview Nina Wilkes, Faith Newman and Vicky Cordero. We were supposed to start locating friends and co-workers of Leslie Watson and determine if anybody would know why somebody would want to kill her.

We first contacted Nina Wilkes and she agreed to meet with us for lunch at 11:30 at a Mexican restaurant near her work. We made sure to be on time.

"Hi, Nina, I'm Officer Hollings. Do you recognize me? I was one of the officers at your house."

"Yes, Officer, of course I do. And thank you for all your help. That was a tough time for me."

"I understand. Let me introduce Detective Mannings. We're part of a task force that the police department has put together to catch this guy."

"Well, that's great that you're giving this so much attention. I don't want anyone to go through this if we can stop it."

We were talking as we were led to our table by a waitress.

"That's the plan. Hopefully, we will catch him soon, but we do need some help. As I told you on the phone, we want to ask you a few more questions."

"Okay, but please don't ask me anything specific about, you know. I lived through it twice and I don't want to re-live it. I'm still in counseling. It has not been easy."

"We understand that and we're not going to ask any questions like that." Then I hesitated. I wanted Mannings to take the lead now. He was much more experienced at this detective stuff. Besides, I was afraid I might say something to upset her.

"Nina," Mannings filled the void, "one of the things we want to know about is if there are any men that you may have dated, or if you have an ex-husband, or somebody like that, who you feel may have wanted to hurt you."

"Well, first, there is no ex-husband, so we can scratch that. The last steady boyfriend I had, we broke up about six months before the attack. Then I had some dates, here and there. I dated one guy for about a month or so, but he dumped me about four or five weeks ago. Nothing serious with anybody."

"Would you be able to give us their names and phone numbers? We may want to talk to them, but don't worry, we'll respect your privacy."

She looked a little disturbed about that. I guess I could understand a girl not wanting a couple of cops digging into her love life.

"Look, I don't think any of these guys could have done this, but okay," she hesitantly agreed.

"Nina, if I may," Mannings continued," I heard what you just said about these guys. You don't suspect any of them. But let me ask you about other guys who maybe you turned down for a date or have been flirting with you and you've been avoiding them, or any man whose behavior has just made you uncomfortable."

Nina thought for a moment. "Well..." and she looked at me with a half smile, almost like she wanted my approval to say what she wanted to say.

"Go ahead, Nina. It's okay," I told her in the most reassuring voice I could come up with.

"Whew, this is weird, but there was this police officer who came to the first attack, Officer Burkett. He kept coming by to check on me and then he asked me out."

I was frozen for a minute. That came out of nowhere. Mannings looked at me, also surprised, but wanting to see if I knew anything about that, which I didn't.

"Nina," now I took over, "I'm sorry, but we were not aware of that. Has he been around lately?"

"No, I called your station. I spoke to a Sergeant Hughes, I think. He told me he would take care of it."

"And did he?" I asked.

"Oh yeah, the officer never contacted me again."

"When did all this happen?" I then asked her.

"It was after the first attack. And that was the end of it."

Then I had a quick flashback; I remembered on the second rape that Burkett called Hughes on the radio and the case got assigned to me. I never did ask why. Now I knew.

We finished the interview and drove back to headquarters.

"That was surprising about Burkett, though nothing he does surprises me. Burkett was always a bit weird," Mannings said to me as I drove.

"You know him?" I asked.

"Yeah, we were on patrol together for a couple of years, quite a while ago. Is he still living with his mother?"

I had to laugh when he asked that.

"Yeah, he still does."

"Then he goes and asks a rape victim out for a date. How did he ever become a cop?"

I assumed that was a rhetorical question and let it go. Driving back, I asked Mannings to pull off at my bank for a moment so I could cash a check. As the teller punched my account number into the computer, she hesitated for a second. Quickly I asked, "Is there a problem?"

"Seems like your account was frozen. Looks like there was a sub..." and she stopped.

"A what... a subpoena?" I asked a little more aggressively.

"Hold on, let me get a manager." She walked off in a hurry, but I had a pretty good idea of what had happened. I watched the teller speak with the branch manager; they looked back at me and, as the manager went back to an office, the teller returned asking me to have a seat and pointed to the waiting area. Within a few minutes, the bespectacled manager, in a gray pin striped suit with a blue shirt and blue tie, with a balding head, politely addressed me. It was all a mistake, he explained and he handed me the cash for the check.

"Did the police department serve a subpoena on my account?" I asked.

"It was just a mistake, sir. There is nothing else to say."

That said it all. IA was looking into my finances, trying to see if I was stocking away ripped-off drug money. I think my $118 balance and the fact that I just cashed a $100 check from my grandmother may have shed some light on my financial condition. That should have made me feel better, but it didn't. No cop wanted IA breathing down his neck. Sometimes IA would see what IA wanted to see.

Chapter 21

Another police funeral descended upon us. Two funerals in a relatively short period of time were not just sad, but professionally embarrassing. All the other police departments must have been wondering what was going on in Westland Park. I was starting to wonder myself and was sure that I was only one of many Westland Park cops thinking the same thing. My uniform would have probably been the more appropriate attire, but I opted for a dark suit. This was not the right time or place, but I wanted to send a message that I was in plain clothes now, albeit temporarily. That separated me from Thompson and the squad.

Hughes' funeral proceeded not much differently than Stryker's, at least from the perspective of appearance. The honor guard, the bagpipes, even a prayer from Edmonds, were all too familiar to us. There was something about a suicide that loomed over funerals. It made the death seem more wasteful than being killed in the line of duty, which had at least a sense of honor and dignity. Anyone close to the deceased wondered what warning signs they should have picked up on and an aura of guilt permeated the funeral. Thompson again escorted the grieving widow, which reminded us of Stryker's funeral. He didn't know what I knew.

Melinda's relatively young face looked as if it had aged since I last saw her at the barbeque; it was noticeably wrinkled by her profound grimace. The tears rolled out from under her sunglasses that she wore on this overcast day, which only made the funeral seem even gloomier. While she wore black and was appropriately dressed with nothing showing, I was inappropriate in my mind, admiring her slim waist accentuated by those great tits. She walked slowly and weakly, almost collapsing before making it to her seat, where Thompson sat beside her. This time, Thompson was different. There was no sense of ego emanating from him. Thompson's movements were calm and controlled and his face reflected a calm that belied his true feelings. He too wore dark sunglasses, and still appeared to be avoiding eye contact. I noticed the deputy chief standing in front of the casket. He was at Stryker's funeral, but now he seemed much more personally involved, showing a sadness that went beyond a professional relationship. I did not know if they had been friends or not, but this death obviously was hard on him.

We had all been switching off going to Hughes' house every day to help Melinda out with whatever she needed. Right after the funeral, she thanked us and told us we could stop. She knew she had to get on with her life on her own. She was probably right. Our showing up was getting awkward for her and us; the conversations were becoming strained and there did not seem to be much that we could really do anyway.

*****

Only one day after Hughes' funeral, IA was preparing to interview some of the squad to talk about Hughes. Though homicide detectives and the coroner's office had determined that he died of a self-inflicted gunshot wound, they did have to do some investigation. What would have driven him to suicide? He seemed to be bouncing back after the suspension, becoming the Sergeant Hughes who once commanded a SWAT team. What set him in reverse? Could it have been guilt over the death of Stryker catching up to him? The department wanted to know if there were warning signs they should have picked up on. Learn a lesson and maybe prevent another police suicide.

IA Commander Jensen walked over to Chief Harper's office.

"Hey, Lee, you got a minute?" Jensen asked Harper from the doorway.

"Sure, Tim, come on in and have a seat."

Harper got up from behind his desk and walked over to the sofa and two chairs surrounding a coffee table. He didn't want to keep it formal by sitting at his big mahogany desk; he and Jensen went back many, many years.

"I'm sure you know we're having a few of the Third Precinct Baker squad in today to talk about Dave's suicide, just to get some background."

"Yes, very good, Tim. That certainly was a tragedy. Do you think the suspension and probation pushed him over the edge or what?"

"I don't know, Lee. Maybe we'll have some answers after we talk to his squad, but there is something else I want to talk to you about."

"Go ahead, Tim. You have my undivided attention."

"Well, after we finish the inquiry into Dave's suicide, I'm going to be retiring."

"What! Why would you do that?"

"I guess it's just time. I mean, Dave's suicide certainly gave me reason to pause and reassess everything. I had many questions that I couldn't answer, so I think my time with this department should come to a peaceful and quiet conclusion."

"Tim, I hope you're not serious. You know that all this introspection and self-doubt stuff always happens when we lose a friend; it's only natural. But stop and think for a minute. The department still needs you. You have a lot to offer."

"I'm not so sure about that anymore."

"Come on, Tim, this is ridiculous. Look, I'm upset too that Dave ate his gun. He and I go way back, like you did with him, and like you and I do. But just because he couldn't take the pressure anymore is no reason to end your career prematurely. That's being weak, like Hughes was. Weakness is hardly one of your traits, Tim."

"Lee, I think I'm a little past a play on my machismo. I outgrew that years ago."

"Well then, let's look at this in more practical terms. I'm retiring in a year or two. You know you're the frontrunner for this job. Isn't that what you worked so hard for, to become chief one day? Why give that up?"

"Probably because I don't deserve it."

"Oh, Tim, please. This is getting sickening. A friend killed himself. I understand that. So we're sad. We give him a proper funeral, we mourn him, and then we move on, just like we would for anyone of us. This is the world we live in. You'll see, even that pretty little wife of his will be out boinking somebody new before he's cold in the grave. Get real, Tim. Life moves on."

"Lee, I'm not naive. I know all about death and how life goes on. That's not the issue."

"Then what is the issue?"

"Let's be honest here. After Dave had that shooting years ago, he was never the same. We both knew it. It was a clean shoot, and he should have been promoted to lieutenant after that. But look what happened; he became withdrawn and wasn't tuned into what was going on around him. We knew there was something wrong. And what did we do? We put him right back on duty, in the street, before he was ready. We should've known that sooner or later things would catch up to him and he would snap. We have some culpability here, Lee. We should just admit it."

"I'm not admitting shit. Look, you remember how all this played out. He was cleared by the shrink. What were we supposed to do? There is no one to blame here. Shit just happens sometimes."

"I don't see it that way. I was his lieutenant at the time. I should have done something. I could have put him in some admin job or anything. Instead, we just left him there in the street in charge of a squad of patrol officers — right where all the shit breaks loose. That was wrong. You were the zone commander. We both should have seen this coming sooner or later."

"This is crazy talk, Tim. Just take some time to think about it. Remember, once you retire, there is no coming back: no changing your mind. Why don't we talk again in a few weeks? I am sure you'll feel differently once you've had a chance to settle down and think things over. You'll see. The shock of this will wear off and everything will look differently."

Jensen stood up and laid his retirement papers on Harper's desk. "I appreciate what you're saying Lee, but I don't think so. It's just time. But thanks."

*****

As Jensen went back to his office, I was arriving at the IA conference room to talk about the little I knew about Hughes, or at least the little I would tell them; I did not know who to trust. Two IA detectives and their sergeant were sitting at the long desk as I came in. They greeted me and motioned for me to take my seat. After some brief, light conversation, they got right into what they wanted to know. The sergeant led their questioning.

"Officer Hollings, how well did you know Sergeant Hughes, on a personal level?"

"Hardly at all, sir. The only time I saw him socially was at the barbeque he threw at his house a couple of summers ago. That's it."

"Okay. Had you heard any rumors going around about anything? You know, even mere gossip that didn't seem like anything at the time."

"No, sir, I really didn't interact much with the sergeant."

"Did you notice any changes in him? Anything unusual?"

"No."

"Well. Let's not drag this on unnecessarily. Is there anything you can tell us about Sergeant Hughes that might help shed some light on why he would commit suicide?"

"No, sir. I have absolutely no information about that. I'm sorry."

"Okay, then."

I sat for a moment wondering if I should bring up their investigation of me and that money that Hughes told me about. Trying to get some non-verbal signal from them I realized that I would not play poker with those guys. Their faces showed nothing. I let it go.

That was brief. I was glad it was early in the morning and I was able to get it out of the way. Maybe if I called Janie, I could talk her into meeting me for brunch. Then she would have to go back to get some sleep for her late shift. I walked to my car and just sat there for a few minutes thinking about Hughes.

*****

While I was reflecting on a lost life, Thompson came into the IA conference room. If the IA detectives knew Thompson like the rest of our squad did, they would've seen a man much different than before Hughes' suicide. He was subdued, he was polite and all his arrogance seemed to have dissipated. Was it real?

"Good morning, Officer. Thank you for coming in."

"Certainly," Thompson answered.

"I think you know why we are here. We are just trying to get some background information on Sergeant Hughes to see if we can determine what might have driven him to suicide."

"I understand."

"How well did you know him outside of work?"

"We socialized some. We went out to dinner with our wives on occasion."

"Did you two ever go out together, just the two of you?"

"We'd meet for dinner during the shift once in a while, but outside of work it was always the four of us."

Thompson's answers were slow and deliberate. He was thinking out each word.

"Okay, in your conversations with him, did you pick up on anything that may have caused him a lot of stress... you know, kind of pushed him over the edge?"

Thompson sat there thinking, and thinking. He looked as if he were lost in his thoughts. His body was bobbing slightly back and forth. He was not answering. The detectives looked at each other in wonder about Thompson's reactions.

What Thompson was thinking about was Hughes' last view of his wife. Naked, at the edge of their bed on her hands and knees, her beautiful, plump breasts dangling down, almost hitting the mattress; it was straight out of a porno flick. She was letting out gentle moans, her head swaying side to side, with Thompson drilling her from behind. Thompson was trying not to smile at that pleasant memory and the look in Hughes' eyes when he walked into the room.

"Officer, are you okay?" the sergeant asked.

For a moment Thompson did not even answer that question. He was staring at the ground. Then he looked up.

"I'm fine. I just get upset when I think about it. Seeing him in the car, it was just a bit much."

The remaining questions got the same Thompson bullshit answers. Finally, IA decided to wrap it up.

"Officer, we didn't find Sergeant Hughes' cell phone at the scene. Did you happen to see it when you were in the car?"

"His cell phone? Detective, I was pretty shaken up. I don't really remember anything about his cell phone."

After Thompson left, the sergeant turned to his IA detectives. "Cops die and their cell phones just disappear. Something is fishy in Westland Park."

Chapter 22

"We got it programmed like you asked. So you take out this chip and put in this chip, just like this. Got it?"

"I got it," Bergman answered as he practiced carefully removing and inserting a chip into the cell phone. "Thanks, guys."

"When you moving back to the city, Berg?"

"I think I just remembered why I had to leave. Forget I was here, okay?"

A handshake and a man hug and then Bergman went out the back door, down the alley to the waiting cab. He was taken to LaGuardia airport and headed back to the Kansas City airport and then back to Westland Park.

We had not made any significant progress on the rape investigation. Another rape brought us another bad rap in the press. That resulted in an angry call from the chief.

That night, while we were still chasing leads on the serial rapist in Westland Park, another strange scenario was unfolding over in Kansas City.

*****

"Okay, Patty, now make the call. That's part of the deal. If you do anything different than usual or we even suspect that you're trying to tip him off, the deal is out the window. Understand?"

"Yes, I got it," Patty answered.

The DEA agent placed a tape recorder on the telephone and then taped an introduction, giving his name, date, time, the number being called, who was called and the purpose of the call. Patty dialed the number and the phone rang.

"Hello," the voice on the other end of the line answered.

"Hey, it's me," Patty responded.

"What's up?"

"We got a big one."

"How much?"

"Probably five grand in cash. Not sure how much product."

"Okay, give me the info."

"Tonight at three in the morning. Name is Frank Swanson, white male, 32 years of age. He'll be meeting with two unknown males at the back parking lot of 1435 Killington Ave." Patty gave that information and description.

"Got it."

"Okay, talk to you later." Patty hung up the phone.

*****

Lieutenant Dickson made it work for himself; the chief assigned him as the Third Precinct lieutenant. There he was, back on the street, having gotten there by stepping all over his old friend Hughes. Hughes' suicide was a distant memory for Dickson. Sergeant Bob Nelson, recently promoted from patrol, took over the squad.

"Okay, let me have your attention." Sergeant Nelson began roll call. "I'm sure you all know Detective Mike Gillis here. He's got something going on tonight in our precinct and we want to make sure you are all aware of it, just in case."

"Hey, guys, good to see you again," Gillis greeted the squad. Pointing over to the man standing on his right, Gillis continued. "This is Detective Jackson, who will be assisting me. We have information that tonight there is going to be a drug transaction at three a.m. in the back parking lot of 1435 Killington Ave. We know that one Frank Swanson, a white male, approximately 32 years of age, will be meeting with two unknowns. Jackson and I will set up surveillance from a predetermined spot behind that parking lot. Officer Bergman will be with us to serve as a uniformed presence when we make the arrest. Sergeant Nelson and Officer Fiero will be set up just across the street behind the gas station convenience store and will move in by car as the arrest is made. Sergeant Nelson will be the on-scene supervisor, if and when any drugs or money get seized. We ask that no other patrol cars come into that area a half hour before, unless there is an emergency. Sergeant Nelson, do you have anything?"

"Thanks, Mike. I don't really have anything to add. It's pretty straightforward. Just keep your ear tuned to the radio, in case we need you, but stay in your sectors. That's all."

*****

By 2:30 a.m. Bergman was set up in the bushes overlooking the back parking lot where the deal was to go down. Nelson and Fiero were across the street as planned. At 10 minutes after three, one car pulled into the lot. Gillis quietly whispered that information into the headset attached to his handheld police radio. Bergman could see one white male sitting in the driver's seat. At 3:15 another car pulled into the back lot with two Hispanic males in the front seat. Gillis again radioed in that information. Simultaneously, all three got out of the cars. The Hispanic male who had been driving walked over to the white male. They spoke softly, but only for a few moments. Casually scanning the area, they then made the exchange. Money from the white male was placed into the hands of the Hispanic male, who walked back to his car and got in. The second Hispanic male, holding a brown paper bag, got out of the car and gave that to the white male.

"That's it. They made the deal," Gillis said to Jackson and Bergman. They leapt from the bushes yelling, "Police, freeze!" and made the arrests. Gillis called in for Nelson and Fiero, who responded within seconds with their red lights flashing. The three subjects were being held at gunpoint. As for a drug bust, that went fairly smooth.

"Okay, Jackson, you search this guy, Fiero this one, and Bergman this one." Gillis gave directions pointing to each perp. "If you get anything, let the Sarge and me know."

Naturally, they recovered a bag that was filled with a white powdered substance and wads of cash. The white male was Frank Swanson. The arrests were made, the drugs and money seized and the cars impounded. Another good drug bust for Gillis. All the drugs and money were sealed and put into evidence that night. The three hapless drug dealers were locked up. This drug bust was by the book.

*****

Back in Kansas City, a tall and thin senior DEA agent, whose gray pin striped suit and white shirt matched his salt and pepper hair, stood over Patty as she sat in a chair with a sullen face and asked the question, "Okay, how did you tip him off?"

"I didn't. You were right here with me. I did everything you said," Patty replied with exacerbation.

"Well, either you somehow signaled him, or you're full of it and he's straight. Either way, this is not going to help your cooperation agreement any. You're a disgrace to this agency."

Patty Moore, Gillis' girlfriend, had been arrested with the rest of her federal task force. DEA had gotten wind that this task force had been ripping off drug dealers in Kansas City. They set up a series of undercover sting operations and got evidence on the three DEA agents and five cops on the task force. Patty decided to cooperate, hoping for some leniency, and told them how she was feeding information to Gillis that she would get from one of her informants, whenever a drug deal was happening in his area. Gillis would steal some of the money and they would split it. That romantic relationship was not long for this world.

Tonight's plan was a sting operation. The three drug dealers were actually undercover DEA agents. The Westland Park Police Department Internal Affairs was out there watching the whole thing unfold; they were cooperating with DEA. They must've been pretty good at hiding in the bushes. Nobody saw them.

This was a good operation, but there was one problem, at least from an IA perspective — Gillis did everything by the book. All the money, drugs and evidence were seized right in front of a sergeant and taken to the evidence vault. There was no rip off. The next morning, Gillis arrived at the jail to pick up his prisoners and take them to court. There were no prisoners. Gillis was met by IA. With contrition, they explained that it was an undercover operation because they had information that Gillis was ripping off drug dealers and they had an obligation to follow it up. They called it an integrity test.

"I guess you gotta do what you gotta do. No harm, no foul. I understand completely. I'm just glad we were able to clear this up. Now, can I go back to work?" Gillis said to the IA detectives, not waiting for an answer, as he walked away with a smirk that turned into laughter.

*****

I was back at headquarters, reviewing the interview reports of the latest rape victims, seeking any information that may look like a pattern and give us a lead, or anything that we may have overlooked. I was determined to find something. I got a little startled when my cell phone rang. Janie was probably still sleeping and she rarely called me at work.

"Hollings," I answered.

"Hey big guy, it's Berg."

"Yo, Matt, what's happening? When did you get back?"

"I flew in a couple of nights ago. How's it going on the task force? Any good leads yet?"

"Nah, nothing solid. Everyone is pretty sure that the perp lives or works in the Third Precinct. He's much bolder there than anywhere else he hits, so we're focusing most of our efforts there right now."

"That's interesting. Just wish we could do something with that tidbit of information," Bergman answered.

"Well, you may want to let the squad know. Tell 'em to keep their eyes open, and think about some of the dipshits they dealt with who might be capable of this. What's up with you?"

"I've got something that I thought may interest you."

"I'm listening," I told him, with curiosity.

"I went out on a Gillis drug bust last night."

"No fuck'n way," I said, in a rather loud voice that caused some heads to turn in my direction. "Hold on, let me get somewhere a little quiet." I walked out in the hallway and ducked into a corner with my cell phone held tight to my ear.

"Let me hear it. Was it one of his fucked-up deals?"

"No, not at all. That was the strange thing about it. It was completely straight. It was planned out. The sergeant was there... kind of the way police work is supposed to get done."

"Shit. Whadda ya think that was all about?" I asked in astonishment.

"I don't know. Maybe he learned his lesson. Well, listen, I'll let you go. I thought you'd enjoy hearing that."

"Yeah, that's something, but listen, the pressure is mounting a bit," I told him, referring to IA being at my bank. He knew that we were not going to talk in detail over the department's phones.

"Well, I got some ideas. Things may let up soon. Let's try to get together."

"You got it, my friend."

By the afternoon, I heard about the sting operation on Gillis and how he beat the whole thing; all sorts of rumors floated around HQ. The rumors were usually more fact than fiction. Nobody knew if Gillis had been tipped off or not, but I was not surprised. He was slick; he probably smelled the set up and turned it around on them. Now, IA had nothing to show for their efforts. With Hughes dead, Gillis blamed everything on him; he told IA that Hughes approved every drug bust he was on. Thompson backed him up. IA had nowhere to go with that. And now, with all their cards on the table, there wasn't any hand left to play against Gillis. He was here to stay. I called Bergman to tell him what happened.

"Un-fuck'n believable. He's good. He must have seen it coming. What do you think?" was his reaction.

"Yeah, that would be my take on it. IA has really got some egg on their face now. DEA busted up one of their own task forces that Gillis' girlfriend was on. What a mess."

"Hey, I guess being at HQ, you get all the good gossip, huh?"

"Yeah, I do. I kinda like it."

"Why don't you solve that rape thing already so we can get your ass back here on patrol?"

"If I solve this thing, you ain't seeing my ass back on patrol."

"Amen, brother. I'll talk to you later. Hang in there." He tried to encourage me to stand tough in face of an IA investigation.

Mannings and I had two interviews. Our first one was with a woman named Robin MacDonald. As I was driving, Mannings was reading from her investigative file. He told me how she wound up at a high school football game naked from the waist down.

"Holy shit, I remember that. I was still in training, riding with Thompson that night."

"Looking back, the Detective Bureau thinks she may be Ground Zero. They haven't tied her rapes to the others, but it was shortly after hers that we started seeing this as a serial rapist."

"Did they have any suspects for that one?" I asked.

"Not really, though interestingly they did take a look at her live-in boyfriend."

"And?"

"And nothing. They ruled him out. He shared a quick beer with a neighbor, and then they confirmed he was online while everything was going down."

Robin greeted us with a warm, friendly smile and a firm handshake; she invited us to sit at the dining room table. She now lived in a modestly decorated third floor, one bedroom apartment. Wearing a black business suit with a white shirt and her hair pulled back in a ponytail, she looked as if she had just gotten home from work. She was slim and fit, which was no surprise as there was a treadmill in front of the television. On the walls, framed photos of her with friends smiling in front of different landmarks certainly led us to think that she had moved on with her life.

Composed and confident, she explained what happened, from the little she could remember. I could only imagine the psychological healing that she must have experienced since that night. We asked about her boyfriend Brian; her relationship with him had fallen apart not too long after the rape.

"He was so angry at me. His hostility got worse and worse," she told us.

"Did he ever hit you?" Mannings asked.

"No, nothing like that. But he became so verbally abusive. All we did was argue. When I told him I couldn't take it anymore, I think he was happy to see it end, and he could blame me for the break-up. The way he acted, you would've thought he was the one who got raped."

Then, her green eyes lost their sparkle as she drifted off into some unpleasant memories.

"Well, Ms. MacDonald, we didn't mean to churn up the past, but we had to make sure that there was not any more information that could help our investigation," Mannings said, picking up that we were now trespassing onto territory where we should not be.

Robin was patient and polite, but it was readily apparent that to continue this interview would serve no purpose but to cause Robin to relive a painful past that was probably better off forgotten. A little smile of relief sprouted on her face as she saw us to the door and into the hallway. As I followed behind Mannings into the stairwell, I stopped and looked back at Robin. She was not looking back at us and firmly closed the door.

"Sweet girl, huh?" Mannings asked during our ride to our next interview.

"Yeah, pretty cute too."

"Hey, hey young man, you're not thinking of hitting on a rape victim now. Are you? That sounds like another cop we both know."

"No, no. I got my girl Janie. I'm a good boy."

With Mannings driving, I was thumbing through Robin's file. Would I have called Robin for a date if Janie were not in the picture? Then I started thinking about all I knew. I read the police reports and the hospital records, in vivid detail. I saw all the pictures. In my mind, I could envision some dirty scumbucket sliming all over here. That was a major turn-off; sometimes you can know too much.

This was a troubling thought. More troubling was my realization that I was viewing Robin through the same eyes as her ex-boyfriend. Was I not more of a man than that?

Our next interview was with Faith Newman. She had been putting us off, but finally agreed to talk to us. She was sure that she had nothing more to offer. It was going to be another long day. I would not get home in time to have dinner with Janie before she went in to work. She was starting to get annoyed by my new schedule. We would have to work through it. As we drove over to Faith's apartment, I asked Mannings his opinion of this investigation.

"This is a tricky one, Gary. I kinda think the guy is a police buff, as we mentioned when you brought up the hoax calls."

"So what turns a cop wannabe into a rapist?"

"Ya know, there is usually a trigger that causes this kind of rage. Could be a lot of things. Some kind of rejection, which could be real or imagined. That sets him off. Remember, rape is not as much a sex crime as it is a crime of violence with a sexual mode. It's more the control and imposition of will that is the motivator than the sex. Not trying to be funny, but a rape is a felonious assault with a penis."

I knew he was serious, but hearing it put that way made me laugh a little, although I didn't want to. I truly felt for these girls and didn't want to give any impression that I didn't. If Janie got raped, I didn't know how I would react.

We made it over to Faith Newman's place. Her sister Charisse was there. That was not a good sign.

"Look, Officers, my sister tried to tell you that she had nothing more to say, but you kept on pushing her to meet with you, so let's get this over with," was Charisse's opening comment.

"Okay, Charisse, but I need you to work with us here. We're all on the same side. If we work together, maybe we'll come up with something to help us catch this guy. Isn't that what we all want?" I said as gently as I could and I think Charisse calmed down. We gave Faith the same line about the men she either dated or thought were strange, or maybe an ex-husband. She did have an ex-husband who she divorced more than two years ago, but as far as she knew, he had moved somewhere in the Carolinas. She wasn't sure; they hadn't been in contact.

"As much as I can't stand that bastard, he ain't the rapist. First of all, he's black, and I am real sure the guy who attacked me was white and about 50 pounds heavier than my ex."

"Is there anybody else you had any trouble with or anything out of the ordinary?"

"Well, about six months ago, you guys had to come out here and throw my old boyfriend out; he was drunk and wouldn't leave."

"Do you remember the name of the officer who responded?"

"No, just a couple of you white guys," Faith answered quickly, looking at Hollings.

"Well, we're not all white guys, Faith. I'm sure you can see that," Mannings responded with obvious sarcasm.

Faith and Charisse actually let out a little laugh. That was a good icebreaker for Mannings to throw in.

"Okay, sorry. That's just what I'm used to. I don't remember their names, but they arrested him and everything."

We took the information on her old boyfriend and the rest of the conversation did not yield anything new or valuable to us. We were heading back to headquarters at about 8:30 in the evening, when we heard a call on the radio. Another rape had occurred on the footpaths, this time in the Fourth District's territory. It was dark out; we had been trying to put out the message for women not to be out alone on those paths alone after dark, but it was not working. Those paths were very popular for those who wanted to jog. Mannings radioed in to dispatch to see if there was anyone from the task force close to that location. There was not. He advised that we'd be responding. Another long night was about to get longer.

Arriving at the scene, we saw two patrol officers from the Fourth Precinct taking the victim's statement. We got one of the officers aside. He described the perp to us, at least what the victim knew. Dark clothes and a dark ski mask and hood covering his face. It was our man again. He just came out of the bushes, and grabbed her from behind. He dragged her back in the bushes and held the knife against her throat. Mannings called in for Crime Scene. The Crime Scene Unit was handling all rape scenes now. The Sex Crimes detectives were working full time on the task force. They did not have the time to process a rape scene. Bringing out the Crime Scene Unit for every rape was like upping the ante. Mannings also asked for some patrol units to cordon off the area. The victim was extremely shaken, sitting on the path, crying, her arms wrapped around her legs, rocking back and forth. Leaves were caught up in her hair, which was now a mess.

It was clearly not the time to interview her.

The female officer was about to escort the victim to the hospital. Mannings called the officer aside and told her about some of the things she needed to ask the victim if the opportunity arose. We told the other officer that we would secure the area and wait for Crime Scene to arrive. He did not blink an eye and he was gone.

Like little puppies, we followed around the Crime Scene technicians trying not to get in their way, but getting a jump on any evidence they collected that may have helped us out. It was difficult to search bushes in the dark. Never at a loss for high-tech solutions, the Crime Scene Unit deployed their high intensity lamps on yellow tripods, which really lit up the area. They moved slowly and methodically, conducting a grid search of the crime scene. The area where the actual rape occurred was obvious. The brush and grass were compressed almost in the shape of a body. In a thin crevice where the dirt met the macadam, an earring was found. It could have belonged to the victim or it could have just been some lost property that meant absolutely nothing.

"Okay, partner, we need to get home. The sergeant wants a full task force briefing tomorrow morning. We don't want to be late," Mannings reminded me.

"That's a big 10-4, buddy. Let's go."

The next morning, the entire task force showed up. We were all going to find out what the other teams had, and what the strategy was. Sergeant Moran called the meeting to order.

"All right, here's where we stand. We had another rape, and it was the same old story, same M.O. The good news, if you can call it that, is that there was no murder, no excessive force. By that I mean that he used only the force necessary to commit the rape. He didn't beat the crap out of the victim just for the hell of it. Having said that, the lab finished its report of the Leslie Watson murder. Forensics found a small silver disk — looked like one of those watch batteries, but it was on a key chain. It turns out that it was one of those electronic devices for opening a locked door. It belonged to the Summers victim who was raped on the footpaths. She had it in her fanny pack which the perp emptied out. So, the question is, why is this puke carrying around things from one rape to the next rape? Is he hoping to get caught or something?"

"So, Sarge, what do we make of this odd behavior?" an officer asked.

"Good question. It's so good, I'm gonna turn it over to our profiler, Detective Peters." Moran looked over at Peters and waved his hand, inviting her to take center stage.

"Thank you, Sergeant. The best profile we can come up with now is a man who is driven to rape by two different motivational factors. One is clearly to carry out this violent act as an outlet of aggression that was caused by a specific trauma, at least something that he sees as traumatic. It may be social rejection or a very painful experience with a significant woman in his life that he has been unable to reconcile. Remember, it is more a crime of violence with a sexual mode, than a sexual crime."

Mannings and I smirked at each other as I glanced over at him. I had heard that before. Peters continued.

"But, then we also see an almost different personality. Committing a murder after the rape was completely inconsistent with his prior acts. Now escalation of violence, in and of itself, is not unusual, but then in subsequent rapes, he does not display that level of violence. This kind of inconsistent behavior is an anomaly for a serial rapist. It's almost like he is two different people at different times."

"So, what are you saying? He's a schizo?" someone else asked.

"Well, schizophrenia is not exactly what most of us think it is. He is someone who displays some very different personal characteristics in his life. To his peers and colleagues at work, he probably comes off as an ordinary guy, maybe a little quirky and a bit of a loner, but not a rapist. In other social situations, he may act more confident, maybe playing out some sort of fantasy role."

After some more meaningless chatter and stupid jokes, Moran got us back on track.

"Patelli has the name of all sex offenders released from prison about the time the rapes began. Find out where they've been and what they're up to. And that's what you'll be doing in your spare time. The rest of the time you'll be staked out in the woods of the jogging paths. Let me introduce Officer Benson."

Officer Benson stood up. She was tall, slender, shoulder length blonde hair and generally pretty good looking. She was about the age of the other rape victims.

"Officer Benson is a jogger. She will be jogging every night at different parts of the park. She will be wired and we will hear her at every moment in the surveillance van. At the first sign of trouble, we'll broadcast it and you come out of hiding and help her. Now, listen, this is high risk. The rapist is attacking from behind. He may get Benson before she even knows what hits her. So, every few seconds she will count out numbers sequentially, so we know she's okay. First time we don't hear her, you will know. We risk burning the operation that way, but Officer Benson's safety is first priority. Each night we go out, you will be given a map of the path she will be running and your positions. As she passes you, call it in. We have no room for error here. This will begin in two nights."

The next few weeks were very hectic. We hunted down sex offenders, ex-husbands and old boyfriends. Nothing in particular was developed by any of the teams that appeared to be a hot lead. Most of us started working in the afternoons chasing leads and then the evenings working in the bushes. It was a pretty sophisticated operation. We were all staked out in the bushes, sitting there for one hour before our bait started running. She would only jog for about a half mile in one direction and a half mile back. We always knew where she was, and whoever was in the car with the receiver could hear her on the transmitter. Not once had we lost contact with her.

What began as an exciting operation, that everyone thought would succeed, started becoming discouraging. After three weeks on the jogging paths, not one rape occurred there. Some of us did manage to attract ticks on our bodies. While we were out in the park, two more rapes occurred in ground floor apartments, one in the First Precinct and one in the Fifth Precinct. It started looking like the rapist knew where we were, and went elsewhere. The press at first touted the formation of the task force as a great effort to attack this scourge of Westland Park. Now, the press was beating us up for a lack of success. How could one rapist elude us for so long?

Today was another all task force meeting. Sergeant Moran called it to order. You had to only look at the faces of everybody there. We were becoming discouraged, embarrassed by our lack of success and just getting worn out.

"Folks, here's the latest. That earring found at the last rape at the jogging paths belonged to a previous victim, Vicky Cordero. Once again, it appears that evidence is being planted by the rapist himself — very strange. Again, the evidence that was planted was from a previous rape in the Third Precinct, but unlike the other two times, now it showed up at a rape outside the Third Precinct territory. What does that mean? I don't know. If anyone read the *Kansas City Tribune* this morning, the fact that the rapist has been leaving evidence behind was leaked to them. The rapist is clearly trying to make us look bad, and he is succeeding. I don't like this, the chief really doesn't like it and we had better do something about it."

The sagging morale of this task force did not benefit from having its lack of success rubbed in its face. There were a lot of years of experience there. It was not likely that we couldn't break this case.

"First of all, we need to put a gag order on all our operations. I am sure you are talking to your friends back at the precincts or your other units. Stop it. Somehow, I think this guy knew we were in the park, and he knew we were focusing on the Third Precinct. We can't afford that. From now on, everything we say and do does not get shared with anybody who is not on this task force. Understood?"

There were grunts and low toned responses of "yes" and "understood" and just head nodding. We all got the message. I hoped I was not the only one feeling a little guilty. I had been telling Bergman almost everything and I actually thought he should share that information with the squad. Obviously, not the right call, though I doubted anyone on the squad was leaking information. With all they had been through, there were probably a lot of other things on their minds, but who knew?

Moran ended the meeting and then called out to Mannings, motioning for us to come over.

"Hey guys, we got a lead to follow. I want it done quietly. One of the first rapes occurred during a high school football game. The victim turned up at the game naked from the waist down. It was quite a scene!"

"Yea, we just interviewed that victim. We didn't get anything." Mannings said.

"Right, but there is a little more. A security guard threw his jacket over her, which seemed like the decent thing to do. Forensics found some hairs on the victim's body which they matched to the security guard, Jason Brooks. They assumed they came from the jacket, so no big deal."

"Okay, Sarge. So, what's up then?"

"Well, through a little luck, we hit on something. My secretary was reading the lab's report and she recognized Brooks' name from when she was a precinct secretary. A couple of years ago, Brooks washed out as a rookie. He had a number of complaints from females claiming he was inappropriate with them. We had to let him go. Peters jumped all over this. Fits the profile and everything. You two track this guy down and get an idea of what he is up to."

That seemed like a good lead. It was ironic that we got it from a secretary who just happened to remember something and not from the last few months of trying to track this rapist down, through the real police work — interviews, stake outs and stuff like that. This was possibly the break we were looking for. First, I would get to solve this case, even if it was from just chasing a lead. Second, that would hopefully lead to a promotion to detective and I could start working burglaries or something like that. This assignment was getting stale and the hours were long. I needed a change; that was strange considering only a few months ago, this task force was the change from patrol that I was looking for. And third, I needed some more regular shift work. Janie was getting pissed about the small amount of time we had been spending together. She was happy for me — she knew I liked being selected for the task force — but, as I already knew, she took relationships seriously. She did not want to play second fiddle to my ego.

Jason Brooks had been a Westland Park cop for a little more than nine months. After a number of IA complaints against him, he was fired. Having not made it past his one year probationary status, it was a summary dismissal. Apparently, he had been a good cop and had a decent number of arrests. One month, he led his squad in traffic tickets, which could be interpreted in different ways, and he once stopped a bank robbery in progress. He tried to appeal his dismissal citing his good work record, but questions of a cop's moral turpitude were hard to overcome; his appeal was denied.

Tracking him down did not prove very difficult. He had a driver's license and was living in a Kansas City suburb. That evening, we paid him an unexpected visit. We pulled up on a square, one story house with light blue aluminum siding. His black two-door car was parked in the one lane driveway, with multiple cracks, leading to the detached garage. We parked on the opposite side of the street and had to walk over muddy water puddles to get to the two steps.

Our visit not only was unexpected, but was quite unwelcome. When we introduced ourselves, holding up our badges and identification, Brooks' grimace sent a clear message that he was not happy to see us. He did not even pretend. Probably just as Mannings was doing, I was sizing him up, both physically and personality wise, to see if he fit what we were looking for, and maybe assessing what we would do if he broke bad on us. Physically, he was probably an inch or two shy of six feet. That would put him in the height range. He looked like he was a little thin and in pretty good shape. That did not jive with the description of a guy who was heavyset. As we already knew, nothing ever fit perfectly. His dark curly hair was inconsequential since nobody saw his hair because of the ski mask and hood. He let us walk only a few feet into his house and we stood in the living room area talking.

"Can I help you, gentlemen?"

"Good evening, Jason. Sorry to bother you." Mannings tried to be polite.

"I'm sure you are. Listen, if you want to thank me again for helping that poor girl while two asshole cops let everyone stand around and take pictures of her pussy, that's okay. That was a while ago."

"Well, while we do appreciate it, that's not why we're here."

"Well then, what the fuck do you guys want? You already fired me. Unless you're here to apologize, I don't really want to talk to you," was his angry response to our introductions.

"Is everything okay, honey?" asked his petite wife, with short brown hair, dressed in an oversized blue sweatshirt and jeans, walking over to the door while wiping her hands on a red and white plaid dish towel.

"Everything is fine. These are guys from my old police department. Would you mind? Give us a few minutes."

She looked at him for a second or two, a little curious; although her face remained stoic, she seemed to understand. She walked away on the worn-out, gold colored carpet and went back to the kitchen. He did not invite us any farther or ask us to sit down, so we stood there talking.

"What could you guys possibly want with me? Didn't you ruin my life enough already?"

"Hey, I know what happened, and while we are not here to apologize, I'm sorry that things didn't work out for you."

"Okay, and...?"

"Jason, was there any reason you did not tell the detectives about being on the department when they first interviewed you about that night at the football game?" I asked him.

"Yeah, like maybe I didn't feel like bragging that I got fired. How's that for a reason?"

Actually, that was a pretty good reason: better than I had expected. For a moment, I did not know what else to ask. But Mannings did.

"What are you doing these days since you left the department?"

"I'm doing just fine, thank you. I'm a sergeant for the mall security force. And I got married eight months ago. I survived what you fucks did to me."

"And you look like you're staying in pretty good shape."

"Yeah, I work out and run. I'm doin' okay. What do you care about what kinda shape I'm in?"

"Oh, so you like to jog. Where do you jog?"

"Never mind where I jog. What the fuck are you guys up to?"

"I was just making some conversation. You know, seeing how things are going for you."

"Somehow I don't think you really give a rat's ass about me. What do you want?"

The moment Mannings opened his mouth to talk, Brooks looked over at me with a strange expression. Mannings stopped whatever he was about to say and stared back. Now I watched Mannings, as he slowly stepped backwards. He started moving his hand to his weapon. That stressed me. I did not perceive the potential danger as did Mannings. I quickly looked back at Brooks. Brooks held up his hand and pointed his forefinger at me. Now, I felt it. I bladed my body in a defensive position and waited for him to attack.

"Don't I know you?" he asked me in a somewhat aggressive tone, but not aggressive enough to sound like he wanted to fight.

"I don't think so."

"No, I do. What did you say your name was?"

"Hollings, Officer Hollings."

"Officer Hollings, oh yeah. Didn't you get the Medal of Valor for that shooting a while back?"

"Yes, I did. It was a very small article in the paper. I'm surprised you even read about it, never mind remembering it."

"Oh, I didn't read any article. I was at the ceremony. Very impressive."

"You were at the ceremony? What were you doing at the ceremony?"

"It was a public event. Wasn't it?"

"Yes, it was. But if you didn't read about the ceremony in the paper, how did you even know about it?"

"I still have a few friends on the department. Not everybody there turned on me. I like to know what goes on. Now, shooting a robber right in the ass, that's a good story. I wanted to be there. Any problem with that?"

"No, no problem."

An eerie silence took hold for a few seconds. Mannings and I had puzzled looks on our faces. Brooks looked just fine.

"Anyway, what I was about to say," Mannings spoke up at a good time, "is we've had a few things happen that we think maybe only someone with police knowledge would know how to pull off. Do you think if we gave you some dates, you could tell us where you were at the time?" Mannings asked, starting to get to the point.

"I think if you gave me some dates, I would tell you to shove them up your ass. How about that? Now you can leave, and if you have any more questions, call my attorney."

"And who is your attorney?"

"You're a detective. Go figure it out. Maybe ask some of those bitches who lied and got me fired. You didn't listen to me back then and I'm done talking to you now."

He walked over to the door and opened it; the message was clear. We had no legal authority to stay and pursue this matter. We left and drove back to headquarters.

"That worked well," I said to Mannings, trying to be funny.

"Yeah, he really enjoyed seeing us."

"Whatcha make of him as fitting the perp's description? I thought he was in the height range, but he looked a little thin. I don't think anyone would describe him as heavyset."

"No, not in the white t-shirt he was wearing. But if he had a couple of layers of clothes underneath that black sweatshirt he was always wearing, he might come off as a little heavy. Witness descriptions are not an exact science and aren't usually that reliable. Though, in this case, they have been relatively consistent."

"You're right. So that makes him a definite maybe?"

"Maybe." After a brief chuckle, Mannings continued.

"Well, there were some other interesting observations to make."

"Like what?"

"First, and quite obvious, he has not forgotten things and has not learned to forgive and forget. He is still carrying a big grudge around. Not just for us, but for those women as well. That kind of rage, well, seems to fit."

"I agree. That is obvious." I hadn't picked up on that, the way Mannings had.

"Okay," Mannings went on, "if I asked you to explain where you were on certain dates, what's the first thing you would ask?"

"I guess, um, I guess I'd want to know why you were asking."

"Exactly. And he didn't ask. He didn't really care. Almost as if he knew why we were asking."

"He must've known we were there about the rapes. I mean, you asked him about the rape at the football field."

"Maybe. But still, he should've responded differently, at least asked what we were getting at. He seemed to know that it was time to shut us down. He was prepared for us."

"So, he knows that we know that he's the rapist. Right? You think he's it? You think he's our serial rapist, getting back at us for firing him?" My childish enthusiasm became a little too obvious.

"Slow down, young man. Let's not get too excited, but this is definitely the hottest lead we have going, at least for the moment."

That was it. Mannings and I had identified the serial rapist. We were gonna catch the bastard and I was making detective. This was too good to be true.

The next day we met with Sergeant Moran and Detective Peters.

"This certainly would be consistent with what we've seen. It doesn't explain some of the anomalies, but the unabated anger at the department, the fact that women had something to do with his firing... it would all make sense.

"Then I think the next step is very obvious," Sergeant Moran said to us, though I did not get it.

"See you tomorrow at 8 p.m. Be ready for a long night," Mannings told me.

It took me a second to figure out where we were heading, but I got it.

"How do we know that's a good time to start?" trying to sound as if I had something to offer.

"We don't. But I'm not risking things and making any inquiries. He's already gonna be paranoid from our visit. We start tomorrow and keep changing our shifts until we hit upon his schedule. Gas tank full, stomach full, bladder empty. Got it?"

"Got it. See you tomorrow."

I was too excited to sleep that night and was anxious all day wanting to get started on surveillance.

"You set up, young man?" was Mannings' opening line when I walked in.

"10-4" was my response to Mannings.

"Okay. Sitting around in a car in these neighborhoods eventually attracts someone's attention. If you think someone is looking at you, just let me know before you move. We don't want to lose the eye on his house. Got it?"

"Got it."

This was my first surveillance. Mannings briefed me on the challenge. We needed to stay close enough to Brooks' car so we didn't lose him. But we also had to be sure that he did not detect us following him. Either way, we could screw the investigation up.

"Subject on the move. Get ready."

Mannings spotted Brooks coming out of his house's side door and going into the garage, while I had let my mind wander off. It was 10:30 at night.

"I'm gonna circle the block and try to pull behind him after he leaves his garage. Let me know when the garage door opens. Just don't let him see you pull away from the curb. That's a dead giveaway."

Brooks was wearing jeans and a dark jacket and carrying a small gym bag. Surely, that bag was holding the dark clothes that he would change into before the next rape.

"I got him going north on West Terrace," I radioed to Mannings.

"Okay, stay about three cars behind us, and get ready to pick him up when I peel off him."

"10-4."

"All right, he's making a right onto the highway entrance. I'm gonna let him go and you take over. I'll catch up," Mannings directed me.

"Okay, I see his car. You can go."

Mannings went straight as Brooks made the right turn. That would relieve Brooks of any suspicions if he thought that he was being followed.

I followed behind Brooks for about two miles when he signaled he was getting off the highway.

"Looks like he's getting off at Exit 66B. What's the call?" I radioed to Mannings.

"I'm back with you. Let him go and I'll follow. You take the next exit and circle back."

"All right."

We did just that and followed Brooks into a mall parking lot. Driving around the outer perimeter of the parking lot, he seemed to be conducting his own counter-surveillance. After two rounds around the lot, he eventually pulled into an employee-only parking garage. The yellow, black striped gate opened, and a uniformed security guard waved to Brooks as he drove in.

"Whatta you think?" I asked Mannings over the radio.

"Good chance he's just going to work. Guess he's on the midnight shift. Ain't that a kick in the ass? Leave patrol to go to another midnight shift, like the proverbial jumping from the fire into the frying pan."

"Yeah, but that's perfect. The mall closes at midnight. He and a few other guards probably walk around the big mall with nothing to do. That's a great opportunity to sneak away and do a rape. I think this is falling together nicely."

"Maybe. Let's see how it goes."

There was no way to get in to that garage to watch Brooks' car. We could not sit in the parking lot past closing. That would only draw the attention of the security guards. We stationed our cars outside the mall parking lot, trying to watch the two exits, looking for Brooks' car. That was not a great plan, but we could not think of a better one. We were not going to talk to anybody in the mall to try to find out more about Brooks; we could not risk him being tipped off.

We did this for three very long nights. I drank a lot of coffee. Each morning, as the mall employees started to trickle in around 7 o'clock, we saw Brooks leave the mall and head home. It was daytime and he and Mannings and I all needed our sleep. The fourth night came and Brooks did not leave his house. Mannings called the mall security office, pretending to be a friend. We called that a pretext call. We were told that he was off until Sunday. It was Thursday. We kept our surveillance on Brooks' house all night. Nothing happened. We were tired.

Brooks was a good lead. Sergeant Moran put on two other detectives to watch Brooks while Mannings and I took a couple of days off. Sunday night came and we were back. While we had been off, Brooks had not been seen doing anything at night. No rapes had occurred either. Two weeks later, we were still there, watching Brooks, but seeing nothing.

Tonight started the same. We followed Brooks to work. We drove around outside the mall and kept an eye on the employee parking garage where he parked his car. About two o'clock in the morning, we heard something we did not expect. Another rape had occurred. It was in the Third Precinct. It was the serial rapist again.

"Okay, this could be a problem," I called to Mannings.

"A problem or an opportunity? Maybe he got out without us seeing. But he's gotta make his way back. Let's keep our eyes open. If you see him coming back, jump his ass. We'll have him."

My heart began pumping. I was excited. This was it. Brooks snuck out on us. But he was not going to sneak past us again. He was mine.

That enthusiasm lasted until about 7:00 in the morning. As the sun was breaking through, Brooks' car left the parking garage and headed home. We never saw him leave the mall or come back. If he committed the rape, he did it right while we supposedly had him under surveillance. Either way, this was not good.

Mannings and I came in about an hour early the next morning to discuss our strategy with Sergeant Moran.

"Whatta you guys think? Could Brooks have pulled this off last night? Could you have missed him?" Moran showed true concern with our plan.

"I don't know, Sarge. There was absolutely no traffic coming in or out of the mall that time of night. Unless he went on foot, somehow and maybe had a car stashed somewhere... anything's possible, I guess."

"Maybe he's just not our guy."

"Maybe not, but everything does seem to fit, Sarge. He's got all that bottled-up rage, he knows police work and he works at night. It sure looks good." Mannings was sounding more confident that Brooks was the rapist and now was trying to convince Moran.

"All right, we'll have to see what Sex Crimes gets from last night's rape. If we think there is any chance that this fuck Brooks is the perp, then we gotta ratchet things up. We can't have rapes occurring right under our noses. We may have to take some chances. Look, Brooks starts his shift about an hour before the mall closes, right?"

"Yes, sir," I answered, trying to have some part in the conversation.

"Good. You two get to the mall before he does. You don't have to follow him from his house; you know where he's going. See who he talks to and what he does. I'm not sure what we're hoping to find, but maybe you'll come up with something. He knows you now, so don't let him see you."

Mannings and I got to the mall early. We knew that around 11:00, the mall's pedestrian traffic would be thinning out and Brooks would be starting his shift. We were hoping to figure something out. Mannings waited outside in the parking lot and would call me on the radio when he saw Brooks' car pull in.

I was looking in the window of a jewelry store when I got a tap on the shoulder with a hard object. Turning around, I was taken aback by the sight of Brooks in his security guard uniform, resting his baton on his shoulder.

"Officer Hollings, what a surprise."

"Oh, hi, Mr. Brooks."

"Mr. Brooks? Please, Officer, don't be so formal. What brings you here?"

"Oh, I, uh, was just looking for a gift for my girlfriend."

"That's nice. I know the owner of this store. Maybe I could help you out. What's your girl's name?"

"Janie, um, I mean." Then I stopped. I had already said too much and there was no way to retract that statement. I tried to change directions.

"Well, I wouldn't want to ask for any favors. You know, being a cop and all, it wouldn't look good."

"I understand. You're a hero cop. You've got a reputation to maintain, right?"

"Yeah, right. Well, listen, nice seeing you."

"Yes, nice seeing you, Officer. Maybe I'll see you again soon."

I had no idea how to read that statement. Last time we saw Brooks, he was angry and on the defensive. Now, he was secure and at ease. The tables appeared to have turned — and not in my favor. Leaving the mall in a hurry, I called Mannings to meet me.

"What happened? Brooks snuck right up on me. Why didn't you call?" I asked Mannings, trying to be polite and respectful, but clearly aggravated.

"Gary, his car never pulled in to that lot. I was right there. He never drove in. I don't know what he did, but he is fucking with us, plain and simple."

"That didn't help any," was Moran's response the next day back at the task force, as we discussed my encounter with Brooks and the next step.

"He's not gonna strike now while he knows we're looking at him." Moran tried hard not to show his frustration. "Look, you guys need to catch up on your paperwork anyway and help us follow-up on a few other leads. It probably wouldn't hurt to lay off this scumbag for a while. Marsha, what do you think?"

"I agree," Peters answered. "Obviously we don't want to let a suspected rapist free to go around and rape, but he is not yet a real suspect. You two don't believe that he could have snuck past you leaving the mall the other night; we don't have any forensic evidence against him and clearly no probable cause to search his house or car. I think we need to keep him on the list of potential suspects, but not to the exclusion of everybody else. We are far from being sure about this. There are other possibilities."

Were there other possibilities? I did not think so. Brooks was the rapist, and now we would not be there to grab him when he struck again. I felt like I screwed up, at least in Moran's eyes, but this was Mannings' fault; he did not see Brooks arrive. I had to fix this.

Saturday night was coming and I was off. Janie was scheduled to work, but she took the night off so we could meet Bergman and his new girlfriend Mindy. We met at a quiet restaurant in downtown Kansas City. It was a little pricey, but the ambience was nice, and it was a good place to sit and talk. The food portions turned out to be quite light. Something funny about restaurants. It seems the more you pay, the less you get.

Mindy struck me as an unusually pretty girl: not the traditional model-like beauty, but the girl next door fantasy. Her straight brunette hair rested on her shoulders and her tight silky shirt hugged her round, firm breasts. Her shirt buttons were open just enough to check out some decent cleavage. Bending down to get into our seats, I tried hard to not be obvious in my attempt to peek farther down her shirt; those babies were hanging nicely. Bergman's tight and mostly unbuttoned shirt was open even more than Mindy's, flaunting a hairy chest that I did not appreciate having so exposed over our dinner table. With his thick, brown hair slicked back, he looked more like a New York mobster than a Westland Park police officer. As we made some small talk, I was taken by Mindy's soft voice, but she spoke with an air of confidence and self-assuredness that I found attractive. Bergman and I tried not to talk about work. We knew that would bore the girls and probably bore us even more. The girls complimented each other's jewelry and talked about some matters relating to shopping.

"So I heard that you're on the rape task force, Gary? That must be exciting," Mindy said.

"Yeah, but we're getting frustrated. It's no secret that after all these months we haven't made an arrest." I wanted to get off the subject in fear I would say something I shouldn't, but I needed to keep her engaged in conversation, just to have an excuse to look at her and listen to her.

"Tell us about your work," I asked Mindy.

"I'm a psychologist. I work in a practice downtown."

"Oh, do you do any of that profiling stuff, like the detective they have on the task force?" Janie asked.

"No, I don't do criminal profiling like they do, but I do form profiles of people all the time trying to understand what is at the root of their troubles. Sometimes they are aware of what things are bothering them and we work towards finding a coping mechanism. Other times, they can't figure out what it is that's troubling them. That's when they need us to help them understand themselves, before we can determine a coping strategy," Mindy explained.

Just at that moment, Berg's cell phone rang. He looked at the number with a strange expression and looking at Mindy, told us, "I'm sorry, I really gotta take this." He got up and walked away.

"So, can you give these guys some advice? I think they need it," Janie said, grabbing my leg and bumping her shoulder into mine, giggling a bit, just to let me know she was teasing me. It also appeared that she seemed to like Mindy. That was good in that Bergman and I were good friends. Things with me and Janie, despite the pressures of work, were going well, at least I thought. I had given up my apartment. We were shooting the "L" word at each other. I was starting to think that marriage was at least in the realm of possibility.

"How is the investigation going? Is it okay that I ask?" Mindy asked.

"Yeah, I guess. We have a good suspect, but the shrink working with us is not so sure. He's got all the personality traits: you know angry about things, like women and his job."

"Well, anger does not make a rapist. I hope you have more to go on than just that."

"There are a couple of other things. I think if we really dig deep into this guy's personality, we'd see a rapist."

"The only thing I can tell you, especially cops who are driven to make an arrest, is to be careful. Sometimes you see what you want to see. There are occasions when we miss the obvious because we have become so focused on one idea — usually an idea that would prove us right. Many times the answers are so simple that they are staring us in the face, and we just don't see them because we won't open our minds even a little bit," was Mindy's answer.

That struck a nerve, because I knew that at that moment I was focused on an idea that I should not have had. Janie was my girl and Mindy was Berg's girl. Enough said. When Berg made it back to the table, I was a bit relieved, knowing I could not let him sense my fascination with Mindy.

On the way out of the restaurant, Berg pulled me aside.

"Hey, I saw some old high school buds back in New York."

"Great. Have a good time?"

"I wasn't there for a good time. I was grieving, remember?"

"Yeah, okay. So how did you cope with your pain?"

"Let's just say I let my friends tinker with the cell phone — you know, that cell phone that we don't have. Are you with me?"

"Kinda."

Actually, I had no idea what Bergman was getting at. But, most importantly, he did not seem to have picked up on my attraction to Mindy. Or maybe he did and just did not care. The night ended and we began the drive home.

"She was quite pretty. Wasn't she?" Janie asked me.

"Huh, who?"

"Oh, come on, you were staring. It was embarrassing."

"Staring at what?"

"Oh, please. The way you looked and talked. I'm surprised your tongue wasn't hanging out of your mouth."

"What are you talking about?"

"You're a pig. Bad enough you don't respect me enough not to ogle Mindy, but she's your partner's girlfriend. Don't you have that code of honor amongst all you cops?"

"You're doing that jealous thing again. I don't like it."

"Oh really, well I'm sorry that I don't appreciate you slobbering all over another woman, right in front of me."

What I thought had been a pleasant evening out was followed by a ride home without a word spoken. When we got home, I sat up in bed thinking about Mindy. She was beautiful. I also was thinking about what Mindy had said — sometimes the answer is so obvious it is staring us in the face. Janie probably had the same thought.

Chapter 23

Mannings and I got in early on Monday morning to start our administrative tasks. Not that conducting surveillance on Brooks was all that exciting, but it beat sitting behind a desk. Around noon, Janie called.

"I just had a strange phone call," she told me.

"What happened?"

"Some guy said he was calling from Oak Hill Mall and was packaging a gift you bought for me. He said he couldn't read the address you gave him, so he wanted to make sure he mailed it to the right place."

"What did you do? Did you give him the address?"

"No, something sounded weird. When I told him I wanted to call you first, he almost yelled at me saying 'no.' You wanted it to be a surprise. That didn't make any sense, so I just hung up."

"That motherfucker."

"Who you talking about, Gary? What's going on?"

"Nothing, nobody. Did caller id get the number?"

"No, it was blocked."

"Okay, just pack a few things and get out of the house. Go to your mother's or sister's or something. Just get out and I'll call you later."

"But…" Janie started.

"But nothing! Go right fuck'n now!"

Mannings and everyone in the office heard me and saw me standing at my desk, waving my hand and walking around.

"What's up, buddy?" Mannings came over to me putting his hands on my shoulders to calm me down.

"It's that fuck Brooks. He needs a visit. C'mon, I'll tell you in the car."

Mannings pushed me aside as I tried to get in the driver's seat.

"I think I'll drive. You just sit there and fill me in."

Reaching my hand out of the window, I placed the red revolving light on the car roof.

"Just fuck'n move it." Then I added, "Please."

Mannings listened to what just happened. Cops take their lumps, but do not tolerate threats on their family. Janie was family.

As we pulled up to Brooks' home, he seemed to be expecting us. He opened the door and stood in the doorway, watching us approach him. He did not move.

"Let's talk inside," I said to Brooks.

"No, I don't think so. Unless you have a warrant, you're not coming in here. You got something to say, say it."

"Fine. Don't be fucking with me. You don't call my girlfriend. You don't show up in my personal life in any fuck'n capacity whatsoever. I'd better not see you around her or anywhere she goes. Are we communicating?"

"Well, I don't know what you're talking about. But, since we're talking about personal lives, what about what you're doing to me? You don't think me and the neighbors saw you guys parked out here watching me and following me? Then you show up at my work. Look, you guys fucked my life once; you're not doing it again."

"Hey, fuck you. Whatever happened in your career is your problem; I got nothing to do with that. Now I'm warning you, stay away..."

"Are you threatening me, Officer?" Brooks yelled out and looked at the small number of neighbors who had gather around to watch what was going on. He continued. "You come to my house with no warrant and threaten me, telling me where I can go and not go. Does everybody hear these officers threatening me?"

Mannings and I turned around and saw a small crowd gathering and heard the buzz of people murmuring to themselves and each other. Brooks was clever; he had this planned. Mannings walked up behind me and whispered in my ear.

"Let's not make any mistakes. Go to the car. I'll handle this."

Hesitating, I quickly mulled over what Mannings was saying. I knew I had stepped knee dip in shit and there was no graceful way out. I stared at Brooks' smug and smiling face and walked off slowly. Mannings approached him.

"You got lucky now. Don't push it." Mannings gave what Brooks knew was an empty threat.

As we drove off, we heard the crowd applauding, and it was not for us. Brooks walked out onto the street pumping his fists in the air.

We drove back to the office to lick our wounds. After that, the week dragged on slowly. We poured over records, call-in complaints identifying who people thought the rapist might be, and other crap like that. The weekend came and Janie and I did not do much. I met her over her mother's house. She was mad. She was having trouble coping with my job threatening her and coming into our lives. Being at her mother's house gave her a great excuse for no sex. But an excuse was all it was. Things between us were tense since the night out with Bergman and Mindy. She was right on this one — but there was no way I could admit that.

"Listen, maybe we should move to a different apartment or something."

"Not now, Gary. I'm going to stay here for a while. You can stay at my place for now. I'll come by Monday and get my stuff. Let's just take a break for a while."

"Take a break? I know what that means. What..."

"Don't, Gary," she interrupted me. "It can't always be your way and on your terms."

I knew what she was saying and I knew what taking a break meant — I understood where that was heading. I was not giving up that easily. I was not losing Janie because of some dickhead like Brooks, or over my stupid inability to reign in my horns.

Before we knew it, we were getting in early on a Monday morning again. Mannings and I found that another rape had occurred over the weekend. It was our serial rapist again. It happened just after that confrontation with Brooks, and he knew we were not watching him. That was way too coincidental for me. It was just plain obvious what had happened. When Sergeant Moran got in, we sat down with him to discuss these developments.

"Okay, I guess we have to see Brooks and get an alibi for Saturday night, though there is no way to force him to cooperate," he told us.

"Whoa, sit down," he ordered as Mannings and I got up from our chairs to interview Brooks.

"You guys ain't going anywhere. Brooks called into IA to complain about you two and what happened. You are ordered to stay away from him. Now you're both under IA investigation."

"Oh great, another IA investigation."

Mannings looked at me and mouthed, "Another IA investigation?"

I just waved my hand, signaling that I did not want to discuss that stupid remark.

"Sarge, we gotta get back on this guy."

"Look, we have nothing on him. The only thing we can say is that we had him in the mall during one rape and we have no idea where he was during a second rape. We got nothing. I'll send another team to interview him. But you two back off. Besides, nobody is even convinced that he is the rapist. He's a possible, at best. Keep working other leads. Got it?"

"Yes, sir," we said in unison.

The rest of the day went downhill from there. My phone rang only a few times; each time I hoped it was Janie. It never was. I wanted to call, but knew that would not help. She was going to decide whatever she was going to decide. Could anything else go wrong?

The shift was almost over. Moran called us into his office.

"Carlson and Benton called in; they just finished up with Brooks."

"And?" Once again, Mannings and I spoke in unison.

"And he had an alibi. They checked it out. He was out with his wife, and another security guard buddy and his wife. There were other witnesses who remember them too. He's threatening legal action if we don't stop harassing him. Brooks is off our list. He is to be left alone. Am I clear?"

Mannings was the first to respond with, "Yes, sir."

I just sort of mumbled.

"Hollings, did you hear me?"

"Yes, sir, sorry."

As we walked back to our desks, heads hanging, I stopped and grabbed Mannings by the arm to stop him too.

"This is nuts. What do we do now?"

"What do we do? We do what Moran just told us to do. We forget Brooks and start working some new leads. What don't you understand?"

"What I don't understand is how we just let the rapist go about his business."

"Hey, nothing is saying that this guy is the rapist."

"Yeah, I know, alibi and all that bullshit..."

"Hold up, young man. The evidence is the evidence. That's that. Now I've been in this business a long time. Showing up at Brooks' house the way we did was stupid. I don't feel like ruining the last years of my career with any more asshole moves. I'm glad you're driven and determined, but your ambition is gonna get you in trouble. I'm not going there with you. Now either you do things like we were told, or find yourself another partner, and good luck with that."

"Okay, I'm sorry. I'll see you tomorrow."

Chapter 24

My cell phone rang. It was Janie's number calling.

"Hey, baby, I miss you," I whispered into the phone.

"Hey, baby, yourself, and I miss you too," came the deep voiced response.

"What the fuck, who... Berg, is that you?"

"Fuck'n A, my friend."

"Whatta you doing with Janie? What's going on?"

"Nothing, relax. I'm not with Janie. I'm calling from that certain cell phone you gave me, remember."

"Yeah, but the caller id says it's Janie's number." It took me a moment to realize that he was talking about Stryker's cell phone.

"Ain't that cool? I can program the phone to show any number I want."

"Well, any other time this might have been funny. How the fuck did you do that, anyway?"

"Hey, nothing a couple of my goombas back in New York couldn't take care of."

"Wow, I'd like to use that phone sometime."

"Well, that ain't happening.

"Huh?"

"Don't worry. You'll figure this out. And when you do, don't thank me. Just forget everything."

"Okay."

"How's the rape investigation going?"

"Sucks. I know I got the right guy, but got this one little problem. It's called no evidence."

"Well, my friend, just remember what Mindy told you. You probably got blinders on. We cops do get like that. Step back and take a breath. You're a smart guy. You'll figure it out."

"Thanks, buddy. Talk to you later."

Another night was spent just sitting up in bed, alone with my troubling thoughts. Why was this all happening? Why was nothing working out? I did not deserve this. Or, maybe I did.

The next morning I approached my work with a new, albeit forced, sense of energy and enthusiasm. Berg was probably right; I could figure this out if I just opened my mind a bit; we cops do tend to put blinders on when we get an idea in our head.

I was reading the chief's report from the day before. My eyes were drawn to the chief's message of condolence for Officer Jim Burkett on the passing of his mother. There was no way I would be going to that funeral. There was also no way I could ignore this. Burkett would probably be lost without his mother.

Just as a few neighbors were leaving, I made my way to Burkett's door.

"Hey, buddy, thanks for coming," Burkett greeted me. Then we shared an awkward man-hug.

Food and flowers were all over the house as Burkett led me in to the living room. Naturally, he tried to steer the conversation to the rape investigation. I tried to avoid that.

"I gotta grab that. It's been going all day," Burkett said as he went to the kitchen to answer the phone.

From the conversation he was having, I could see that Burkett was going to be on the phone for a little while. Had I not just gotten there, I would have used that as an excuse to leave. I started to meander around the house and found myself in a small room that looked like Burkett used as a study. Newspapers covered the desk. Picking them up just to see what Burkett was reading, I saw that articles had been cut out. Not just any articles. I knew which ones, because I had read them. They were articles about the rapes. Reading them is one thing, but cutting them out? I looked around and did not see that he had the articles on the wall or anything, but he must've been keeping them somewhere. I didn't have the balls to start opening drawers. I sat at the desk, looking and thinking.

Out of the corner of my eye, buried in the dark brown shag of that disgusting carpet, I saw some light reflect. I looked closer. It was a small, plain, gold-plated earring. I grabbed it and put it in my pocket like a kid stealing candy from the counter. Then I started to look around more. That desk drawer became the focus of my attention. I turned around to watch the doorway and with my hands behind my back, I wiggled that drawer a little at a time and opened it just a bit. Then I turned back around. Sitting in the drawer was a brown scrunchie: those little elastic things girls use to put their hair in a ponytail. I picked it up and started staring at it. I became transfixed on it.

"Whatta ya doing, Gary?" Burkett managed to scare the crap out of me.

Nervously dropping the scrunchie, I picked it up and tried to not act as nervous as I was.

"I just saw this on the desk and was wondering…"

"I thought it was in the drawer," Burkett said.

"No, JB, it was on the desk. I wouldn't open your drawers. Shit, why would I do that?"

"Don't know. Yeah, some babe left that here a few nights ago. Chicks are always leaving things behind. To be expected. They ain't thinking straight after I fuck their brains out."

"Yeah, I guess. Anyway, I gotta get going, J.B. I just wanted to pay my respects."

I walked out still holding the scrunchie.

"Well, thanks for coming. I don't think you'll need that. Besides I gotta give it back." Burkett took the scrunchie right out of my hand. He was smiling, but this time it wasn't that stupid grin he usually had. It was smug, more like the look Brooks gave me. But this time I was right; I knew it.

Chapter 25

Too many sleepless nights. At least Janie and I were talking. Even though the Brooks' matter had died down, Janie still hadn't moved back. I had made too many mistakes recently. I needed to move more cautiously. Starting tonight, I had to time my trips just right.

"You know nobody can know about this, right?"

"Of course, Gary. I understand," Mindy said as we slurped cups of coffee at her dining room table.

"Not to rush you, but I do have to get to work," she continued.

"I know. I'm going. Look, I just had to come here. I wanted to be sure before I said or did anything stupid."

"I know. Now go do what you gotta do."

"Good night," I told her as we hugged at the door.

The next few days at the task force were tense for me. Mannings could see that I was distracted. I blamed it on things being stressed with Janie. We were pursuing a few more leads one night when another rape occurred. I called Bergman.

"Is Burkett working tonight?" I asked him.

"No. Why?"

"Never mind. Just a hunch. I'll talk to you later."

"C'mon, Hollings. We need to get out to the rape scene."

"Listen, can I catch up with you? I wanna stay back for a few and call Janie. See if I can clear things up a bit. OK?"

"Seems like a strange time to do that, but I guess I've forgotten what young love is like. Don't take too long."

Young love? Was this really that simple? What was Janie thinking? Was she out screwing some other guy? I couldn't take that thought. Calling Janie was not on my agenda tonight, but I thought maybe it should be. While driving I called her and told her the things I knew she wanted to hear. I apologized for making her uncomfortable when we were out with Berg and Mindy. I didn't admit anything, but the apology seemed to work, with the promise of never again. When I arrived at my destination, she ended the call with "I do love you, you know." That was what I needed to hear.

The house looked dark and empty, but I walked up to the door and rang the bell. There was no answer. Two more tries — nothing. Out of frustration, I sat on the steps. Within minutes I was hit by headlights as Burkett pulled up into the driveway.

"Hey, Gar. Whatta ya doing here?"

"Hi, JB. I don't know. Just wanted to see how you're doing. I kinda had to rush off the other day."

"How'd you know I wasn't at work?"

"I, uh, I called over to the precinct. I was gonna hook up with you on the side channel. That's all. So what were you doing?"

"I was out getting a few things at the C store." He then opened the rear car door and took out a white plastic bag with some milk and cold cereal. "Why you asking, Gary? What's going on?"

Unsure what to say, I just kinda mumbled. I didn't expect Burkett to challenge me. Maybe he was sharper than I gave him credit for.

"Nothing, JB. I know how close you were with your mom. Wanna talk for a little bit or anything?"

"No, Gary, I don't. As a matter of fact, Gary, I thought we were friends; you come to my house and say you want to visit, but all I see is you snooping around. That's really weird, Gary. You go back to your task force buddies and I'll be fine. See ya." Burkett walked into his house, letting the door slam shut with me staring, like a lover who was just dumped.

Catching up with Mannings at the scene of the last rape, I found myself not paying attention to the investigation. It seemed to be the same story. A heavyset, white male broke into a ground floor apartment where a female lived alone. As she got out of the shower, the rapist attacked her from behind. No strong leads to act on. I was completely dispassionate to the victim.

The next day, I woke up early expecting an exciting day. Janie invited me over; we were on the way back. Before that, I had something I had to do. My old squad would be getting off their shift in a few minutes. I headed for the Third Precinct, timing it so that everybody would be changing back into their civilian clothes — lockers open, goofing around and not really paying attention to me.

"Hey, Mr. Hotshot Task Force Man" was my greeting in the locker room.

I worked hard to convince everyone that I was paying a friendly visit to my squad. Bergman looked at me with a very jaundiced eye. After a few minutes of shooting around sophomoric locker room jokes, I made my exit.

Walking down the hall, I ran in to Liz, who was brushing her hair back with her fingers as she headed for the door. I gave her a friendly hello and started to imagine that she would invite me into the storage closet for a quickie. Instead, she gave me a casual and polite, "How ya doing, Gary?" as she continued to walk off, clearly not sharing my thoughts. My fledgling erection quickly petered out.

My next call was to Sergeant Moran. It was urgent that I meet with him. I included Mannings in the meeting; after all, he was my partner.

"So, you saw the articles cut out of the paper on his desk, right?"

"Yes, sir."

"And why were you at the precinct at that moment?"

"Just following a hunch, sir. I wanted to get a glimpse of what was in Burkett's locker. I didn't really know what to expect, but when I saw that earring there, I just knew I was right. Besides, I figured that as soon as I left his house, everything I saw was gonna disappear."

Moran looked at Mannings and asked him, "What do you think?"

"Well, Sarge, between that and the hair thing Hollings found, it sure looks suspicious. I mean, look, we focused on Brooks because of his police background. I have to admit, I am a little biased; I know how weird Burkett is. Certainly sounds like probable cause to me."

"It does. Good work, Hollings. I guess we made the right choice when we invited you on to the task force."

We walked out knowing that this would be turned over to IA. Mannings smiled and patted me on the back, like a dad proud of his son hitting the winning shot at the buzzer.

The scene was ugly and I was not enjoying watching it play out; IA served a search warrant on Burkett's locker and found the earring of one of the rape victims. A veteran police officer being led out of the precinct, still in uniform, stripped of his weapon and handcuffed behind his back. A squad of officers stood in line watching the parade to the unmarked cars. Burkett was muttering incoherently; the shock of this left him dazed and on the verge of collapse. The two detectives straddling him had trouble holding up that large frame of Burkett's.

After arresting Burkett, IA searched his house and found nothing. It was cleaned out as I suspected. That earring was going to be critical to our case. No DNA, fingerprints or other physical evidence could tie him to the rapes, so there would be a lot more work before trial. Hopefully, some skilled detectives would persuade him to confess. As much as the department wanted to keep Burkett's arrest hush-hush, that was not going to happen. It was all over the news. The Westland Park rapist had been arrested. And it was a cop. This was some story. Could things get any worse for the Westland Park Police Department?

My sense of righteousness did not keep me calm for long. I still had IA looking at me. I knew that they hadn't found anything on me; there was nothing to find. Yet, I realized just how far a cop would go when he thought he was right. Our ability to justify our actions, at least to ourselves, was nothing less than shocking. The sleepless nights only got worse. How would this all end?

While I was home awash in my problems, Thompson was also sitting home when he got a text message. It was from Gillis. Gillis had become a folk hero of rogue cops. He beat the IA investigations. He smelled the setup at the drug bust and he knew how to blame everything on Hughes. Dead men can't defend themselves.

"What the fuck?" Thompson mumbled to himself. "That's Union Station. Why the hell are we meeting there?" he texted back.

"It's important. Just be there" was Gillis' text response.

Thompson put on his shoulder holster and threw on his jacket as he headed to Union Station to meet Gillis. Maybe there was trouble. Maybe there was a big score.

"Charlie 15," the two Kansas City plain clothed cops called in.

"Charlie 15, go," the dispatcher answered.

"We are at the location. We have a white male matching description of the anonymous call. Just confirming — caller advises that this is the shooter of Detective Barstow. Is that 10-4?"

"That is 10-4, Charlie 15."

"Any further information?"

"Negative, Charlie 15."

"Be advised, we are approaching subject. Have units move in this direction."

"10-4, Charlie 15, back-up units en route."

"Freeze...police," was all Thompson heard when the bright light hit him. Startled, he was not sure what had just happened. Was Gillis busting his balls with a stupid joke?

Blinded by the spotlights, Thompson kept moving forward, not responding to the demands that he stop and raise his hands. He was not accustomed to being on that side of things. The siren gave a short blast. The tone of the police officer's voice was more stern, and higher pitched. Thompson realized that this was possibly a mistake, but did not know the heightened level of fear and suspicion behind those lights. Thompson's calm arrogance ruled his response.

"No, I'm a cop. It's okay."

"Freeze," screamed the voice, now with more fear, as the four eyes of the two officers trained on the gun, which could be seen through the opening of Thompson's jacket.

"Gun, he's got a gun," yelled one of the officers.

"No, I'm a cop," Thompson yelled wildly, reaching for his badge.

Five shots, maybe six rang out.

In the marble wall at the southeast doors to Kansas City's Union Station, two more bullet holes joined the ones memorialized there from the historic Kansas City Massacre where three cops, one FBI Agent and one mobster were killed. Now, more than 75 years later, another cop fell dead.

The next morning was a busy one, not just at the task force, but for the entire Kansas City Police Department and the Westland Park Police Department. A cop getting gunned down by a neighboring police department was more than anyone could imagine. As Bergman tossed a cell phone out of his car window and into the Missouri River, the Kansas City cops had fun looking through the pictures on Thompson's cell phone of him screwing Melinda Hughes in different positions. What gave them a few laughs pushed another cop to take his own life.

Another IA investigation. Another police funeral. This was getting old. The next few days for me were spent doing some of the mundane tasks of detective work. We had solved the whodunit, at least for some of the rapes. Now we just had to put the final touches on the investigation — collecting reports, cataloging evidence, court appearances and other administrative matters. The task force was closing shop.

I gave a lot of thought to Burkett and could not understand how his life could have devolved the way it did. I wondered how he managed to pull these rapes off and keep us at bay for so long; but of course, he was a senior police officer. He knew what our approach would be and what we would and would not be looking for. When I thought back on everything, I could not believe that I didn't see it earlier. Would any police officer have suspected that of a fellow cop?

I knew how strange Burkett was. His admiration of the rapist, his sexual excitement at the victim's telling us about the rape. It just was not right. Maybe if I had told someone —Hughes or anybody — about those strange things Burkett used to say, a few less women might have been raped. Maybe even Leslie Watson would still be alive. But what about all the other things I had seen? Thompson making his play for Hughes' wife and Gillis' questionable police tactics. I never opened my mouth. Maybe if I had, two cops would be alive now. Speaking up was a big part of being a cop. As Bergman so pointedly told me, we were cops first and foremost. I had to deal with my own feelings of guilt. I had screwed over Burkett after the shooting. Then there was Brooks. I was wrong. I almost fucked up his life for no reason. I would have to remember all of this the rest of my career.

I assumed that Burkett would seek an insanity defense. I'm no shrink and no lawyer, so I didn't know whether that would work or not. You gotta believe that a career cop who starts to rape, and then kills someone, had gone off the deep end. Even if he did play the insanity card, then he'd go to a psycho ward for who-knows-how-long.

Detective Peters had talked with Burkett several times over the winter months to understand what happened and to draw her profile. Today, the sun was shining in a cloudless blue sky, though a nasty wind was bringing the temperature down. I was heading downtown to see Peters. The visit was under the guise of trial preparation, but I just really wanted to know what she had learned. During the drive over, Berg called me.

"Hey, buddy."

"Hi, Gar, what are you up to?"

"On my way to see the KCPD shrink who was working with the task force. I'm trying to just wrap up a few things."

"You think you might confess your own guilt?"

"What guilt?"

"About Mindy."

"What, wadda ya mean?"

"Oh, I bet you never told anybody what you did with my girlfriend. She told me how you came over that night and she psychoanalyzed all your thoughts about Burkett. Using a civilian to do your police work — shame on you."

"Oh, she told you about that, huh?"

"You know there are no secrets around here."

"Sure seems that way."

"Anyway, what's up with you and Janie?"

"I think we're on our way back. We had some issues, but we're getting past them. I know this — she's the one."

"Then go get her, my friend. I'll talk to you soon."

Berg was a good friend. I looked forward to working with him during my career. I arrived at the Kansas City Police Department.

"Good to see you again, Gary."

"Same here, Marsha. Thanks for making time for me."

"So, I guess you want to know what we've learned about Mr. Burkett."

"You can say that." She ushered me to a chair in the corner of her small, windowless office.

"It was all very interesting. In many ways, he fit a classic profile of a certain kind of rapist. He was awkward socially and very insecure. He had experienced numerous rejections from women, and he saw some of those experiences as very painful and embarrassing. He talked about being scorned by some girl when the two of you were together at some night club."

"Yeah, I remember that. Wow, that was quite a while ago. He couldn't shake that off?"

"No, he could not. Not only was he humiliated by the girl, but having it happen in front of you was salt in the wound. There is a lot of rage inside of him."

"We all get rejected by girls at night clubs when we're out with our friends. It's not the kind of thing you carry around for so long."

"Well, Gary, maybe it's not a big problem for you, but for him it was."

Peters hesitated, and she did not appear to want to say much more. Obviously, there was more to be said.

"Marsha, what else? What are you not saying to me?"

"Well, Gary, he mentioned you several times."

"Me? Why would he mention me at all?"

"Oh, there were a number of things. He felt that you betrayed him with IA during the review of the shooting and that's why he didn't get any recognition. Then you and Thompson got medals and he was disciplined. You even met your girlfriend as a result of getting shot; I think that's what he said."

I just nodded and she went on.

"After that, you got selected for the task force. Even with all the rapes happening on your beat, you were still chosen for an assignment he felt he should have gotten. The same night you were picked for the task force, there was a murder in your sector. He thought for sure that would make you look bad, and you would be knocked off the task force."

"Holy shit, that's right. Watson got killed the night I was told that I was on the task force. Don't tell me he killed some poor girl because I..."

"No, Gary, stop. First of all, until I hear it from Burkett himself, or see some definitive evidence, I am not saying he raped or killed anybody. We still have no physical evidence and none of the victims can identify him."

"Wait a minute. Burkett hasn't admitted to raping these women, or killing Leslie Watson? Then what the hell have you been talking to him about?"

"Mostly about himself and what makes him tick. My job is to build a profile, not solve the crime. It's up to your department to put the case together. Detectives figure out the 'who did it' and I figure out the 'why he did it' part."

"Well, that sucks. We don't have a confession, but we do know that I was probably half the reason for Burkett doing whatever he's done."

"C'mon, Gary. You're not the reason for anything. Only Burkett is responsible for Burkett's choices."

"Somehow, that is not making me feel much better."

We spoke for about another 30 minutes: some specific about Burkett, some just generalities about the various rapist profiles. On the drive home, I could not rid myself of some guilt. What Marsha did not know was that Burkett was not completely wrong — I had screwed him during the IA review of that shooting incident at the convenience store. Burkett probably deserved the Bronze Medal more than I did. I did not do shit except get shot; it was all political and I played the game for my own gain.

Look at what happened.

Things had to change. I had to change. I had to be a better person and be a better cop. I remembered a flow chart I drew with lines and arrows that showed how Burkett was linked to the rapes. If I did that again for all these tragedies — Burkett, Hughes, Stryker and Thompson — I would find that somehow, I was a common denominator. And, I would have to learn to live with that.

Epilogue

Not only was the task force disbanded, but the chief broke up my squad; he had to. Too much damage had been done.

"Okay, good evening, everyone," Sergeant Harris said to the squad.

He was met by grunts and groans. Much to my discontent, I was back to patrol. I had been transferred to the Fourth District and put on another midnight shift. I put my name on the waiting list for day work; midnights were getting weary. I heard a lot of talk and rumors that I was going to get promoted to detective any day now. I was still waiting. After a few weeks, I called Mannings just to touch base and get together. Having since been promoted to sergeant, Mannings was on a midnight patrol shift in the Second District. We met for a late dinner.

"Good to see you, Gary. How's it going back on patrol?"

"Ah, you know. Patrol is patrol. I'm really hoping to make it to detective sometime soon. I was kind of figuring that my work on Burkett would do it for me."

Mannings knew I was fishing for information.

"Yeah, I do hear your name being knocked around a bit. But be patient. IA is still clearing up everything they found after looking into Thompson's activities. You were never really a strong suspect anyway."

"Really?"

"Yeah, I heard that when they did a financial background on you, they found so little, it looked more like you were getting ripped off than ripping off drug dealers."

"Oh, and how do you know that? I thought IA investigations were top secret."

"C'mon, young man, you know there aren't many secrets in this department."

"So I keep hearing."

"Besides, how important is it to be the youngest detective in the department?" Mannings asked to my shock.

"How did you know that? Am I that obvious?" I felt myself blushing at having been so transparent.

"No, but you are talking to the man who was going to be the first black detective on the department, no matter what."

"I guess I should've seen that. I've learned a lot from you."

"Anyway, that was strange how Thompson got killed. Wasn't it?"

"Yes, it was." I watched Mannings' reaction as I answered him. Somehow I felt that Mannings expected me to shed some light on the strange circumstances surrounding Thompson's death."

"Looks like Thompson was one fucked-up cop. That must've been some experience getting trained by him."

"I don't know. I was too naive to see what was going on. What about Gillis? Do you hear anything about him and how he fits into this whole thing?"

"Well, I did hear that they found a text message on Thompson's cell phone from Gillis' cell phone, asking Thompson to meet him at Union Station. Next thing you know Thompson gets plugged by KC cops. Gillis is going to have to explain that."

A few seconds were needed for that information to sink in. In my mind, I saw Berg with one shit-ass grin across his face.

"Anyway, you'll be cleared and then they can start thinking about you for detective. Ya know, you should've told me about that dirty money IA was looking at you for at the outset. We were partners. And who knows? Maybe I coulda helped you."

"I know. I just figured it was better left unsaid. I didn't know where it was heading. It's kinda scary being investigated for something you didn't do."

"Well, just keep that in mind next time you're out investigating someone and throwing around accusations."

"Message received. I'm just glad all that trouble is behind me."

"So, any other good gossip going around the department?" I asked him.

"I'm sure you remember the arrest that was made on the Stryker shooting, right?"

"Of course. I'm not about to forget that."

"Anyway, I heard from the Detective Bureau that one of the guys who was arrested is cooperating. He gave up the shooter and some dope dealers in New York and LA; this may go federal," Mannings told me.

"That's good news."

"Well, for the most part. But there is some really fucked-up stuff coming out of it. Apparently, these guys had girls working at Triple 7s all over the area. These babes would get bullets from cops for either screwing them, or giving a BJ or things like that. Then anytime the bullets were used, they were traced back to a police department. That tends to fuck up an investigation. Those bullets were probably used to kill Stryker."

"No shit," I answered with true surprise.

Of course, I knew Bullet Brenda all too well. I did not know where my blood went, but it had drained out of my head; I could feel myself turning white.

"Yeah, and apparently, these girls secretly videotaped themselves doing it, just in case. Now, they're trying to bargain their way out of trouble by agreeing not to let out those tapes. That's some good pre-planning for you."

"Wow, that is something," was the most I could say at the moment. I swallowed hard and felt sweat developing on my forehead and on my palms. I felt like Willie Dixon, with that twitching eye. My heartbeat was in my ears with a deafening loudness.

"Sure is. Our department can't get a friggin' break. Just one crisis after the next."

"How many tapes do they have? Who's on the tapes?" I began asking questions as I became more nervous.

"Can't answer that. The department is being real tight-lipped on this one. I can't blame them. This is going to really hurt. A lot of guys are gonna get whacked — not just professionally, but I see a lot of personal lives being ruined from this."

I rushed us through the rest of the meal, trying to act as if I was still paying attention to our conversation, but I wasn't. Now, I really had trouble to face. There was a strong possibility that I was on a videotape getting a BJ from Bullet Brenda. What if this did get out? What would happen to my career? I only did it once and I was a rookie. Surely they would not come down heavy on me for one stupid mistake. What about Janie? How would she handle this? I swore to her that I was not that kind of cop. I'm not, at least not anymore. I couldn't go back there either. Janie finally agreed for us to move back in together, but this time, we used the "m" word. As I told Berg, she was the one.

Now I wondered what I should do. I could wait to see if I was implicated in this Bullet Brenda thing. Maybe I wouldn't be. Maybe there was no tape of me. Or, I could be the kind of cop I knew my good friend Bergman was, and just come forward and tell IA what I did and what I knew. Then, there was Janie. I had a couple of choices. I could be the kind of man Janie expected of me — just be honest with her and let her make her own decision as to what this may mean for our future. Or, I could just wait and see what happened. Actually, there was a more important question I needed to ask myself. That was, why was I having any indecision about what I should do? With all that had happened, had I not learned anything over the past few years?

I got back in my patrol car. The dispatcher was on the radio. *Did I hear that correctly? That can't be. Not now, not again.*

Lights and siren and I knew exactly how to get to that address.

There were already two patrol cars there. She was wrapped in a blanket being led into the back of the police car. Crying, hysterical, walking like she was drunk, she sensed my presence. Her reddened eyes screamed out in pain and her pain pierced my heart like a lightning bolt. I knew what that rape would mean to her and to me. I knew my Janie and I knew me.

###

Walking the Corporate Beat:
Police School for Business People

- Paperback: 316 pages
- Publisher: BookSurge Publishing
- November 17, 2009
- Language: English
- ISBN-10: 1439255601
- ISBN-13: 978-1439255605
- Product Dimensions: 8 x 5.2 x 0.7 inches

Walking the Corporate Beat: Police School for Business People is former FBI Special Agent in Charge and businessman Michael Tabman's gift to all executives and business professionals seeking new and effective ways to recognize and prevent problems. Readers will be intrigued by parallels between police work and business, and how basic law enforcement concepts resolve management problems. Whether the focus is managing risk or team building, defining company objectives or discussing ethics, the parallels are compelling.

Tabman explains the similarities with candid descriptions and dramatic, and often humorous, vignettes from his days on the force. In an approach that captivates the reader, he juxtaposes such challenges of law enforcement and business as multitasking, conferences, relationships, and strategizing. The concept that rushing into a melee without stopping to think is as dangerous in police work as it is in business is one example of how this book will open new and energizing doors.

Review

This is an awesome book! It is filled with great stories written by a seasoned and very accomplished Law Enforcement Officer and Executive. Agent Tabman shares with the reader plenty of examples of problem and crisis solving which he learned in his many years of service to both the FBI and the Police Department and how one can apply them to those problems encountered everyday in the business world. This book is a "must read" by all upcoming executives and those who face critical and important management decisions on a daily basis. Agent Tabman teaches executives how to safely go "Walking the Corporate Beat" by avoiding problems and embarrassing and tough situations. Thank you for your service to our country Agent Tabman!

CPSIA information can be obtained
at www.ICGtesting.com
Printed in the USA
LVHW010255080120
642889LV00001B/20/P